Also by Sharon Sala

The Next Best Day

Don't Back Down

Last Rites

Heartbeat

LEFT BEHIND

SHARON SALA

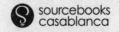

sourcebooks
casablanca

Published by Sourcebooks Casablanca, an imprint of Sourcebooks
P.O. Box 4410, Naperville, Illinois 60567-4410
(630) 961-3900
sourcebooks.com

Printed and bound in the United States of America.
BVG 10 9 8 7 6 5 4 3 2 1

Chapter 1

IT WAS LINETTE ELGIN'S DAY OFF, AND SINCE SHE WAS a nurse, days off rarely came two in a row. This morning she was hustling, getting ready to walk out the door, get all of her errands over with, so she could clean her apartment and do laundry later.

The day was already hot, but it was June in Jubilee, Kentucky, which meant if you wanted to stay cool, you either looked for shade or went where there was air-conditioning. She had dressed for the weather in old jeans and a lightweight gray T-shirt with the word *no* printed on it in bloodred ink before she headed for the elevator. When the doors finally opened, she found herself face-to-face with Cecily Michaels, one of the women who'd rudely interrupted her first date with Wiley Pope.

Cecily looked startled, and then frowned. "What are you doing here?"

"I live here," Linette said, and then saw the shock spreading on Cecily's face and grinned. "Welcome to the neighborhood."

Cecily was horrified that she'd moved into the

enemy's camp and still pissed that Wiley had blocked her calls. So, being the utter bitch that she was, she couldn't keep her mouth shut.

"How's Wiley?" she drawled.

Linette pivoted so fast Cecily flinched, and in the sweetest voice, put her in her place.

"Bless your heart, honey. You must be the most miserable little thing to have nothing better to do with your life than interfere in someone else's, so because I am a really nice person, this is just a friendly little warning." Then she leaned forward. "Don't fuck with me."

The elevator stopped. The door opened, and then she was gone.

Cecily was in shock and just a little bit cowed. Every woman in the South knew *bless your heart* was code for *kiss my ass*, and Linette was taller and scarier up close. By the time Cecily gathered herself and got to the parking lot, Linette Elgin was nowhere in sight, and that was just fine with her.

━━━━━━

Linette had already forgotten the new neighbor and was on her way to the bank. Traffic was already getting heavy, which was par for the course in a tourist town like Jubilee, and she was grateful to find a parking place. When she entered the bank lobby, she was thinking about making meat loaf later and what she needed to get at the supermarket. She had personal business to attend to and sat down in one of the chairs outside the vice president's office to wait her turn. She was reaching for her phone when she heard a sudden commotion at the front entrance.

To her horror, three men came charging into the lobby, wearing surgical masks, waving guns, and shouting. A big heavyset man wearing gray coveralls and a Texas Rangers baseball cap issued the first order.

"Everybody down! Get down on the floor now!"

People started screaming and panicking, and one lady fainted where she stood.

Texas Ranger fired a shot into the ceiling. "Shut the hell up! Next one screams is dead! Belly down on the floor and don't look up!"

There was a mutual gasp, the quick shuffling of feet as people dropped down onto the floor, and then silence.

Linette was horrified. Her phone was in her pocket, but she was belly down and couldn't move. Mr. Trotter, the vice president she'd been waiting to see, wound up lying right beside her. She could hear the rapid, shallow gasps of his breathing and knew he was as frightened as the rest of them.

Texas Ranger shouted at the two men with him. "Get the money!" Then pointed at the tellers, who'd frozen in place behind the plexiglass windows. "All of you! Empty your tills into the bags and no funny business!"

The tellers began cramming the money from their drawers into the bags they'd been given as fast as they could.

One of the gunmen, a short, skinny dude, kept pulling up his pants and dancing from one foot to the other, then trading his gun from right hand to left hand, and back again.

Linette's best guess was that he was high on something, which didn't bode well for any of them.

"Hurry up, bitch!" Skinny Dancer shouted and pounded his gun on the counter in front of the teller.

Texas Ranger shouted again. "Who's in charge?"

"That would be me," Randall Trotter said, and held up his hand.

"Then get the hell up and open the vault," Texas Ranger ordered.

"Yes, sir!" Randall said.

"Be careful," Linette whispered, as they shared a brief look.

Randall was in the act of getting up when Skinny Dancer swung around, saw Randall getting to his feet and shouted, "He told you not to move!" and shot him in the face.

Randall Trotter was dead before he hit the floor.

More screams, then moans of dismay rolled through the lobby. Linette was in a state of disbelief. Randall's body had fallen across her outstretched arms, pinning her to the floor. She was screaming inside so loud her ears felt numb, but in actuality, she was lying in frozen silence, watching the blood pooling around his head.

"God damn it!" Texas Ranger shouted. "What did

you do that for? Now how the hell are we gonna get in the vault?"

The third man, who was standing lookout at the entrance, was distracted by the disruption of the killing and didn't see the cop coming in the door behind him, but Linette did, and this time, her heart nearly stopped.

———

Jubilee police officer Wiley Pope was unaware of the robbery in progress, or that the silent alarm had been activated at the PD, until he entered the bank lobby. Within a heartbeat, his brain registered the customers in total panic, belly down on the floor with their arms stretched out before them.

The frantic expressions on the teller's faces.

And the three armed men in the act of robbing the bank.

Wiley was already drawing his weapon when Lookout Man finally spotted him, yelled, "Cop!" and fired off a shot.

Wiley ducked behind a pillar and fired back. Lookout Man dropped, and the other two robbers were scrambling, which gave every teller in sight the opportunity to hit the floor below the counters.

The robbers were firing off shots at Wiley as they scrambled for cover, and he returned fire in rapid succession.

Skinny Dancer dropped.

Wiley and Texas Ranger were the last men standing, and a heartbeat later, both aimed and fired.

Texas Ranger's shot hit Wiley's chest and sent him flying backward, while Wiley's shot ripped through Texas Ranger's shoulder, splattering blood all over the plexiglass window at the tellers' stations behind him.

The silence afterward was as frightening as the robbers' entry had been.

The three men were unconscious and bleeding on the floor, and Wiley was staring up at the ceiling, reeling from the impact and trying to catch his breath.

All of a sudden, people began screaming.

Tellers came running out from behind the counters, and a teenage boy was on the phone calling 911, unaware the silent alarm had already been triggered.

Wiley was still struggling to breathe and grabbing at his shirt when a woman ran into his line of vision.

Oh my God! Linette!

"Help…" Wiley gasped, trying to unsnap his shirt to get to the bulletproof vest beneath.

———

Linette was in a panic. From the moment the robbers entered the bank to when Wiley was shot, every dream she'd ever had for a happy-ever-after life flashed before her eyes. It seemed like a lifetime, but it was, in fact, mere seconds. She knew how deadly a chest wound would be and was up and running toward him when she realized he was tearing at his shirt and struggling to breathe.

Body armor! He was wearing a bulletproof vest! Thank you, God!

Without saying a word, she grabbed at the front of his shirt, knowing the vest that just saved him was now impeding his ability to catch his breath.

Wiley was fighting her, grabbing at her hands, when she grasped his wrists.

"Wiley, don't fight me! Relax. It knocked the breath from your lungs. Relax and it will come."

Even as he was struggling to breathe, her voice and her face splattered with blood shocked him out of his own panic, and then he realized she was mobile and talking, and he was not, so he leaned back against the pillar and tried not to pass out as she unsnapped his shirt and began yanking at the Velcro straps to loosen the vest.

His heart was pounding; the room was spinning. It felt like he'd just been hit in the chest with a sledgehammer. And then all of a sudden, the vest was loosened, his lungs inflated, and he was finally able to inhale. The look of gratitude that passed between them was telling.

"I hear sirens," she said. "You're doing great, Wiley. My God, my God, you saved us."

"Check pulses," he mumbled.

Her voice was shaking. "I hope they're dead. All of them. They killed Randall Trotter and were fighting among themselves when you walked in."

He grabbed her wrist. "Check…please."

She cupped his cheek, then did as he asked, moving from body to body.

"They're alive," she said.

"Shit," Wiley muttered, rolled over onto his hands and knees, and finally staggered to his feet. His hand was splayed over the center of his chest, afraid to move it for fear he'd fall apart, while he waited for the room to stop spinning. Once he could breathe and stand up at the same time, he reached for his radio.

"Officer Pope reporting. Attempted robbery at Jubilee Bank. One bank employee dead. Three perps down, but still have pulses. I took a shot in the chest. Suggest haste."

Aaron Pope was on patrol when dispatch notified them of a silent alarm at the bank. As they were responding, they also heard Wiley radio in.

"Holy shit," Officer Bob Yancy said, giving his partner, Aaron, a quick glance.

Aaron's gut was in a knot. "At least he's alive and conscious enough to make the call."

———————

But inside the bank, Wiley was already in containment mode, trying to get everyone away from the perps without passing out in front of them.

"What do you need? I'll do it," Linette asked.

"Move the customers to the front of the lobby."

Linette turned around and began issuing his orders, loudly and firmly.

"Can we leave?" one man asked.

"Nobody leaves," Wiley mumbled, then doubled over as a wave of pain rolled through him. He needed to get the weapons contained, but he couldn't bend over for the pain.

Linette slid her arm beneath his shoulder to steady him and was moving him toward a chair when the police began pouring into the lobby to contain the scene. Once they had retrieved the weapons, they gave the all clear to the EMTs. After that, Rescue moved inside in teams and did what they did, readying the wounded for transport.

Aaron came in running, headed straight to Wiley, and then knelt beside his chair. "Damn it, Brother, are you okay?"

Linette recognized him. "Your brother was our hero. He took a bullet in the chest. The body armor stopped it, but he's hurting. Steady him. He's dizzy. I'm going to get an ambulance for him." Then she passed Wiley off to Aaron without another word and ran.

"What happened?" Aaron asked as he slipped his arm beneath Wiley's shoulder.

"They killed Trotter before I got here," Wiley said, holding his hand against his chest. "Body armor saved me. Feel like I've been hit with a sledgehammer. Can't breathe. Sick to my stomach. Perps still have a pulse."

"Stop talking, buddy," Aaron said. "We'll figure it

out," he added and started walking Wiley toward the door.

At that point, Linette sped back into the lobby. "The first ambulances are here. Walk him out. They're waiting to take him to the ER. I'm staying here to help."

Wiley started to thank her, but she was already gone.

Aaron helped him out of the bank and loaded him up into the back of an ambulance.

"Don't tell Mom. She'll fuss," Wiley said.

"You don't get to choose," Aaron said. "She'll kill the both of us if I don't. I'll get there as soon as I can," he said, then stepped back as they closed the doors and took off to the hospital. At that point, he called home.

━━━━━━

Shirley was mopping the kitchen floor when her cell phone rang. She saw Aaron's name on caller ID, leaned the mop against the wall, wiped her hands, and then answered.

"Hello, honey. You caught me in the middle of mopping. What's up?"

"There was an attempted robbery at the bank. Wiley walked in on it. He's okay, but on the way to the ER. He was wearing his body armor but took a bullet in the chest. It never penetrated, but he's hurting. Just wanted you to know."

"Oh my God," Shirley said. "What about the bank robbers?"

"He took down all three of them, but they'd killed Mr. Trotter before he got there. The perps were all still alive when we got to the bank and are in the process of being transported to the ER. I've got to go."

"I'm leaving now," she said. "Thank you for calling me. He wasn't going to, was he?"

Aaron chuckled. "What do you think?"

Shirley sighed. "Right. Does B.J. know?"

"Not yet, but I'm calling him next," Aaron said, and disconnected.

At that point, Shirley dropped her phone in her pocket and took off through the house to Sean's office while Aaron was calling their youngest brother. He was the head pastry chef at the restaurant in the Serenity Inn, and most likely elbow-deep in sugar and flour, but he had to let him know.

———

As Aaron predicted, B.J. was in the hotel kitchen when his cell phone rang. He started to let it go to voicemail, and then noticed it was from Aaron and stepped out into a hallway to answer.

"Hey, Aaron. What's up?" he asked.

Aaron repeated everything he'd just told their mom.

B.J. was stunned. "He shot all three of them? Are they dead?"

"No. They were all still breathing when the EMTs transported them."

"Is he conscious?" B.J. asked.

"Yes, and talking once he was able to breathe again."

B.J.'s eyes welled. "All this shit was happening while I was baking bread."

"And I was sitting in a police car on patrol. And Mom was mopping the floor, and Sean is likely in his office, and that's how life works. Don't go there. We live our lives by our choices until we're done. Wiley is damn good at what he does. He saved a bunch of lives today, okay?"

B.J. took a breath. "Yes, okay. It's just overwhelming to think about. I'm not sure if I can get away. I'll call Mom first, and if he's in trouble, I'll be there. Thank you for letting me know."

"Of course. Just take a breath for Wiley, and one for yourself. I'm sure he's okay. I walked him out to the ambulance myself."

"Right," B.J. said, but the moment he disconnected, he called his mom.

———

Within minutes of receiving the message, Sean and Shirley were in the car and heading into Jubilee, with Sean behind the wheel and Shirley riding shotgun. They'd barely left the driveway when her phone rang. She glanced at caller ID and then answered.

"Hello, honey."

B.J. was shaking inside, but trying to hold it together.

"Aaron just told me what happened. I'm not sure I can get away without bringing the whole pastry line to a halt. Will you tell Wiley I'm saying prayers and let me know if he's not okay?"

"Of course. Sean and I are already on the way into Jubilee. Wiley was wearing his bulletproof vest. He'll be bruised and hurting, but I'm sure he's going to be fine. I'll keep you updated, okay?"

"Yes, okay. Love you," B.J. said.

"We love you, too. Go back to work, and I'll call you when I know details."

"Thanks," he said, then hung up and hurried back into the kitchen, waved at three of his sous-chefs, and pointed at the timer. "Get the pans ready. The rye dough is on its last proofing. And this time, remember to braid the loaves before you set them to rise. The dough for the baguettes is also ready, and for the love of God, delicate cuts, delicate cuts on the baguettes this time. Last time they looked like they'd been run through a guillotine. I want them as perfect as that diamond in your fiancée's engagement ring, understand?"

"Yes, Chef!" they all echoed and jumped to obey, while B.J. fretted that he was here and not there with the rest of his family.

———

By the time the ER staff had Wiley's upper body devoid of clothes, the contusion on his chest was turning a

deep shade of purple, and they were moving in a porta-
ble X-ray machine to check for broken bones, followed
by a CT scan to check for internal bleeding.

Blood tests on the wounded men revealed high
contents of meth, which explained the manic behavior
they'd exhibited. They were all still alive as they were
being taken to surgery, and if they survived, they would
be moved to a prison ward for recovery, then to court
to face charges of attempted bank robbery, murder, and
the attempted murder of a law officer. They were going
nowhere fast, and the coroner was on his way to Jubilee,
while outside the bank, officers were stringing crime-
scene tape across the sidewalk.

———

Sean and Shirley Pope walked into the ER and straight
to Wiley's exam room. His chest was bare, revealing the
dark-purple contusion. They'd raised the head of the
bed to make breathing easier, and Police Chief Sonny
Warren was with him as they entered.

When Sonny saw Wiley's family walk in, he waved
them over.

"Shirley. Sean. I was just commending Wiley for the
body armor. He's going to be miserable for a few days
and will need to rest. He'll also be off duty until the
doctor releases him."

Shirley nodded, then walked straight to Wiley's bedside, kissed his cheek, then eyed the spreading bruise in

the middle of his chest. But for the vest and the grace of God, he could have died today.

Wiley patted Shirley's arm. "I'm okay, Mom. Just a cracked rib and a bruise that hurts like hell, but as you always say, 'This too shall pass.'"

Shirley cupped his cheek. "I honor you and the job you chose, and I'm so grateful you're okay."

"You and me both," Wiley said, then grinned at Sean. "So, I had to get shot to get you out of your cave."

Sean grinned. "I had no idea you were yearning for company, considering all those women you have on speed dial."

Wiley frowned. "They've been blocked."

Shirley's eyes widened. Something had happened, but now was not the time to ask.

Sonny Warren decided it was time to make an exit. "They're getting his release papers ready. I am assuming you will take Wiley home. Wiley, we'll get your patrol car back to the lot and your personal car back to your house. Consider yourself clocked out until further notice, and take care of yourself, Pope. I don't want to lose you."

"Thanks, Chief," Wiley said.

Moments later, Sean's wife, Amalie, appeared, wild-eyed and breathless as she hugged Sean, then hurried to Wiley's bedside. There were tears in her eyes and her voice was trembling. The bruising on his chest was shocking and the pain in his eyes was visible.

"Wiley, honey! I heard gunshots from my office. I

didn't know until then that the bank was being robbed. I didn't know you were in the middle of it. Then they wouldn't let any of us out of the building until they'd cleared it for accomplices. I'm so sorry you were hurt. What can we do to help?"

Wiley patted her hand. "I'll be okay, but thanks for caring. I am one lucky dude. I have the best family."

"Do you want to come home with us for a few days?" Shirley asked. "At least until you're a little more comfortable?"

"I'll be okay, Mom, but thank you for the invitation. However, I won't say no to receiving home cooking you care to share."

Shirley smiled. "That, I will gladly do."

A short while later, Wiley was waiting for his release papers when Linette appeared in his doorway.

"Hey, you! Come talk to me," he said.

She hesitated, eyeing the family around him, then slipped past them to get to his bed.

"What's the verdict?" she asked.

"Cracked rib. Big-ass bruise. They're getting the paperwork ready to sign me out." Then he reached for her hand. "Thank you for everything. You are one cool lady under fire. Please tell me none of that blood is yours."

She glanced down at the gray shirt with the big red *no* and realized the word was a good statement for the hell they'd lived through.

"It's not mine. It's Mr. Trotter's."

Wiley frowned. "I'm so sorry. And this isn't how I imagined introducing you to my family, but you already know my brothers. This is my mom, Shirley Pope. Mom, this is Linette Elgin. She was in the bank, and the first one I saw coming toward me after I was shot."

Linette smiled at Shirley. "We've met. I was Sean's nurse when he was shot."

"Oh yes! I remember," Shirley said. "And here you are again, helping another one of my sons. We are so grateful."

"We're the ones who are grateful," Linette said. "He saved our lives." Then she realized Wiley was still holding her hand, and gave it a squeeze before turning loose. "I should go. I just wanted to make sure you were okay before I went home. Take care of yourself."

And then she was gone.

Wiley sighed. Other than the bank, this was the first time she'd spoken to him since their disastrous first date a year ago, and with family all over the place, he couldn't say what he wanted to say.

And then a nurse came in with his release papers, followed by an orderly with a wheelchair, and he was on his way home.

———

Aaron's wife, Dani, had been in Bowling Green when everything happened, and by the time Aaron found time to call her, she was already on her way home. She met him at the door when he got off work that evening, wrapped her arms around him, and held him without speaking until he could talk without choking up.

"Is he okay?" Dani asked.

"He will be. He has a big contusion on his chest and a cracked rib, and feels like shit."

"Everyone's saying he saved a lot of lives," Dani said.

"It appears so, but they killed Mr. Trotter before he even knew it was happening.

"Why was Wiley even there?" Dani asked.

"He went in to tell them someone had damaged their ATM."

She shuddered. "Go shower and get out of uniform. Supper is almost ready."

Aaron tunneled his hands through her hair and kissed her. "I won't be long," he said, and took off up the hall as Dani went back to the kitchen to finish up their meal.

———

Linette's plans for the day were over. She was on the verge of coming undone as she drove home, and as fate wasn't through ruining the day, Cecily Michaels was right behind her, loaded down with grocery bags, when she got on the elevator.

Linette saw the look of horror on Cecily's face and rolled her eyes.

"Get in. I'm not going to kill you. Someone tried to

rob the bank. I was there when it happened, and I'm not in the mood to deal with you."

Cecily entered the elevator in disbelief. "Is that your blood?"

"No. It's Mr. Trotter's. He's dead," Linette said.

Cecily blinked, and then said nothing more.

Linette didn't know there were tears rolling down her face and wouldn't have cared. The doors closed. She pressed the fourth-floor button and then leaned against the wall, exhausted emotionally and physically, as the car began to rise.

She got off on her floor without looking back and headed for her apartment, but was sobbing by the time she unlocked the door. The familiarity and the silence were a blessing as she headed straight for the laundry area and stripped. She tossed everything she'd been wearing into the washing machine, then made a beeline for the bathroom.

As a nurse, she considered herself capable of setting aside emotions to deal with emergencies, but today had been different. It was going to be a long time, if ever, before she forgot the sound of the bullet ripping through Trotter's head, shattering bone and brain, then seeing Wiley lifted off his feet and falling backward from that shot in the chest.

She started to take a bath, and then opted for the shower instead and turned on the water. It ran cold before it got hot, but it didn't matter. She just needed to be clean.

Before she went to bed that night, she scrolled through her contact list, glad she hadn't deleted Wiley's number after all, and sent him a text.

> I know you're hurting. Don't be a tough guy.
> Take the pain pills and thank you again for what
> you did today. You saved a lot of people's lives,
> including mine.

Sean and Shirley stayed with Wiley until they were certain he was able to get up and down on his own, and left him to rest with a promise to be back tomorrow with food.

Finally, the house was quiet, and Wiley didn't have to think or talk. The pain pill he took was kicking in when he stretched out on the bed to sleep. He woke up a couple of hours later when his phone rang.

Pain rolled through him as he reached for it, then waited for the pain to pass before he answered.

"Hello?"

"Hey, Wiley. It's me, B.J. Is your extra key still under the frog statue on your back porch?"

"Yes, why?"

"Because I'm coming over, and I don't want you to have to get up to let me in. I'll be there in about five minutes, okay?"

"Okay," Wiley said, and then laid the phone back down without noticing he had other messages.

Minutes later, he heard his brother coming in the back door, then moving through the house to his bedroom. The worry on B.J.'s face was evident as he walked in, then pulled up a chair beside the bed.

"Wipe that look off your face. I'm okay. At least I will be," Wiley said.

B.J. leaned back in the chair, managed to smile, and then shook his head. "Huff and puff all you like. I'm staying the night with you."

Wiley frowned. "What the hell for?"

"For the hell of it," B.J. countered. "And I brought food."

"Well, all right then," Wiley said, but he was secretly glad not to be on his own. He didn't like being helpless, but he was close to it. "What time is it?"

"After six," B.J. said. "And I'll be leaving early in the a.m., so I won't mess up your beauty sleep, and be glad it's me and not Mom. She was already fretting until I told her I was coming. She would have been up every hour, on the hour, feeling your forehead for a temperature."

Wiley chuckled, and then groaned as he reached for his chest. "Shit. Don't make me laugh. It hurts."

"I know how to be an asshole. It's the least I can do," B.J. said.

Wiley stifled another laugh and groaned again. "Evidently," he muttered, and eased himself upright, then swung his legs off the side of the bed.

"Where are you going? What do you need?" B.J. asked.

"I'm going to wash up and eat what you brought. I'm

starved, and I'm not supposed to be taking the pain pills on an empty stomach."

B.J. helped Wiley stand. "Are you okay to get around on your own?"

Wiley nodded.

"Then I'll be in the kitchen," B.J. said.

The food was good, but the brotherhood was better. B.J. was still the same little brother inside, who now towered over all of them in height. He didn't pry. He also didn't comment over the fact that Wiley had shot three men today, or that he was also the hero of the hour.

Instead, he served up a second bowl of gumbo to Wiley, along with another hot crusty slice of a buttered baguette for dipping.

Finally, Wiley put down his spoon and put a hand on his chest as he leaned back in the chair. The cracked rib was as painful as the contusion area from the impact of the bullet, but his belly was full, and the room had quit spinning.

"Thank you, little brother. That was so good. I guess I should have said a prayer of thanksgiving before I ate, but I have too many drugs in me to think straight right now."

"Today, I am most thankful for the person who invented body armor," B.J. said. "The rest goes without saying."

Wiley grinned. "I have a question."

"What?" B.J. asked.

"Are you as big a wiseass in the kitchen as you are off the leash?"

B.J. shrugged. "I hated being yelled at when I was a sous-chef. I never saw the point in being loud, or being a jackass to people. So, I don't yell. I don't curse. But I have been known to point out the error of their ways in terms that illustrate my disgust or dismay, without hurting their feelings."

"Like how?" Wiley asked.

"Oh, I don't know…like the sous-chef that showed up last month. First day on the job, he's cutting off pieces of dough for French baguettes, and rolling them to size to set in the baguette pans to proof. They were abysmal, and I walked over to where he was working and quietly told him they looked like limp dicks and were never leaving my kitchen."

Wiley burst out laughing, then grabbed his chest and his stomach at the same time.

"Oh lord, that hurt, but the laugh was worth it! What did he do?"

"He just whispered, 'Yes, Chef,' without looking up, pulled the dough out of the pan, and the rest of them turned out fine. Now, I think you've been up enough for today. I'll help you in and out of the shower, then into bed. If you want to watch TV, you can do in lying down."

Wiley didn't argue. "You sound like Mom."

"We all still answer to her, and I don't want to be on her bad side. I promised I'd take care of you, and you're going to have to deal with it."

"Understood, and I'm too miserable to argue."

A short while later, Wiley was stretched out in bed again, fresh from a shower and satiated from the food in his belly. He'd taken another pain pill and B.J. pulled up the covers and handed him the TV remote.

"I'll be across the hall in the pink room," B.J. said.

Wiley grinned. "It was already pink when I moved in. Mom offered to decorate, and I didn't want to, so that's what she picked out, and I'm fine with it."

"It's all good. I was just teasing you," B.J. said. "Besides, I've never slept in such a girlie room in my life. Maybe it will speak to my feminine side."

"So says my Harley-riding brother who spent all of high school in silver-studded black leather and Wrangler jeans with the knees worn out."

B.J. shrugged. "It was a phase. Sleep well, and give a shout if you need me. I'm leaving the doors open between us." He headed out of the room, then paused in the door-way. "I am so very glad you're still alive, Brother," he said, then turned off the light and walked out.

Wiley closed his eyes. Moments later, tears rolled from the corners and onto the pillow beneath his head. All he could think was, *So am I.*

Chapter 2

B.J. GOT UP WITH WILEY ONCE MORE IN THE NIGHT, and when Wiley woke up again, it was daylight and his brother was gone.

He thought about seeing Linette at the ER. He'd wanted so badly to talk to her, but the timing was off. He still regretted what had happened between them and the disaster their first date became, and all because of two jealous women—Cecily Michaels, who he first met while working at Reagan Bullard's music venue, and Rhonda Tiller, who worked as a desk clerk at Hotel Devon.

He'd dated Cecily once and Rhonda twice, and then never called them again, although they'd chased him around town for a few weeks to no avail. He was polite and friendly, but they were a little too into themselves to suit.

Then on his first date with Linette, they made it their mission to mess it up for him. All he could figure was they'd gotten together to do it, because seeing both of them show up on his first date with Linette was no accident. One of them showed up at Trapper's

Bar and Grill, where he'd taken Linette, and flirted with Wiley in front of Linette without even acknowledging she was sitting there, and then blew him a kiss and left.

He was stunned and embarrassed, and trying to explain when the second one showed up and did the very same thing. To his dismay, Linette got up and walked out, and he hadn't seen her since—until yesterday in the bank, blood-splattered and coming to his aid.

He was still in bed, trying to work up the courage to move when his phone signaled a text. It was from his mom.

Text me when you wake so I'll know you're okay. Whatever you need, just let me know and I'll bring it. Love you.

He smiled, then responded.

Just woke up. I'm okay. B.J. spent the night. He's gone to work now. I'm just lying around taking it easy. Don't worry.

It was only after he hit Send that he realized Linette had texted him last night. The fact that she'd followed up gave him hope that he might have a second chance with her after all, and he responded.

Sorry I missed your text. My brother B.J. came

to babysit me and I fell asleep. I promise I'm not
messing around. I'm too sore to blink. Thank
YOU for helping me. Scariest shit in the world to
be conscious and unable to take a breath. I owe
you. Maybe one day you'll let me try that dinner
date with you again, but without the bullshit. They
thought it was funny. I didn't. It was unforgivable.
I've blocked their calls.

Linette was already at work when she got the text.
She felt the phone vibrating in her pocket, but had to
ignore it until she had a free minute to check it, and
then her heart skipped when she saw it was from Wiley.
She read his message, then smiled. Best news she'd had
in weeks.

———

As always, B.J. was at work early, and when the first
croissants came out of the oven, he boxed up six of
them, along with a small jar of honey butter, and called
DoorDash to come pick it up from the Serenity Inn and
deliver it to Wiley's house, with instructions to hand it
to him personally.

Then he sent a text to Wiley.

DoorDash delivery coming your way. Breakfast on
me. Take care, big brother.
B.J.

Wiley was sitting on the edge of the bed, contemplating whether to get up and shave, or live with the black whiskers, when he got the text. He smiled as he read the message. No cold cereal for him. He managed to pull on a pair of sweatpants and a T-shirt before making his way to the front of the house.

The cool floor felt good beneath his feet as he went to the kitchen to start coffee, but he needed no reminders to go slow. Everything hurt.

A few minutes later, his doorbell rang. He was sweating by the time he got to the door to retrieve the box, then headed back to the kitchen.

"Oh man," he said when he saw what was inside, then grabbed a butter knife and carried the whole box to the table. He picked up a croissant and took the first bite plain, reveling in the flaky exterior and the melt-in-your-mouth interior. After that, it was honey butter on every bite.

He quit at four. Eyeing the remaining two with regret and a promise to himself to finish them later, he poured himself a second cup of coffee and downed a pain pill, then sent a quick text back to B.J.

Thanks for breakfast! It was amazing, and so are you.

Then he eased back down the hall, decided to keep the whiskers, and crawled into bed, hoping he'd get a text back from Linette giving him the okay to call. And at the same time, Linette was impatiently waiting for that second invitation, without realizing she hadn't responded to his text.

━━━━━━

Rhonda Tiller was at the nail salon when Cecily Michaels walked in. They gave each other a wary glance, but when Cecily sat down at the station next to Rhonda, Rhonda leaned over and whispered in her ear.

"Did you know Wiley was shot during that bank robbery?"

Cecily nodded. "Did you know Linette Elgin lives in the same apartment building that I just moved into?"

"No way!" Rhonda said.

"Yes, way," Cecily muttered. "She was also at that bank when the robbery happened. I saw her in the elevator when she was leaving the building, and when she came home later, she was covered in blood and very shaken."

Rhonda frowned. She didn't want to empathize. "So what? She's a nurse."

Cecily frowned. "You know...she never did anything to us, but she got hurt because of what we did to Wiley."

Rhonda shrugged. "I don't care. We got back at him."

Cecily sighed. "I know, but for what? All that just because he didn't ask us out again?"

Rhonda sniffed. "Nobody blocks me and gets away with it."

"It happened because of what we did, and in the process, we made an enemy of him. I'm mad at myself for ever agreeing to do it," Cecily said.

Rhonda ignored her. They'd bonded over a mutual issue, but Cecily Michaels could walk out of her life today and Rhonda wouldn't miss her.

―――――――

Pope Mountain: A week later

The rain came before sundown. A hard but steady downfall with only the distant grumble of thunder. No wind. No lightning. Just a blinding sheet of water, but Carey Eggers couldn't stop. She was running for her life. She'd taken a wrong turn on her way back to Bowling Green and didn't know where she was, other than she'd been driving up a mountain, and now she was driving down.

Her fingers were numb from gripping the steering wheel, and she kept watching for headlights behind her while trying to keep her eye on the road. But the rain made it hard to see the white line on the blacktop, and the windshield wipers were a continual squeak— the only sound within the car other than her short ragged breaths. Her brother was dead, she just knew it And, if she couldn't lose the killer behind her, she would be, too.

If only she could take back her decisions.

The windshield wipers were worthless, but mesmer-
izing. And she kept remembering waking up this morning with nothing but Johnny's welfare on her mind.

———————

Bowling Green, Kentucky: Hours earlier

Carey helped her fiancé, Johnny Knight, into bed,
gave him his pain pills, and sat beside him until he fell
asleep. As soon as he was out, she grabbed her purse
and phone and left the house to catch the city bus. She
needed to go to a suburb of the city, where her brother,
Billy Eggers, lived.

She got off the bus at her stop, then started walking
to his house to ask for help. It never occurred to her that
he might be gone until she was almost there, and then
she began to panic. What if he wasn't home? Then what
was she going to do? But when she got closer and saw
his car parked in the yard and saw him coming out of
the front door, she started running.

Billy saw her, then stopped and raised a hand in
greeting.

"Little sister! Are you lost?" he said as she ran into
his arms.

"No. But I need help. I don't get paid for another
week, and Johnny's out of pain meds. Can you loan me
money to get them refilled?"

Billy was just a head taller than her, and both of

them bordered on the edge of skinny as he put his arm around her.

"Bless your heart, sugar! Why didn't you call me?"

She ducked her head. "I don't know. I guess because I didn't want to ask for money and then ask you to deliver it?"

He hugged her again. "Truck on the fritz again?"

She nodded.

"Come inside," he said as they walked in together. "How much do you need?"

"The meds are almost a hundred dollars," she said. "He's getting better I think, but I can't stand for him to suffer."

Billy nodded. "Get yourself something cold to drink. I've got to open the safe."

She headed for the kitchen and was drinking Pepsi from a can when he returned and handed her a wad of bills. "Here's five hundred to tide you over."

"Oh my God! Thank you, Billy! You're the best," Carey said.

He ruffled her blond curls. "At everything, and don't you forget it," he said. "Oh, and you don't pay me back. This is a gift from me to you."

Carey threw her arms around his neck. "Thank you. You're the best brother ever."

He grinned. "Yeah, I know. I can give you a ride back to the bus stop, but I can't take you home. I'm heading the other way, and already late," Billy said.

"It's okay, and thanks," Carey said. She stuffed

the money in her purse and slung the strap over her shoulder.

But the sound of an approaching car shifted Billy's mood as he glanced out the window.

"Shit."

"What's wrong?" Carey asked.

He handed her the keys to his car. "Get in the utility room. If you hear gunshots, go out the back door, take my car, and don't look back."

"No, Billy, how will you—"

"Just do it!" he said, and shoved her hard. "And hurry!"

She tightened her grip on the keys and bolted, closing the door to the utility room behind her, and then unlocking and opening the back door, just in case she needed to make a quick escape. Her heart was hammering as she hunkered down in a corner to listen.

Seconds later, she heard someone pounding on the front door, and then loud voices. Billy was yelling at someone, and they kept shouting something about acting on orders, and Billy was yelling back and said a word that sounded like *gunny*, or *money*, and the other person said something about invading someone else's territory, and then a gunshot, followed by a horrifying silence. That's when Carey knew Billy was down. That's when she got up and ran.

Every step she took across the yard, she imagined that it would be her last, but that didn't happen. She made it to the car and sped up the driveway, in a panic to put as much distance between her and the man who'd just shot her brother. She glanced up once and caught a glimpse of a man running out of the house, then stomped on the accelerator, heading back toward the little town just as the sun was going down. If she could get out of sight before he caught up, she might be able to get away. She was scared and crying now, fearing that what had happened to Billy was going to happen to her.

She blasted through the suburb, ignoring the speed limit, and made an instant decision not to lead him straight to her house. Johnny was already hurt. The last thing she wanted was to get him killed, so she took a turn that led her away from the city. Barely two miles further, she drove into the storm. The rain was a deluge. Wind was blowing it sideways, but since she couldn't see a car length behind her, she reasoned the man wouldn't be able to see her either and kept driving.

About a half hour later, she finally accepted she was lost and called Johnny just to let him know what had happened. When he didn't answer, she guessed he was still asleep and left a frantic message about where she'd gone, what had happened, and that it was raining so hard, she couldn't tell where she was. She was crying when she said, "I love you," afraid that she'd never see him again.

———

Two hours later, she was driving down a two-lane road on a mountain she'd never seen before, and as lost as she'd ever been. All she saw behind her was the horizontal rain and a night so dark there was no definition. Had it not been for the car's headlights, it would have been like driving into oblivion.

She shifted slightly in her seat and, as she did, glanced up in the rearview mirror again and caught a flash of light a distance behind her. When it disappeared, she guessed the car had just taken the curve on the road that she'd left behind only minutes earlier.

She panicked, and then immediately began trying to reassure herself.

Calm down. It could be anyone. But her gut instinct was to speed up. She stomped on the gas, and when she did, the car fishtailed slightly. She overcorrected, hydroplaned, and all of a sudden, she was off the road and heading straight for the trees looming in her headlights.

She screamed, and then IMPACT!

The world was spinning, the rain was still coming down, and through the illumination from the headlights, she could see the wind whipping the tree limbs. She was hurting all the way to the bone when she remembered the car behind her and looked back, just as headlights became visible in the distance.

In a panic, she began scrambling to get out and then couldn't move. It took her a few moments to remember she was still buckled in.

Seat belt. Seat belt.

Her fingers were shaking as it came undone, and then her door was jammed and wouldn't open. In a panic, she pocketed her phone, grabbed the flashlight from her console, then crawled over it and out the passenger door that had come open upon impact.

Despite the pain, she was still mobile, and she took off into the forest without turning on a light, blinded by the wind and rain. She looked back only once and saw a light bouncing around the crashed car, and then gasped when the light moved into the woods.

Oh God! Somebody was following her! It had to be him!

She turned left to dodge a tree and increased her speed and, as she did, realized she was running up an incline, going back the way she'd come. She didn't know what was out here in these woods, but anything was better than what was behind her. In her panic, she ran headlong into brambles before finally tearing herself loose, then a hundred yards farther, nearly knocked herself out when she ran into a low-hanging limb. She didn't know if she'd lost him. She just kept running with the wind and rain blasting her, knowing the storm was drowning out all sound.

When Lonny Pryor came over the hill and saw taillights off the road and into the trees, every thought within him focused.

I've got her.

He pulled off the side of the road and, as he did, saw a flash of movement and then nothing. He pocketed his weapon, grabbed an LED flashlight, and got out and started toward the car. He was so focused on the tail-lights that he didn't see the ditch until he stepped off into it and went belly down in the mud and rain.

"Son of a bitch!" he yelped as his knee landed on a rock, but he was back on his feet and moving within seconds.

When he reached the car and found it empty, he cursed again and aimed the flashlight down, catching a glimpse of footprints washing away in the rain. But they were going into the forest, and he had no option but to follow. This night just kept getting worse. What should have been an easy job had turned into a clusterfuck.

Nobody told him Billy Eggers had a woman. Nobody even warned them of the possibility of one. He hadn't gone there to do anything but ask Eggers if he knew anything about a new crew dealing drugs in town. But Billy had been confrontational, telling him he knew nothing and to get the hell out of his house. In frustration, Lonny pulled his gun, just to threaten him. He hadn't expected Eggers to grab the gun Lonny waved in his face, and the rest was history. He didn't know anyone was in the house until he saw the woman running across the front yard. When she jumped into Eggers's car and sped away, he was in shock.

That was over four hours ago, and if he hadn't taken Eggers's phone to use as a GPS locator, he would never have found her. Only now the car was in the trees, and she was long gone. All he could do was keep running, in hopes she'd hurt herself bad enough in the wreck to finally stop on her own. He was dodging trees and undergrowth, but his knee was throbbing, and when he fell and banged it again, he got up slower, cursing.

After that, it was slow going, looking for any kind of sign that the rain couldn't wash away. Ten minutes into the search, he found a small piece of cloth hanging from a bramblebush. The same color as the jacket the woman had been wearing. He was on the right track!

A short while later, he found another piece of denim fabric hanging from a broken branch on the trail. She'd been wearing jeans! It appeared he wasn't the only one falling. Ignoring the pain, he hastened his speed.

Carey's head was throbbing so badly she couldn't think. She turned on the flashlight to get her bearings and then reached for her head. Her fingers came away red with blood, and then she watched in horror as the rain swiftly washed it away.

Am I running for nothing? Am I going to die from a head wound and blood loss before he catches me? Why, God? Why me? But she knew the answer before she took her next breath. *Because I was there.*

She aimed the flashlight in the direction she'd been running and saw nothing beyond the beam of light. She was too tired and weak to keep going up. It was time to start moving downhill. Hopefully she'd see a house or a place to hide. She knew she was taking a chance using the flashlight now, but it was still raining so hard that he'd have to be standing beside her to see the beam. She kept moving forward, slowly angling downhill as she went.

But the farther down she went, the harder it was becoming to breathe, and she wondered what she'd done to herself when her chest hit the steering wheel. She was beginning to get dizzy. Half-blinded by the rain, she found herself staggering and once thought she'd been walking in circles.

She stopped to rest against a tree, grateful for the brief shelter beneath the branches. Once she'd caught her breath, she started off again and, within moments, stumbled and fell. Her phone fell out of her pocket, and she dropped her flashlight. She crawled to where it had fallen, picked it up, and was struggling to stand when a bullet tore through her shoulder. The impact threw her forward into the underbrush, and then everything went black.

Lonny grunted with satisfaction. He'd stopped her, but he needed to make sure she was dead. He aimed his flashlight down at the compass on his watch and was starting toward where she'd fallen when a shaft of lightning came down in the trees so close to where he was standing that the hair rose on the back of his head. He saw flames through the rain, followed by a crack of thunder so loud his ears popped.

"To hell with this," he muttered, and headed back

the way he'd come, running as fast as he could move through the trees.

By the time he got back to the road, the lights had gone off on her car, which was good. It would be daylight before anyone could possibly see the wreck, and thanks to the rain, no one would ever know he'd been there.

But he had a problem. He'd wrecked his knee. He was bleeding like a stuck pig and in serious pain. No way was he going to be able to drive like this. He knew Jubilee was further down the mountain and he needed help, but he couldn't call an ambulance, and he wasn't sure he wanted to walk into the ER and show his face. He didn't want anyone to be able to say they'd even seen him in the vicinity.

He sat for a few moments, frantically going through the contacts on his phone when he saw the name Lilah Perry and paused. They'd parted company over two years ago, but not in anger.

Impulsively, he called her number, listened to it ringing, and sighed, fearing she wasn't going to answer, and then she did.

"Hello?"

"Lilah, it's me, Lonny."

"What the hell, Lonny? It's blowing up a storm down here."

"Are you still in Jubilee?"

"Yes, why?"

"At the same place?" he asked.

"Oh, for God's sake, Lonny, just spit it out," Lilah snapped.

"I got caught in the storm and had a flat. I slipped changing it and hurt my bad knee. I need to get it patched up before I drive home. I was wondering if you would—"

"Can't you just go to the ER?" she asked.

"That's money I don't have," Lonny said.

She sighed. "Yeah, well, I understand that. Yes, I'm in the same place. Can you drive well enough to get here?"

Lonny breathed a sigh of relief. "Yeah. I really appreciate this, Lilah. I'm not asking to stay. Just long enough to get it bandaged up and stop the bleeding."

"Jesus, Lonny! Are you bleeding bad?"

"Enough, but not enough to kill me. I'll see you soon," he said, and hung up, then put the car in gear and took off down the mountain.

The lights of Jubilee were a welcome sight when he finally drove through town. The streets were empty. No one in their right mind would be out on a night like this, and he kept going east on the main drag until he came to the oldest residential area of Jubilee and turned left. Lilah Perry's house was the last one on Thornehill Drive, and she'd turned the porch light on.

He pulled up into her driveway, stuffed the gun beneath the seat, and hobbled through the rain and up the steps to her front door. She opened it before he could knock.

Without makeup and her hair all sleep-squished

on one side, Lilah looked every day of her forty-seven years and then some.

"Come inside before you drown," she said. "And stand on the doormat and strip. I don't want you dripping all over my house."

He didn't hesitate and stripped down to his underwear. The deep cut on his knee was plainly visible, as was the rapidly spreading bruising around it.

"You did mess that knee up," she said. "Here. Lean on me. You need a warm shower. Scrub soap in that cut while you're at it, and then I'll doctor it when you're all dry."

Lonny was hurting too bad to argue. As soon as she got him in the shower, she disappeared, and he went about the business of washing the evidence of two murders off his body, while thinking it was unfortunate the shower could not cleanse his soul.

Lilah picked up his clothes, wrinkling her nose at the smell as she carried them to the utility room. She wasn't going to wash them, but she would toss them in the dryer. She got a glimpse of herself as she passed by the mirror in the hall and rolled her eyes.

"I look like shit, which should work in my favor. I don't want him getting interested again. It took too long to get rid of him the first time," she muttered, and headed into her bedroom.

As soon as she heard the water turn off, she went into the bathroom with a handful of old towels.

"Dry off in the tub. I can wash the blood out easier than mop it up."

Lonny did as he was told, feeling slightly emasculated as she eyed his nude body. He never had been buff, but he'd let his belly go to paunch and couldn't even see his dick anymore.

"Step out easy," Lilah said, and held his arm to steady him. "Now, wrap this towel around you and sit down on the toilet lid, and we'll see to this knee."

Lonny sat. The cut was bleeding. His knee was throbbing. His head was pounding. He was at the feeling-sorry-for-himself stage when she poured alcohol into the cut. He yelped.

"Holy shit, Lilah! That burned!"

"You need stitches," she muttered.

"Well, that ain't gonna happen," he said, and then moaned when she doused the cut with alcohol again.

"It's not going to heal without them. Every time you bend your knee, it's going to bust open and bleed."

"Well, can you at least bandage it up good enough that I can get home without bleeding out? I'll get my Medicaid card from the house and go straight to the hospital there."

She frowned. "Yes, that'll work. I need one of those stretchy bandage things to hold the gauze pads in place, but I don't have any. Wait a second. I have something that will work," she said, and ran into her bedroom.

He heard her banging doors and drawers and then she was back.

"I haven't worn these in years, but I thought I still had a pair," she said, and dropped down on her knees and began tearing open packets of gauze pads until she had eight of them sandwiched together. "Straighten out your leg," she said, and as soon as he did, she placed the pads on top of the cut and pulled a pair of pantyhose from the pocket of her robe. She folded the panty part, pressed it tightly over the gauze pads, and then began wrapping the legs around his knee in opposite directions, pulling tightly with each rotation, until she ended up with the feet on top and tied them as tightly as she could pull, then stood him up. "There. That'll hold until you can get home."

Lonny groaned again. "Got any over-the-counter pain meds?"

Lilah took a bottle from the medicine cabinet, shook three five-hundred-milligram capsules into his hand, and ran tap water into a glass and handed it to him.

He downed them in one gulp and emptied the glass.

"Just sit. And keep your leg as straight as you can. Good thing it's your left knee. I'll go see if your clothes are dry enough to put back on."

Lonny stared at his wet underwear lying on the floor. No way was he putting those back on. He was going home commando.

Lilah returned a few minutes later and handed him his shirt.

"They're still damp, but you can at least get them back on."

"I don't see as how it matters," he muttered, as he pulled the shirt over his head. "It's still raining like a big dog. I'm just gonna get wet all over again."

"You can have my umbrella. And don't bother

bringing it back. Consider this a random moment in time that shall never be repeated," she said.

"Yes, ma'am."

Then she leaned over, helped him get his legs into the pants, then stood him up.

"Okay. You're done. Your boots are by the door. Let's get you shod and on your way."

Lonny stiff-legged it through the house, leaned on her as he stomped his feet back into his boots, and picked up his car keys from the table where he'd dropped them when he'd dropped his drawers.

She walked him out onto the porch and handed him the umbrella.

"Looks like the rain is letting up some. Drive safe. There are all kinds of crazy people out there," she said.

And I'm one of them, he thought as he hobbled down the steps and to his car. By the time he got situated inside the car, she'd already closed her door and turned off the porch light.

He started the car, backed out of the drive, and headed back through town and up Pope Mountain. When he passed the scene of the wreck, he never even looked in that direction. He was bothered by the events of this day, but what was done was done. He also knew that when Billy Eggers's body was discovered, his DNA would be all over it.

This shit show was far from over.

Lilah Perry walked back into the bathroom to clean up, saw Lonny's sodden underwear lying by the shower, and carried it through the house and tossed it in the garbage can off the back porch. She went back inside and cleaned up her bathroom until there wasn't a remnant of Lonny Pryor left, then went back to bed. Her alarm would go off at 5:00 a.m., and she'd be clocking in at work at the Jubilee PD by seven. She had been working as a clerk in records for almost two years. It was the best job she'd ever had.

Chapter 3

LONNY PRYOR GOT BACK TO HIS APARTMENT JUST after daybreak. He'd driven straight to the ER to get his knee fixed and sat stoically through it all while the doctor and nurse razzed him about the pantyhose bandage as they applied surgical glue to close the cut. He nodded and laughed with them and was grateful for the prescription for pain pills when he walked out.

His visit to Billy Eggers had gone south, but he thought he'd cleaned up the witness. He didn't know who she was, but he figured she'd bleed out or exposure would finish the job. He entered his apartment, weary to the bone. Stowed the handgun in his safe, then called in. The phone rang three times before it was answered.

"Hello?"

"This is Gunny."

"Yeah?"

"Shit happened," he said.

Junior Henley paused. "What kind of shit?"

"Eggers got violent. We got into a heated argument. I pulled my gun. We wrestled with it, and it went off. He's dead."

"Dead! You weren't supposed to kill him!" Junior shouted.

"Yeah, well, it happened. And that's not all. There was a woman at the house, and I didn't know it until I saw her running to his car. I gave chase, but I had to run her down across two counties to shut her up. You never told me he had a woman."

"Son of a bitch! He didn't have a woman. What did she look like?"

"A skinny little blond with curly hair."

"That's his sister, or should I say, 'She was his sister'? So, she's out of the picture, too?"

"She is now," Gunny said.

"You're sure?" Junior asked.

"Well, I chased her through a freaking forest in a rainstorm and shot her in the back," Gunny said.

"What did you do with the body?"

"Nothing. I missed getting struck by lightning by about fifty feet. I messed up my knee and got my ass out of there. She'd already wrecked the car. She was disoriented and walking in circles when I caught up to her," Gunny said.

"How the hell did you find her?"

"Eggers had a tracker app on his phone for his own car. All I had to do was follow the blip."

"What did you do with the phone?" Junior asked.

"Busted it into pieces and threw it out the window on the way home."

Junior sighed. "Yeah, okay. What about the gun?"

"Yes. I'll bring it over tomorrow."

"No. You bring it over now. It's Dad's. I need it back," Junior said.

Gunny frowned. "Dammit, Junior! I just got the cut in my knee glued shut. I hurt like hell, and I'm beat, and you gave me a registered gun? What the fuck's wrong with you?"

The line went dead in his ear.

He went back to the safe and got the gun, then stopped at the kitchen table and broke it down, wiped his prints from every piece, and then wiped the ammo before reassembling the gun and reloading it. Then he hobbled back to his car and drove all the way across town and into the ritzy part of the city to Henley's estate, pulled up in front of the iron gates across the driveway, then waited.

Moments later, the gates opened. He drove through, then around to the delivery entrance, got out with the gun, and rang the buzzer.

Seconds later, the door opened. Junior Henley was in the doorway. Gunny handed the gun over. "Are we good?" he asked.

"We're good," Junior said.

Gunny went back to the truck and drove home, but Junior's troubles were just beginning. He had to get rid of his father's gun and deal with the wrath of it going missing, and he had to let him know what had happened with the visit to Eggers. The lucky part for Junior was Daddy wasn't home, so he loaded everything up in his Porsche, made a call, and left the property.

———————

Johnny Knight was groggy from the pain pills he'd taken after lunch and lay down to sleep about midafternoon. Carey had tucked him in and told him she loved him, and that's the last thing he remembered until he woke to a dark house. Surprised that it was so late, he rolled over to check the time and frowned. It was fifteen minutes after 3:00 a.m. and Carey wasn't in bed beside him. He threw back the covers and sat up on the side of the bed until he got his bearings, and then grabbed his crutches and stood. The room was spinning, but it would stop, so he waited until it did and then went to the bathroom, sloshed some water on his face, and opened the bottle of pain meds. Only two left.

He replaced the lid and put it back in the cabinet. There was no money for refills, and the titanium rods and screws in his leg weren't going away. He'd been a lineman for the electric company for almost ten years, and the fall he'd taken should have killed him. Instead, it had shattered his right leg from the knee down. The bones would knit back together, but he'd never climb another power pole or walk with ease again.

They'd been living off of Carey's tips from waitressing while waiting for workman's compensation to start paying out, and she wasn't getting paid for five more days. He wasn't sure he could hold out that long without pain meds, but he was about to find out.

He grabbed his crutches and headed for the living room, thinking Carey must have opted to sleep on the sofa to give him room in the bed. But the living room was empty, and when he began turning on the lights, it didn't take long for him to realize her purse and phone were gone.

He hobbled back to the bedroom to get his phone, then sat back down on the side of the bed to call her and realized she'd left him a voicemail.

"Johnny, I caught the bus to Billy's to borrow some money to get your meds refilled. He was just about to give me a ride home when someone drove up. Johnny gave me his car keys, told me to hide and, if I heard gunshots or fighting, to take his car and run."

When she paused to take a breath, Johnny's heart stopped, too. The panic in her voice was more than he could bear.

"There was a horrible argument, a lot of shouting, and I heard Billy say something that sounded like gunny or money, *and the man said something about new men in the territory, then sounds of a fight and furniture breaking, then a gunshot. I ran out the back door, jumped in Billy's car, and drove away. I know the man was following me, but the sun went down and now I'm driving in this terrible rainstorm. I don't know where I am, and I think Billy's dead, or he would have called."*

When she choked on a sob and paused, he wanted to cry with her, and then she continued.

"I think I took a wrong turn. I just wanted you to know. I'll try to call again, but the cell service is spotty. I think I'm in the mountains. I love you."

Johnny Knight was so scared he couldn't breathe. His hands were trembling as he called her number over and over, but it kept going to voicemail, so he called his best friend, Thomas Wheaton. Tom was a cop. He would know what to do. But the phone rang and rang, and just as he thought it was going to go to voicemail, he heard Tom's voice, short and bordering on aggravation.

"Damn it, Johnny. This better be good."

"I just woke up. Carey's gone and there's a hell of a voicemail from her on my phone. She was at Billy's. She thinks Billy's dead, and she's on the run from the man who shot him. She's driving Billy's car. She drove into a rainstorm in the dark and she's lost. It's all on the voice-mail. I don't know how to report this. I can't fuckin' walk, and our car is in the shop. I need help."

Tom was already out of bed and pulling on clothes.

"I'm on the way. Hang in there, buddy. I need to hear the message to figure out who to report this to, and we'll go from there. Give me fifteen minutes. Unlock your front door and turn on the porch light."

"Thank you," Johnny said, and then the line went dead.

He hobbled to the front door on his crutches, unlocked it, then turned on the porch light. He was hurting, but he wasn't taking anything that would put him to sleep, so he popped three over-the-counter pain pills and sat down to wait.

Thomas Wheaton pulled up into the driveway at Johnny's house, got out on the run, and when he walked in the house and saw the look on his buddy's face, his heart sank.

"Have you heard back from her yet?"

Johnny shook his head and gave him the phone.

Tom listened to the message, and then handed it back and pulled his notebook and pen out of his back pocket. "What's Billy's address?" he asked, then wrote it down when Johnny told him. "What time did Carey leave?"

"I don't know for sure. She helped me into bed a little after three p.m., I think. I'd taken pain pills and fell asleep. I woke up to this message, but she sent it just after eight p.m., and I didn't wake up until just before I called you. I tried to call her over and over, but it just goes to voicemail."

"What kind of car does he drive?" Tom asked.

"Last I knew, it was a white 2019 Jeep Cherokee," Johnny said.

"Billy's got priors," Tom said. "If he's dead, it's likely drug related."

"Oh, hell, we both knew that. But he's all the family Carey has, and Billy practically raised her. He worships the ground she walks on."

"Are you out of pain meds?" Tom asked.

"I have two left. I've been saving them for when it gets really bad."

"Shit, Johnny. You could have asked me. Sit tight. We'll deal with your meds in a minute. Right now, I need to call all this in."

Johnny leaned back and closed his eyes as Tom walked out of the room to make the call, but he couldn't stop the tears. Carey was his life, and he was scared to death that hers was already over. He could hear Tom's voice in the other room, but let the sounds roll over him. All he wanted was for Carey to walk in the door with that beautiful smile on her face.

A few minutes later, Tom came back. "Here's what's happening," he said. "The first thing they're doing is a welfare check at Billy Eggers's residence. If he's dead, they'll go from there. We put out a BOLO for his car. And the detectives are running the name Gunny through the system on the off chance there's actually someone in the system with that alias. We'll see how many hits we get on that. Now tell me where the bottle is with your pain meds."

"In the bathroom medicine cabinet," Johnny said.

Tom headed for the bedroom and then into the en suite bathroom. When he came back, he laid the two remaining pain pills on the table.

"I'm going to get this refilled. I'll be back."

Johnny wiped the tears off his face and nodded. "I owe you."

"You owe me nothing, John Knight. Nothing. We're friends. We'll get through this together. Understood?"

Johnny nodded.

"Take the pain meds," Tom said.

"Can't. Not until I know what's happened to my girl."

"Jesus, Johnny. It could take—"

Johnny looked up.

Tom sighed. "Right. I think there's a twenty-four-hour pharmacy not too far from here. I'll be back as soon as I can. Do you need help getting back to bed?"

"No. I can manage. But take my house key with you. It's in that dish on the hall table. Lock the door when you leave."

———————

The welfare check at Billy Eggers's house yielded exactly what Carey had described. The front door was ajar. The living room was a disaster, and Billy's body was lying in a pool of congealed blood. The back door to the house was open, and his car was missing. Crime scene investigators were called to the scene, as was the county coroner. The can of Pepsi that Carey had been drinking was bagged along with everything else, including a spent cartridge shell.

———————

It was just after daybreak when Annie Cauley left her house on Pope Mountain to make her daily drive down into Jubilee. There would be people waiting in line for her baked goods by 6:00 a.m., and she needed to have Granny Annie's Bakery open for business. She knew her daughter, Laurel, would have driven in before daylight and already be at the shop setting dough to rise.

She hadn't slept well because of last night's storm. The rain had been a deluge, and when she walked out onto the back porch to watch the sunrise, she could hear the water coming off Big Falls and roaring down the creek that ran through Jubilee, even from this far away.

She and her husband, John, were one of the families living highest on Pope Mountain, so the drive down every morning was a long one. She was coming up on the road leading to her nephew Cameron's house when she caught a glimpse of a white vehicle off into the trees on the south side of the road. It was obvious it had crashed, and the passenger door was standing open.

Annie slammed on the brakes and killed the engine, then got out on the run, taking care not to slide as she moved down into the ditch. Her worst fear was that she'd find a body. She saw a purse lying on the floorboard, but the car was empty. Knowing better than to disturb anything that might turn into evidence, she ran back to her car and made a quick call to Cameron. It rang a couple of times before he answered.

"Hello."

"Cameron, this is Annie. There's a wrecked car off in the trees a couple of hundred yards up from your driveway, but no driver in sight. Do you know anything about this?"

"No! It rained so hard last night the only thing I could hear was Ghost whining. He hates storms. So obviously no one has reported this, or the police and a wrecker would already be on the scene. You call it in. I'll take Ghost and see if he can track whoever was in it."

"Yes, okay, but I can't imagine how there'd be a scent left after all that rain," Annie said.

"It won't wash it away. It just disperses it a little. Ghost is good. Maybe we'll get lucky. Thanks for letting me know, Auntie." Cameron said.

"Of course," Annie said, and after they disconnected, she called the Jubilee police.

"Jubilee PD, Sergeant Winter speaking."

"Walter, this is Annie Cauley. I just found a wrecked car off in the trees just up the road from Cameron's driveway. The car is empty; the door is wide open. I saw belongings in the car but no sign of the driver. It looks like a bad accident. Has anyone been picked up from here in the night?"

"Let me check the log," Walter said, and then came back. "No, ma'am. There was not. I'll get dispatch on this. Thanks for calling it in," he said.

"Sure thing, and Cameron's taking Ghost to the crash site to see if they can find the missing driver," Annie added.

"I'll make a note," Walter said.

Satisfied she'd done all she could, Annie continued her trip into town, as Cameron headed for the bedroom to change his clothes. Ghost sensed an outing and followed him.

Cameron's wife, Rusty, was getting their little boy, Mikey, dressed, when she heard Cameron coming toward the bedrooms.

"We're in here," she said.

He paused in the doorway to Mikey's room, and couldn't help smiling. Their son was growing so fast. He'd be in first grade this year and, like every other Pope, was tall for his age. But he was arguing with his mother about going out to play.

"Michael! What did Mama say?" Cameron asked.

Mikey ducked his head. "Too wet to go outside."

"Then why are you arguing with her? You're not in charge around here, boy. You do what Mama says, understand?"

Mikey frowned, but the tone in his daddy's voice was the one that meant business. He nodded.

"And what do you say to Mama?" Cameron prompted.

Mikey looked up and smiled at Rusty. "Mama's pretty."

Cameron grinned.

Rusty snorted. "Lord. Like father, like son."

"Well, you are pretty, so there's no arguing that," Cameron said, and gave her a quick hug. "On another note, Aunt Annie just called. Somebody wrecked their car just up the road from our driveway, but nobody's in it. She's already called the police and a wrecker, but I'm going to take Ghost and see if we can figure out where the driver went."

LEFT BEHIND 59

Rusty frowned. "Oh no! I hope it's just a case of someone picking them up and already taking them into Jubilee."

"Me too, but I need to check. If the driver was injured,
there's no telling how disoriented they could have been,
or how far they might have wandered into the woods."

"Yes, I understand, but be careful," Rusty said.

Cameron slid his arms around her and nuzzled the
back of her neck. "Always. I'm taking my sat phone, and
I have Ghost. We'll be fine."

A few minutes later he went out the front door with
Ghost on a leash and headed up their driveway. Once
they got to the road, they turned left and started walking up the mountain. It didn't take but a few minutes
to reach the wreck, and then he jumped the ditch with
Ghost and headed for the car.

Like Annie, the first thing he saw was the purse lying
on the floorboard. But he wasn't as cautious as Annie.
He wanted to know who he was looking for, opened
it, found a wallet, and the driver's license for a young
blonde woman named Carey Eggers. He put everything
back in the purse, then let Ghost get the scent.

"Seek, Ghost, seek!" The giant German shepherd
whined as his ears came up.

Cameron dropped the purse where he'd found it and
gave Ghost his head. When the dog went straight into
the trees, it answered one question for Cameron. Carey
Eggers was somewhere in the woods.

Ghost turned into the heat-seeking missile that he
was and started running, keeping Cameron on the move

behind him. Twice, the dog was confused by the scent and circled until he keyed in on it again.

By the way Ghost was tracking, Cameron feared the woman was disoriented, or she would have had no reason to go into the trees. She would have either stayed in the car or started walking down the road.

Then Ghost whined and began straining at the leash to go faster. Cameron unclipped it from the shepherd's collar and let him go, then had to run even faster to keep up. Minutes later, Ghost disappeared, and Cameron kept running toward the place he'd seen him last.

He was coming upon a small clearing when he saw something on the ground up ahead. A cell phone! Then he heard Ghost whining, followed the sound, and walked up on his dog lying with his head across the legs of a woman's body.

Damn it. "Good boy," Cameron said as he knelt beside the body and laid his hand on Ghost's head. He was about to reach to check her pulse when he saw the bullet hole in the back of her shirt. "What the hell?"

He slid his hand down the side of her neck and was shocked she had a pulse. It was faint and thready, but she was alive. He rolled her over and saw bruises on her face, a cut on her forehead, and when he pushed her shirt aside to look for an exit wound, he saw bruises on her belly. That had to be from the wreck.

"You ran into the trees because someone was after you, didn't you, Carey? Hang in there, girl. I'm calling for help."

He grabbed his sat phone to call for an ambulance and then called the county sheriff's office.

───────

Sheriff Rance Woodley was writing up a maintenance request to get plumbing repaired in two of the jail cells when the dispatcher buzzed his desk. He picked up the receiver.

"This is Woodley."

"Sir, we just received a call from Cameron Pope on Pope Mountain. He and his dog found a woman in the woods up above his house. He thought he was looking for the driver of a wrecked car up in the trees, but when he and his dog found her, she had a bullet wound in her back. She has head wounds and bruises, likely from the wreck. He thought she was dead, but then realized she still had a pulse. He's already called for an ambulance to take her in to Jubilee Hospital, but since she was shot in our jurisdiction, we caught the case."

"Shot! Well, damn," Woodley said, remembering another shooting up on the mountain a couple of years back. "Okay…get the directions to the crime lab and get them on the scene, dispatch a couple of officers, and call a tow service for the wrecked car, too. I'll be en route to the hospital to see if she's regained conscious-ness, and then I'll contact the team on the ground."

"Yes, sir," the dispatcher said, and disconnected.

Woodley glanced at the paperwork. The plumbing

request was going to have to wait. He picked up the phone.

———

Jubilee Police Chief Sonny Warren was at his computer when his phone rang. He hit Save and then reached for the receiver.

"Hello."

"Sonny, it's Rance. I'm about to invade your world again. Just got a call about a shooting victim in the woods just up from Cameron Pope's place."

Sonny frowned. "Who found her?"

"Cameron and his dog. I'm told your ambulance crew will be picking her up, but I'm towing in the car the driver wrecked before it was abandoned. I'm on my way to Jubilee in the hopes she regains consciousness. She left a purse in the car. Cameron checked the ID. It matches the woman he found. Her name is Carey Eggers. When he found her, he thought she was dead, so she's probably not in good condition. Do me a favor. It'll take me a while to get there, so would you please go meet the ambulance when they bring her in and see if she's talking? I don't want to lose the chance of getting any info in case she passes. You know the drill."

"Yes, I can do that," Sonny said.

"Thanks. I'll see you soon."

———

Sonny was in the ER when they brought in the woman from the wreck. She looked dead, so it was no wonder Cameron thought she was, and as soon as they had her stabilized, she went straight to surgery. Her condition was dire, and surgery was her only option for survival, so an interview was not going to happen. Disappointed, he sat down to wait, and shortly thereafter, Sheriff Woodley arrived in the lobby.

"Anything?" he asked as he sat down beside Sonny.

Sonny shook his head. "She's in bad shape. Never did regain consciousness before they took her to surgery."

"Well, thanks for covering for me. I'll take it from here," Rance said.

"No problem," Sonny said, then went back to the precinct, while the team from the county crime lab arrived on the scene of the accident.

Cameron took them back to the area where he found her. They bagged her cell phone and the flashlight she'd dropped, and bagged a shell casing found nearby, but the rain had destroyed any other signs or clues that might have been helpful.

———————

A couple of hours later, Carey's surgeon, a doctor named Kline, came into the waiting room looking for the sheriff. There was only one man in the waiting room wearing a uniform, so he headed for him.

"Are you here for Carey Eggers?" Kline asked.

"Yes. I'm Sheriff Woodley. How is she?"

"I'm Dr. Kline, her surgeon. She's in recovery, but in critical condition and will be going straight to the ICU."

"Did she ever regain consciousness?" Woodley asked.

"No, and if she does regain consciousness, it's going to be a while before you can speak to her."

"Understood, but I'll be needing the clothes she was wearing to take back to the lab," Woodley said.

"When we saw the bullet wound, we assumed you would. They're already bagged. I'll have one of the nurses bring them to you," Dr. Kline said.

"Thanks," Woodley said. "And keep me updated on her condition. As soon as she wakes up, I need to talk to her."

Dr. Kline nodded and left, and a few minutes later, a nurse came looking for the sheriff.

"Sheriff Woodley? Dr. Kline asked me to bring these to you."

"Thank you," Woodley said. He left the hospital with the clothes and headed back to his office to turn them over to the lab.

It was midday when Woodley got back to his office and began going through the papers that had been left on his desk. Within moments, he came upon the BOLO regarding Billy Eggers's missing car. He immediately checked the report on the vehicle towed in and, when he realized it was the same one, called the contact number.

"Bowling Green PD. Detective Gardner speaking."

"Detective, this is Sheriff Woodley out of Jubilee, Kentucky. I just received your BOLO about a missing car belonging to a Billy Eggers. We towed that car off Pope Mountain this morning. It was wrecked during a rainstorm sometime last night."

"Who was driving it?" Gardner asked.

"A woman named Carey Eggers. Her purse and identification were found in the wrecked car, but the car was empty. However, we were notified later of a woman who was found unconscious up in the woods and it was her. She'd been shot."

"Shot! Damn," Gardner said. "Where is she now?"

"The hospital in Jubilee. She's undergone surgery. I don't know anything more. She has yet to regain consciousness."

"Thank you for your information. There are people who've been looking for her for hours," Gardner said.

"What happened?" Woodley asked.

"It appears she was a witness to her brother's murder. Looks like the killer ran her down."

The skin crawled on the back of Woodley's neck.

"Do you know who it was?"

"No, and I'd appreciate it if you didn't advertise the fact that she's still alive," Gardner said.

Woodley frowned. "I'll call the Jubilee PD and ask Chief Warren to make sure nothing is put in the local paper, but I can't promise word doesn't spread locally."

"Thanks," Gardner said. "If we can find the shooter, we'll let you know, and if she wakes up and is able to be interrogated, let me know."

Chapter 4

TOM WHEATON HAD TAKEN PERSONAL LEAVE AND was at Johnny's house when his cell phone rang. His heart skipped as he glanced at caller ID. It was coming from the precinct. He'd left his number as contact for updated information regarding Carey's disappearance.

"Hello, this is Tom."

"Tom…Detective Gardner here. I have news. Eggers's car was found early this morning, wrecked on Pope Mountain, and with the driver missing. A local resident found her in the woods. It's Carey. She'd been shot in the back, which indicates she was running, and she had not regained consciousness before they took her to surgery. It's not good, but last I heard, she's still alive."

"Oh my God," Tom muttered. "Where is she? What hospital?"

"She's in Jubilee. There's only one hospital there," Gardner added.

"Thanks for the update. She mentioned something about Billy arguing with someone called Gunny, or something about money in her text to Johnny. Did you get a hit on the alias?"

"Nothing as of yet, but they are still running tests on evidence from the crime scene. We're hoping to get a hit on some prints. The living room was destroyed in the fight, so there should be prints all over the place, and hopefully we'll pull some DNA from Eggers's body to point us in the right direction."

"Got it. Thanks again. Keep me updated," Tom said, and breathed a sigh of relief as he hung up. This wasn't the best news, but it also wasn't the worst news. Carey was still alive.

He googled the number for the Jubilee Hospital, then asked for the nurses' desk at the surgical wing and got the runaround about not giving out information to anyone but family, but he persisted.

"Yes, ma'am, I know that. But I'm a police officer with the Bowling Green PD. I gave you my name and badge number. You can confirm that with my commander. I gave you his name and number. Carey Eggers's only family member was murdered last night, and I am standing in her house with her fiancé, who is recovering from very serious orthopedic surgery. So, at this moment, I'm the only upright and mobile person on this earth who gives a shit about what's happening to her. All I need to know is if she's still alive. Because if she's not, I'm not driving a man on crutches all the way to Jubilee to look at her body."

"Please hold," the nurse said.

Tom took a breath and waited, and then waited, and finally, the nurse was back online.

"She is in the ICU. Her condition is grave. That is all I am allowed to tell you."

"Thank you," Tom said. "That's all I needed to know. The next time you hear my voice, you'll be looking at my face, and I'll be pushing a man in a wheelchair. His name is John Knight. And don't fuck with him like you just did with me. She is his world."

He was shaking when he hung up. Now he had to tell Johnny, help him pack a bag, then go home and pack for himself and rent a wheelchair. The last time he and Johnny had gone on a trip together was their long fishing weekend just before his fall. And now this. Life had a way of lifting you up so high, just to see how well you fared after you were dropped.

And then Johnny hobbled into the living room. "What's going on?"

"Sit down," Tom said.

Johnny paled. "Just say it!"

"They found the car. It had been wrecked. They found Carey in the woods on Pope Mountain. She'd been shot in the back, which means she was running when it happened. She had not regained consciousness when they took her into surgery. She is out of surgery and in critical condition. That's all I know."

Now Johnny sat. "Where is she?"

"In the hospital in Jubilee."

"The big tourist town?" Johnny asked.

"Yes. I know you want to go. I'll take you. I'll pack your bag; then you sit and wait while I go pack mine and rent a wheelchair. I'll be back within a couple of hours. Okay?"

There was a muscle jerking at the side of Johnny's jaw, but he was scary calm and quieter than Tom expected.

"You okay, buddy? She's still alive. We have to hang on to that."

"Just get my suitcase out of the back bedroom. It's in the closet. I can pack it myself," Johnny said.

Tom didn't argue, and when he carried the suitcase back to their bedroom, Johnny was already stacking a few things on the bed. Tom opened the suitcase, then stepped aside.

"I'll be back as soon as I run down a wheelchair and pack a few things," he said. "Take a pain pill before we go. That's a long ride and you're gonna be hurting before we get there."

Johnny shrugged off the concern. "I know how to hurt. I just don't know how to live without her. Hurry back."

———

Wiley had been back at work for days, but he was riding a desk, which only exacerbated the funk he was in. He'd hoped for a positive response back from Linette Elgin about going on another date, but heard nothing. The going phrase for being dumped was *being ghosted*, and that's how he felt. He didn't blame her. Their first attempt at dating had been sabotaged by two of his ex-acquaintances, and it had hurt her. Coming out on the

good side of being shot had given him a whole new
aspect of life. It was short. And it mattered. People mattered. And if paperwork was part of being a cop, then he
could do it with his chin up and his mouth shut, which
was what he was doing, when the phone rang at his desk.

"Jubilee PD. Officer Pope speaking."

"Hi, Wiley, it's me, Cecily. I wanted you to know how
sorry I was about the bank thingy. I tried to call you at
home, but the calls never went through."

Wiley frowned. *Bank thingy?* "That's because I
deleted and blocked you and the other clown you hang
out with. I consider the brief acquaintances I had with
both of you to be severe lapses of moral judgment on
my part," he said and hung up in her ear.

He was still muttering beneath his breath when the
chief walked in and paused at his desk.

"Morning, Wiley. How are you feeling?" Sonny
Warren asked.

"Good, sir."

"Good enough to make a run to the hospital for
me?" Sonny asked.

Hot damn! Wiley stood. "Yes, sir."

"Good. Do you know about the woman your cousin
Cameron found this morning?"

"I heard," Wiley said.

"Well, it turns out she's a witness to her brother's
murder, and it appears the killer chased her down to
silence her. Only she's still alive. Sheriff Woodley asked
us not to advertise the fact, and I'd like for you to swing

by the hospital and let the nurses' station know the situation. I think it's prudent that we have someone on duty."

"Absolutely," Wiley said. "How do we know the killer was a man?" he asked.

"Because she left a message on her fiancé's phone about what had happened. What I can't figure out is how the shooter trailed her from the east side of Bowling Green all the way to Pope Mountain in the dark and in that storm."

"If the shooter had her brother's phone, there's a good chance he was using the GPS on it to track her," Wiley said.

Sonny blinked. "There are days when I think I'm aging out of this job."

"Sean keeps us all up-to-date on tech stuff," Wiley said.

"Right," Sonny said. "This isn't going to be a simple job, because the hospital isn't going to let us into the ICU to guard her bed, so you're going to be outside of the ICU, checking off the people who do go in. Get a list of patients in the ICU and then a list of people allowed to visit those patients, and if somebody's not on the list, they don't get in."

"So, since her brother's dead, who's on Carey Eggers's list?" Wiley asked.

"I checked with Woodley. There's a fiancé named Johnny Knight and Tom Wheaton, a cop from Bowling Green, who's likely bringing Johnny here."

Wiley frowned. "Knight can't bring himself?"

"He was a lineman for an electric company. He fell

off a high-line pole about six weeks back and shattered his leg. It's being held together with rods and screws, so he's not driving or walking right now."

Wiley frowned. "That's tough. He probably feels like the whole damn world is falling down around him. Text me photos of both of them from the DMV. Do you want me there now?"

"Yes. I'll have someone from the hospital get the patient names and visitor list to you," Sonny said.

"Do I stay, or are you spelling me off?" Wiley asked.

"I'll send someone to relieve you in the morning."

Wiley looked up. "What if she doesn't make it?"

Sonny nodded. "It's a possibility. She was already injured from the wreck before she got shot. She must be a tough little thing to have run that far through the woods in that storm before he ran her down."

Just thinking about that happening made Wiley's gut knot.

"I'm on it, Chief. I'll pick up a cruiser from the lot. No need dragging someone in from patrol just to give me a ride."

Sonny smiled as Wiley bolted out of the room. Probably wanting to escape before Sonny changed his mind. He admired the Pope family. And Aaron and Wiley were two of his best officers. The brothers all looked alike, but Wiley was different. A bit wilder and far less likely to suffer fools.

Linette was on duty in the surgical wing when she saw Wiley Pope coming up the hall. The width of his shoulders was almost as broad as his stride was long. He needed a haircut and a warning label, but the wild side of her longed for the wild side of him. He was walking toward her with a fixed look at everything in front of him, which at this moment included her. Here she was, still waiting for that phone call and a second date, and like the proverbial bad penny, he'd turned up on her turf.

Then, before she knew what was happening, he stopped in the middle of the hall, slid his hands up the sides of her cheeks, and kissed her. Square on the mouth, with purpose and intent. Within seconds, she'd lost all sense of self.

She was in a state of shock and had forgotten to breathe when he ended it and started talking.

"I've been needing to do that since the moment you came running toward me at the bank. I saw all that blood on your face and thought you'd been shot, and all I could think was I'd never got the chance to say I'm sorry, or to thank you for what you did. The ICU is that way, right?" he asked, pointing up the hall.

Speechless, she nodded.

He brushed the back of his hand against her cheek again. "Sorry you weren't up for another dinner date. Gotta go. I'll catch you later."

What? I never said… I didn't.… But she never uttered the words. Instead, she turned to see where he was going and caught him standing in the hall watching her.

Damn the man. He knew I would turn around. Disgusted with herself, she turned and walked away.

I knew you'd do that, Wiley thought and kept walking until he was at the entrance to the ICU. He knocked on the door, and when a nurse opened it, he flashed his badge.

"Office Pope, reporting for duty. I've been assigned to guard Carey Eggers. Chief Warren told me you would furnish me with a patient list and a visitor list. And you need to know that anyone who's not on that list will not be going into the ICU for visits as long as Carey Eggers is a patient here."

The nurse blinked. "Uh…"

Wiley kept talking. "She's a witness to a murder. Someone tried to kill her. I'm here to make sure that doesn't happen again. I need to see where she is, and if she's too close to other patients, you'll need to move her."

"I'll get my superior," the nurse said, and closed the door. A few moments later, another nurse came out. "My name's Norma. Follow me and please keep your voice down."

"Yes, ma'am," he said, and walked in behind her, quietly moving past eight other patients before they reached a bed at the far end of the room. "Doctor requested she be kept away from the others a bit. Is this okay?"

Wiley eyed the setup, then the woman in the bed. He could see the staples in her head where they'd shaved away her hair. A bandage across her shoulder, and so many cuts and contusions on her face and arms that he could only imagine what the rest of her body must look like. He turned to the nurse, nodded, and followed her out.

"I'll get that list for you and a chair," she said.

"Thank you, ma'am," Wiley said.

"Just call me, Norma," she said.

"Yes, ma'am," he said again.

She rolled her eyes and disappeared, then came back a few minutes later with both lists on a clipboard and a folding chair.

"Sorry. It's the best I could do," Norma said.

"It's fine. Thank you. Do you have visiting hours on the hour only?"

Joan nodded. "Yes. Two people per patient, and only for ten minutes, then visiting hour is over."

"When do you change shifts?" he asked.

"Midnight. All four of us here will leave then, and four more will come on. No more. No less. Hospital rule."

Wiley nodded and settled in. He could see the waiting room through the glassed-in enclosure in which he was sitting, and as time grew closer, people began to gather in the outer lobby. Some of them were silent. Some of were visiting quietly. One was crying, and at one time or another, they were all on their phones.

When the clock rolled around to the hour, the visitors found themselves face-to-face with a uniformed policeman.

"Who are you visiting, and name please?" he said.

Taken aback, one man started to argue, when Wiley held up his hand.

"I know this is new, but there's a reason for it. It has nothing to do with your loved ones, but it involves the safety of someone else."

After that, they gave up their names, and who they were visiting, without meeting his gaze. And when every patient had been marked off, Wiley went inside and straight to Carey's bed.

She didn't know him, but he felt bad thinking of her lying in here so hurt and so alone. He put a hand on her arm and then spoke softly near her ear.

"Miss Eggers, I'm a police officer. My name is Wiley Pope. You're in the hospital and you're safe. Now fight your way back, like you fought to stay alive."

He patted her arm, then stayed at her bedside until every visitor was gone before he left the unit. As soon as he exited, he resumed his seat at the door and pulled out his phone to check for messages. There was one from the chief with two photos. One of Carey Eggers's fiancé, and one of the cops who was accompanying him. He already knew their names. Now he knew what they looked like.

The routine of hourly visitors came and went two more times with Wiley giving the same speech to different people, but as the third hour approached, he saw two men entering the waiting area. One was pushing the other in a wheelchair, and he recognized their faces.

Eggers's fiancé and the cop had arrived, and Wiley knew within moments that John Knight was in misery.

Pain was etched on his face, and yet he sat motionless, stoic in his suffering. Tom Wheaton went for water, handed a pill and the drink to his friend, and then gave his shoulder a squeeze before sitting down beside him. At that point, Wiley looked away. Carey Eggers was a train wreck, and he was already empathizing with Knight for their first viewing.

When the clock finally moved to the hour, the visitors stood and began filing into the outer area of the ICU. Knight and Wheaton were at the end of the line, but heard Wiley's declaration as he checked people off. When they reached where he was standing, John Knight looked up.

"You're guarding my girl."

Wiley nodded. "Yes. I told her you were coming. I thought it might help."

John grabbed the arms of his wheelchair as if he wanted to get up and run. "She's awake?"

"No. But I told her anyway. From what we know, she fought really hard to stay alive. I just wanted to encourage her to keep fighting. Nobody is to approach her bed but you two and the nurses. She's the one at the far end of the room. You both have ten minutes. Make them count."

Then he followed them inside the unit, but stayed up by the nurses' desk with his focus on Carey and her visitors.

Just being in a hospital again was a cold reminder of his situation, but when Johnny saw the bed at the far end of the room, and all of the machines surrounding her, and how tiny and alone Carey looked beneath the sheets, he nearly lost it. By the time Tom rolled him up to her bedside, Johnny was blind with tears.

Carey was so battered he barely recognized the woman he loved, and so still. She was never still. He touched her hand, expecting her fingers to curl around his, but they were limp.

"Carey. It's me, Johnny. I'm here, baby. I'm here. We found you. I know you've been hurt, but you're safe in a hospital now. I love you. So much. Tom's here. He brought me to you."

Tom leaned over the bed. "Hey, pretty girl. It's me, Tom. We're here and we're not leaving you. We know what happened. I've got Johnny's back, and he's got yours."

They paused, staring at her face, hoping for a miracle, that she'd just open her eyes and talk. But their only answers were machines beeping back to let them know she was still alive. When the ten minutes were up, all of the visitors filed out. Johnny and Tom were the last ones to leave, and Wiley followed them back to the waiting room.

"Do you have a place to stay yet?" he asked.

"No, I was thinking we'd just bed down here and—"

Wiley shook his head. "According to my information, she's not going to wake up anytime soon. They put her in a drug-induced coma to lessen the stress from all her injuries. I can't tell you what to do, but it's obvious you're in bad shape, and you won't do her any good if you mess yourself up. Get a room. Get some food and rest, and come back whenever you want, but you need some place to shower and sleep, too."

"I don't want to leave her," Johnny said.

Wiley understood, but he wanted to reassure them. "Just so you know, I was visiting her every hour on the hour until you two arrived, and either me or whoever replaces me in the morning will continue to do that because we're under orders to guard her. So, when visitors are in the ICU unit, even when you're not there, one of us is by her bed. Understand?"

Johnny sighed. "Yes, understood and appreciated."

Tom eyed the tall dark-haired cop and read him as sincere. "That's good to know. By the way, could you recommend a place to stay?"

"Sure thing," Wiley said. "There are two large hotels in town that cater to tourists, and Reagan Bullard's Campgrounds two miles east, outside of town. Those are little cabins, but out there you'd have to fend for yourself when it comes to food. The hotels have cafés and restaurants in them, and they're closer. There's Hotel Devon and the Serenity Inn."

"Thanks," Tom said.

Wiley nodded. "Did you leave your contact information at the nurses' desk?" he asked.

Johnny frowned. "No, I didn't think to do that."

"Both of you give it to me. I'll make sure they have

it," Wiley said. He grabbed a little notebook and pen from his shirt pocket, took down their info, and went back to the ICU to leave it at the nurses' station, while Tom wheeled Johnny out of the hospital and went to find them a place to stay.

———

Linette made it her business to find out why Wiley Pope was in the hospital and was surprised to learn he was guarding a patient in the ICU.

She didn't have much willpower when it came to the man. He was aggravating and sexy, and she'd already been burned once. She didn't want to get her heart broken, but if it happened, he would be the man to break it, and she was still confused about his comment about not going to dinner because he had yet to ask.

She was getting ready to clock out for the day when she got a text from Norma, the RN in charge of the intensive care unit.

Linette, are you still in the building or have you already left?

Linette responded, Clocking out but still here. Why?

Would you mind running down to the cafeteria and picking up a food order for me? It's for the cop who's guarding one of our patients. He's not

asked for a thing since he got here, and I know
he's got to be hungry.

Linette sighed and returned the text. I don't mind a
bit. Do I pay for it, or...?

Norma texted back, It's already charged to the police
department.

So much for keeping her distance. On the way.

Linette clocked out, grabbed her things, and took
the elevator down to the cafeteria, trying to ignore what
she was feeling. *Damn man. Damn gorgeous, aggravating
man. Now I have to face him again.* She exited the elevator and went into the cafeteria.

"Dolly, I'm supposed to pick up a food order for the
cop on duty up in the ICU."

"Oh, sure thing," the hostess said. "Hang on a sec.
I'll go get it."

Linette slung her purse strap over her shoulder,
combed her fingers through her hair, and wished
she'd thought to brush it and put on some lipstick, but
whatever.

Dolly returned with a sack and a drink with a lid.

"Here you go. I hear he's a looker," Dolly said.

"Really?" Linette said, and went back to the elevator
and rode it up to the ICU floor.

Her heart was pounding as she walked down the
long hall with the food and then to where Wiley was
sitting. When he saw her, he looked up and smiled.

"Hey, Linnie."

She didn't blink. "Norma asked me to bring this up for you."

He stood, took the food, and then didn't want her to leave. "That's really kind of you. I'll be on duty until morning, so I really appreciate it."

"No problem. I'm already clocked out, but don't get too excited. It's hospital cafeteria food."

"Still better than my cooking," he said.

Her eyebrows rose just enough to exhibit surprise. "You cook?"

Wiley could tell she was still pissed at him, and she hadn't replied after he'd sent that text about taking her out again, so he didn't know where they stood, but he resented the tone of her voice just enough to fire back.

"I'm not a complete ass. I also do laundry, clean house, am kind to animals, and love my family," he said.

Linette blinked. She heard hurt in his voice and was immediately sorry, but it was too late to take back what had already been said. She walked out feeling like a fool.

Wiley sat back down with his food and ate because he was hungry, but he was bothered. He didn't like people being upset with him. And at the same time, he knew she had every right to feel how she felt.

———————

Linette was teary-eyed all the way to her car. As soon as she slid in behind the wheel, she laid her head down on the steering wheel and cried, then wiped her eyes, blew her nose, and drove home. She couldn't keep doing this—resenting a man she'd only had half a date with. And he'd said in his text that he'd been appalled at what had happened and blocked them from contacting him again, and she'd been happy when she read that.

And then all of a sudden, it hit her! She'd never responded. She'd just assumed he would call her again, while her silence must have given him the impression she wasn't interested.

"Oh lord. I am such a dumbass," she muttered.

But how did she correct this?

Had he given up on her?

After the snotty attitude she'd just copped, was it already too late?

Before she could talk herself out of it, she sent him a text.

I think I messed up. I read that last text from you as a heads-up to an incoming invitation after you healed, then heard nothing, and you read my idiotic mistake in not responding to your text as I wasn't interested. Nothing could be further from the truth. I'm still here. You still make me crazy. But dinner sometime would be nice.

Then she hit Send.

Wiley had just finished off his burger and was

working on the last of his fries when he got a text. He wiped his hands before checking his phone.

As he read, he knew he was smiling, and when he got to the end of the message, he was smiling inside as well.

"Hot damn," he said softly, and sent her a thumbs-up emoji and a smiley face. Life was looking up.

———————

Tom Wheaton was at the front desk of the Serenity Inn, requesting a handicap-accessible room on the ground floor for him and Johnny Knight.

"How long do you plan to stay?" the clerk asked as they were checking in.

Tom glanced down at Johnny and then sighed. "We're not sure. We're here because his fiancée is in the hospital in the ICU. We don't know what's going to happen because she hasn't recovered consciousness."

The clerk blinked. "Oh my. So, you're in Jubilee just because of this family emergency?"

"Yes," Tom said.

The clerk paused. "Excuse me a moment," he said, and slipped into the adjoining office.

Tom saw him pick up a phone and wondered what was going on, but when he came back a few moments later, he soon found out.

"Mr. Wheaton, your room and two meals a day have been comped for the duration of your stay. That includes the cold drinks and snacks available in your room." He handed Tom two card keys. "All you have to do is charge the meal to your room and it will be picked up by us, along with the room charge."

Both men were in shock, but it was Johnny who spoke first.

"I have no words to explain what a gift this is. You have my undying gratitude for such kindness."

The clerk nodded. "You're welcome, sir. It's our policy to accommodate families now and then in emergencies such as this. We're sorry for what's happening and wish your fiancée a speedy recovery. Follow that hallway, and take a right. Your room is about halfway down on the left."

Tom pocketed the card keys, shouldered his travel bag and put Johnny's bag in his lap, and then wheeled him away. As soon as they got to the room, he gave Johnny the bed closest to the bathroom, then helped him into bed. It was midafternoon but he felt like he'd been awake for days.

Johnny was in so much pain that he was ashen. Tom helped him undress and then got him to the bathroom, gave him two pain pills, then helped him back into bed.

"Rest easy, buddy," Tom said. "We're here, and with some luck and a few prayers, Carey will wake up and get well. But you've got some healing to do, too, so we're gonna be smart about these visits. Morning. Noon. Evening. Not every hour on the hour. Understand?"

"Yes, and I appreciate what you've done by taking off from your work like this for us."

"You would have done it for me,' Tom said. "Get some rest. I'm gonna shower. Do you want a snack or something to drink from the fridge?"

"No. I just want the pain to go away so I can sleep."

Tom patted his friend's shoulder, then stripped and walked into the bathroom and closed the door.

Johnny heard Tom turn on the shower, and then the pills kicked in.

He was asleep when Tom emerged with a towel wrapped around his waist. He glanced at Johnny, then got a cold Coke from the fridge, and stretched out on the bed to check messages. When he was finished with his drink, he crawled into bed so damn tired he couldn't think and closed his eyes.

———

Wiley was relieved of duty just after eight the next morning. He checked in at the precinct before going home to get a few hours of sleep. As soon as he got to his house, he showered, ate some breakfast, then sat down and called Linette, hoping it wasn't against hospital rules for nurses to take personal calls because he was done with texting. It was too freaking impersonal and too easy to be misunderstood.

When his call began to ring, he half expected it to go to voicemail, but instead he got her.

"Hey, you."

He grinned. "Hey, back," Wiley said. "I just got off

work and am going to catch a few hours' sleep. I don't go back on duty until eight p.m. What time do you get off work today?"

"I came on at six. I get off at four today."

"Are you free for dinner this evening?" he asked.

"For you, yes."

He closed his eyes, thanking God for a second chance. "I know it's short notice and a short date, but I can pick you up at five and spend a couple of hours with you."

"I would love that," she said.

Wiley exhaled, grateful she didn't know he was grinning from ear to ear.

"Awesome. See you at five."

He set his alarm for 4:00 p.m. and crawled into bed. Thinking about Linette made it easy to go to sleep.

When he woke up hours later, he was excited by the thought of spending time with her. He already admired her dedication to her job, but there was something about her that spoke to his heart.

Chapter 5

LINETTE WAS A BUNDLE OF NERVES BY THE TIME SHE clocked out. She flew home, jumped in the shower, and then once she was out, did her hair and makeup before going to her closet. She couldn't decide what to wear, and time was getting short. Finally, she settled on a pair of gray slacks and a pale-blue blouse with elbow-length sleeves.

As she was dressing, she kept remembering the first time she'd dressed for a date with Wiley. She'd been so smitten with the man that she'd been expecting too much, and then had been humiliated by the two women who'd ruined it.

But after the attempted bank robbery, her perception of what mattered most in life had changed. They'd survived the tragedy together, and experiencing firsthand how swiftly a life could end had changed the whole dynamic of her life. Now all that remained was to see if the chemistry from before was still there, too. She was pacing the living room, anxiously awaiting his arrival when she heard a knock at the door.

He's here!

She opened it to tall, dark, and handsome, and then realized she was holding her breath, and exhaled.

"You look beautiful," Wiley said. "Are you ready, or do you need a minute?"

"I don't want to waste a minute. I'm ready to go," she said, then grabbed her purse and pulled the door shut as they headed for the elevator.

There was an awkward moment when the elevator doors shut them in. He pressed the button to take them back down to the lobby and then glanced at her. She was watching everything he was doing when he caught her staring and winked.

She blushed, then laughed, and the doors opened. They walked out of the apartment building to his car and were soon headed downtown to the tourist strip. When he pulled into the parking lot at the Back Porch, Linette sighed.

"I love this place. The food reminds me of my grandma's cooking," she said.

"What about your mama's cooking?" Wiley asked.

Linette wrinkled her nose. "We don't talk about it."

Wiley grinned. "That bad, is it?"

"Daddy cooks. Mama does dishes. It works out better that way," Linette said.

"Where do they live?" Wiley asked.

"St. Petersburg, Florida. I grew up there," she said. "Let's get out. We can talk inside. You don't have much time to eat before you have to go on duty."

They both exited the car and hurried across the parking lot and into the restaurant.

"Wiley Pope. Reservation for two," he said, when the hostess approached.

She checked his name on the computer, then led them to a table beside a window. "Your waiter will be with you shortly," she said, then left the menus on the table and walked away as Wiley seated Linette, then sat down and shifted his legs a little sideways to make them fit beneath the table.

She noticed his dilemma. "They don't leave enough legroom for guys like you, do they?"

He shook his head. "Or beds long enough, or headroom in some of the older buildings. But we're really handy at changing light bulbs. We rarely need a ladder. What sounds good to you?"

"I'm going for shrimp scampi with wild rice," she said.

"And I've been thinking about chicken-fried steak all day," he said.

Linette deadpanned. "And here I thought you were thinking about me."

He had a moment of panic, but then realized she was teasing and sighed. "For a second there, I thought I was in trouble all over again."

She laughed, which intrigued Wiley even more. Linette was a dark horse. She was gorgeous and smart, and now he was discovering that she has a wicked sense of humor, too.

He loved it.

The waiter arrived and took their drink orders and, when Wiley told him they were pressed for time, took their food orders, too. After that, they sat back and stared at each other from across the table, almost as if they were memorizing each other's faces. Finally, it was Wiley who broke the ice.

"So? Do I pass muster?" he asked.

"Do I?" she countered.

The teasing slid out of his voice. "You already did the first time I saw you. I wanted to ask you out even then, but you were so far out of my league that I didn't think I'd stand a chance. And then when I finally got the nerve, well, we both know what happened. Thank you for the second chance."

She rolled her eyes. "It would have happened sooner, but I missed the cue, then had to get out of my own way."

He shook his head and reached for her hand. "It no longer matters. Tell me about Linnie Elgin. Why did you want to become a nurse, and how did you wind up in Jubilee when you grew up in Florida?"

"I always wanted to be a nurse. I was always putting bandages on my dog or on Daddy. Mom had to put Band-Aids on the grocery list at least once a month because I used them all up on Dad, dolls, and dogs."

Wiley smiled, trying to imagine her as a child, and listened intently as she continued her story.

"As for how I wound up in Jubilee, it's because we came here for my sixteenth birthday to see the music shows and do the tourist thing, and I fell in love with the place. After I graduated from nursing school, this hospital was the first place I applied for a job. I don't know what I would have done if they hadn't hired me. I never saw myself anywhere else."

"I'm really glad you did," Wiley said.

She gave him another long, steady look. "So am I. Now you. What's your story, other than being related to most of the local residents?"

He hesitated. But if they were going to have the relationship he wanted, he had to be honest from the start.

"Mom was born here. She was a Pope before she married. We grew up in Conway, Arkansas, and before we came here, our last name was Wallace. We changed it to Mom's maiden name just before we came back, which was about a year after our father went to prison. He abused Mom and us throughout their entire marriage, up until we were old enough to fight back or move out. Then one day when he was high on drugs, he beat her so badly she nearly died, then left the house and murdered two strangers in cold blood. Sean found Mom and called an ambulance.

"The cops arrested Clyde and put him in jail. He went to prison for life, and we were vilified for being related. Aaron's first wife divorced him after only a year of marriage because of it. We were all let go from the jobs we had. Then Grandma Helen died. Mom inherited her homeplace, and we moved back to Jubilee with her. She's living in the house in which she grew up. I know it's an ugly story, but I don't want any surprises between us."

Linette was in shock. She'd thought of him as a man just looking for a good time when they first met. Her opinion had already changed, but now she was seeing a whole other side of Wiley Pope. He already knew how to survive long before she saw him get shot.

"Oh, Wiley...I'm so sorry. What a life for all of you. But you've all risen above his crimes. You should feel no shame, and you're the hero for so many here in Jubilee already. I hope you know how indebted we all are to you for your bravery."

"I wasn't being a hero. It was a knee-jerk reaction to what I walked in on. I didn't see you until you were running toward me, but I will never forget how you stepped into the gap for me, and then for the victims, with no thought for yourself."

She shrugged. "Oh, I fell apart. I just waited until I got home."

He reached for her hand. "I'm sorry."

"So am I. Mr. Trotter was a really nice man. The last thing he did before he got shot was look at me. We were belly down beside each other. I could see the fear in his eyes even then, and then seconds later he was dead. It was so random, and those men were high as kites."

"Like Clyde Wallace," Wiley muttered, and then changed the subject. "What do you want out of life?"

She let go of his hand, took a sip of her sweet tea, and then looked up.

"I already have the job I want. But I want a family. I love children. I often work on the children's ward. I don't want things. I just want to be happy with the man I love. And you?"

"Same. Aaron and Sean are head over heels in love with their spouses. I want that. Brendan—we call him B.J.—is also looking for Miss Right, but he's the head pastry chef at the Serenity Inn, and right now, he doesn't have much of a social life."

She shrugged. "I never did believe in looking for love. Daddy always said when it's right, love comes to you."

"That's beautiful, Linnie…just like you," Wiley said.

She smiled. "You talk as pretty as you look, and there comes our food. I think you're going to be good to go on time after all."

"Next time, I won't be cutting it so short," he said.

She liked the thought of "next time," but the waiter was already putting their food in front of them, and their focus shifted to the meal. She would think later how easy he was to be with. There was no pretense. Just two people playing catchup on who they were and what they'd been before they met.

It didn't take long for her to realize how solidified the bond between the brothers really was. Maybe it had to do with growing up in an abusive home, or maybe it was due to the strength of the woman who'd raised them. But by the time they were back in the car and on the way to her apartment, she knew she wanted more of Wiley Pope.

"We cut it close. I don't want you to be late clocking in. You don't have to go inside with me," Linette said as Wiley pulled up to the apartment building.

Wiley shook his head. "No, ma'am. I'm not dumping you out in the parking lot."

They both exited the car on their own, but when they started toward the building, Wiley reached for her hand.

It was an innocent gesture, but it meant everything to her. She hadn't held hands since high school. The men she'd dated were always reaching for something else. He was still holding her hand as they rode the elevator up, and when she unlocked her apartment door, he walked her inside.

The moment the door closed behind them, Wiley stopped.

"Linette, I've been heartsick ever since our first date, and tonight meant everything to me. Thank you for the second chance."

She slid her arms around his neck. "Thank you for asking," she whispered.

Moments later, she was in his arms. Her heart was racing, and the kiss was all that she'd imagined and more. The moment he pulled away, she regretted it was ending.

"Be safe," she said.

Wiley ran a finger down the side of her cheek, then brushed his lips across her mouth one last time.

"Always. I'll call you," he said, and then he was gone.

———————

The next day, Wiley sent flowers to her at the hospital and signed the card, *Two hours was not enough. Let me know your next day off.*

Linette came by the nurses' station just after the flowers arrived, and when she found out they were for her, she blushed, knowing she was going to get teased all day. And then she read the card and quickly slipped it in her pocket, prompting every nurse on duty to ask the same question.

"Who are they from?"

And she gave all of them the same answer, "None of your business," which only amped up the prying, and the smile on her face was all they needed to know the flowers were from a man.

As soon as Linette had a moment, she sent him a text.

You have caused a sensation at my work today. The flowers are beautiful. And you're right. Two hours was not enough. I'll check my schedule and you check yours, and we'll meet in the middle.

Wiley got the message and sighed. Their jobs and schedules were going to be a headache to work around, but she was worth it. He was off today, and tomorrow he'd go back on days and someone else would guard Carey Eggers, and he wouldn't be in the hospital with Linette anymore.

He sent her a message to that effect, then grabbed his car keys and headed out the door. He hadn't been to the supermarket since the bank robbery, and while his family had kept him in food, he needed to do laundry and was out of detergent. Once there, he plowed through the deli section, stocking up on food that was already cooked and would freeze well. He wasn't too proud to thaw and nuke.

He was coming around the corner of the aisle when a lady pushing a shopping cart came from the other direction and bumped into his cart.

She looked up. Her eyes widened as her lips parted, but she never got the chance to utter a word.

Wiley lowered his voice and pointed his finger straight at her. "No, ma'am. Whatever you were going to say, stuff it. I don't want to even hear the sound of your voice."

At that moment, Rhonda Tiller realized how utterly stupid it had been to make an enemy of a cop. A dark-red flush crept up her neck and onto her cheeks as she yanked her cart aside, made a one-eighty pivot, and headed down another aisle, afraid to look back for fear that he was following her.

As for Wiley, his shopping experience was over. He headed straight for checkout with his jaw set. He'd had plenty of guys pissed off at him in his life, but a bloody nose or a black eye had solved it on both sides. Women with an agenda were a whole other subset of humanity. They were scary mean and didn't care who they hurt when they didn't get what they wanted. He paid for his purchases and headed for the parking lot, and by the time he was driving away, he'd dismissed Rhonda's existence.

A short while later, he was home and putting up the last of his groceries when his phone rang.

"Hello?"

"Wiley, this is Sean. I can't find Mom. She said she wanted to get some air, and I thought she was going outside to the back porch. I went to check on her about thirty minutes later, and she wasn't there. I've looked all over—in the barn, around the outbuildings. I've called and called, and she doesn't answer and she's nowhere in sight. I knew today was your day off and thought maybe…"

Wiley didn't hesitate. "Call Cameron. Tell him to bring Ghost to track her. I'm on the way." He grabbed his car keys and bolted out of the house, calling Aaron and B.J. as he went.

He was halfway up the mountain and almost to the house when he heard a siren and knew it was Aaron in a patrol car. By the time he pulled up in the yard, Aaron was behind him, with B.J. at his side.

B.J. had flashbacks of finding the remains of their ancestor Meg in an abandoned cellar a few years back and knew the remnants of other old homesteads were scattered all over the mountain. He couldn't bear the thought of his mother falling to her death in a place like that. He was grim-lipped and silent as Sean came running out to meet them.

"Nothing?" Wiley asked.

Sean was flushed and sweaty from searching and could only shake his head. Moments later, Cameron came flying into the yard in his Jeep, with Ghost riding in the seat beside him.

"Thank the lord. That dog could find God if someone would give him a trail to follow," Aaron muttered.

Cameron clipped a leash on Ghost and hurried to join the others. "Tell me what you know," he said.

Sean was bordering on panic as he explained what had happened. He'd made a conscious choice to stay on the mountain to watch over her, and now he'd lost her. "I've searched the entire property around the house. I can't imagine her wandering off without letting me know first."

"So, to confirm, she went out the back of the house and you haven't seen her since," Cameron said.

"Yes," Sean said.

Cameron nodded. "I need something with Shirley's scent."

"I knew you would. It's in the kitchen," Sean said.

They followed Sean through the house. He gave Cameron the nightgown his mother slept in, then grabbed a backpack from the counter and slipped one strap over his shoulder as they exited the house.

Cameron thrust the gown beneath Ghost's nose. "Seek, Ghost. Seek!"

Ghost whined, lifted his nose, and then went straight out across the yard, out through the back fence, past the barn, and headed into the forest beyond the pasture without wavering. They were at least a half mile from the house when Ghost began straining at the leash. Cameron unclipped it and let the big dog run, then they lengthened their stride to follow.

The brothers panicked when they lost sight of Ghost, but Cameron didn't hesitate. He knew his dog and just kept running in the direction they'd last seen him until he ran up on Ghost lying beside Shirley's body.

"Oh my God! Mom!" Sean cried as they all rushed forward.

Cameron was already on his knees checking for a pulse. "She's alive. Her pulse is steady."

But it was Wiley who keyed in on the root of the problem. She was missing a shoe, and her foot and leg were already turning purple. Then he saw the missing shoe half-buried in a pile of leaves. When he went to pick it up, he discovered it was wedged beneath a protruding tree root.

"Look! She hung her toe and fell. From the looks of her foot and leg, she'll be lucky if she didn't break a bone. Check to see if she has any head injuries!"

Cameron ran his hand beneath her head. "I don't feel anything obvious, but she could have passed out from the pain. Call Medi-Flight."

But Aaron was already on it.

Sean was sick at heart. "This is my fault. I'm supposed to be watching out for her. Why the hell did she go all the way out here?"

Wiley frowned. "Sean! None of this is your fault.

Mom is a grown woman. There will be a reason, and when we find out, it will make sense."

"I hope so, because right now, none of this makes sense," he said. Then his phone began to ring. "It's Amalie," he said, and answered, but all he could hear was the frantic tone in his wife's voice and that she was skipping words as she spoke. He knew what this meant. She'd just had one of her visions, but he couldn't make out what she was saying and put her on speaker. The moment he did, they all paused to listen. "Honey, slow down! I can't understand you. Mom went missing. We just found her unconscious out in the woods behind the house."

Amalie shuddered, then took a deep breath, making herself calm.

"That's part of what I was trying to tell you. I was working in the office when I heard someone say my name. I looked up and Ella was standing in the doorway. She said, 'Help Shirley,' and then she blew me a kiss and disappeared." At that point, Amalie burst into tears. "So now that you've found Shirley, someone needs to go to Ella's house. I think she's dead."

Sean froze. "You're serious?"

"Yes, I swear, I swear. She disappeared in front of my eyes. Just check on Ella, and call me when you get Shirley to the hospital."

"Yes, yes, I will," Sean said.

Cameron was sick to his stomach, thinking of the welfare check he was going to have to make, but right now, Shirley came first.

"Anybody got any water on them?" he asked.

Sean reached for the backpack he'd dropped and pulled out a bottle of water. As he was kneeling beside his mother's body, he had a moment of déjà vu, remembering the day he'd found her sprawled out on their kitchen floor back in Conway, unconscious and bloody from the beating their father had given her. Then he shook off the memory, soaked his handkerchief with water, and began wiping her face and neck, repeating over and over, "Mom! Mom! Can you hear me? It's Sean. Can you open your eyes for me?"

He dampened the handkerchief again, and this time gently wiped her lips, then her neck, and when she began to stir, he breathed a sigh of relief. "She's coming to, but she's going to be in agony," he muttered.

The brothers knelt around her, holding her hands, patting her, and talking to her until she suddenly gasped and opened her eyes. The moment she did, the sound that came out of her mouth was a long, high-pitched cry of pain.

"Mom, it's us. We've got you," Wiley said. "Aaron called Medi-Flight. We're going to have to carry you out, and it's going to hurt."

She moaned, clutching their hands so tightly that her knuckles went white.

"What happened, Mom? Why did you leave the house?" Sean asked.

Shirley moaned again. "Ella. Saw Ella…lost. Didn't think. Just ran."

Shock ran through every Pope there.

"What do you mean, you saw Ella?" Cameron asked.

Shirley grimaced as a wave of pain washed through her. "She was standing in the pasture looking toward the house. Too far from home. Went to check on her."

The brothers eyed each other. It was as Wiley said. When they knew why she left, it would make sense, and it did.

"Did you talk to her?" Cameron asked.

Shirley started crying. "No, she disappeared."

"Aaron, where did you tell the chopper to land?" Cameron asked.

"Back pasture behind the house, but we have to get her out of the woods," he said.

"Then let's get moving, because one of us is going to have to go check on Ella, and you four need to be with your mom, so it's going to be me."

Aaron stood. "Thank you for coming to help. We'll get her to the pickup site. Mom carried each of us for nine months before we were born. It's our turn to carry her."

Cameron took off at a lope, with Ghost right beside him.

When Wiley began taking off his belt, B.J. frowned.

"What are you doing?" he asked.

"I'm going to buckle her good leg to her injured leg and use it as a brace."

"Good move!" Aaron said.

Aaron and Sean held her legs together while Wiley

wrapped his belt around them, just above the ankles, then B.J. buckled it down. Once they had immobilized her injured leg, they stood. Aaron squatted down, slid his hands and arms beneath her body and picked her up, and the moment they moved her, she screamed again and passed out. It was heart-wrenching, knowing that to help her, they had to hurt her again.

"Sorry, Mama," B.J. said.

"Let's go," Wiley said, and then turned and led the way. Before they reached the clearing, all four brothers had taken a turn carrying her. When they finally came out of the woods, B.J. had her in his arms, and they could hear the inbound chopper.

B.J. turned his back to the chopper to shield her from the rotor's blast as it began to land. After that, the paramedics took over, and once Shirley was loaded into the chopper, it lifted off and headed down the mountain to the hospital in Jubilee. Her sons were not far behind.

But Cameron and Ghost were going up the mountain on a welfare check for Ella.

———

Ella Pope's land was near the top of Pope Mountain, between John Cauley's homeplace, and Marcus Glass's property. It was where she'd been born, and if Amalie was right, where Ella's life had ended.

All the way there, Cameron kept wanting to believe this would be a fool's errand, that Aunt Ella would come out to meet him, sit him down in her kitchen with a cup of coffee and a gingerbread cookie, and before he left, impart a bit of mountain wisdom to keep his feet on the right path. But it didn't bode well for that to happen. They had already accepted Amalie had the gift of sight and Ella had appeared with a message to "help Shirley." The part of the scenario that didn't fit was that Shirley didn't have that gift, and yet she'd seen Ella, too, standing in the pasture. When he finally reached the road leading to Ella's home, he turned north off the blacktop and stopped at the mailbox, gathered up her mail, and kept driving.

The lane was graveled and bordered on both sides by trees and bushes. By the time he got to her house, Ghost was halfway into the front seat with his head on Cameron's shoulder.

"It's okay, boy," Cameron said. As soon as they got out, he clipped the leash on Ghost and headed for the porch, but before he could even knock, Ghost was whining the same way he used to in Iraq when they would find a body in the rubble. "Dammit," Cameron mumbled, and knocked, but no one answered. He knocked one more time and then tried the door.

It swung inward.

Ghost got to the threshold, looked up the stairs, then whined and went belly down.

"Okay, boy. I get the message," Cameron said. He tied the dog to the porch post, then went inside. He could see the kitchen from where he was standing, and there wasn't a cup or a plate sitting out on the table or anything out of place. He left her mail on the hall table and headed up the stairs to her bedroom.

Even though he'd been expecting it, finding her like this was a gut punch. She was lying on her back, her long white hair in a braid draped across her shoulder. She was covered only with a sheet and a light coverlet, and the windows had been opened to catch the night breeze. She looked like she was sleeping, but when he checked, her body was already in rigor mortis.

"Ah, Aunt Ella, we were never going to be ready for this." The sense of loss Cameron felt was overwhelming. The family elder—the last of her generation—was gone. He laid a hand on her forehead, then bowed his head. "Bless you on your journey, Ella Pope. You were so loved and are going to be so missed."

He was blinking back tears as he headed back downstairs, then walked out onto the porch to call 911.

"911. What is your emergency?" the dispatcher asked.

"This is Cameron Pope. I just did a welfare check on an elderly relative and found her in her bed, deceased. I'll need an ambulance sent to her residence. She wasn't suffering from any disease, but she was in her late nineties. It is my understanding that in instances like this, she must be transported to a hospital for a doctor to officially pronounce her dead."

"What's her name and address?" the dispatcher asked.

"Ella Pope, 10085 Pope Mountain Road. Once you reach the mailbox with that address, you'll turn north. It's the only one at the end of the lane."

"Yes, sir. Are you going to be with her?" the dispatcher asked.

"Yes, I'll be here," Cameron said, and disconnected, then began making calls, beginning with Rusty, his wife, so she'd know why he was delayed coming home, and then he started with Aunt Annie.

After that, word spread across the mountain like wildfire, and by the time the ambulance arrived, the front yard of Ella's house was filled with cars, and family members were sitting quietly on the porch and around the yard.

Ella had died just as she'd lived.

Alone.

But family was with her now, all the way to the grave.

————————

Shirley's sons and wives were in the ER waiting room when Aaron received Cameron's text. He sighed, then looked up at his brothers.

"Amalie was right. Aunt Ella is gone, probably sometime early this morning."

Amalie started to cry. Dani reached for Aaron.

The brothers lowered their heads. This was a hard blow for the family, and Shirley's injury just made it worse. They'd all just learned she had a hairline crack in her tibia and a severe sprain. The doctor was putting her ankle in a cast, while her sons were making plans as to how to help Sean care for her, when Linette came running into the waiting room.

"Hospital grapevine! I just heard they brought your mother in," she said, and sat down beside Wiley. "What happened?"

Seeing her at this moment was an emotional boost as he reached for her hand.

"She was out in the woods behind the house, hung her toe on a tree root, and fell. She has a severe sprain and a hairline crack in her tibia. They're putting on a cast. Scary part was not being able to find her. She'd passed out," Wiley said.

"Oh, no! That was likely from the pain. I can't stay and talk because I'm on duty, but after I heard the news, I had to come check on you." Then she stood and looked around the waiting room where all the family was seated. "I didn't mean to interrupt," she said, then gave Wiley one last glance before leaving the area.

"Is this one a keeper?" B.J. asked.

"If she'll have me," Wiley muttered. "The votes are still out on that."

A short while later, a nurse came to tell them the cast was on and Shirley's doctor wanted to talk to them, so they followed her back to the exam room and were relieved to see their mom sitting up in bed and talking.

The doctor turned as the sons filed into the room.

"Dr. Kline, these are my sons and daughters-in-law. I'm afraid I gave them quite a scare."

"That's the understatement of the week," Sean said.

The doctor's eyes widened at the sight. "My goodness, Shirley. You have passed on some remarkable genetics to your boys. And I know it comes from the Pope side, because I've treated several of them since I've been here."

"Thank you, Doctor. I'm proud of all my family," she said.

"As you should be. Shirley tells me one of her sons lives with her. Which one would that be?"

"That would be me, and my wife, Amalie," Sean said.

Kline nodded. "Okay, then you need to know she's not to put weight on that foot for at least four weeks and then check in with her regular doctor. Get her one of those knee-leg scooters so she can put her knee on the pad and then propel it with her good leg. It will save everybody trying to move her and be safer than crutches. I don't know where the nearest medical supply is, but it's likely Bowling Green. And Shirley, I'm saying this in front of your family so you can't tell them different later. Do not try to cook on one foot. Figure something else out, or let your family feed you for a while. I don't want you back in here with grease burns or the like, understood?"

Shirley rolled her eyes. "Fine. Whatever."

"We hear you loud and clear," Sean said.

"Okay then. They'll be bringing your release papers soon, and you can take her home. There will be a prescription for pain meds with the papers. I'd suggest getting that filled before you leave Jubilee. She'll be needing them for a few days." Kline touched her shoulder and smiled. "Take care, Shirley, and you'll be dancing again before you know it."

As soon as he was gone, Shirley leaned back in the bed. "I'm so sorry. I still can't believe this happened," she said.

Wiley moved to the foot of her bed. "Mom, you said you left the house because you saw Ella."

Shirley frowned. "Yes, that's right, I did see her out in the pasture. I couldn't imagine her being this far down the mountain and afoot. It worried me, but then she walked into the woods and disappeared, and I kept looking for her."

Aaron reached for her hand. "I'm so sorry to have to tell you this, but Aunt Ella passed away sometime this morning."

Shirley gasped. "Oh no! She was lost! If only I could have found her before—"

Amalie stepped up between the brothers. "No, Mom. Ella was already in spirit when you saw her. She was walking the mountain, telling it goodbye, and had no idea that you would be able to see her."

Shirley gasped. They all knew Amalie had the same gift of sight that Ella Pope had been born with. "Oh my God. How did you know this?"

Amalie's eyes welled. "Because Ella appeared in the doorway of my office and called my name. As soon as I looked up, she said, 'Help Shirley' then blew me a kiss and disappeared...like smoke. I heard the rest of it in my head after she was gone and I called Sean, but they'd already found you. I told them to go check on Ella. Cameron found her in her bed. She'd been gone for a few hours."

Shirley was weeping. "She was so dear to all of us and the last of the old ones."

"No, ma'am," Amalie said. "She's not the last of anything. It's just a shift in generations. Uncle John and Aunt Annie Cauley are now the elders, right?"

Shirley swiped at her tears. "Yes, you're right, and thank you for that. Perspective is often a blessing, but we're so going to miss her."

B.J. was standing at the foot of her bed with his hands in his pockets, staring blindly at the wall above Shirley's head.

"Ecclesiastes 3: 'For everything there is a season, and a time for every matter under heaven: a time to be born, and a time to die.' Nothing can change that outcome, Mom, and God knows Ella was given more years than most, but we aren't going to forget her. Look how long we've hung on to Brendan and his Meg."

Shirley smiled through tears. "Oh, B.J., when did you get so wise?"

He looked away, and when he finally answered, there were tears in his eyes.

"When I found the remains of our ancestor Meg. She'd been lost to us for so long, and in those few moments when I saw her like that, I felt the weight of a thousand years upon my shoulders, like I'd been born for that purpose, and that nothing I ever do will top the importance of bringing her back to bury her beside her loving husband, Brendan."

Total silence followed, as everyone thought about Brendan Pope, the very first man to stake a claim on

Pope Mountain, and his beloved wife, who had been kidnapped. Brendan had mourned her loss for the rest of his days, which none of the family knew until his journal had been found a few years earlier.

The silence was broken only after the nurse came in with a wheelchair and Shirley's release papers. "Time to go home!" she said, unaware of the gravity within the room.

Sean and Aaron helped Shirley into the wheelchair, and then everyone headed for the exit.

Aaron took B.J. back to work.

Wiley headed to the pharmacy with the prescriptions.

Ella was already in her heavenly home. It was time for Shirley to get back to her earthly one, but she was quiet and tearful all the way back up the mountain.

"I can't believe Aunt Ella is gone," she said.

"I know, Mom. She was such an institution, I think we all thought she was immortal," Sean said.

Shirley sighed. "I can't believe what I saw was her spirit, though. She looked so…so solid…so real."

"Until she disappeared," Sean said.

"Yes. Until she disappeared," Shirley said, and glanced out the window. "Looks like clouds are building up over the mountain. It might rain tonight."

"Good. Maybe it'll cool things off," Sean said. "Dani is coming to stay with you for a while tomorrow until I can get back. I have two business appointments in the morning, both in Bowling Green, and then I'm going to pick up that knee-leg scooter Dr. Kline recommended before I come home."

"I hate being helpless and dependent on other people. I've sure gone and messed everything up," Shirley muttered.

Sean gave her hand a quick squeeze. "No way, Mama. After all you do, and have done for us, we are blessed to be able to return the favor. And you'll heal and be good as new soon enough."

"I guess," Shirley said. "But just for the record, I'm sorry I won't be able to help out with Ella's funeral, or the family dinner, or anything."

"Maybe not, but we can get you there. Don't fret about that, okay?" he said.

"Thank you, Son. I appreciate that," she said, then leaned back and closed her eyes.

"Are you hurting?" Sean asked.

She nodded.

"Wiley will be along shortly and we'll get those pain meds started, and when Amalie gets home this evening, she and I will be making supper. You will be in bed with your foot on a pillow and the TV remote. I have some handheld two-way radios. When you need help, just give me a shout. We can do this, Mom."

"I don't know how lucky I became to have such wonderful sons, but I would marry Clyde Wallace all over again just for the blessing of being your mother," she said.

Sean shook his head. "Thankfully, you'll never have to do that again. Once around the block with Clyde was enough for all of us."

Chapter 6

WILEY MADE A FLYING TRIP UP THE MOUNTAIN WITH Shirley's meds, then headed back into Jubilee. He knew Ella's body had been sent to the funeral home and that extended family members were still being notified. He also knew that John and Annie Cauley were making the arrangements, and Marcus Glass was coordinating with Preacher Farley at the Church in the Wildwood regarding services. Everyone on the mountain was in mourning.

As soon as he got home, Wiley sent a text to Linette to let her know about Ella Pope, and that for the time being, his time was going to involve work, helping with his mother's care, and burying the family elder. And then he ended the text with a promise.

> Hold my place, Linnie. I'm coming back for more if
> you'll have me.

Linette was shocked to hear about the passing of the Pope family member and felt nothing but empathy and regret for all they were going through. She wished she could help, but at this point, she was still on the outside looking in at the Pope family circle.

By the time she got off work she was exhausted and grabbed some smoked ribs from Emory's Barbecue before going home. Not having to cook for herself was just one thing less to do before she could go to bed and, hopefully, dream of the man who was laying claim to her heart.

It rained in the night and was still overcast and drizzling when Dani arrived early the next morning at Shirley's house, leaving Sean free to make his appointments and get the scooter from a medical supply company in Bowling Green. Amalie had made chicken and dumplings last night, so there would be food ready for lunch today, and Shirley was restless and achy and relying on the pain meds.

The overcast day stayed with them through nightfall, but the next day dawned with clear skies and sunshine. The families on the mountain were hustling from one task to another, and baking and cooking for the meal after Ella's funeral service, and on the third day after Ella's passing, they laid her to rest in the blue bridesmaid dress she'd worn to Sean and Amalie's wedding.

She'd looked like an angel the day of that wedding, tall and regal with the sunlight pouring in through the windows behind her, and now she had become one. They buried her beside her parents and covered the freshly turned earth with flowers, cried through Brother Farley's shaky, heartfelt prayer, then headed into the church for the family dinner. The atmosphere was somber. Only rarely did a laugh sound above the murmurs of conversation across the dining hall, until John Cauley stood.

"Could I please have your attention for a moment?" he said.

The room went silent.

"We're all adrift, and that's as it should be today. Ella was our anchor to the past, but there's something we're not acknowledging here that I think matters. Ella always considered us her link to the future. No one lives forever, but from the time we are born, we are standing in the footsteps of our ancestors. They're within us and around us, and what we do now is honor Ella Pope's place in our history. She loved these family gatherings at the church more than anything. Share your Ella stories with each other. Tell your children about the woman who could see into the past as easily as she could see what was ahead of her. It's how we keep those we've lost with us—by keeping them alive in our hearts." Then he picked up his glass. "To Ella. May she rest in peace!"

"To Ella!" they echoed, and after that, the lull in conversation lifted and the people who loved her most began their conversations with, "Remember when…" and stories were told, and laughter ensued.

Once the day of the funeral had passed, life settled back into daily routines.

Dani came up the mountain to help Sean during the day, and Amalie was home from work in the evening to help Sean at night.

B.J. and Wiley made regular trips up to check on their mother and bring grocery orders to save Sean having to go get them. Shirley was looking forward to having the cast removed and her life back to normal, and Wiley's free time was finally his own again.

He sent Linette a text while he was on break.

> I'm free after six tonight, if you're free. I miss you. My place? We can order in and pretend we live really normal lives. Please say yes. You're my safe place to fall.

Linette read the text with tears in her eyes and responded.

> Yes. After six.

"Hot damn," Wiley whispered.

Wiley's partner, Doug Leedy, looked up. "Were you talking to me?"

"Nope. Just to myself," Wiley said, and smiled.

Wiley was barely out of the shower and buttoning up his jeans when the doorbell rang. His hair was still damp, and he was minus a shirt, but he didn't want to leave Linette waiting on the doorstep, so he grabbed a T-shirt as he ran to let her in.

The door swung inward. A greeting was on the tip of his tongue. Their gazes locked for a second, and then hers raked him from head to toe. He saw her nostrils flare, and her eyes narrow as they centered on his broad shoulders and flat belly.

"Ah...to hell with propriety," he muttered.

The door swung shut behind them as she crossed the threshold, and then she was in his arms, sandwiched between the door and his chest. She slid her arms around his neck and lost her mind.

He took her standing up, then carried her to bed and made love to her again, without a stitch of clothes between them until she was completely exhausted, numb to everything but the thunder of her own heartbeat in her ears. Long moments of silence ensued within his embrace, and then he broke it with a question.

"Are you okay?"

She shuddered. "I knew it would be like this, and I will never be okay again. You're my drug, Wiley Pope. I will never not want you."

He raised up on one elbow, needing to see her when he said it.

"As in *forever* want? Because that's what I want with you."

Linette put her hand in the middle of his chest, feeling the steady thump of his heartbeat against her palm. "I thought when I watched you get shot that every happy-ever-after dream I had had just ended before it began. I'd never even kissed you, and when you flew backward, my heart stopped. I thought I was dying with you. Your face is what I see when I close my eyes at night. I love your laugh. I love that you're impulsive and honest to a fault, and I love that wild streak in you. Yes, forever. Forever in my heart. Forever yours."

"Then it's settled. How long do you need to be courted before you will marry me?"

Linette blinked, and then burst out laughing. "Our second real date has barely begun, and you have already proposed. Oh, I don't know. Let me check my schedule."

He grinned. "Was that too much, too soon?"

"Not really. You're damn good at the too-much part, but I would like for you to meet my parents."

"What if they don't like me?"

She heard the worry in his voice. "They don't have to. I just want them to meet the man who keeps a permanent smile on my face and who will father their grandchildren."

He brushed his lips across her mouth. "I love you very much."

"I love you, too, crazy man."

"I want to give you the world," Wiley said.

"Thank you, sweetheart, but right now, I'd settle for food."

"I can make that happen," he said. "Did you bring your toothbrush?"

"Uh, no."

"No matter. I have new ones. Will you stay the night with me, too?"

She slid her hand up the side of his cheek. "Yes, and thank you for the invitation."

He smiled, and her heart skipped.

Stay wild, my beautiful man. Crazy looks good on you.

They ordered in fried chicken and biscuits, and gravy for dipping, and made love in the kitchen and again in his bed. Falling asleep in his arms was the cherry on top, and she never wanted it to end.

But when the alarm went off the next morning, yanking them back into the reality of their worlds, he loved her awake. She had to go back to her apartment to get ready for work, and he had to let her go.

"Are we a secret?" he asked.

"Not in my world," Linette said.

He nodded. "And not in mine. Be careful today. I love you."

"You're the one with the gun. *You* be careful."

"Are you coming back?" he asked.

"As often as you'll have me," she said.

He opened the dresser drawer and pulled out a spare house key and laid it in her palm.

"You already hold the key to my heart. Now you have a key to the door. Come when you can. When you want to. And take a break for yourself when you don't. I have no expectations beyond what you're willing to give me, but if I had my way, you'd already be here."

She wrapped her arms around his neck. "Love you, Wiley Pope."

"Love you more, Linette Elgin, and don't you forget it."

A few minutes later, she was gone. The house was quiet, but Wiley was as happy and as at peace as he'd ever been.

———————

Two mornings later, just as the nurses were changing shifts, Carey Eggers regained consciousness. She wasn't cognizant enough to talk to, but it was the first sign of recovering. The hospital notified Johnny Knight, and he and Tom were the first ones in on the next visiting hour.

When they opened the ICU to visitors, Tom and Johnny got in line, and once inside the critical care unit, Tom rolled Johnny up to the bed. The first thing Johnny did was stand up, using the bedrail as a crutch to steady himself, and stroke the side of her face.

"Hey, sweetheart, it's me, Johnny. Tom and I are here. We've been here for days, waiting for you to wake up." Then he gently clasped her hand and just held it as he talked.

———————

Carey didn't know where she was. Her last memory was running in the dark, and even as she was beginning to be conscious of sound and pain, she was still in the dark, unable to wake up enough to open her eyes. She continued to drift in and out without knowing what was happening, until someone stroked her cheek, then clasped her hand.

The rumble of the voice felt like love. She thought she was underwater, yet could see light, and kept trying to swim up, even as something was holding her down. She was afraid to open her mouth, for fear she'd drown, and so she moaned, wanting them to pull her up into the light.

Johnny jumped when he heard her moan.

"Oh my God, Tommy, did you hear that?"

Tom nodded. "I did, buddy. She's fighting. That's all you can ask of her."

Johnny leaned down close to her ear. "I know you can hear me, love. It's me, Johnny. You're in a hospital. You're safe. Just come back to me, baby. I can't do life without you."

Carey moaned again. She knew that voice. Johnny! It was Johnny! She needed him to know that she heard and, with all of the strength she could muster, curled her fingers within his palm.

"She just moved her fingers in my hand! She heard me!" Johnny said as a nurse approached.

The nurse checked all of the readings, making note of them in the log on her computer, and then eyed the time.

"Time to tell our sleeping beauty goodbye," she whispered, and pointed to the clock.

Johnny nodded. "Just rest, Carey. Tom and I will be back. Just keep fighting, girl. I love you forever."

Carey sighed and sank back into the dark, but the awakening had begun, and over the next two days, she finally reached the point of being moved out of the ICU into a private room and was alert enough to be questioned by the authorities. She was anxious about the guards in the hall and about what would happen to her when she went home, when she would be well enough to go back to work, and couldn't believe this nightmare was still ongoing.

———

Sheriff Woodley arrived at the hospital with Carey's personal belongings. Detective Gardner, the detective in charge of Billy Eggers's murder, was with him as they made their way to Carey's room. Even though they'd read the reports, they were not prepared for her appearance.

She was covered in bruises, healing cuts, and scratches, with visible staples in her head and the bandages still on her upper body from the gunshot wound. Johnny was sitting in his wheelchair beside her bed, and Tom was at the foot.

After the introductions were made, Rance Woodley held up a paper bag. "Miss Eggers, we're returning your purse. It was on the floorboard of the car you wrecked and has nothing to do with either of our cases, so we're returning it to you intact."

"Is the money still there?" she asked.

"There's money in there. I don't know the amount of which you're speaking."

"Five hundred dollars. Billy gave me five hundred dollars," she said. "Give it to Johnny. It was for his medicine." And then she started to cry.

"I'm sorry this is upsetting. Is it still okay that we do this today?" Woodley asked.

"Yes, I want to get it over with and get well enough to go home. Give Johnny the bag, please. I don't want it here in the hospital with me. Have you caught the man who shot Billy?" she asked as Woodley set up the video equipment.

Gardner shook his head as he handed the bag to Knight. "Not yet, but we have an ID from prints and DNA."

Woodley fiddled with the focus until he was satisfied, and then began.

"Miss Eggers, since this is going to be your official statement as to all that transpired to get you where you are today, we'll be recording it. Detective Gardner is investigating your brother's murder, and I'm investigating what happened to you after the wreck and the attempt made on your life. If you get tired or need a break at any time, just let us know, okay?"

"Yes," Carey said, and felt Johnny reach for her hand.

"Will you state your name, occupation, and where you're from for the record?" Woodley said.

"Carey Jean Eggers. I'm a waitress at an IHOP in Bowling Green, Kentucky. I also live in that city."

"Are you married?" Woodley asked.

"No, sir, but I am engaged to Johnny Knight. He's a lineman for BGMU… That's Bowling Green Municipal Utilities in the city. We live together."

"For the record, Detective Gardner will begin the questioning."

At that point, Gardner already had tests results from the crime scene, including Carey's and her brother's DNA at the scene, and fingerprints and DNA taken from beneath Billy's fingernails belonging to man named Lonny Joe Pryor, a.k.a. Gunny, from Sparta, Tennessee, but he needed her verification on some details.

"Miss Eggers, why were you at your brother's house on the day of the murder?" Gardner asked.

"Johnny was recently injured on the job and had surgery on his leg. He suffers a lot of pain. His workman's comp hadn't come through, and my payday was about five days away when we ran out of pain pills. I'd gone to my brother, Billy, to borrow money so I could get Johnny's pain meds refilled."

"Did you drive there?" Gardner asked.

"No. Our only vehicle was in the shop, so I caught the bus, then walked the rest of the way to Billy's house. He was coming out of the house when I arrived, and of course, he immediately offered to help when he heard why I was there."

"What happened next?" Gardner asked.

"We went inside together. He told me to help myself to a cold drink, so I got a Pepsi from the refrigerator while he went to open his safe. I asked to borrow a hundred dollars. Johnny's meds were over eighty dollars. But Billy gave me five hundred dollars and told me it was a gift, not a loan. I was so grateful, and just as we were getting ready to leave the house, someone drove up."

"Did you see the person or the car they were in?" he asked.

"I only heard the vehicle. I didn't see anything when they drove up. I'm not even sure the driver was alone. I did briefly see one man come running out of the house from my side mirror as I was driving away, and I saw the man's vehicle when I was getting into Billy's SUV. It was a black Chevrolet short-bed pickup with a set of fancy mag wheels and a decorative rebel flag sunshade on the back window."

Gardner frowned. Lonny Pryor didn't own a vehicle, but they still had the DNA. "Okay, so what did Billy do when the person drove up?" Gardner asked.

Carey's eyes welled. "He cursed. I knew it meant trouble. Then he handed me his car keys and told me to go to the kitchen and hide, and if I heard fighting and gunshots, to take his car and run and not look back. I argued. I didn't want to leave him stranded, but he was firm, and I was scared and did what he said. I went through the kitchen into the utility room and shut the door between, opened the back door in case I needed to run, and waited."

"What did you hear?" Gardner asked.

"Loud voices. Cursing. Something about invading someone else's territory. I heard my brother say something about the man being full of shit...then something about gunny or money, I couldn't really tell which, and then fighting, then a gunshot. I held my breath, listening, but it had gone quiet. I went out the back door on the run, got in Billy's car, and drove away. As I stated, I had a glimpse of the man running out of the house, but I was over a hundred yards away by that time and couldn't identify him if I had to."

Then she covered her face and wept. "I knew Billy was dead."

"How did you know that?" Gardner asked.

"Because he never called me afterward. Billy was fifteen years older than me and mostly raised me. He loved me and was the only parental figure I ever had."

Johnny gave her a handful of tissues to wipe her face and stayed silent. He'd heard the story before, but it still made him sick to his stomach, knowing how much danger she'd been in, and how alone and scared she was.

"What happened after that? Did the shooter chase you?" Gardner asked.

"I was sure he would, but I had a pretty good head start, and then I drove into a thunderstorm and took a wrong turn in the downpour, and it got dark, and I was lost and still driving."

"Did you ever call your brother again?" Gardner asked.

"No. I called Johnny and left a message with him. He

was asleep when the call came and saw it after he woke up, but by then, I'd already wrecked the car, been chased through the woods, shot in the back, and left for dead."

At this point, Woodley picked up the questioning and identified himself on the recording before going forward.

"Did you know you were on Pope Mountain when you wrecked?" he asked.

She shook her head. "No, sir. I could barely see the road in front of me, but I kept watching the rearview mirror. I thought I'd lost him, and then I caught a flash of headlights in the rearview mirror, panicked, lost control of the car, and wrecked. When I came to, I could see headlights in the distance behind me. I had hit my head in the wreck, and my chest hit the steering wheel, and then my door was jammed. I came to enough to get myself out by crawling over the console, grabbed a flashlight and my phone, and staggered into the trees, then started running."

"When did you know you were being followed into the woods?" Woodley asked.

"Almost from the start. I saw a flashlight at the wreck, then someone carried that flashlight into the woods after me. I just kept running. I thought I'd lost him, and then I fell. Dropped my phone and flashlight. I crawled to pick up my flashlight, and as I was getting up, there was this sharp pain in the back of my shoulder like I'd been stabbed."

"And you never saw him," Woodley asked.

"I don't remember anything until waking up in the ICU days later."

"Could you identify the man?" Woodley asked.

"No, sir, I could not," Carey said.

"Would you recognize his voice if you heard it again?" Gardner asked.

"No, sir, I don't think I could."

Both officers looked at each other, and then nodded.

Woodley ended the recording by stating the time, and turned it off.

At that point, Tom Wheaton stepped forward.

"Now what? When Carey gets released, is it safe for her to go home?"

Gardner knew Tom. They'd been in contact from the beginning of this case, and he could see how invested he was in his friends' welfare.

"You know the drill," Gardner said. "What I can say is that I will make it known that the witness could not identify anyone but that we have gathered sufficient DNA from the scene to issue an arrest warrant for an individual. That will take the heat off of her. And hopefully, by the time Carey comes home, we'll have the shooter in custody. If not, it will serve no purpose for the killer to want her dead because she poses no threat to him."

Tom sighed. "That's good enough."

Gardner nodded.

Woodley gathered up his recorder. "Thank you for your statement, and my deepest sympathies for the loss of your brother," he said. "I hope you can get some rest now. We shouldn't be needing to speak to you again."

As soon as they were gone, Carey sank into the pillows.

"Oh, Johnny…why is all this horrible stuff happening to us? You got hurt. Billy was murdered, and here I am, in the same boat as you. What are we going to do?" she wailed.

"I have a little information that might help," Tom said. "I know for a fact that Billy had a will. I know he owned that house and the property it sits on. And we all know he had money. I'm just throwing this out here now, but I'll bet a month's wages that you inherit everything, honey. Billy didn't stop taking care of you after you grew up."

"How do you know that?" Johnny asked.

Tom shrugged. "I grew up with Billy. I've arrested him more than once, but he never held it against me. Before Johnny came into the picture, Billy gave me a heads-up one night when I was taking him to booking and said that if anything ever happened to him, to make sure I told you to go to Williams and Williams, Attorneys at Law. They have a copy of his will and information Carey will need to know."

"Oh my God," Carey muttered. "I never thought… I never dreamed. I thought whatever he owned would just be confiscated."

Tom shrugged. "He wasn't being arrested. There were no warrants out on him. Technically, someone just walked into his house and shot him. That makes him a victim of a murder. He loved you, and you're his heir. You and Johnny are going to be okay."

———

Junior Henley was still in cleanup mode and had been checking every news outlet in the state for days, looking for any mention of a body being found on Pope Mountain. But when there was none, he called Gunny.

Gunny was lying on the sofa with an ice pack on his knee and frowned when he saw caller ID. He wanted to ignore it, but knew better than to skip the call.

"Yeah, what do you want?"

Junior didn't mess around with niceties. "Why is there no mention of a woman's body being found on that mountain?"

Gunny was immediately on the defense. "Because it may never be found? Because animals dragged it off? How do I know?"

"But there was a wrecked car, you dumbass. Authorities won't quit looking until they find the driver."

Gunny frowned. "I'm nobody's dumbass, and if I am, what the hell does that say about you for hiring me? Even if I had removed the body, I couldn't have gotten rid of the car. It was wrecked and in a torrential downpour. I did good to even find her afterward. She was hurt in the wreck. I shot her in the back and nearly got struck by lightning in the process. A damn tree was on fire in the rain when I booked it, and I was bleeding all over the place. Thank God for the rain. It washed it all away."

Junior frowned. He understood the situation, but it didn't make him feel any easier.

"Yeah, well, you better be right, because if any of this comes back on me, you're gonna be the first to pay."

"I did exactly what you sent me to do, with all the information you gave me. I went to deliver a message. Eggers is the one who freaked out on me. I shot in self-defense and, on my own, followed a witness in a fucking storm and took her out. You don't blame me for this shit."

"You don't talk back to me, boy!" Junior shouted.

Gunny went silent.

"Did you hear me?" Junior asked.

"I'm nobody's boy," Gunny whispered.

When the line went dead in Henley's ear, his skin crawled. He'd heard stories of what had happened to people who crossed that man, and he didn't want to be on the receiving end of a grudge.

"Whatever," he muttered, and went to look for his daddy. It was time to let him know what was going on. At least up to a point.

Moments later, Junior sauntered into the library. "Hey, Daddy?"

Carl Henley was in his favorite easy chair, typing out a text. There was a glass half-full of his best bourbon on the table beside him, and a half-smoked cigar smoldering in an ashtray. He looked up when Junior walked in.

"Yes?" Carl asked.

"I need to fill you in on some stuff. Remember when you told me to go talk to Billy Eggers about that new crew coming into your territory? Well, I sent Gunny to do it instead."

Carl frowned. "But I told you to do it."

"Well, I didn't. I sent Gunny, and he and Eggers got into an argument. Gunny pulled a gun on him, just as a threat. Eggers grabbed at it. They were wrestling with it when it went off, and Eggers is dead."

Carl shot up from the chair so fast that Junior jumped a good three feet back.

"You fucking idiot! Why am I just now hearing about this?"

Junior shrugged. "You were gone when it happened, and I guess I let it slip my mind, but that's not all. Gunny said there was a woman hiding somewhere in Eggers's house, and after Eggers dropped, Gunny saw her running out of the house. She got in Eggers's car and escaped. He went after her. Tracked her down in that rainstorm up on Pope Mountain and shot her, and left her body in the woods."

Carl stared at his son as if he'd never seen him before. "Who was she?"

"From Gunny's description, I'd guess it was Eggers's sister."

Carl was in shock. "Is there more?"

"No," Junior said. "I just told Gunny he was a dumbass for being so careless."

"You're the dumbass for sending someone else to do something I told you to do. Do we even know if the witness is really dead?" Carl asked.

Junior shrugged. "Gunny said..."

Carl held up his hand. "Between you and Gunny, you have turned a simple task into a nightmare. You get your ass to Jubilee and see what you can find out. See if there was a body found on the mountain. I don't like loose ends."

Junior ducked his head and left the library. He didn't want to go to some hick tourist trap. This was all Gunny's fault, but nobody bucked Carl Henley. Not even his son.

The next morning, Junior Henley was en route to Jubilee. He was in trouble with his old man, but it was no big deal. All he had to do was poke around a bit, see if there was any gossip about a body being found up in the woods, eat some barbecue, drink a few beers, and see the sights—maybe even have a funnel cake. He hadn't had one of those since he was a kid.

But completing his quest was going to be tricky. He had to find out what he needed to know without asking outright, and in his experience, the best place to loosen lips was at a bar. Find the locals who've been at the bar too long, buy another round of drinks and strike up a conversation, get them to the point of trying to one-up each other, then ask the right questions. And after a quick cruise of the area, he headed straight for Trapper's Bar and Grill, parked, and went inside.

He moved to the end of the bar, giving himself a

clear view of the place and the customers and ordered a beer. After it came, he turned on the charm to the bartender who served it.

"Nice place you got here!" Junior said. "I drive through here sometimes, but I've never taken the time to stop."

Louis Glass eyed the man as he slid a little bowl of pretzels toward him, wondering where the hell the man would be coming and going from to use this off-the-beaten-path highway to get there.

"Oh really? So, where are you from?" Louis asked.

"Originally? Frankfort. How about you? Lived here long?" Junior asked.

"All my life," Louis said, then moved down the bar to serve new customers.

Junior kept striking up conversations with the people around him, feeding them the same line and questions, and as Louis slowly made his way back down the bar to where the man was sitting, he noted the man's glass was nearly empty and so was the bowl of pretzels.

"Want another?" Louis asked.

"Yeah, and how about an order of nachos this time around?"

"Coming up," Louis said. He turned in the order, then brought a second beer. As he was reaching for the empty bottle, the stranger leaned in.

"You said you've lived here all your life, and I always wonder about that mountain. Every time I drive up on my way to Bowling Green, I see signs of people who live there, but I don't ever see houses. It's really creepy."

"Why do you say that?" Louis asked.

"I don't know. It just looks like a dangerous place to live. You can't see shit through those trees. Are there wild animals up there?"

"Of course," Louis said. "There are wild animals in every part of rural America. They just vary from place to place."

Junior nodded. "Yeah, right. Stupid question. I guess I mostly mean carnivores. I'd hate to get lost in those woods and get eaten by a bear or something like that."

Louis laughed, but he knew the guy was feeling him out for a reason. "You're safe sitting right here, mister. I'll go check on your order."

Junior frowned when the bartender walked away, then took a drink of his beer. The bar was filling up, and soon another guy slid up to the barstool beside him.

"Hey, Louis! My usual," he yelled.

Louis waved to indicate he'd heard and came back carrying a dark ale in a longneck bottle and a bowl of pretzels.

"Hey, Gus. How's the family?" Louis asked.

"Good. My oldest boy cut himself on some glass. He took a shortcut through the woods on his way back to the house and tripped and fell on it. Four stitches. We reckon it was from that wrecked car up there by Cameron's place."

"Sorry to hear that," Louis said. "I'll say something to Cameron. He'll want to get that cleaned up."

Gus nodded. "Yeah, I heard him and that big dog of

his found the driver. That dog's something. I remember when Cameron and Ghost tracked down that man who took your Lili."

Louis nodded. "That was a nightmare we won't soon forget." Then he glanced at Junior. "They're bringing your order out now."

"Thanks," Junior said, and as soon as the bartender moved away, Junior leaned back to let the server deliver his food, took a bite, and then moaned in delight. "Dang, these are good."

Gus glanced at him and nodded. "Yeah, they do good stuff here."

It was Junior's opening. "I couldn't help but over-hear what you said about your son. Hope he's gonna be okay."

"Oh sure. Kids are resilient."

"Right," Junior said. "So, there was a wreck, and a body was recovered? How sad."

"Oh, she ain't dead. They just found her."

Junior's heart sank, but he plastered on a smile. "Oh my God! A miracle. And right here in this hospital! Amazing."

Gus nodded. "They happen now and then."

Junior was in shock. Daddy wasn't going to like this one bit. He sat there eating his nachos, knowing he wasn't going to have time to get that funnel cake after all. This was stuff Daddy needed to know now. He fin-ished his food, waved two twenties at Louis, gave him a thumbs-up, and walked out.

Chapter 7

LOUIS PICKED UP THE MONEY AND THEN GLANCED AT Gus Walters. "Saw you talking to that dude who just left. What were you saying?"

Gus shrugged. "He just heard me talking about my boy, asked if he was okay, and how sad it was about the wreck and a dead body being found."

Louis stilled. He already knew through the family that they had purposefully not made mention of this in any of the papers for a reason.

"And...?" Louis asked.

"Oh, I just said she wasn't dead when they found her."

Louis's skin crawled. "What did he say?"

"Something about it being a miracle, then he finished eating and left."

"Oh, yeah, a real miracle," Louis said. "Give me a nod if you want a refill."

"I'm good. I'm gonna quit with the one and get on home," Gus said, and put some money on the bar. "My best to Rachel and Lili."

"Thanks," Louis said. He took the bills to the register, paid them with the money that had been left, put the change in the tip jar, then glanced up at the security cameras to see which ones were aimed at the far end of the bar.

A couple of minutes later, the next shift arrived, readying for the evening rush, and Louis clocked out, then went to the back room and called the police station, asking to speak to Sonny Warren. As soon as Sonny answered, Louis began to explain.

"Chief, it may be nothing, and it may be something, but I just had a stranger at the bar who fed me a line and then began questioning me about Pope Mountain, and people getting lost up there, and how scary it would be to get eaten by a wild animal. I got busy, and then Gus Walters came in and sat down beside him at the bar. I'm taking Gus's order, and he tells me about his oldest boy taking a shortcut across Cameron's land and falling on some glass from that wreck and having to have stitches. I walk off. See the dude head-to-head with Gus, then he pays and leaves. I ask Gus what they were talking about. Gus told him about the driver's body being found in the woods and now the man knows the driver is alive. As soon as he found that out, he left."

Sonny's skin crawled. "Tell me he's on your security footage."

"There were two cameras aimed in that direction," Louis said.

"I'm sending an officer down there right now. Tell Waylon Parker to make me copies, and thanks," Sonny said.

"Sure thing," Louis said. "I just clocked out. I'll help him find the guy on the footage before I leave."

As soon as they ended the call, Louis headed straight for the manager's office, knocked, then walked in and told him what they needed and why. Minutes later, they were in the back room of his office going through the most recent footage from those two cameras.

"There! That's him walking in," Louis said. "And that's him walking all the way past all those empty stools to the one at the far end. The chief is going to want everything he's on, okay? And if you can find him driving up or driving away, it would help them identify what he was driving as well."

"Got it!" Waylon said, and sat down at the computer as Louis walked out.

When the officer arrived and asked for the manager, Waylon came out carrying a flash drive. "This is what Sonny wanted," he said.

"Thanks," the officer said. He dropped the drive into an evidence bag and left.

Waylon wondered what was going on, and then shook it off. Anything to do with criminal activity made him nervous.

As soon as the flash drive landed on Sonny's desk, he quickly plugged it into his computer and started watching. Almost immediately, he thought the man looked familiar. He cropped a headshot and ran it through the database.

It didn't take long for facial recognition to make him.

"Holy shit," Sonny muttered. "That's Carl Henley's boy."

Henley was a well-to-do businessman in Bowling Green, but long suspected to be involved in the drug trade, although they'd never been able to pin anything on him.

Sonny saved the footage, then emailed it to Sheriff Woodley with a long detailed message, then sent the screenshot of Henley's face to the guard on duty at the hospital with a warning, then sent the same thing to hospital security, with a warning not to let that man in the hospital or give him any indication that Carey Eggers was even there.

This was a worst-case scenario evolving before their eyes, and the moment Rance Woodley got the message and saw the footage, he sent it straight to Detective Gardner.

———————

Junior was on his Bluetooth, talking to his daddy as he headed out of Jubilee.

"Daddy, it's me. I'm headed back," Junior said.

"What did you find out?" Carl asked.

"The woman's not dead. Some people found her and she's in the hospital in Jubilee. I don't know details."

There was a long silence.

Junior got antsy. "Daddy? You still there?"

"Yes. I'll tend to it from here. Just get on home."

"On the way," Junior said, disconnected, then burped. The jalapeños on his nachos were playing hell. His belly was starting to burn, and so was Carl's, but for a different reason.

Carl picked up the phone to call Gunny, then stopped.

The worst that could happen was Gunny being identified and picked up for the murder. If that happened, it put Carl in jeopardy, because Gunny could link him. What he needed to do was get rid of Gunny and let the woman alone. He needed to think about this. Whatever happened to Gunny needed to look like an accident.

———

Gunny felt the walls closing in. He didn't know where the woman was, but she surely had to be dead. But the longer he sat, the more uncertain he became. He knew his DNA was going to be on Billy, because he hadn't gone in there to fight with anyone, let alone kill them, so he hadn't gloved up. He could explain away his DNA being there because he and Eggers were acquaintances. He could even sell the story that they'd had an argument, but nothing he would have ever killed him for.

He'd already removed his prints from the gun and the remaining ammo before he took them back to Henley. And the truck he'd been driving for the past month was not his. It belonged to Junior Henley. He'd won it from him in a poker game, but Junior had only given him the keys and never signed over the title. It seemed like a good time to return the truck to its legal owner—after he had it wiped clean of his prints. Then everything connected to the Eggers murder would be on Henley premises. Henley had called him dumbass, then called him boy. Henley had, by God, threatened him. He didn't take that shit from anybody.

Gunny's knee was mostly healed, but a little stiff. He winced as he stood up, glanced around the apartment, and knew it was time to disappear. All he needed to take were his clothes and his money stash. The furniture was used when he bought it, so he took a deep breath and headed for the bedroom, thinking, *There's no time like the present.*

He got his money first, put it inside the lining of the duffel bag, rolled up the clothing he was taking, and packed it in the bag, then proceeded to shave himself bald and shave his facial whiskers into a vandyke beard. He owned two pairs of shoes. One pair was blood-splattered, so he put them in the bottom of a garbage bag, then stuffed the garbage from his kitchen in on top of it, emptied all of the disposable food from the fridge into a box, and carried it all out to the dumpster.

Then he carried his things to the truck and drove to the bus station, rented a locker, and stashed his belongings until he had time to get back, and headed for a car wash with a pair of gloves in the seat beside him.

The sun was going down when he finished cleaning the truck, both inside and out. He got back in, still wearing the gloves, and drove the truck to the alley behind Henley's estate and parked it, threw the keys beneath the mat, locked the truck, and took off walking.

His knee was throbbing, and as soon as he was far enough away, he called a cab to take him to the bus station. After his arrival, he retrieved his belongings, bought a ticket to Miami, Florida, and some food to tide him over on the ride, then sat down to wait. It was just over an hour and a half before that bus departed.

When it finally arrived, Gunny loaded his suitcase. When he boarded the bus, he went all the way to the back, chose a seat in the dark in the far corner, and settled in. Less than fifteen people boarded with him and scattered about the bus to suit themselves. It had been years since Gunny had been on a bus, and he wasn't talking to anybody. He didn't want to be remembered. He wasn't here to make friends.

Once the bus was on the road, and Bowling Green was behind him, he pulled out his burner phone and made a call to the Bowling Green PD.

As soon as the call was answered, he started talking.

"I got a message for the cop in charge of Billy Eggers's murder, so either record this or start writing. Billy Eggers was a friend. DNA don't prove anything except me and Billy had a fight, and it wouldn't have been the first time. It don't prove who shot him. The gun that killed him belongs to Carl Henley. The truck the shooter drove belongs to his son, and I ain't goin' down for their deeds."

Gunny hung up, even as the person on the line was trying to talk to him. He'd just leveled the playing field. It was time for the Henley duo to sit in the hot seat and see how they liked it.

———————

When Detective Gardner received the email and the security footage of Trapper's Bar from Sheriff Woodley, he was shocked, but after hearing the phone call they got from Lonny Pryor, he realized Pryor's phone call might be on the level, and all of this had just blown a great big hole in their theory. In all the years they'd been trying to find something to link Carl and Junior Henley to illegal activities, this might be the first break they'd been given.

After running info through the DMV, the description Carey Eggers had given of the truck the shooter was driving turned out to be a match for Junior Henley's truck. And after some online research, they had found photos of Junior standing beside that truck, with the rebel flag in plain sight.

Then Gardner began checking gun registrations and learned Carl Henley owned a number of guns, one of which *was* a Beretta M9, an older model from the 1990s. Casings from that gun would match the type of one found beneath a chair near Eggers's body and another found near where Carey Eggers was shot.

Knowing he was skating on thin ice, Gardner wrote

up a search warrant for Henley's home. And a warrant to search Junior's truck for DNA, using the security footage from Trapper's Bar and Grill as proof that Junior Henley was fishing for information about Carey Eggers. The warrant pointed out that the only way Junior would have known to ask about her welfare was that he already knew what had happened to her and Billy and was trying to find out if the witness to Billy's murder was still alive.

───────

Lilah Perry brought doughnuts to work, and after taking one for herself, left the rest of them in the PD break room. She knew the officers were already in the morning briefing, but they'd find the doughnuts. They never lasted past noon.

She sat down at her desk with the doughnut and a cup of coffee and booted up her computer terminal. There were always files to be entered and records to update, and after finishing her sweet, she wiped her hands and got to work.

It wasn't long before she came across a report from an ambulance run up on Pope Mountain that brought in a young woman who'd been shot in the back. She grimaced, thinking about the brutality of humanity, and then noticed the date. It was the night of the big rainstorm. The same night Lonny had shown up at her house with his injured knee. Then she shrugged it off. One thing had nothing to do with another. One of the officers even commented about having some roof damage from the wind, and the clerk where she bought groceries mentioned the wind broke a limb off in their backyard and fell on their roof. It had been a bad night for a lot of people, and with that thought, she went back to work.

Conway, Arkansas: July 5

Seven-year-old Ava Dalton learned a long time ago how to shrink herself up as tiny as a mouse by staying silent in the background of her mother's life. Today Ava was wishing she'd learned how to become invisible, too, because Corina had been raving and throwing things for an hour, all because Miss Mattie dropped dead.

"Most inconsiderate bitch I ever knew!" Corina shouted, and threw a shoe across the room. "I finally get the best gig of my life and now this!"

Ava wanted to slip into the bathroom and close the door, but she was afraid to call attention to herself because *she* was the problem in Corina's life.

She had known all her life that Corina never wanted to be a mother, and yet, here they were. Before Miss Mattie dropped dead, Corina used to dump her at Mattie's house for days, sometimes weeks, before she'd show up again. And when Mattie was unavailable, like the times when she was in the hospital for her asthma, Corina would call everyone she knew until someone said yes, and that's where Ava would be.

Ava didn't have a home, and everything she owned fit in a single garbage bag. Corina had given birth to her as a ploy to get child support and more welfare money, but then the father bailed on her, and all she had left was a kid she didn't want. Ava wasn't sure what was going to happen to her now, but it didn't look good, and she was as scared as she'd ever been, watching Corina going through her call list.

Corina was pretty frantic, too, but in a whole other way and for a whole other reason. She needed a place to dump the kid, but nobody was taking her calls. Maybe she'd overplayed her poor-single-mother hand once too often. She turned, glaring at the tiny blond huddled in the corner.

"Why me, God!" she screamed. "Why me?" and threw the other shoe.

She was at her wits' end when someone knocked on her door. She ran, flung it open, and in grand drama fashion, threw her hand up in the air. "Junie! Am I glad to see you! I thought you and Pete were on vacation!"

Junie Sumner strolled in with an unlit cigarette in one hand and her cell phone in the other, wearing the remains of a healing sunburn beneath a skin-tight white tank top and cutoff jean shorts.

"We just got back, and you will not believe who we saw!"

All of a sudden, Ava was forgotten as Corina and her drinking buddy cozied up to the kitchen table.

"Tell me," Corina said.

"I'll do one better. I'm gonna show you," Junie said, and pulled up the photos from their trip, scrolled through them until she found the ones she was looking for, and slid the phone across the table. "Who does that look like to you?"

Corina frowned, tapped the photos to enlarge the images, and then gasped. "You are fucking kidding me!"

"No. Swear to God," Junie said. "Right there, big as Dallas, Aaron and Wiley Wallace, both in police uniforms. At first I thought they was just look-alikes 'cause their names was different. They wasn't goin' by Wallace. Pete went up and said hi, and sure enough it was them, but they're goin' by the last name Pope. Apparently, it was their mother's name before she was married. Can't blame them none. Who would want to claim kin to Clyde Wallace, right?"

Corina frowned. "Where was it you said you went?"

"Jubilee, Kentucky, to see Reagan Bullard in concert. Pete loves his music."

"They're both cops now?" Corina asked.

"Obviously, girl. Look at their uniforms," Junie said.

"Did you ask them anything or, like, talk to them?" Corina asked.

"Not really, and they didn't look pleased to see us, either. Anyway...I just wanted to show you. Figured you might be interested, considering...well...you know..." she said, and glanced at the little girl in the corner.

Corina started her pitch. "Junie, Miss Mattie

dropped dead this morning. I don't have anybody to watch the kid, and I got the gig of my life! I'm going to be working on a cruise ship sailing back and forth along the Mexican coast."

"Great news! You'll find someone," Junie said. "I gotta go. Still need to unpack."

Corina turned on the whine. "I need help bad. I don't suppose you'd be…?"

Junie shook her head. "No, I got my own job."

"Pete doesn't work. He could keep her," Corina said.

Junie frowned. "Pete doesn't do kids. That's why we don't have any," she said. Then she got up, blew Corina a kiss, and walked out.

"I don't do kids, either," Corina muttered, but Junie had already shut the door. She sat for a few minutes, thinking, then got up and poured herself a shot of whiskey, tilted her head, and downed it in one gulp. When she looked up again, the kid was gone. She heard the bathroom door close and then threw the glass against the wall.

She stared out the window, and then it hit her! She did have another option. But she was going to have to take Ava with her on the trip to make it happen. She began throwing all of Ava's clothes into a trash bag.

———————

Corina had left Conway late in the evening and driven through the night with Ava in the back seat, using her bag of clothes for a pillow.

Ava didn't ask for anything. Not food or water, or even admitting when she needed to pee. She just held it until Corina had to stop for herself and ate whatever Corina gave her, which was usually the leftovers from what she didn't finish. She didn't know where they were going or what Corina was going to do with her when they got there, but she was scared.

It was just after 8:00 a.m. when Corina drove past the city limits sign in Jubilee, Kentucky. She was primed for war and absolutely certain her luck was about to change. She pulled into a gas station to refuel, then took herself and Ava to the toilet, washed up, and gave Ava a hairbrush.

"Get those damn tangles out of your hair. You look like some homeless kid," Corina snapped.

Ava didn't argue. She just brushed her hair, then waited for food to be the next item on the agenda, but that didn't happen. Instead, Corina asked for directions to the police station, and then they got back in the car and drove away.

Corina was pleasantly surprised by the charm of the tourist attraction, but she wasn't here for pleasure. She had business to attend to, so when they pulled up in front of the police station and parked, she grabbed Ava by the arm and stormed into the station, heading straight to the front desk.

"I need to speak to Aaron Pope!" she said.

Desk Sergeant Walter Winter glanced up. "He's in a meeting. Just have a seat."

Corina glared. "I didn't come all this way to wait!"

"Is he expecting you?" Winter asked.

"No, but—"

Winter's eyes narrowed slightly. "Then have a seat, ma'am."

Corina snorted beneath her breath, yanked Ava's arm hard enough that the little girl winced, and then sat down to wait.

Fifteen minutes went by, and Corina was getting angrier by the minute. Finally, she stood and stomped back to the desk.

"I demand to speak to your police chief! I want to file a grievance against Aaron Pope!"

Winter stood up. "Lady, you don't demand anything here. Sit down."

Corina stomped back to her seat and then slapped Ava's leg.

"Sit up straight!" she hissed.

It was the unnecessary abuse of the child that made Sergeant Winter get up and go into the briefing room just as the meeting was breaking up.

"Chief! We have a problem out front. There's some woman with a kid, and she's waiting to talk to you. Said she wants to file a grievance against Aaron."

Wiley was on his way out the door and pivoted when he heard that. "What the hell? Who is she?" he asked.

Aaron was frowning, wondering who he'd come in contact with in the last few days who could have taken offense at anything he might have done. "Did she give a name?"

Winter shook his head. "I didn't ask. The little girl with her is covered in bruises. I watched her yank the kid's arm so hard she almost pulled her off her feet, and just now, she slapped her leg so hard I heard it from where I was sitting."

Chief Sonny Warren's face turned red. "Bring her and the child into my office. Now."

"Yes, sir," Winter said, and hurried back toward the lobby.

"Aaron, with me," Sonny said.

"I'm coming, too," Wiley said.

"Whatever," Sonny said, and headed for his office.

A few moments later, Winter escorted the woman and child into the police chief's office.

Sonny glanced at the woman, but didn't recognize her. "Thank you, Sergeant Winter. Please close the door on your way out," Sonny said, then focused on the woman. "I'm Chief Warren. You asked to speak to me. Please have a seat and state your name."

Corina blinked. This sounded too much like interrogation.

"My name is…"

But it was Wiley who took a step forward. "Her name is Corina Dalton. She's the hook…I mean, cook from Melvin's Diner in Conway, Arkansas."

Corina glared. Wiley Pope wasn't her target, and she didn't want anything to do with him. He was just enough like Clyde to make her nervous.

"Yes, I'm Corina Dalton."

Sonny was eyeing the woman, but Wiley was looking at the little girl beside her and realized how terrified she was.

"And who is the child with you?" Sonny asked.

Corina pointed. "She's Aaron Pope's child. Her name is Ava!"

Aaron was stunned. "I'm sorry, but I don't know this woman and have never seen her until this moment."

"You're lying! You just want to get out of paying child support! You went and changed your name and skipped out of Conway when she was just a baby, and I didn't know where you went until the other day!"

Wiley snorted. "Now, *that's* a lie."

"It's no such thing!" Corina shouted and pulled an envelope from the depths of her tote bag. "And this here proves it. It's Ava's DNA test I had run when she was a baby to claim child support."

Aaron looked lost. "Wiley. What the hell's going on? Do you know who...?"

"I know exactly who she is. And there's a real good possibility that DNA test will prove we're related to that little girl, but not as a father. We're likely her brothers. Corina Dalton was one of Clyde Wallace's side pieces for at least four years before he wound up in prison."

Corina gasped. "How do you—"

Wiley's eyes narrowed. "How do I know? Because I saw you two together all over Conway, that's how. Our DNA is on file here. Compare it, Chief!"

Corina paled. This wasn't going as planned.

"So, what kind of scam are you trying to pull here, lady?" Sonny asked.

Corina glanced at Ava, and when she did, Wiley saw sheer terror on the little girl's face, and in that moment saw a tiny, unwanted child—a victim, just as they had been. Only Corina was her monster, just as Clyde had been theirs, and if she was truly Clyde Wallace's child, then she *was* their sister.

Corina and Aaron and Sonny Warren were arguing, but it was Wiley who knelt down beside Ava. When he started to put a hand on her shoulder, she flinched as if bracing herself for the blow.

"I'm Wiley. What's your name?" he asked.

She glanced at Corina, and then whispered, "Ava."

"Where do you and Mama live?"

"Mostly, Corina leaves me with people like Miss Mattie, but she dropped dead, and now there's no one."

Wiley blinked. She didn't even call her Mama. He looked up at Aaron, and then Sonny. "Ava looks hungry. Okay if I take her to the break room for a doughnut and milk?"

Sonny looked at Corina. "Is it all right with you if—"

"I don't care where you take her," she said. "I need to get this straightened out. I got a job waiting."

Wiley's skin crawled. *Jesus wept. What the hell has been happening to this child?* He held out his hand. "Want a doughnut?"

She glanced at Corina again, and then got up and followed him up the hall without touching him. As soon as they were in the break room, she crawled up in a chair and watched him take a doughnut out of a box, put it on a paper plate, and get a carton of milk from a dispenser. He opened the milk, popped in a straw, and then sat down on the other side of the table.

"Dig in, Ava."

She ate like she was starving, biting off big bites, barely chewing before swallowing, as if afraid the doughnut would be taken out of her hands before she was through. Watching her eat like this hurt Wiley's heart. He took a picture of her while she wasn't looking and sent it to his mother with a brief text.

Pretty sure this is our half sister. Corina Dalton just sailed into the PD this morning from Conway, trying to claim Aaron as the father to scam money, and I know you know who she is. The child is covered in bruises and scared spitless of her mother. She's so tiny. And she's breakin' my heart. I'm about to go to war for her, Mom. Will you hate me if I do?

He hit Send and waited. Within a minute, he got a response.

God in heaven. No, I won't hate you. What can you do?

He texted back.

Corina doesn't want her. I do. Her name is Ava. I
will never sleep again knowing she's somewhere
in the world without us.

He waited. Shirley Pope responded again.

See if she'll sign papers to terminate her parental
rights. We'll go from there. If this child has been
abused all her life, she won't be easy to raise.

He sent one last text.

We were abused all our lives, but we had you.
Until today, she had no one. Now she has four
brothers. I need to know she's fed and safe at
night. She's too quiet. I don't want her to be afraid
again. I can't be her daddy, but I can stand in for
one. I'm going to give Corina Dalton a deal she
won't pass up. Thanks for understanding.

Wiley put the phone back in his pocket, and when
Ava glanced up at him, he winked. The thought went
through his head that this might complicate matters
with Linette, but he'd never be able to live with himself
if he let this child go.

When he winked, Ava looked startled and ducked
her head, and then a few moments later looked up again.
He was still smiling. Maybe he wasn't going to yell.

"That's a pretty good doughnut, isn't it? It came from

a bakery here in town. Our aunt Annie owns and runs it. She's a really good baker. We have lots of family here. Do you have family back in Conway?"

She shook her head.

"Not anyone?" Wiley asked.

She ducked her head.

"Why not?" he asked.

"Corina only likes men. I'm a mistake."

The smile slid off Wiley's so fast that Ava froze. She was waiting for an explosion of rage that never came.

"Nobody is a mistake," Wiley said. "If you had a wish, where would you wish to live forever?"

Her eyes widened and, for the first time, welled with tears. "Where nobody yelled. Where I had a bed and a pillow."

Now Wiley's eyes were full of tears. "And who would you live with in this wonderful place?"

"With someone who wanted me."

"What if I wanted you?" Wiley asked.

Ava's lips parted, but all she could do was stare.

"I know we don't know each other yet, but I might be your brother, and if I am, then so are Aaron, and Sean, and B.J., my other brothers. You could live with me, and we would learn to be friends, and then maybe one day you would learn to love me…to love all of us."

"Do you have a wife?" Ava asked.

He thought of Linette. "Almost."

"Does she live with you?"

"Not all the time. But she stays at my house a lot. You would like her. She's a nurse at the hospital in Jubilee."

"Then who would take care of me when you're not there?"

"Who takes care of you now?" he asked.

"Miss Mattie, only she dropped dead. Other people do sometimes, but I stay quiet so they forget that I'm there."

"Well, that's not happening anymore," Wiley muttered. "You'd be in school part of the day, and I'll find you the best babysitter in the world for when I'm at work, and it would be your home forever."

Her eyes got wider. "With a bed and a pillow? I've never had a bed and a pillow."

"Yes, and so much more, and I'll read you bedtime stories and cook your favorite foods and—"

"Do you yell?" she whispered.

He shook his head. "Never. I promise."

She sighed. "Corina's going to work on a big boat."

Awesome. "Are you finished with your milk?"

She nodded.

"Let's wash the sticky off your face and hands and go back now, okay?"

While she was washing, she glanced up at Wiley.

"Are you a giant?"

"No, just a really tall man."

She nodded, satisfied with that answer. "If I lived with you, what would I call you?"

"Well, I'm your brother, and my name is Wiley."

"I can't call you Daddy, can I?"

His heart broke a little bit more. "Your daddy and my daddy are the same man, so I don't think that would work."

"A girl at my school has a big brother. She calls him Bubba."

Wiley was watching every nuance of her expressions. "Would you like to call me that?"

She looked doubtful. "What if Corina won't let me stay?"

"Don't worry, sugar. I've got this," Wiley said, and this time when he held out his hand, she took it.

Chapter 8

Aaron was standing at the door to keep Corina from bolting. She'd already figured out she was in trouble, and Chief Warren had taken Ava's DNA report and walked out. She didn't know what was going on.

A half hour passed before Sonny came back, and when he did, he was frowning. Corina saw the look and, as always, chose offense before defense and became indignant all over again.

"I'd like to know what the hell is going on here, and where's my kid?"

"You know where your daughter is. You gave Wiley Pope permission to get her some food and specifically said you didn't care where she went. As for where I've been, I took Aaron Pope's DNA report and your daughter's DNA report to one of the doctors at the hospital, who verified that they are definitely related, but on the level of siblings, not parent and child, which you already knew, didn't you? Because I had one of the officers look up your daughter's birth certificate and it specifically names Clyde Wallace as the father. This constitutes fraud. You, lady, are in big trouble here. I don't take kindly to anyone accusing my officers."

Before she could answer, Wiley and Ava walked in. Aaron saw the look on Wiley's face and knew he was about to blow the lid off somebody's pot, most likely one belonging to Corina Dalton.

"Have you charged her yet, Chief?" Wiley asked.

Sonny blinked. "Uh…"

"I have a proposition. Aaron won't file charges if she's willing to terminate her parental rights. Ava tells me Corina calls her a mistake, and Ava is covered in bruises, which points to child abuse. Ava also informed me that she does not, nor has she ever, had a bed or a pillow of her own. That she just sleeps where she's left. So, there's that."

Corina's heart was hammering so hard she couldn't breathe. If she got in trouble now, she'd never make that cruise.

"How do I know you won't hurt her?" Corina asked. "I mean, you're a man alone and—"

Aaron snapped. "Shut your mouth now, lady, before you say something you're going to regret. You didn't give a shit where you left her before, and since she's part of our family, she'll be treated as such, which means loved, cared for, and protected with our lives."

Corina didn't even look at the child. She was just looking at the door.

"Yes, hell yes, I'll sign anything it takes to be rid of her. But you don't charge me with anything, right?"

Sonny had seen some hard women in his life, but this one might just be the worst.

"Sit down, Miss Dalton. I will take your statement to this effect. You will sign it, and I will have it notarized before you leave the building. You will state the name of your child's doctor so medical records can be retrieved. You will state the name of the school she's been attending, so those records can be requested. Before you leave for your cruise, you will be served with official papers to this effect and have to appear before a judge. Make damn sure you are available for that, or I will make it my personal responsibility to have you pulled off that ship at its first port of call and hauled back to the States for child abandonment. Do you understand me?"

Now Corina was whining. "Yes, gladly, but what if it takes longer to get the paperwork done? I leave in a couple of months."

"I know people," Sonny said.

"And so do we," Aaron added.

"Where's her suitcase?" Wiley asked.

"Her things are in my car. You can get them when I leave. I'll be glad to be done with her," Corina said, and glared at the little girl all but hidden behind Wiley Pope's legs.

Suddenly, Ava stepped out from behind Wiley's legs and stared Corina straight in the face. "Somebody wants me."

Corina blinked.

Wiley knew the courage it took for Ava to even speak, and reached down and picked her up.

"A whole bunch of somebodies want you," he said.

Ava was startled at being touched, and then it dawned on her how high off the floor she was, and she gasped.

"We're high up," she whispered.

"Too high?" he asked.

Her eyes were huge. "Maybe."

"Then we'll sit," Wiley said, and carried her to the back of the room to the sofa and sat down with her in his lap.

At first, she was stiff, almost uncertain how to relax, but for the first time in days, her tummy was full, and her Bubba's arms were so strong that she knew he wouldn't drop her. Finally, she leaned her head against his chest and watched the grown-ups across the room and, as always, made herself as small as she could be. And closed her eyes.

She was asleep when Corina signed her declaration and still asleep as the notary notarized it.

"Am I free to go?" Corina asked.

"Yes," Sonny said.

"I'll follow you out to get Ava's suitcase," Aaron said.

She headed for the door without even looking at the child asleep in Wiley Pope's arms.

"Don't you want to tell her goodbye?" Wiley asked.

Corina felt the dig for what it was, lifted her chin, and kept walking.

It was just as Wiley expected. Ava had no bond with that woman. In time the bruises she'd given her would fade, but it remained to be seen what had been done to the little girl's fragile ego.

Wiley looked down at the sleeping baby in his arms, marking the tilt of her nose, her white-blond hair and the reddish cast to her brows and lashes. She was malnourished and emotionally frozen. What was it going to take to find the child hidden within?

Aaron came back with a disgusted look on his face and carrying a black garbage bag. "These are her worldly belongings."

Wiley sighed. One hurdle down. A million more to go. He glanced at Sonny. "Chief, I'm gonna need a few days off."

Sonny was still flushed with rage. "The way I feel, so do I. I have never encountered anyone like her. Take the time you need to get situated, find yourself a good babysitter, and get her enrolled in school, and without asking, I'm telling you now you are officially on the day shift and weekends off unless there are dire emergencies."

"This is definitely not what I expected when I woke up this morning, and I don't know how to thank you, but it is much appreciated," Wiley said.

Aaron was still reeling from the initial accusation and in shock at Wiley's reaction. He'd never seen this side of Wiley, and he was a little bit in awe.

"You're not in this alone, little brother. We have to tell Mom and—"

"I already told Mom I was going to fight for her, and she told me to go for it."

Aaron sighed. "I should have known. Then we'll

have a family meeting at Mom's when you're ready. Your little girl needs to know who her brothers are, the sisters who will have her back, and a grandma who will rock her world."

———————

Corina Dalton was beside herself with glee. The trip hadn't quite turned out how she'd planned, but was ending better than expected. She wasn't getting the payoff money she'd planned on, but she'd gotten rid of the unwanted burden of motherhood. She was tired of driving, but the need to get as far away as possible before they changed their minds was uppermost, so she grabbed breakfast to go and ate on the road. She was still surprised Wiley knew who she was and, if she'd known, would never have had the guts to try this, which proved sometimes a wrong thing can turn out right.

———————

Wiley's thoughts were in free fall as he took Ava and her things to his car. He wasn't one bit sorry for the decision he'd just made, but he was scared as to how he was going to make it work. He didn't know squat about kids, but he'd been one. He knew what it felt like to be afraid of who was coming in the door. And he knew what it was like to be ridiculed. He wanted to carry her, but she was very protective of her personal space, and he was afraid to find out why. As soon as they got to the car, he put the sack with her clothes in the seat beside her, then buckled her into the back seat.

"Are you okay, here? It's not too tight across your chest?" he asked.

"Not too tight," she whispered, and pulled the sack with her things into her lap.

Watching her clutch at the only things in the world that were hers hurt his heart. "Okay then, I guess we're ready to go."

"Where are we going?" she asked.

"Home, sugar. We're going home."

She looked up. "Your apartment?"

"No, it's a house," Wiley said.

Ava blinked. "You have an all-by-yourself house?"

He smiled. "I do, and it has two bedrooms. One will be all yours."

She hugged the bag with her clothes a little tighter. "Is it far?"

He lifted a lock of hair from the corner of her eye and pushed it back into place. "No. You'll see."

He got into the car and drove out of the parking lot, wondering if she had even grasped the reality of what had just happened. If she was always getting dumped wherever, did she know Corina wasn't coming back? One thing was for damn sure about his new arrangement. The only girl who fit into his world now was the little sister sitting in the back seat with that frozen look on her face.

When he pulled up to the little house, he paused to open the garage door, then drove inside.

"We're here," he said, as the door rolled down behind them.

He helped her out, grabbed her belongings, and opened the door, turning on lights as they went. The house still smelled like breakfast, but the kitchen was clean. He didn't like clutter on the counters and kept stuff put away when it wasn't in use. A holdover from lessons his mother had taught all of them.

Ava was standing in the middle of the floor, eyeing the white cabinets with gold knobs, the big island with the tall chairs, and the shiny stainless-steel appliances.

"This way, Ava. I'll show you the house as we go. This is our living room. It has a gas fireplace for when winter comes." As they started up the hall, he pointed into the bedroom on the right. "This is my bedroom, and there's a big bathroom in it with a tub and a shower. Do you like bubble baths?"

"What's that?" she asked.

He stopped. "You never played in a bathtub that had soap bubbles in it?"

She shook her head.

He grinned and held out his hand. "Oh, Sister, you are in for a treat," he said. "Come with me and I'll show you your bedroom. It's right across the hall."

This time, when he held out his hand, she took it. Wiley opened the door and turned on the light. From the look on her face, the pink bedroom might as well have been a palace. They walked inside, and then he opened the door beside her bed. "This is your bath-room, but it has two doors so someone can get to it from the hall, or you can use it from your room."

She nodded, looking in at the tub and the shiny faucet and the white bath towel hanging on the towel rack, and then back at him.

"So, what do you think?" he asked.

"I can take a whole bath?"

"Absolutely," he said. "Now let's go back to your room."

"This is all mine?" she whispered.

"All yours," Wiley said.

"Pink is my favorite color," she whispered.

He picked her up and sat her down on the pink quilted bedspread.

"You don't have to whisper. You don't have to be afraid. You are safe here, honey. This is your room, in your home, with a bed and a pillow, and soft sheets and warm blankets. You have a closet and a dresser for your clothes. You can put your toys wherever you—"

She shook her head.

Wiley's heart sank. "What? You don't like—"

"I don't have toys."

He couldn't take it. He picked her up and sat her in his lap and just held her until he could talk without cursing.

"Well, you will have some before bedtime tonight. A plushie to sleep with. A dolly to play with. And any-thing else that catches your fancy. Okay?"

She looked up at him, this giant of a man who said he was her brother. She wasn't even sure what all that meant, and what her role would be in this place, but for the moment, she didn't care. Nobody was screaming at her. Nobody was throwing things at her. And she had a bed and a pillow.

"Is that okay?" he asked.

She nodded.

"Now tell me," Wiley said. "Who am I?"

"My Bubba?"

"Yes! I'm your Bubba. That's me. Say my name."

"Bubba," she whispered.

"Nope, can't hear you," he said. "Say it louder."

Her eyes suddenly lit from within. "Bubba."

He winked. "That's better. Now…how about we put up your clothes and then go shopping?"

"Corina shops, but she's gone. Is she coming back to take me away?"

Wiley's eyes narrowed. "No. Are you going to be sad?"

Ava shook her head. "No. I'm a mistake."

"No, you're not, baby. You're a gift. A teeny-tiny gift we never saw coming. We're sorry we didn't know about you before, or we would never have left you behind. Okay?"

She nodded.

"Now, show me what's in this bag. We might need to buy some new clothes, too. Who knows?"

Her eyes widened, and for the first time since he laid eyes on her, she smiled, and he was done for.

He dumped the contents of the bag onto the bed and then stared.

"Are these the only clothes you own?"

She nodded.

Wiley took a deep breath. "Then let's get them folded up and put away," he said, then opened the lowest dresser drawer. "I'll fold. You can put them in the drawer, okay?"

"Corina just throws everything in together," she said.

"Well, Corina isn't the boss of us anymore, is she?" Wiley muttered. "We're doing stuff our way now."

Ava leaned against Wiley's leg. "Our way," she whispered.

Wiley folded clothes with a knot in his gut. He had to let go of the rage he was feeling on Ava's behalf and just be grateful that she was finally safe.

It didn't take long to fold and put away her clothes because she only had three complete outfits, counting what she was wearing, three changes of underwear, and a couple of extra T-shirts. No jacket. No pajamas or nightgown. No other shoes but the little sandals on her feet. No hairbrush. No toothbrush. Not even a remnant of anything that a child might cuddle to sleep with. He could easily take her shopping, but he didn't know if she was up to it. He sat down in the chair beside her bed and leaned forward, his elbows on his knees.

"Okay, everything is put away. When you go to bed, what do you sleep in?" he asked.

"What I wear," she said.

He frowned. "That's not gonna happen here. You get clothes for sleeping, and playing, and school and church."

"What's church?"

Wiley stifled a curse. "A place where we go on Sunday to hear Bible stories and sing songs. You'll like it."

Ava had no clue as to what Bubba was talking about, but she wasn't going to make waves. "I will like it," she echoed.

Wiley picked her up and hugged her. "I hope so, but it's okay if you don't. Nobody will be mad at you. There are things I don't like, and that's fair. People aren't alike. Now we're going to town to buy you stuff you need." He slid her off his lap and patted the back of her head. "Go wash, and use the bathroom before we go, and scoot! I'll be in the kitchen."

She giggled. The word *scoot* was a new one, but she knew what it meant and hustled herself into the bathroom.

Wiley scrubbed his hands across his face, then stood. Resolve was etched on his face as he headed for the kitchen to make a grocery list. But the first thing he did was send Linette a text, along with the same picture of Ava that he'd sent to his mom.

Family crisis. Big shock. This is Ava. She's seven years old and she's our half sister. Her mother called her a mistake and just dumped her. Something inside of me broke when I saw her. She's scared of everything. She's been neglected

and mistreated, and I'm keeping her. I plan to
become her legal guardian, and if this isn't in your
wheelhouse, now's the time to bail. Otherwise,
she's just been added to our plans. I won't hold
anything against you for how you feel. This came
out of left field and I'm still in a bit of shock myself.
But I know this is the right thing to do. Love you
forever. Me.

He hit Send and then started checking out the contents of his refrigerator. He had plenty of beer and cold
cuts, but no milk and no real food in sight. Life was
about to get real in this house. Then his phone signaled
a text. It was from Linette, and he was almost afraid to
read it.

Bless her heart. As for you, I'll pretend I'm not
pissed that you doubted me. This is just part of
what "for better or for worse" means, even if we
aren't really married. You already know I love
children. I will help you every step of the way and
hope she learns to love and trust me more than
you do... You're an ass, but you're mine, and I will
keep you anyway. Love, L.

Wiley grimaced. "Thank God," he muttered, and a
few minutes later, they were back in his car and headed
uptown. First stop was for clothes. There wasn't a real
department store in Jubilee, but there were enough

kids' clothes in the tourist shops to cover immediate needs, and he'd talk to Linette about online ordering. As soon as they reached the tourist strip, he parked, then turned to look at her. She was big-eyed and staring out the window at all of the sights.

"Ava, honey, are you okay?" he asked.

She nodded.

"Will you promise to tell me if you need to go to the bathroom, or if you get hungry?"

She nodded.

"Will you promise to tell me if you get tired and want to go home?"

She nodded again.

He grinned. "Is that a yes, because I can't hear you."

"Yes," she said, and then almost smiled.

"Good. Thought for a minute my ears had quit working," he said.

She giggled, and startled herself when the sound came out of her mouth and clapped her hands over it.

"Don't you hide that pretty smile," Wiley said. "You're my girl, remember? We're making new rules, and the first one is how to be happy." When he got her out of the car and turned to face the throng of tourists in the plaza, he frowned. "How about I carry you through the crowd, and then we'll walk when we get into a store?"

She eyed the people all around them and nodded, then slid her arm around his neck as he picked her up.

Wiley winked at her, and then they were off.

There were people everywhere, walking in all

different directions, going into different shops around the plaza, and coming out of others. She saw kids like her with families, and they were laughing and squealing and carrying stuffed toys or eating as they walked.

At first, Ava was nervous. Her Bubba was tall, and she was really high off the ground, but then it dawned on her that she'd never seen the world like this before. She had no memories of being carried, and Bubba made her feel safe, and he smelled good, and she had a pink room with a bed and a pillow, and they were shopping. She wasn't sure what *shopping* meant, but Corina liked doing it, and she was about to find out if she did, too.

Chapter 9

WILEY HAD NO IDEA WHAT WAS GOING THROUGH Ava's head, but he was on a mission and headed straight for one of the shops that sold souvenir tees and shorts. It was called Something Extra, and Georgia McKay, who was related to the Cauley family, ran it. She'd know what little girls needed better than he did, and hopefully she'd have some of it in stock.

The store was crowded when they entered, but it was cool, and it smelled like the cotton candy that was being sold from the kiosk just outside the entrance.

Georgia spotted Wiley almost instantly, and two things went through her mind. Not once had she ever seen Wiley Pope inside this store, nor had she ever seen the little girl in his arms. He looked a little out of his element, so she headed straight toward him.

Wiley saw her coming across the room and breathed a sigh of relief. Help had arrived.

"Hey, Wiley! Good to see you," Georgia said.

"And you," Wiley said, and then gave Ava a quick hug. "Ava, honey, this is Miss Georgia. Georgia, this is my little sister, Ava." He saw the shock on Georgia's face and quickly added, "We have the same daddy. And… Ava's gonna be living with me now. It was a bit sudden, and Ava needs some clothes. Right, baby?"

Ava held on a little tighter to Wiley's neck and nodded.

Georgia could tell the child needed way more than clothes. She looked like she'd been mistreated and starved, and she was more than uneasy.

"We can sure help with some immediate needs, and then you can either make a trip to a department store in Bowling Green or do some online ordering later." But when she reached out to pat Ava's arm and saw the child flinch, her heart broke. She could tell the child had been abused as well.

"What's your favorite color, Ava?"

Ava looked at Wiley.

He winked. "Remember. You have to speak up to be heard."

"Pink. I like pink," Ava said. "And yellow, and blue."

"Follow me," Georgia said, and led the way to the children's corner. She eyed Ava's size and then picked up a size small T-shirt. "How old are you, honey?"

"Seven," Ava said.

Georgia hid her shock. She would have guessed five.

Wiley put her down and watched as Ava and Georgia searched the T-shirts folded on the tables and the shorts shelved in little cubbies according to size.

Georgia looked up at Wiley. "How many outfits do you want?"

"At least eight. She has two plus the one she's wearing. Do you have underwear for kids?" he asked.

Georgia nodded. "Not a huge selection, but yes."

"A dozen pair to start with, in her size," Wiley said.

Ava kept looking back at Wiley, afraid to lose contact, and finally, Wiley just picked her back up.

"You showed Miss Georgia what you like. Now we'll let her gather it all up, okay?"

Ava nodded and hid her face against Wiley's neck.

Poor baby, Georgia mouthed.

"You have no idea," Wiley muttered, and then saw a shelf of stuffed toys. "Go ahead and take those to the register," he said. "We're going to the stuffed toys."

Ava heard the word *toys,* and when she saw where they were going, she couldn't imagine one being for her.

Wiley heard the catch in her breath and swallowed past the lump in his throat. She wasn't begging or whining for anything, but the disbelief and desire in her eyes were there for the world to see.

"Look at all the stuffed animals," Wiley said. "Teddy bears, rabbits, little squirrels, puppies, kittens, and all these colors. Oh…and there are rag dolls. Those are the old-fashioned kind of dolls that my mother would have had when she was little. They're soft, too, and good sleeping buddies. Let's look, okay?"

He set her back down in front of the shelves. "You pick out whatever you want, honey."

Ava's eyes widened. "I can have one?"

Wiley squatted down beside her. "You pick out a

dolly and as many stuffed toys as you want, and I'll buy them for you."

Tears rolled.

Wiley was lost. "Don't cry, baby," he whispered.

"I don't know how to choose," she said.

"What color of teddy bear do you like best?" he asked.

"The white one with the pink bow?"

Wiley pulled it off the shelf and dropped it in a shopping basket sitting on the floor. "What next? What color of kitty?"

And down the row they went, until Ava was almost giddy from the game and the growing pile in the cart.

"Now, do you want to pick out a dolly?" Wiley asked. "Here's one with short red hair, and one with long brown hair, and… Oh wow! Look at what I see hiding back here on the shelf!"

He pulled aside a handful of dolls, revealing one with big blue eyes and blond curls, just like Ava. The doll was wearing a pink gingham dress and a petticoat with ruffles visible beneath the gingham hem.

"Her! Can she be my dolly?" Ava asked.

"Absolutely, but you have to pick her up yourself so she'll know you chose her, just like I chose you."

Ava reached for the doll with both hands as she lifted her off the shelf, looked the doll straight in the face, and then hugged her.

Wiley breathed a sigh of relief. So far, so good. He picked up the basket of toys and held out his hand.

"Let's go pay Miss Georgia for all your clothes and toys, and then get something to eat, okay?"

Still clutching the doll, Ava nodded.

She was still clutching dolly when Wiley buckled her in the back seat. "Remember to tell me when you need to go to the bathroom, and we'll find one."

She nodded.

He paused. "Are you hungry?"

She nodded again.

He tweaked her nose. "I can't hear you."

She giggled. "Yes!"

"What do you like to eat, baby girl? What are your favorite foods?"

She shrugged. "I have mac and cheese in the blue box, and sometimes chicken nuggets."

Wiley blinked. "Anything else?"

"Ummm, sometimes Miss Mattie gave me a pudding cup."

"What about burgers and fries, or fried chicken, or soup, or mashed potatoes and meat loaf?"

"Oh, soup. Yeah, soup in a can."

Wiley sighed. "Hot dogs?"

She frowned. "Maybe I've had those. Is that the weenie wrapped in bread sandwich?"

"Sort of. I know you have to like french fries."

She frowned. "Corina only gives me her cold ones. I don't like them so much."

"Corina was an ass," Wiley muttered.

Ava blinked, then grinned.

At that point, Wiley realized what he'd said, but it was too late to take it back.

"Sorry. I shouldn't call people bad names. Even when they deserve it," he said. "But you need to know right now that how you were treated was wrong, and I won't let that happen again. None of us will. You have four big brothers who will always take care of you. Understand?"

She nodded.

"Good. Better be thinking of what you're gonna name dolly. We can't go around calling her dolly forever, right?"

Ava giggled.

Wiley brushed the top of her head, then shut the door to the back seat and got in the car. The best place he could think of to take her to eat on short notice was Granny's Country Kitchen. It was the closest to home cooking in Jubilee, and if she was used to doing without, then stuffing a bunch of food in her belly all at once would only result in making her sick. But they'd figure it out after he got there.

They were pulling into the parking lot when he saw Linette and two other women walking toward the entrance. Talk about luck.

"Maybe we better leave dolly here," he said as he helped Ava out.

"She's taking a nap," Ava said, and grabbed his hand as they headed up the steps and then into the café.

"Table for two, and we're gonna need a booster seat," Wylie said.

"Coming up," the hostess said. She grabbed a menu

and a booster from a stack by the door and led the way through the dining area.

Wylie knew Linette had seen them, but she was obviously giving them space and he purposefully didn't look her way. When Ava came close to getting stepped on, he swooped her up into his arms and carried her the rest of the way across the floor, then settled her into the booster seat.

"How's that, sugar?"

She smiled. "Good."

He pulled his own chair as close to hers as he could, just in case, and then opened the menu.

"Let's see what's on the menu, okay?"

"I like mac and cheese in the blue box," she reminded him.

He nodded. "I remember. We'll make that at home, okay? They cook other things here. Okay, here's chicken nuggets and french fries, and they won't be cold. Wanna try those?"

"Yes."

"And you can have bites of my stuff, too, just to see if you like it, and then we'll know what not to buy at the supermarket."

"Sometimes I went to the grocery store with Miss Mattie," Ava said.

"Oh yeah? What all did Miss Mattie buy besides mac and cheese in the blue box?" Wiley asked.

"Umm, Coca-Cola in a can. Soup in a can. Burglar meat, and ciggies."

Wiley didn't know whether to laugh or cry.

"Well, I don't smoke, but we can get soup in a can and burglar meat. I know how to make meat loaf and hamburgers, and spaghetti sauce for spaghetti noodles."

Her eyes widened. "I had s'gettie in a can before."

"Mine's better," Wiley said. "Promise."

She nodded.

The waitress arrived with two glasses of water, one of which was in a small paper cup with a lid and a straw. "Hey, Wiley, look at you. A new girl on your arm, already."

"Hi, Diane, this is Ava," he said. "Ava, this is Diane. She's a cousin, so she'll be part of your family now."

Diane blinked. "Is this your girl?"

"Half sister. She's living with me now."

Ava didn't look up. She just sipped some water through the straw in her to-go cup.

Diane's eyes filled with tears and then she looked at Wiley. He winked and shook his head and gave her their food and drink orders.

"Okay then. I'll turn these in. It shouldn't be long," she said, and hurried away.

Ava sat for a few moments, then leaned over and patted Wiley's arm.

"Bubba, I need to go to the restroom now."

"Okay, honey," he said. He got up with her and took her across the dining room to the hall leading down to the restrooms. But almost immediately, he realized he didn't know if she was tall enough to manage what was in there, or if it was safe to let her go in alone. Wiley was still debating with himself when Linette walked up behind him.

"Hey, you!" she said, and smiled at both of them.

Fabulous! Just when I needed her. "Linnie! Sweetheart! I need a favor. Ava needs to go to the bathroom, but I don't know if it's safe, or if she's too small to reach everything. Can you check for me?"

Linette looked down at the tiny blond clinging to Wiley's hand and smiled.

"Hello, Ava. I'm Wiley's friend. How about you and I go in together and I can help if you need me. Would that be okay with you?"

Ava glanced up. "Are you Wiley's almost wife?"

"I suppose I am," Linette said, and took Ava's hand as if it was something she did every day.

Wiley sighed. Ava was so used to being dumped on total strangers that she had no concept of stranger danger, which meant she would be a prime target for all kinds of things he hadn't thought about, but Linette had just passed her first meeting with flying colors.

———————

There were six stalls in the ladies' room, and three were empty.

Linette quickly checked the height of the toilet stools and then opened a door for Ava. "Can you manage or is that seat too high?" she asked.

"I can manage," Ava said.

"I'll be in the one right next to you," Linette said. "When you finish, just wait for me and we'll wash up together, okay?"

"Okay," Ava said, then went inside and pushed the door shut but didn't lock it.

Linette hurried and was waiting when Ava emerged from the stall. "Oh…forgot to flush," Ava said.

"It's okay, honey. They automatically flush themselves," Linette said.

"Really?" Ava asked.

Linette smiled. "Yes, really. Let's get washed. We don't want to keep Wiley waiting."

"Bubba will wait. He's gonna take good care of me."

"Your Bubba is a really good man," Linette said, and turned on the water for Ava to wash.

She thrust her little hands beneath the water and started talking. "Corina didn't want me. Bubba does. I have four brothers now, and a bed and a pillow. Bubba bought me clothes today and a dolly. I never had a dolly before. I have to pick a name."

The matter-of-fact tone in the child's voice was as horrifying as what she'd just said, and Linette couldn't begin to imagine what hell this child had been through. Her hands were shaking as she handed Ava a handful of paper towels to dry off.

"I'll bet you pick the best name for your dolly ever," Linette said, and then opened the door.

Wiley was standing in the hall. They locked gazes.

Linette handed Ava over without a word, then put her hand in the middle of Wiley's chest.

"You rock, and so does she," she whispered, then brushed the hair away from Ava's eyes and walked away.

Wiley felt like he'd just been struck by lightning. *Thank you, God, that Linnie didn't balk on us.* Then Ava reached for his hand and pulled him back to earth. They went back to their table and settled in, and a few minutes later, their food arrived. He wished Linette was sitting with them, helping him through this transition, but one thing at a time. Nothing mattered today but Ava, so he put a tiny bite of his meat loaf on her plate and a spoonful of mashed potatoes and gravy, while Ava watched in silence.

"Those are little bites so you can taste my stuff and see if you like any of it," he said.

Ava nodded, then immediately put a chicken nugget and three french fries from her plate onto his.

"And you can taste mine," she said.

"Thank you, baby. We're sharing, right?"

She almost smiled. "Yes," she said, and as soon as he popped a french fry in his mouth and rolled his eyes at how good it was, she picked one up from her plate and took a nibble. Then another, and another until the whole french fry was gone.

"That's good," she said. "I like them when they're not cold."

"Right," Wiley said, and took a bite of his meat loaf and rolled his eyes again. "Mmm, good stuff," he said.

Ava scooped up her bite of meat loaf with a spoon

and cautiously slipped it in her mouth, chewed, and swallowed.

"So?" Wiley asked.

"I like it!" she said, and ate the mashed potatoes and gravy next. "And this, too," she said.

"Awesome. You can taste a green bean, too, if you want," he said, and pushed his plate close so she could fork one, then watched the expression on her face change from distrust to delight.

"You choose good stuff!" Ava said, and took a bite of a chicken nugget.

"Do you like to dip your chicken in a sauce?" he asked.

"I don't know? What's a sauce?"

"My gravy is a sauce." He spooned a little on her plate, then opened a honey packet on the table and squirted a tiny bit on her plate. "Swipe your next bite of chicken through one of those before you eat it, and then tell me what you think."

Ava didn't hesitate. She was used to doing what she was told and completely unaware she had choices in the world. She tried the gravy first and gave him a thumbs-up, then swiped the last bite of nugget through the honey.

Wiley watched her eyes widen as she chewed and swallowed.

"I like both of them, but the last one best!" she said.

"Want some more of my meat loaf?" he asked.

He gave her one more bite, and then they both settled in to eat, while every now and then stopping for him to wipe a drip of honey from her chin or remind her the napkin was handy for wiping her fingers.

By the time they were finished, Wiley had fallen the rest of the way in love. He knew there were bound to be rough days ahead, but considering they had known each other less than a day, this child was a gift to all of them. They still needed to go to the supermarket, and he had a feeling she was going to crash long before dark, so he hurried through cleaning her hands and face and paying the bill.

Only after they were leaving, did he glance across the room at the table where Linette was sitting, and caught her watching them. She blew him a kiss. He gave her a thumbs-up, and then they were gone.

One of Linette's friends saw the byplay between them and grinned.

"Who's the hunk?"

"Wiley Pope. He's my hunk and a police officer here in Jubilee."

"Is he the one who sent the flowers?" she asked.

Linette nodded.

Her other friend frowned. "But it appears he's married, or was."

"She's not his daughter. She's his little sister. End of story."

———

After Wiley's phone call from the police station, Shirley knew their lives were about to change. She was in a walking cast now and finally mobile again, so she headed for Sean's office. The door was open. She knocked.

"Got a minute?" she asked.

Sean immediately stopped and turned around. "Sure, Mom. What's up?"

"This," she said, and showed Sean the photo and then told him about Wiley's call.

"Holy shit! Are you serious?" Sean said. "Who the hell is Corina Dalton?"

Shirley sighed. "One of Clyde's women."

"You knew?" Sean asked.

Shirley rolled her eyes. "Son, a woman always knows if her husband is cheating on her, and vice versa. But I had no idea there was a child. I don't know details, and I never expected Wiley would react as he has, but I'm proud of him. I told him I would back any choice he made. Look at her. She's so tiny and looks half-starved. God only knows what her life has been like, but I can tell you now, her days of want are over."

"You know Amalie is going to immediately empathize. One unwanted child to another kind of thing," Sean added.

Shirley nodded. "I don't know how Wiley thinks he's going to manage, but I'm not butting in with any advice unless he asks for it. He'll find his own way through this decision, and they'll both be the better for it."

Aaron was still reeling from Corina Dalton's initial accusation. Those few seconds before Wiley spoke up had been every man's nightmare, to be unjustly accused of any kind of abuse or mistreatment of a woman or a child. Thank God for Wiley!

He was shocked by his brother's instant decision to become their sister's guardian, but immeasurably proud of him, too. When he called home, he unloaded the whole story on Dani before heading out on patrol.

Dani was stunned.

"And you had no idea?" she said.

"No. If it hadn't been for Wiley, this could have gotten nasty. Honestly, I've never seen a more cold-hearted woman. God only knows what that child has been through."

"How old is she?" Dani asked.

"Seven, according to her birth certificate, but she's no bigger than a five-year-old. She's malnourished and scared of her own shadow. Wiley took one look at her and turned into some superhero on her behalf. I've never seen him like this, but I think he's found his calling."

"That's wonderful, but it's going to be hard for him, too. We can all help. When school starts again, she can come home with me until he gets off work, and I'll be there at school for any problems that might arise. She's your little sister, which makes her mine, too. We all have his back."

"He's going to need it. And the chief has already put him on days with weekends off, except for emergencies."

"That's really good of Chief Warren," Dani said.

"I've never seen the chief so pissed," Aaron said. "He was about ready to throw the book at her for intent to commit fraud and for child abuse and neglect when Wiley waded in with a solution. The deal was that I wouldn't press charges if she'd relinquish her parental rights to him. She signed those papers so fast it made our heads spin, and never even looked back at her daughter asleep in Wiley's lap when she left. All I have to say is Clyde met his match when he hooked up with her."

"I'm sorry," Dani said.

"Don't be. It's a miracle we found out she even existed. But if Wiley has anything to say about it, she's lived her last day of need or want. I've got to go. Talk to you later. Love you, honey."

"Love you, too," Dani said.

———

Unaware that his family was already making plans to help him, Wiley and Ava were in the supermarket, going up and down the aisles, looking for mac and cheese in the blue box and soup in a can, as well as kid-friendly foods he guessed she would eat.

Getting to pick out her own box of cereal was such a big deal to Ava that she teared up. Going home with ice cream was unheard of. She'd never had options. She'd never been asked to make a choice. She'd just done what she was told. Ate what she was given, and had learned a long time ago that her life was easier if people forgot about her, but right now, everything happening to her felt like a dream. Corina had never wanted her and told her so on a daily basis. Then her brothers found out about her, and they wanted her, and Wiley called Corina an ass, then gave Ava a pink bedroom with her own bed and pillow. They were standing in the cookie aisle, looking at all the choices when Ava reached for Wiley's hand.

Wiley looked down. "You can pick out what kind of cookies we take home."

"Are you gonna keep me?" she asked.

The fear was back in her eyes. Without saying a word, he picked her up, settled her on his hip so she could see the cookies on the top shelves, too, and hugged her.

"Yes, baby. All the way to grown-up and forever."

"What if you change your mind?" she whispered.

"But you don't change your mind about people you love. I love that you're my little sister. I want to take care of you. I want to keep you safe. I don't ever want you hurt again. We're partners, you and me." He reached for a package of chocolate sandwich cookies, and put them in the shopping cart.

Ava was worn out from the drama of the day and from making choices, and laid her head on Wiley's shoulder.

He knew when she fell asleep because she went limp in his arms, so he shifted her to a more comfortable position and finished shopping with her head on his shoulder.

Seeing the big good-looking man with the tiny blond asleep in his arms, drew many longing glances from women of all ages, but Wiley was oblivious. His entire focus was on the child and her well-being, and figuring out how the hell he was going to make good on his promises. By the time he checked out, all he wanted was to get her home.

He led the way to his SUV, with the kid who'd bagged his groceries now following him with the purchases. The boy loaded them into the rear hatch as Wiley laid Ava down in the back seat. He drove home slowly, parked in the garage, and carried her into the house and down the hall to her bedroom, tucked her and dolly in beneath a blanket, and went to finish unloading the car.

When he finally had everything put up, he checked on Ava again. She was still asleep, so he took off his boots and walked sock-footed through the house with his laptop. He was about to get online to research day cares in Jubilee when his cell phone signaled a text from Dani.

Aaron called me. God love you, Wiley. We've got your back. I am at home all day by myself. I'll gladly be your summer babysitter, and I'll be at school with her if troubles arise, so bring her by tomorrow so we can get acquainted. We don't want to interfere, but we're all here for you and her.

Wiley was overwhelmed and relieved, and sent an immediate text back.

Thank you! More than you will ever know. I'll bring her by in the morning. She arrived with three outfits, including the one she was wearing, three pairs of panties, and the sandals on her feet, and said it was all of her clothes. There's not even a coat or a jacket. She's never had toys. I asked her what she wanted more than anything else and she said a bed and a pillow, and someone who didn't yell. I bought some Jubilee tourist clothes today at Georgia's and a bunch of stuffed animals and a doll. She's never owned toys. She looks like some little half-starved orphan from the streets. She keeps saying she was a mistake. When I asked her what she liked to eat, she said mac and cheese in the blue box and soup in a can. She wanted to call me Daddy. I would have given anything to say yes. Instead, I am her Bubba, and I will slay dragons for her. That is all.

When Dani read that response, she burst into tears. She'd seen children like that walk into her classroom before. She knew how traumatized some of them were. And how distrustful they were of everyone. Someone had done a really good job of breaking this child, and it was going to take the whole Pope family to put that little girl back together again.

After the hospital interview with Carey Eggers, Detective Gardner made sure to spread the news around the Bowling Green PD that Billy Eggers's sister never saw the man who shot him, or her, and that she was useless as a witness. Then he announced that they would proceed with an arrest warrant for a man named Lonny Joe Pryor, based on DNA recovered from beneath Billy Eggers's fingernails and from the fingerprints found at the scene.

The news trickled down to a desk sergeant, and when his lunch break came, he went to his car, pulled a burner phone from the console, and made a call to Carl Henley.

It rang three times before Carl picked up.

"This is Carl."

"It's me. They've interviewed Eggers's sister and completely eliminated her as a possible witness. She never saw the man who shot her brother and heard nothing but a fight and the gunshot before she ran. She never saw the man who shot her in the back. They have crossed her off the list. But…they have identified the shooter from DNA under Eggers's nails and prints found at the scene. They're putting out an arrest warrant for Lonny Joe Pryor."

"Thank you," Carl said, and hung up, but he was already in cleanup mode, and he wasn't leaving this to chance. His instincts had been right. He had to get rid of Gunny before the cops arrested him. As far as he knew, Gunny didn't know the woman was alive. But he knew how to get rid of Gunny. The man didn't go out to

eat, ever. He ordered everything from restaurants and
had the food delivered. It was the only crack in Gunny's
wall, and Carl was about to slip through it. All he needed
to know was if Gunny was home, so he ordered a pizza
to be delivered in person, as confirmation that he was
home before Carl paid him a little visit. Instead, he got
a call informing him that Lonny Pryor was no longer in
residence at that address, and what did he want to do
with the pizza?

"What do you mean, he's no longer in residence?"
Carl asked.

"You said to hand deliver the pizza, so when he didn't
come to the door, I knocked on a neighbor's door and
found out the man's gone. The landlord already has the
apartment up for rent again."

The hair stood up on the back of Carl's neck.

"Enjoy the pizza," he muttered, and disconnected,
then stared out the window in front of him, trying to
decide if this was good news or bad news, when he
heard the doorbell and then the housekeeper's footsteps going to answer.

Now the foyer was echoing from the loud voices. He
stepped out into the hall to see what was happening and
saw cops swarming all over the entryway.

"What the hell is going on here?" he shouted, then
heard Junior charging down the stairs behind him.

"Daddy! What's happening?"

Detective Gardner took pleasure in handing over the
search warrants.

"Carl Henley, we have a warrant to search your house, and Junior Henley, this is a warrant to search your truck."

"You can't just search my house for no reason," Carl roared.

"We have reason. You own a weapon just like the one used to kill Billy Eggers, and the truck the killer was driving matches your son's short-bed black Chevy truck, right down to the rebel flag sunshade on the back window."

"That's absurd! Guns are everywhere. How dare you assume it was mine?"

"Because you're the only registered owner of a Beretta M9 in the entire city of Bowling Green, and that was the weapon used to kill Billy Eggers. So of course, we have to eliminate you from suspicion, and the only way to do that is to test-fire the gun to see if it matches the cartridges found at the scenes of both Eggers's murder and the attempted murder of his sister near Jubilee, Kentucky."

Carl staggered. "That's impossible. I'm just a collector."

"Then you won't mind taking my officers to your gun collection and turning it over," Gardner said.

Junior was in a panic. He'd already tossed that gun down into the city sewer system, and its absence was going to make his daddy look guilty. He knew this was all his fault, but he had his own ass to cover, too.

"I don't own that truck anymore. I lost it in a poker game to Lonny Pryor last month. You go ask him! You'll find it parked at his place!"

Carl turned and stared at his son as if he'd never seen him. He didn't know what was happening, but from the look on his son's face, he was all too aware of what and why.

Junior's panic was obvious, but Detective Gardner already had a rebuttal.

"No, Junior, the truck in question is parked in the alley at the back gate into this property. And according to our records, the title is in your name. So, if you lost it in a poker game, then why is it hidden behind your residence?"

Junior groaned. His refusal to pay off an honest gambling debt had just nailed him to the getaway car at a murder scene. He'd called Gunny a dumbass, but it appeared Gunny had outsmarted both of them.

Meanwhile, Carl's shock was morphing into panic, and Detective Gardner was still issuing orders.

"Mr. Henley, if you'll escort these three officers to where you keep your guns, we need to confiscate the Beretta for testing, and Junior Henley, these two officers will go with you. The truck is locked. If you have an extra set of keys, we won't have to break it open. We will be towing it to the lab."

Carl glared at his son and then headed for the game room at the back of the house. He swaggered to his desk, got the keys from a drawer, and opened the gun case. But the place where the gun should be was empty, and the moment he realized it, he felt the blood drain from his face so fast he nearly passed out.

"The Beretta! It's not here!" he said, and turned to the officers in a panic. "I don't know where it is! I swear!"

Gardner was waiting in the foyer when Henley returned with the officers.

"Sir, Henley's Beretta seems to have gone missing."

Gardner glared. "Convenient. This doesn't look good, Carl. We'll be needing you to come down to the station to make a statement."

"How can I make a statement about something I know nothing about!" Carl shrieked.

"We need that on record," Gardner said. "And a plausible reason for why you don't know where it's at, since it's the weapon used in a murder."

"I'm not talking to you without my attorney," Carl shouted.

"Fine. But you can ride down to the station with us and wait for him to show up," Gardner said. "Officers, please take Mr. Henley to the station and put him in an interrogation room. I'll be along shortly."

Carl was cursing and shouting as they walked him out of the residence. And at that point, the other officers came downstairs with Junior Henley and the car title and extra keys for his truck.

"Where's Daddy?" Junior asked.

"On his way to the station," Gardner said.

Junior panicked. "But why?"

"Because the gun in question happens to be missing from his collection, which puts the both of you in a very bad light. I'm going to be needing you to come down to the station and give a statement as well. Officers, Mr. Henley needs a ride," Gardner said.

"Fuck off. I'm not going anywhere with you!" Junior shouted.

Gardner pointed. "Handcuff him and get him to the station."

Chapter 10

IT WAS LATE IN THE EVENING BEFORE CARL AND HIS son left the police station. They'd both had to wait for the lawyer, then gave their statements before being released, with a warning not to leave town.

Carl called an Uber to take them home, and the moment they got back to their estate, he lit into his son.

"What did you do with my Beretta?"

"Why are you blaming me that it went missing?" Junior snapped.

"Because you're the only one with access to my things." Junior glared.

Carl moved closer. "Let me phrase this another way. Did you give my Beretta to Gunny?"

"It was just for backup. He wasn't supposed to hurt anyone," Junior said.

Carl's gut knotted. "Hellsfire! You could get a burner off the street. Why the hell didn't you do that?"

Junior shrugged. "I don't know. Yours was here. It was handy, but after he told me what happened, I ditched the gun the same day he gave it back."

Carl stared. "Did you pawn it?"

Junior shrugged. "No. I threw it away."

"Where?" Carl asked.

"Down a sewer grate out in the park."

Carl rolled his eyes. "Did you really lose your truck to Gunny in a poker game?"

"Yes. He's been driving it most of this month," Junior said.

"Then why do you still have the title? Do you not have any honor at all?" He slapped Junior with the flat of his hand and sent him reeling. "A man always pays his debts. It's not like you don't have the money to just buy another truck. Why the hell didn't you just sign it over? We wouldn't be in this mess if you had. There's no way to explain this away."

Junior's cheek was burning. "Gunny's prints will be all over the truck, and we can claim he stole the gun. Surely there will be security footage somewhere of him driving the truck. We can figure something out."

"No. All of this still links us to Eggers's murder. You know, you nearly drowned in the bathtub when you were two. I did CPR and saved your life, and at this moment, I deeply regret that. Get out of my sight."

Junior pivoted on his heel and stormed out of the house.

Carl was on the phone when he heard the roar of Junior's Porsche speeding away from the property. He thought about the possible consequences of Junior Henley having one of his meltdowns, then reminded himself it was nearly sunset, and his son was thirty-two

years old. If he was lucky, Junior would wreck the
Porsche, break his damn neck, and Carl could blame
this whole mess on him.

⸻

At the same time Carl Henley's world was coming
undone, Gunny was at the bus station in Miami, waiting for his cousin Roly. He'd called Roly before he left
Kentucky, making sure his cousin would give him a
place to stay, and then called him again about an hour
outside of Miami to come pick him up. If he wasn't here
already, he soon would be. It had been years since he'd
seen his cousin, but all of the Pryors looked alike, and
Gunny was counting on recognizing him, which he did.

   Roly Pryor had already spotted Lonny the moment
he walked into the station, and lifted a hand in greeting
before heading toward him. They met with a quick hug,
thumping each other on the back.

   "Man, Lonny, it is good to see you," Roly said.

   "You too, cuz," Gunny said. "I hope I'm not putting
you out."

   Roly shook his head. "Naw. My ol' lady left me over
a year ago. I'm just rattling around in that house on my
own. I'll be glad for the company. You got your own
bedroom, and I can always use a hand at work. I take
people out on swamp tours. Got me an airboat and
everything. Are you ready to go?"

   Gunny nodded and followed Roly to an old black

Jeep 4x4, threw his bags in the back seat and got in the front seat.

"Buckle up!" Roly said. "Driving in this traffic is like playing dodgeball with cars."

Lonny sighed and did as he was told. He was about to leave Gunny behind, and it felt good. No one here had ever known him by that name. He was headed to the Everglades. Back to his roots. And if his daddy hadn't moved them to Tennessee when he was a kid, he would have grown up in the swamps and been a whole different man. It was too late to change the past, but he was aiming for a new future.

———

Ava opened her eyes and, for a moment, didn't know where she was until the pink room registered. Bubba! Then she heard music and smelled something cooking. She threw back the blanket, grabbed her dolly, and ran.

Wiley had spaghetti sauce simmering on the back burner and some refrigerated cinnamon rolls baking in the oven. They weren't on the Granny Annie's Bakery level, but they were good enough. He'd washed and dried all of Ava's new clothes and had them folded on the kitchen table, just waiting for her to wake up before putting them away, and was online ordering storybooks, crayons, and coloring books, some colorful wooden puzzles, and a small flat-screen TV for her room. He'd just finished the order when he heard her running up the hall, and then she appeared in the doorway, wide-eyed and verging on panic. Before he could ask what was wrong, she slid to a stop.

"You're still here," she whispered.

Wiley opened his arms as she crawled up into his lap. "Yes, baby, I'm still here. Popes don't lie. Popes keep promises. You're my girl, okay?" He felt her trembling, but she was beginning to relax.

"Did you ever figure out what dolly's name was?" he asked.

She pulled the doll up beneath her chin as she leaned against him. "She said her name was Pinky."

Wiley smiled. Of course, it was. "Ah…what a great name. We should have known, right? I mean…look at that pretty pink dress she's wearing."

Ava nodded.

"Did you have a good nap?" Wiley asked.

"Yes. What do I smell?"

He grinned. "Spaghetti sauce and cinnamon rolls are in the oven. Smells good in here, doesn't it?"

"Do I like cinnamon rolls?" Ava asked.

"I'm pretty sure you do. They're sweet and have icing on the top and cinnamon and sugar swirled in the middle."

"Yum," Ava said.

Wiley laughed. "Definitely yum. And now that you're awake, want to help me put away your new clothes? I have them all washed and ready to wear."

"Yes! New clothes! I never had new ones before. Corina shopped at the army."

Wiley frowned. "The army?"

Ava nodded. "Miss Mattie says it's where they save souls and worn-out clothes."

"Ah...the Salvation Army," Wiley muttered.

"Yes, that's the one," Ava said.

Corina Dalton's soul sure need saving, Wiley thought, but remembered he'd already called the woman an ass. There was no purpose in mentioning she was on the road to hell as well.

"Well, since we're making new rules, we won't be shopping there anymore, if that's okay with you."

Ava nodded. "It's okay," she said and slid out of his lap. "Pinky can help carry."

"Works for me," Wiley said, and handed her the little stack with her new panties. "You two can carry these."

Ava's eyes widened as she felt the silky garments.

"They're so soft," she whispered.

"No whispers, unless needed, and you're right! They are soft," he said.

He grabbed the rest of the clothes and did a march step out of the room, with Ava right behind him, mimicking his every move.

For Ava, the process of filling up her dresser drawers was like burying treasure. And it was all hers to wear when she wanted. She hadn't thought of Conway, or Corina, in hours. Not since Bubba promised he was keeping her. Ava didn't know the word *trust*, or understand its meaning, but without realizing it, she was learning that it did exist.

Wiley had signed up for the Disney Channel while she was sleeping so they could watch movies together and then found a channel on TV that aired nothing but cartoons.

"I'm going to finish making supper," he said. "You and Pinky can watch TV together for a bit, okay?"

She had already zeroed in on the screen and just nodded.

He iced the cooled cinnamon rolls and put some pasta on to boil. When he peeked in later to check on her, she had all of her new stuffed toys lined up on the couch, and she was sitting in the middle of them with Pinky in her lap, still glued to the screen. When he heard her giggle and then laugh out loud, he smiled. Now he knew what her laugh was like, and he walked away.

Supper was a success. Ava liked Wiley's spaghetti better than spaghetti in a can. He took a picture of her at the table slurping up a noodle, with spaghetti sauce on her chin, and sent it to Shirley with a message.

Ava likes s'gettie.

He got a text back in a couple of minutes with a happy face and a whole row of heart emojis.

"Are you too full for dessert?" Wiley asked.

Ava had been eyeing the cinnamon rolls all through the meal and shook her head.

"No, Bubba. I saved room."

He pushed the plate toward her. "You pick out the

one you want," he said, again making the point that she had choices.

She took the one nearest her with the most icing, bit, chewed, and swallowed.

"Yum."

"So, they're good?" Wiley asked.

She nodded.

"Good. Then I'll have one, too," he said. "Hmm, I don't know which one I should choose."

Ava pointed to the one on top. "That one, Bubba! It's tall like you."

He grinned. "You're right! It is pretty high up there, and it's just waiting for me." He took it from the platter. "Cinnamon roll! Get in my mouth!" he announced, and took a big bite.

For some reason, that struck Ava as funny, and she collapsed in giggles. After that, every time she took a bite, she said, "Get in my mouth," and Wiley would laugh like they were the funniest two people they knew.

Finally, the meal was over, and Wiley sent her to wash up while he cleaned up the kitchen. But as it began to get dark, he noticed Ava was getting anxious. She began worrying about the window shades being open, so he pulled the shades, and then the curtains need to be closed. But she was still pacing and uneasy, and finally, Wiley sat down beside her.

"What's wrong, honey? Are you afraid of the dark? Tell me."

"You have to pull the shades and curtains and stay away from the windows. At night, they shoot guns and fight in the street."

A wave of horror washed over him. "That doesn't happen here." And then he thought of the bank robbery and being shot less than two months ago. "And if there ever is a bad man with a gun anywhere in town, the police grab him and put him in jail. I'm a policeman. That's my job. I will always keep you safe, and I will always come to help you when you need it."

She was staring at him intently, watching his face, hearing the words, and he doubted that she believed him. Only time would ease this fear. "Come on, we'll go all through the house and make sure all the shades are shut and the curtains drawn, okay?"

He got up, took her by the hand, and they walked the entire house, checking the windows to make sure they were locked, and the shades and curtains pulled. And then he turned on the little lamp by her bed. The nightlights were on in the hall and in the bathrooms, and she could see all of the corners in all of the rooms and be satisfied no one was there.

"Is that better?" he asked.

She nodded.

He picked her up and hugged her. "I'm so sorry Corina didn't keep you safe, but I will, understand?"

She hid her face in the curve of his neck and said nothing, but he felt her relax.

"Hey, how about I wash your hair at the kitchen sink;

then you can try out your bathtub and have bubbles in it? Does that sound like a deal?"

Ava nodded, intrigued by the idea of washing her hair at the sink, and even more intrigued by the idea of bubbles in a bathtub.

Wiley got a step stool, a towel, and shampoo and headed for the kitchen with Ava at his side.

"You climb up here," he said. "All you have to do is hold on to the edge of the sink and lean over, and I'll do the rest. We'll put this towel around your neck so I won't splash your clothes."

"Miss Mattie did this, too, when there weren't too many dishes in the sink," Ava said.

Wiley winced, wondering how many dirty pots and plates she'd had to dodge and then let it go. That was then, and this was now.

"Good, then you know how this works," he said, and when the water was just right, he draped the towel around her little shoulders and leaned her over.

"Close your eyes. This won't take long," he said.

She flinched when the water hit the back of her head, but she didn't say a word. By the time he got to the shampoo part, she was leaning against him.

"Am I scrubbing too hard?" he asked.

"No, Bubba. It feels good," she said.

When he began to rinse out the soap, he was struck again by how fragile she felt. Her tiny bones were too prominent, but he doubted anyone could match Ava's fortitude. She was the epitome of a survivor.

"All done, sugar!" he said, and pulled the towel up around her hair and gently squeezed until the water quit dripping. To his delight, when he removed the towel, her head was a mass of thick, white-blond natural curls. "Wow. Just look at how pretty you are!" he said.

"I wanna see!" Ava cried.

"Go look in your mirror. You are so pretty!"

Ava's eyes widened. "Am I pretty as Corina?"

Wiley frowned. "She's not the standard by which we judge beauty, little girl. You can't be pretty on the outside if your insides are all mean and hateful."

Ava thought about that, then jumped down and ran down the hall.

Wiley followed. He wanted to see the look on her face when she saw herself in the mirror. When he got to her room, she was standing in front of her dresser, touching her hair all over.

"What do you think?" he asked.

"I like it," she said.

"So do I. Bath next. And we don't get our hair wet in the bathtub, okay? That kind of soap isn't good for your hair. Just your skin." He started the water running in the tub, added a little nonallergenic bubble bath, and let the tub fill to about a foot of water with a thick layer of bubbles.

Ava was beside herself with glee, leaning over the tub and poking her fingers in the bubbles and laughing.

"I can get in the bubbles now?" she asked.

Here's where he ran into another roadblock. Was it

proper to help a little girl bathe, or did they wash themselves at this age?

"Can you get in the tub and wash all over by yourself, or do you need help?"

"I don't know. I never had a bath like this before," she said.

He had to go with his gut on this. She wasn't a baby. She was going to be in second grade. Even if she'd never had the luxury, she'd surely seen other women in bathtubs.

"I know you're old enough to wash yourself, but the bubbles will make the tub feel slick. So be careful getting in, and when you're through, I'll be sitting on your bed waiting. Then we'll get you dried off and into your new nightgown, okay?"

"Yes, Bubba. I can do that," she said, and was already pulling her shirt over her head.

He had one glance at the lack of flesh on the child, the prominence of her ribs and hip bones, and then walked out of her bathroom.

"I'm right here!" he called out as he sat down on the side of her bed.

"'Kay!" she said, and then she was in the bubbles.

He could hear her slapping her hands together, popping bubbles and giggling, and then sloshing.

"Don't forget to wash. Your bar of bath soap is right there in the little shelf," he said.

"I see it!"

Moments later, he heard it thump into the tub and

grinned. Likely slid out of her hands. Now she had to go fish.

He remembered doing that with B.J. when they were little. Mom always bathed the boys two at a time. The two oldest, then the two youngest, changing water between because little boys were always dirty.

And then as he sat, he realized she was talking, but not to him.

"The bubble princess came up from the sea and blew bubbles all over Corina, 'cause she needs a-washin'. Lipstick won't make her pretty. She's mean, and I'm not a mistake. Bubba wants me. I don't never have to go back to Conway again."

His throat tightened with emotion. He couldn't begin to imagine the things this child had seen, and closed his eyes.

God, please help me do this right.

He gave her fifteen minutes and knew the water was probably getting cold and the bubbles were most likely gone. She was still rattling away, lost in her own little world, but it was time to intervene.

"Hey, honey! Time to get out."

"I'm gettin'," she said.

He walked in as she was climbing out, wrapped a giant bath towel around her, then carried her into the bedroom and set her down beside her bed, dried her all over, then slipped one of her new nightgowns over her head. Her hair was completely dry now, and the curls were soft as silk beneath his hands.

"I sleep in this?" she said.

"Yes. It's called a nightgown. That's what it's for. To sleep in," he said.

She ran her little hands down the front of it, then reached for her doll.

"Can Pinky sleep with me?"

"Yes, ma'am. That's why she's so soft, so you can hug her while you sleep."

The whole concept of having something to sleep with was foreign.

"One last thing and you're ready for bed," he said.

"What's that?" Ava asked.

"We have to brush our teeth, right?"

"I don't have a toothbrush," she said.

"You have a new one," Wiley said. "It's in your bathroom. Come on. I'll put toothpaste on it for you."

She was all eyes, watching the ritual. Absorbing the rules of the house. Determined to do everything right so Bubba wouldn't be sorry he kept her.

He was still waiting for her when she came out of the bathroom again, but instead of just putting her in bed and leaving, he tucked her and Pinky in, then leaned over and kissed her forehead.

"Gotta have a good-night kiss for sweet dreams," he said.

"Where will you be, Bubba?"

"Right across the hall in my room. I'm going to shower and brush my teeth and get my pajamas and go to bed, too. I might watch a little TV. Will the noise bother you?"

"No. Corina always slept with the TV on."

"That's not a good idea. Everybody needs quiet time, right?" Wiley said.

She nodded. "Yes. Quiet is magic. Sometimes when I get really quiet, I disappear, and then Corina can't throw things at me."

Jesus wept. Wiley was dumbstruck.

"Did she ever hurt you?" he asked.

"Sometimes. But I didn't bleed."

The fact that Ava thought that was a level of okay was horrifying, and there was another question burning into his gut. He had to ask, but was scared shitless to hear the answer.

"Did she ever leave you with people who hurt you or touched you when you didn't want them to?"

"No. Mostly they forgot about me, 'cept for Miss Mattie. She was nice."

"Okay then," Wiley said. "I'll turn the TV off later, and when the house gets quiet, then just remember it's working its magic, making us safe."

She nodded. "Yes. Quiet is good, Bubba. And we pulled the shades and closed the curtains, so we're safe."

He cupped the side of her face. "Yes, baby, you're safe. I've got this! Now close your eyes. You can hear the TV, and I'm going to get in the shower."

"Okay. Don't worry. I know how to be still," she said, and rolled over onto her side with Pinky tucked beneath her chin.

He patted her shoulder, then walked into his

bedroom, turned on the TV, and then turned the sound down a little and headed for the shower. He hadn't slept in pajamas since he was in middle school, but that was all changing now. He grabbed a pair of gym shorts out of his dresser and headed for the bathroom and closed the door, then turned on the water to let it get warm while he stripped. It was the quickest shower he'd ever taken, and as soon as he dried and put on his shorts, he went to check on Ava.

She was motionless. Like she'd promised. She knew how to be still.

He pulled the sheet up over her shoulder, then went back across the hall and climbed into bed. The television was still on, and he was too antsy to sleep, so he lay there—watching a late-night talk show, missing Linette—and drifted off to sleep.

———

Linette wasn't sleeping well. She kept having nightmares of the bank robbery, reliving Mr. Trotter's murder, then seeing Wiley Pope take a bullet in the chest. In the dreams, she was trying to get to Wiley, but everyone on the floor kept grabbing at her ankles, begging her to help them. She could see Wiley, but she couldn't get to him and kept screaming at them to let her go. Then the dream morphed to Wiley carrying Ava and walking out the door.

She woke up sweating. She knew Wiley wouldn't do

that to her, but right now his focus had to be on Ava. It was a sad thing to accept, but Linette knew, as every parent knows, the children come first, and Ava was an obvious victim of neglect and abuse.

Even though the air conditioner in her apartment was set on morgue-level cold, she got out of bed and made a beeline to the kitchen to start some coffee, then headed for the shower. Her shift began at 7:00 a.m. and she felt like crying, which was not how she needed to begin her day.

Wiley was used to being up early for work and was already waking up when he remembered Ava. She hadn't called out or cried at any time during the night, and the quiet seemed ominous. He leaped out of bed and was across the hall in three long steps, only to find her rolled up in a little ball with Pinky in one hand and the white teddy bear in the other. So, she had been up in the night and had taken teddy back to bed with her, too.

He watched her sleeping for a few moments and reminded himself she wasn't as helpless as she appeared. She'd learned a long time ago how to survive within the environment into which she'd been born, and now that he knew she was fine, he went back to shower and shave, then get dressed. They had a big day ahead of them, and he wanted to make breakfast before they went to meet Dani. While he was cooking, it dawned on him that they should have a party this evening at his house so Ava could meet her brothers, her grandmother, and her sisters-in-law.

━━━━━━━

Ava opened her eyes, blinked sleepily as she looked around the pink bedroom, then remembered yesterday. It had started out scary until Bubba told her he had a bed and pillow for her, and a home forever.

She could smell bacon cooking. She loved bacon. Maybe she would have toast, too. The anticipation of the unknown was too much to ignore. She made a quick trip to the bathroom and then ran barefoot to the kitchen, just to make sure Bubba was still there.

Wiley heard her coming as he pulled the last strip of bacon from the skillet. He turned off the burner and wiped his hands just as she flew into the room.

"Good morning, sunshine!" he said, and swooped her up into his arms and kissed her cheek. "Did you sleep good?" he asked.

She giggled.

"I'll take that as a yes. Are you hungry, sugar?"

Ava nodded.

Wiley pretended to frown. "I can't hear you!"

She giggled again. "Yes! I'm hungry."

"Me too. Do we scramble or fry our eggs?" he asked.

Her eyes widened. "I get eggs?"

He sighed. "Yes, and bacon, and toast!"

"I like them scrambled," she said.

"Then scrambled it is," he said, and put her down. "Why don't you go get dressed first?"

"What do I wear?" she asked.

"Remember where your new clothes are?" he asked. She nodded.

"Then you pick out a pair of new panties and whichever shorts and shirt you want to wear."

Her eyes widened. "I get to pick?"

"Of course, you do. You're smart and little girls your age get to dress themselves. Go surprise me!"

She disappeared so fast he laughed, then reached for the carton of eggs and began breaking some into a bowl, then whipped them up. He poured the bacon fat into a bowl and then put the raw egg mix into the hot skillet and began stirring. As soon as he had the eggs cooked, he turned off the burner, covered them with a lid, and popped some bread in the toaster.

Chapter 11

AVA'S DELIGHT IN WEARING SOMETHING NEW LASTED all the way to opening the drawer. All of the brightly colored T-shirts were folded and stacked so neatly, and her little shorts in the same colors in another stack beside them were so perfect that she hesitated. She picked up a pair of new panties and rubbed the silky feel against her cheek before putting them on, and then took off her nightgown and laid it across the foot of her bed. As she did, she wondered what had happened to her old clothes that came from Conway. Everything she had now was so pretty and perfect, but she didn't know how to be this little girl, because inside, she was still the child hiding in the corner, wearing clothes from "the army" and eating Corina's leftovers.

Bubba was her brother. She needed to believe he meant what he said, but Corina was her mother, and she'd lied to her all the time. She was so scared of doing something wrong and winding up back in Conway that she started to shake, and by the time Wiley found her, she was in tears.

Wiley's heart skipped a beat when he saw her standing in the middle of the room in nothing but panties, crying as if her world had ended. She was so tiny and so thin he was almost afraid to pick her up for fear of hurting her, but he couldn't bear the tears. He wrapped her up in the blanket from her bed and then sat down in the rocker beside her bed with her in his lap.

"Ava, sweetheart! What's wrong?"

Tears were rolling. "Corina always lied."

He didn't know where this was going, or what had triggered it.

"Okay, but she's gone, baby. She can't hurt you or lie to you anymore."

She looked up at him then, tears shimmering, her body shaking, but studying every aspect of his face for so long Wiley became uncomfortable. He didn't know what to say and still didn't know what was wrong until she asked him a question.

"Do brothers lie, too?"

He sighed, pulled her close, and started rocking.

"Some people lie. Some people don't. *Your* brothers don't lie. Not to each other, not to you, not to anyone. What made you scared?"

Her cheek was against his chest, and the rumble of his soft, deep voice vibrated in her ear.

"I don't want to do the wrong thing and make you mad. I don't want you to give me away," she said.

Wiley wanted to cry with her. "Well, that's never gonna happen. We're family. We hold on tight to family and love them forever, and we don't quit the people we love. Today, you and I are going to go to Aaron and Dani's house here in town. You'll never be alone in the world, baby girl. You'll never be left behind again. But the most important thing you need to remember is that I chose you. I wanted you. You are not a mistake. You are a gift. I asked to be your official guardian, which is like being a parent, because I'm older, right?"

She nodded.

"Now, no more tears. Bubba's got you! Want help getting dressed?" he asked.

"Yes," she said and slid out of his lap, then watched as he took out a pair of shorts and a new T-shirt from the drawer.

"This feels like a pink day to me!" Wiley said, and took heart when she smiled.

Within a couple of minutes, she was decked out in pink shorts and shirt and wearing her sandals.

"I messed up your hair," he said, and gave it a quick brush, then held out his hand.

"Bacon and eggs waiting," he said.

"And toast?" she asked.

"And toast!"

When she walked out holding his hand, Wiley glanced down at the top of her curly head and smiled. The fact that she'd initiated the contact was a small victory, and he would take it gladly. He pointed at the table as they entered the kitchen.

"I'll make our plates. Sit wherever you want," he said.

"I sit here," she said, claiming the same chair she'd sat at last night.

"Oh, right! You sure do. What was I thinking?" Wiley said, then grabbed a clean dishcloth and tied it around her neck. "Just to keep the crumbs off your clean shirt, okay?"

"Okay," she said as she climbed up into the chair and plopped down on the stack of books that he'd put there for a booster seat. It was hard to sit still, knowing that the food going on the plate was hers to eat. This was a good place to be.

Wiley knew she was still in starvation mode, so when he gave her the plate, he cautioned her, too.

"Take your time. We don't have to hurry. And quit when you're full. There will always be more."

Ava nodded.

"Want butter and jelly on your toast?" he asked.

Her eyes widened again. "I can have…?" She stopped, then took a breath. "Yes, please."

She's catching on, he thought, as he buttered the toast and then lightly layered some strawberry preserves.

He ate with her and, when she wasn't looking, watched. She was still alternating between cramming everything good into her mouth at once, and then remembering and slacking off, chewing one thing at a time until the meal was over.

"I'm full," Ava said, wistfully eyeing part of her jelly toast that she couldn't eat.

"Me too," Wiley said as he untied the dishcloth from around her neck. "You go wash your face and hands while I clean up the table, and then we'll go see Dani, okay?"

"Will Aaron be there?" Ava asked.

"I doubt it. He's already at work, but it won't matter. You'll see him another time. Dani is a schoolteacher. You will go to school where she teaches."

"Will she be my teacher?" Ava asked.

"No, she teaches first grade."

"I'll be in second grade," Ava said.

"Right. We'll get you enrolled when it's time. Right now, this is your summer vacation time. Time to do fun things."

She frowned.

"What?" Wiley asked.

"Corina hates summer vacation. That's when she has to put up with me."

"Well, she's gone and I'm not, and we don't care what Corina thinks, right?"

Ava nodded. "We don't care."

"Right. Now go wash the jelly off yourself. We have things to do and people to see. This is gonna be a good day! And see if Pinky wants to go, too."

She beamed. "I'll ask her," and ran out of the room.

"Corina is still an ass," Wiley muttered as he cleared the table and loaded the dirty dishes in the dishwasher.

By the time he was finished, Ava was back with Pinky.

"She wants to go!" she announced.

"Awesome," Wiley said. "Let's do this!"

———

Dani didn't know when Wiley and Ava would arrive, but she was ready for them when they did. She'd dug through her office for crayons and paper, used her copy machine to print out some pages to color, and laid out some books from her personal children's library.

She and Aaron had moved things around in their spare bedroom to make it little-girl friendly so that when Ava was here, she would feel comfortable and welcome. Ava's transition wouldn't be easy for her, but every child rescued was a child who'd been given a second chance, and Wiley was dedicated to this. The text he'd sent her last night was proof. Now, it was up to all of the family to back him up one hundred percent. Ava was Aaron's sister, and Sean's sister, and B.J.'s sister, too. And after talking to Shirley, she knew it was a done deal.

Ava Dalton was on a fast track to happiness. She just didn't know it yet, so when Dani saw them pulling up into her driveway, she went out on the porch to meet them.

One look at the tiny blond holding tight to Wiley's hand and Dani was hooked. She loved children anyway, but having this one as part of their family was going to be so special.

"Good morning!" Dani said as they came up the steps. "I'm so happy you're here." She led the way into the house and then the living room and sat down so they would, too.

"Dani, this is Ava Dalton, our sister. Ava, this is Dani. She's Aaron's wife, so that makes her your sister-in-law. That's the same thing as a sister."

Dani held out her hand. "I'm so happy to meet you, Ava. I always wanted a sister."

Ava almost smiled. "Really?"

Dani nodded. "Yes, really!"

Wiley kept a hand on Ava's back, just as a reminder that he was there, and let the two of them chatter. During a lull in their conversation, Wiley spoke up again.

"Guess what, Ava? When I have to go back to work, you won't be going to day care. Dani has invited you to stay with her during the day, and then I'll pick you up and we'll go home together every evening. Does that sound like a plan?"

Ava's heart skipped a beat. She already knew she'd have to be somewhere when Wiley went to work, and she was used to being dumped. But this felt different.

"I am invited?" Ava asked.

"Yes, please," Dani said. "I would be so happy for the company, and I have so many fun things already planned for us to do."

Ava's eyes widened. "You would do things with me?"

"Yes. Like crafts and coloring books, and making cookies together, and so many fun things like that," Dani said.

"I don't have to be quiet in the corner?" Ava asked.

Dani gave Wiley a look and then shook her head. "Never, unless you feel like being quiet, like when we sometimes want to take a nap."

"Do you see cartoons on your TV?" Ava asked.

Wiley grinned. "Disney Plus."

"We'll have Disney Plus," Dani said, "and on Aaron's days off, he'll be home with us, and you'll get to spend time with him, too. He's ever so nice and sweet, like Wiley."

"So, baby girl, what do you think?" Wiley asked.

"I think it's a good idea, Bubba," Ava said.

Dani clapped her hands. "Then it's settled. Wiley is going to be off work for a few more days, but we'll see each other in between. Would you like to see the whole house before you leave? Our spare bedroom will be for you when you want to nap, and there's even a TV in it, too."

Ava's eyes lit up. "I will have two bedrooms!"

Wiley could only imagine what Ava was thinking. She'd gone from nothing to everything in less than twenty-four hours. "You two take your house tour. I have some calls to make."

Dani held out her hand. "Come on, sugar. I'll show you the house and then the backyard, too. We have a porch swing out back and two really pretty shade trees."

Ava was immediately at ease with Dani. She thought she was pretty and had a kind voice, and she was a teacher, which was the gold standard for Ava.

"This will be your spot," Dani said, when she took

her to their spare bedroom. "This bed is where you can come to nap, and this room is where you can play if you just want quiet time. Do you like quiet time?"

Ava nodded. "That's how I make myself go away."

Dani was startled by the phrasing. "What do you mean, go away?"

Ava lowered her voice, as if imparting a secret. "When you don't want people to see you, if you'll be really still and really quiet, they forget you're there, and then you're safe."

The poignancy of this child's life broke Dani's heart.

"Oh, sugar," she said, and sat down on the side of the bed and pulled Ava into her arms. "You'll always be safe with us. We're so happy to have you in our family."

Ava wanted to believe, but words meant little to her. She was waiting for proof. After they left the bedroom, she saw the rest of the house and decided she liked the idea of having two beds and two pillows. And then Dani took her outside, and the moment Ava saw the two huge shade trees and the bird feeders between them, she was entranced.

"Do those birds live here?" she asked.

Dani nodded. "Some of them live in the trees, and some are just visiting, but they all know they have food here. You'll have to help me fill bird feeders, too, when you're here."

Ava's voice slid back into that whisper, "I never fed birds before!"

Dani leaned down and hugged her. "Then I'm happy

to be the one to teach you how to do it. You can walk all the way to the trees. They'll fly away for a moment, but then they'll fly right back. They know we won't hurt them."

"I know how to be quiet," Ava whispered, and moved into the shade, then stood motionless, watching.

Wiley came outside to get them, saw what was happening, and stopped. A huge wave of relief washed over him when he saw the delight on Dani's face and the awe on Ava's.

But it was Ava who saw him first and came running to him from across the yard, talking as she went. He caught her in midleap, still talking.

"Bubba! Dani has birds! They live in the trees, and they visit. I'm going to help feed them!"

"That's awesome! So, you think it's okay to be here when I'm at work?" he asked.

"Yes, I think it's good," Ava said.

Dani was smiling when she caught up. "Little sister is smart," she said.

Wiley put Ava down and watched her run back to the porch and settle herself in the porch swing before responding.

"How so?" he asked.

"She saw some of the books I laid out in the extra bedroom for her. They're children's books, and she can read them. As in, read. Not sounding out words. Not stumbling over some of them. She read two aloud and asked if this school had a library, because her other school did and her teacher let her read lots of books there, because Corina didn't have anything for her to read at home."

"Corina is a disaster. That woman can't even read the writing on the wall," Wiley muttered. "Thank you for this. It means the world to me, and it will mean the world to Ava, knowing there are people who have her best interests at heart."

"You're welcome, Wiley. She's so lost. When she told me how she makes herself disappear, I nearly lost it. The tragedy of a child feeling the need to be invisible just to feel safe breaks my heart."

"All she kept saying when we first met was, 'Corina says I'm a mistake.' Can you imagine being told that every day of your life?"

"Who's Corina?" Dani asked.

"Her mother, but Ava never once referred to her as Mother. She just calls her Corina, and right now, her biggest fear is that I'll give her back."

Dani sighed. "Bless her heart. Well, she has us now, and maybe those awful memories will fade with time. Thank you for bringing her by. I'm looking forward to having her here."

"Thank you for jumping into the gap for us. I'm planning a party for this evening so all of you can come meet her in her house. You can let Aaron know, but I'm calling the other brothers and Mom," he said, then went up the back steps to get Ava. "Tell Dani goodbye, sugar. We're leaving now."

Ava slid out of the porch swing and grabbed Wiley's hand.

"Bye, Dani."

Dani grinned. "Bye, honey," she said, then walked them through the house and waved goodbye from her front porch as they drove away.

"Are we going home now?" Ava asked as she settled Pinky in her lap.

"No, we're going to Granny Annie's Bakery first. We're having a party at our house tonight."

Ava gasped. "A party? What kind of a party?"

"A come-meet-Ava party, and all of your brothers and their wives, and your grandma, Shirley, are coming to meet you."

Ava's voice was trembling. "A party for me?"

"It's a welcome-to-the-family party."

"What do I do?" she asked.

"You don't have to do anything but be Ava. You can show them your new room, and they will talk to you, and you will talk to them, and you'll know just how many people want you."

Ava went silent and tightened her hold on Pinky as they drove through Jubilee.

Wiley glanced at her in the rearview mirror and thought he saw tears in her eyes. "Are you okay, Ava?"

She nodded.

"Are you sad?" he asked.

"No."

"But you're crying," he said.

LEFT BEHIND   233

"I never had a party. Will there be cake?"

Shock rolled through him.

"What about your birthday?" he asked.

She shrugged.

"Do you know your birthday?" Wiley asked.

"June fourth," she said.

He was absorbing her truth all over again. A child without comfort or clothes, or toys, or even a real place to call home. Acknowledged only as "a mistake."

"And nobody ever made you a cake or gave you gifts?"

She thought a few moments then shrugged again. "Miss Mattie gave me chewing gum sometimes if she had any in her purse. And pudding cups. We had pudding cups."

"I'm sorry that happened, but you'll never be ignored again. I promise."

"Okay," she said.

He sighed. Words meant nothing to her. It would be actions that would change her world, so he shifted the conversation as he pulled up to the curb in front of the bakery.

"We're here, sugar. Let's go pick out some yummy stuff for the party, okay?"

Ava nodded. She liked Bubba's idea of yummy stuff, and she was excited about having a party. She latched onto Bubba's hand as they walked into the bakery, and then stopped, stunned by scents of sweets and baking bread.

"What do I smell?" she whispered.

Wiley grinned. "Yummy stuff, sister. Yummy stuff. See that lady at the counter with the pretty white hair? That's our aunt Annie. She owns the bakery and makes all this good stuff to eat." They moved to the display case so Ava could see, but when he realized she was too small, he picked her up for a better view. "Now you can see better. Do we want a cake, or do we want cupcakes and cookies?"

"Cake," Ava said.

"Done," Wiley said. "Now, do we want chocolate or vanilla cake?"

"What is vanilla?" Ava asked.

"The white kind."

"Yes, that. Will it have my name on it?" she asked.

He saw hope and expectation. "Why, I think it should, since the party is for you, right?"

She nodded, then hid her face against his neck.

Like a little turtle, Ava had retreated into her shell, and Wiley let her be. Annie Cauley was all smiles when they approached the register.

"Wiley, it's a joy to see you," she said. "And who is your pretty little friend?"

Ava came up for air, eyeing the lady with white hair as intently as Annie was eyeing her.

"This is our little sister, Ava. We found each other yesterday, and she's going to be living with me now."

Annie's eyes widened and then softened. "There you go, being the hero all over again," she said softly.

Wiley shook his head. "No, ma'am. Just taking care

of family. We're having a party at the house tonight so she can meet her brothers and sisters-in-law and her grandma all at once, and we need a cake."

"I never had a cake before," Ava said.

Annie blinked. "Well, I declare," she said. "How old are you, Ava?"

"I'm seven."

"And a pretty little thing you are," Annie said, trying to hide her shock.

Wiley quickly ended the personal inquisition. "This is just another in a long line of firsts for Ava. We have decided we want a white cake with white buttercream icing. Maybe half a sheet-cake size? And could we have writing on it that says, 'Ava, welcome to the family'?"

Annie's hands were shaking. "You can have whatever you like on it. Is there a color preference for the writing?"

He nodded. "Pink is the color du jour. Would it be possible to have this delivered to my house around five today? I know this is short notice but..."

"If this is her first cake ever, it's not short notice. It's long overdue," Annie said. "Let me write down your address for the delivery."

He handed her a credit card, but Annie waved it away.

"This cake is a gift from me and her uncle John. Ava, honey, from now on, you just call me Aunt Annie, like your brothers do, okay?"

Ava looked at Wiley for approval, and when he winked, she knew it was okay.

"I think you probably need a couple of cookies to take with you," Annie said. "Ava, honey, you pick," she said, and pointed to the sheet pan in the display case. "Sugar cookies, peanut butter cookies, chocolate chip cookies, cherry drop cookies."

"I like peanut butter," Ava said.

Annie scooped two peanut butter cookies from the tray into a little sack and handed them to her.

"I think we need to thank Annie for the cookies," Wiley said.

"Thank you for the cookies," Ava echoed.

"Enjoy, and come see me again soon, okay?"

"We will," Wiley said, and put Ava down.

Ava had the sack of cookies in one hand, and latched on to Wiley with the other as they walked out the door.

"Lord, have mercy," Annie muttered, then grabbed the order and headed to the back room. "Laurel, this needs to be ready and delivered to Wiley's house by five."

Annie's daughter, Laurel, glanced at the order, and nodded. "Simple enough, but who's Ava? Is Wiley finally settling down?"

"All I know is Wiley introduced her as his little sister, and he's taken her to raise. That's about as settled as a single man can get."

"Wow," Laurel said. "So, Clyde Wallace fooled around on Shirley?"

"Obviously," Annie said.

"Do you think Shirley knew?"

"Oh, I know Shirley knew he wasn't faithful, but I

don't think any of them knew about this child. I don't know how this came about, but she looks half-starved and neglected, so she's right where she belongs, with people who want her."

———

But back in Jubilee, Wiley and Ava were still making waves. When he pulled into the gas station to refuel before going back to their house, he left Ava sitting in the back seat with Pinky and rolled down the windows so she wouldn't get too hot. He didn't notice the driver of the truck on the other side of the pumps, until he heard someone call his name and turned to look, then frowned.

Keith Priddy. He used to work security with him at the Bullard music venue. He hadn't liked him then, and he didn't like him now.

"Hey, big shot! I haven't seen you in a while. I see you've recovered from the bank robbery."

Wiley nodded, but didn't respond. He was keeping an eye on the pump and on Ava.

Keith moved between the pumps and then leaned against Wiley's SUV. That's when he saw Ava sitting in the back seat.

"Well, who do we have here?" he drawled. "This your kid, Pope? I always figured you'd have a woods colt or two out there."

Wiley turned on him so fast Keith gasped, then choked on his own spit.

"Priddy, if you plan on waking up tomorrow, then shut your mouth."

"Oh hell, come on, Wiley. Don't be such an uptight asshole. I didn't mean nothin' by it," Keith muttered.

Wiley was in his face, speaking in a low, quiet tone of voice, but Keith knew that if looks could kill, he would already be dead.

"She's our sister," Wiley said. "Mine, and Aaron, and Sean, and B.J. She's living with us now, so if you want to talk about us, make sure it's the truth."

"Yeah, sure, I didn't—"

"And apologize to Ava for the language you used in front of her."

Keith swallowed past the knot in his throat and looked down at the little wide-eyed blond staring up at him.

"Say, kid, I'm real sorry I said some bad words. Okay?"

Ava looked at Wiley.

"She heard you," Wiley said. "Now get on your side of the pumps and stay there."

"Yeah, sure thing," Keith said. "Sorry."

Wiley glanced in the car at Ava again, but she had gone back to playing with Pinky as if none of that had just happened. Only he knew better. Ava had gone quiet. She was hiding from the grown-ups again, and he didn't blame her.

As soon as he got back in the car, he turned on the air-conditioning and rolled the windows back up.

"Ava, honey. Are you okay?" he asked.

She nodded.

"I'm sorry that man was rude."

She looked up. "What's rude?"

"When someone says something mean on purpose."

"Why do they do that?" Ava asked.

"Because, when God was handing out manners, they were picking their nose instead, that's why."

She giggled.

Wiley grinned, then winked. "That's my girl."

"Are we going home now?" she asked.

"Yes, we are," Wiley said. "You're gonna play, and I'm going to straighten up the house and get ready for the party."

They were leaving the station and about to turn left when he saw Linette coming out of an office building. He honked and waved, and she waved back, then blew him a kiss. Wiley had the strongest urge to stop the car, get out, and kiss her senseless in front of God and everybody, but since that couldn't happen, he just kept driving. He was, however, still smiling when he pulled into their driveway.

He opened the garage door with the remote, drove inside, then lowered the door before getting Ava out of the back seat and into the house.

"You can go play now. And if you want to watch TV, come tell me and I'll find your cartoons for you."

"Okay, Bubba. Can I take off my shoes and play barefoot?" she asked.

"Absolutely," he said.

She nodded and skipped off down the hall with Pinky under her arm.

Chapter 12

CAREY EGGERS RECEIVED THE NEWS AT BREAKFAST that she was being released today. They were getting her release papers ready, and all she needed now was a ride out of town. She was so excited she quit her food and called Johnny immediately to give him the news. When he answered on the first ring, the familiar rumble of his voice was in her ear.

"Hello?"

"Hi, Johnny, it's me. I have good news. I can go home this morning."

Johnny let out a whoop. "Best news ever, sweetheart. It won't take us long to pack up and check out. I can't wait to get you out of here."

"Me too," Carey said. "Love you. See you soon, and thank you for the new going-home clothes you brought me yesterday."

"You're welcome. See you soon," he said, and disconnected.

An hour later, she was finally dressed in blue shorts and a blue and white T-shirt with *Jubilee* written across the front. As she waited within the silence of her room, the gravity of her situation fell in on her again.

She was going home to a brother in the morgue and the hopes that there was no one left who wanted her dead. Being hunted down like a wild animal had shaken her to the core. Detective Gardner had assured them again that he'd publicly announced Billy Eggers's sister had neither seen the person who shot him, nor had any idea who'd tried to kill her. She couldn't identify anyone, or know anything of value to the case, and that was all the reassurance she had that she was off the shooter's radar. She also knew that they'd issued an arrest warrant based on DNA found under her brother's fingernails during the fight, so she had no reason to doubt Gardner's word, but the whole debacle was still horrifying.

Then the door to her room opened, and Tom and Johnny came in. She eased herself down from the bed and hugged the both of them.

"You two are my angels. Tommy, I will never be able to repay you for all the days you've sacrificed for us. And Johnny never quit believing I'd survive. I just want to go home, talk to Billy's lawyers to see what I have to do, and find out when I can bury him."

"He's still in the morgue, but I think they'll release him for burial now that you're able to claim the body," Tom said.

Her eyes welled. "He wanted to be cremated. I'll have to find a funeral home for that. I've been so focused on me that I haven't had time to grieve his absence in my life, but I will. I will miss him. So much. He was the last of my family."

Johnny took her hand. "We have each other, and good friends like Tom. We'll make our own family, baby. Just don't cry. Not today. Today is pure joy that you've healed enough to leave."

She nodded. "I'll have to check in with my regular doctor once I get home. They're sending my medical records to his office so that he'll have the full picture, but it's standard practice until I'm released to go back to work."

"We'll figure it out," Johnny said. "Together, we're unstoppable, darlin.'"

Then an orderly came in with a wheelchair, followed by a nurse with Carey's release papers and prescriptions.

"Look at us," Carey said as she settled into the wheelchair. "We have our own handicap convoy. Breaker, breaker, Cowboy Cop. Take us home."

Tom laughed and wheeled Johnny into step behind the orderly who was pushing Carey, and as he did, he realized he hadn't laughed once since learning of her disappearance. It felt good to do it again.

———

It took over an hour for Tom to get them home, and then he helped them inside. The house was hot and musty. Most of the food in the refrigerator had gone bad, and he spent a few minutes cleaning it out while Carey made a list of what they needed. After Johnny forked over some of the money from Billy's gift, he took off to do their shopping.

Word had spread among their friends as to what had happened to Carey, and they'd all donated enough money to get their truck repaired and out of the garage. It was sitting in the driveway, washed and detailed and ready to ride.

They found the truck keys on the floor when they walked in the house. Someone had shoved them through the mail slot, along with a get-well card to both of them, a sympathy card for the death of Carey's brother, and an envelope with three hundred dollars in cash.

Carey cried. Johnny wanted to. But they were home and Carey was upright and mobile, and Johnny was getting there. He still had the cast on his leg, but it was due to come off, and they didn't know if the police were anywhere near closing the case of Billy's murder.

Tom returned about an hour later with fresh groceries and put them up. "I hate to leave you two like this," he said.

"We'll be fine," Carey said. "Tomorrow I'm contacting Williams and Williams, the lawyers you mentioned, to see where I stand, but today, Johnny and I are going to just take it easy and rest."

"I'll talk to Detective Gardner and let you know what I find out, and I'll swing by after I get off work every day to see if you need anything, okay? If you have doctor appointments, use that extra money you were given and call an Uber. Do not try to drive until your doctor releases you, or you'll be liable if you have an accident, understand?"

They both nodded.

Then Tom patted Casey's shoulder. "And no walking a freaking mile to get somewhere, either. This time, you ask for help, girl."

She sighed. "Message received."

"Okay then. I'm headed home, and then I'll probably be back on duty tomorrow. I'll call when I know something," Tom said, and then gave Johnny a quick hug. "You're the toughest guy I know. You bit the bullet for your girl, and dealt with a level of pain I can't imagine, just to be near her. Now figure out what your next move is going to be, because your days as a lineman are over."

"They've already offered me a desk job," Johnny said. "It will be an adjustment, but I'm not going to be unemployed."

"Good deal, buddy. So, I'm leaving now, but promise you'll call if you need me."

"I promise," Johnny said, and then Tom was gone.

Johnny turned his wheelchair toward Carey. "Well, we're home, darlin'. Nobody said life would be easy, but neither of us ever saw this coming. What you need to know is that I'll never quit you. You're my girl, now and always. I thought I'd lost you, and I will never take life for granted again."

Carey moved across the room, then leaned down and kissed him.

"The drive home was exhausting. I missed our bed. I missed lying beside you and listening to you sleep." Then her voice broke. "I thought I would never see you again."

"I can't make love to you yet, but I can hold you in my arms. Come to bed with me, love. You need to rest, and I want out of this chair."

She wheeled him into their bedroom and steadied the chair as he moved himself onto the bed. Then she laid his cell phone by the bed, pulled off his shoes, then kicked off her shoes and eased herself down onto the bed beside him, and groaned.

"Home at last," she said, and reached for his hand. His fingers curled around hers.

"Love you," Johnny whispered.

"Love you more," she said, and closed her eyes.

———

It was a quarter to five when the cake from Granny Annie's Bakery was delivered to Wiley's house, and the food he'd ordered from the local caterer was already on the counter and in the refrigerator, just waiting for guests to arrive.

Ava was playing in her room and didn't know the cake was here and that it was what was in the big box on the counter when she came into the kitchen.

"Bubba, is it time?"

He glanced up at the clock. "They should be arriving

soon. I need to change my shirt. Wanna come with me and help me pick out a good one to wear with my jeans?"

She nodded and ran ahead to his bedroom.

The simple sight of her curls bouncing and the fact that she felt comfortable enough to lead the way gave him hope that she was happy, or at least trusting that he wasn't going to give her back.

"Do you have pink shirts?" Ava asked, when he pulled his T-shirt over his head and tossed it in the laundry.

He grinned. "No. Pink's not my best color." He opened a dresser drawer. "These are my good T-shirts. I'll wear any color you choose."

She leaned over, eyeing the array, then picked a pale-blue one. "I like this, Bubba. It's the color of the sky."

"Good choice," he said, took it out of the stack, shook it out, and pulled it over his head. "How's that?"

She studied his appearance seriously, then nodded. "You look pretty."

"Girls are pretty. Boys are handsome," he said.

"My Bubba is pretty," she stated, and crawled up on his bed to watch as he went to the bathroom to comb his hair. "Are you gonna wear the good smelly stuff, too?"

He laughed. She paid more attention to what was going on than he realized.

"A little, okay?" then he sprayed a little cologne into the air and walked through the mist and picked her up. "Do I smell good now?" he asked, and kissed her cheek.

She giggled. "You smell pretty."

He grinned. "You're something else, Miss Ava. So, pretty it is." He swooped her off his bed, carried her across the hall and into her bedroom, and plopped her down on her bed. "Now you need to put on your shoes."

"For the party," Ava said.

"Yes, baby. For the party," and he picked up her sandals. He was fastening the last Velcro strap when their doorbell rang.

She gasped. "Is that company?"

"I think so. Let's go see."

She slid off her bed and grabbed his hand, but as they were going down the hall, she went quiet.

"Don't be scared, baby," Wiley said.

"If they don't like me, will you still keep me?" she whispered.

"Nobody can take you away from me, so stop worrying. Besides, I know my brothers. I know my mother. They will love you, like I do."

She looked up at him, but said nothing, and then they were at the door. Wiley swung it open to see his entire family standing on the porch.

Ava took one look at the giant people before her and froze. This was where she usually made herself disappear, but Wiley was here, and so she silently moved behind Wiley's leg instead.

Wiley didn't react other than to welcome in their guests. "Come in, everyone. Let's sit for introductions. Ava thinks I'm a giant. Four of us is probably a little intimidating. Right, sugar?" he said, then scooped her up in his arms and held her while everyone walked in carrying gifts.

Ava felt safer in Bubba's grasp, but she was silently staring at all of the bows and colorful wrapping, almost in a state of disbelief that they could be for her, but everybody who walked past said hello and said her name.

As soon as they were seated, Wiley shut the door and headed for the spot they'd left for him on the sofa. He sat, still holding her, then put her down. She backed up between his knees, still watching.

But it was Shirley who broke the ice. She was looking at a beautiful little girl who was half the size of what she should be, obviously in a state of fear and flight. In that moment, she felt the bond every mother feels when they look upon their child's face for the very first time. Ava Dalton might not belong to them by blood, but she already belonged in Shirley's heart.

"Ava, I'm Wiley's mother, and I brought a present for you, but I have a cast on my foot that makes walking a little difficult."

Ava eyed the soft cast.

"I can walk," she whispered.

"Thank you. That is so helpful," Shirley said, and held out the package.

Ava glanced at Wiley. He nodded his okay, and she left the shelter of his presence to cross the room.

Shirley handed her the gift.

"Thank you," Ava said, and clutched it against her

chest as she scurried back to Wiley, then sat down at his feet. "Bubba, can I open this?"

"You sure can," he said.

Ava ran her fingers across the shiny white paper with a perfect yellow bow, and just sat there. It was almost as if the box could have been empty and she wouldn't have cared because the wrapping alone was more than she'd ever had and would have been enough.

"You can open it, honey," Dani said.

"It will tear," she whispered.

When he laid his hand on the top of her head to reassure her, her curls clung and coiled at his touch, as if they were alive on their own. It was a sign. She already had him wrapped around her little finger.

"It's just paper, baby. Think of it like the shell of a peanut. You take off the shell to get to the good stuff, right?"

"The good stuff," Ava whispered, and tore at a corner, and then saw something colorful inside and ripped off the rest of the paper and gasped. "It's a puzzle, Bubba! I know how to do puzzles! Thank you, Bubba's mother!"

Shirley's eyes were shimmering with unshed tears, but she was smiling from ear to ear.

"You can call me Grammy," Shirley said.

Ava looked back at Wiley. "I have a grammy."

By now, everyone in the room was half-afraid to speak to her and all the way in love with her.

B.J. abandoned his chair and sat down beside her. "I'm your brother Brendan, but everybody calls me B.J. My brothers and I always wanted a little sister, and now we have one. Welcome to the family, Ava," he said, and handed her his gift.

Ava glanced up at Wiley again, and when he winked, she giggled and tore into the paper, revealing a small silver box.

"It's a music box," B.J. said. "Open it. There's something else inside."

Ava lifted the lid and saw a shiny chain with a little silver heart lying at the bottom of the box. She gasped.

"Bubba, there's treasure! It's a necklace with a heart!"

Brendan lifted out the necklace, leaned forward, and fastened the clasp around her neck. The little heart fell into the hollow at her throat. Then he picked up the music box and turned it upside down. "Watch me, and you'll see how to wind it up."

She leaned forward, intent on his instructions as he gently twisted the little key beneath, then set the box down and closed the lid. The moment Ava heard music, she froze, and then tears welled.

"It's singing to me," she whispered.

B.J. opened his arms, and to everyone's shock, Ava fell into them, laid her head on his shoulder, and sobbed.

"Don't freak. This is a good reaction," Wiley said. "I think she liked it…and you."

At that point, Sean and Aaron joined the circle, each carrying their own presents. Amalie and Dani stayed back. This moment was for the family reunion.

"Hi, baby," Aaron said. "We've already met, haven't we? I'm Aaron, remember?"

She turned loose of B.J. and moved toward Aaron. "Corina was mean to you. Mean is like being rude. Bubba says rude people were picking their noses when God handed out manners."

There was a moment of silence, and then Aaron burst out laughing and hugged her. "With Wiley for a Bubba, it will be a mystery as to what comes out of her mouth in the years to come. And yes, you're right. Corina was rude."

Ava nodded, then glanced back at Wiley, making sure she wasn't in trouble, and got a grin and a wink from her Bubba. After that, she was fine.

Aaron handed her his gift, then pointed at Dani. "You already know Dani. She helped me pick out this gift. Wanna open it?"

Ava gave Dani a shy glance and nodded, tearing into the wrapping on this gift with more force. With Aaron's help, she got the lid off the box and saw a treasure of another kind.

"Look, Bubba! Two coloring books and crayons. Colored pencils with paper to draw on. My own little scissors! I know how to cut paper! I learned how at school! I will be careful. I will only cut paper…just my paper. I am not a baby."

"I know that, darlin'. You are responsible," he said. "Do you know what *responsible* means?"

She nodded. "That I know how to behave."

"Yes, that, but it also means you know what's right and what's wrong, don't you?" Wiley said.

She was quiet for a moment, thinking about what he said, and then she nodded.

"Yes. I'm not a mistake, am I, Bubba?"

Shock silenced all of them as Wiley leaned over and ruffled the curls on her head.

"No, ma'am, you are not a mistake. What did I say you were?"

"A gift. You said I was a gift," Ava whispered.

"And you are a gift! To all of us," Sean said. "I'm Sean, and I brought a gift, too."

By now, Ava was into the swing of the moment, and the brothers all looked so much alike that she wasn't scared of them anymore, but still reserved the right to back off if the need arose.

She walked over to where Sean was sitting and sat down in front of him.

"Hello, darlin'," he said softly. "See that pretty woman with the white streak in her hair? That's Amalie, my wife. She's also your sister. She helped me pick out our gift to you." He slid the box toward her.

Ava glanced back at Wiley again, but this time her expression was lit from within.

"Bubba! I have another present!"

"I see that! Better open it to see what it is!" Wiley said.

She smiled shyly at Sean and then tore the paper off her gift and lifted the lid from the box.

"An iPad, Bubba, and it's pink! We used these at school. I know how! I know how!" she cried.

"I promise it's only for kids her age. I've vetted the

programs and links. They're fun, but all geared to learning. Gotta make sure our little sister is up-to-date with the world she's growing up in."

"This is awesome," Wiley said.

"We use things like this at school," Dani added.

This time, Ava didn't need any urging. She stood up, hugged Sean's neck, and whispered, "Thank you," in his ear. Then went to where Dani and Amalie were sitting. "Thank you for coming to my party," she said.

Dani hugged her. "We wouldn't miss it for anything."

Amalie held out her hand, and when she did, Ava saw the burn scars on the back of it, and then saw the burn scars on her neck. But instead of the scars, it was the white streak in Amalie's hair that caught her eye.

"You have pretty hair. Thank you for coming to my party," she said.

Amalie had already seen herself in this child.

"Thank you for finding us," Amalie said. "I was lost when I was a little girl, and it took a long time for my real family to find me. I'm so glad we found you now."

Ava blinked. "You didn't have people?"

Amalie shook her head. "No. I didn't have people. And now I have a father and a whole mountain full of family, including you."

"I don't have a mother and daddy. Just Corina." Then she glanced back at Wiley anxiously, as if by even saying the name that she might have conjured her back up again. "Bubba's not going to send me back."

Wiley couldn't take it anymore. He got up from the

sofa, picked her up in his arms, and hugged her. "No, way, baby girl. You're ours forever. Now let's get your gifts off the floor and go find the yummy stuff."

"Do we have cake?" Ava asked.

He grinned. "Oh, Sister! Do we have cake!"

"Amalie and I will get the gifts off the floor. Shall we take them to her room?" Sean asked.

"Yes, please," Wiley said. "Guys, you help Mom into the kitchen so she can oversee what's happening. Ava is going to help me get the yummy stuff onto the table."

"I'm helping Bubba," she said.

Within minutes, the kitchen was full of laughter and talking, and Ava had retreated from the forest of tall people with long legs and was at her spot at the table.

Shirley sat down beside her and patted her hand.

"Your brothers are a little loud, but they're always like that when they're together. They love each very much."

Ava nodded, watching her beloved Bubba interacting with the men who looked like him, then looked at Shirley.

"I have brothers and sisters, and a grammy, and two beds and two pillows, and gifts, and I'm having a party, and a cake. I've never had gifts or a party or a cake before."

Shirley hid her shock of the child's acceptance of her fate.

"This may be your first party, sweetheart, but it won't be your last. We celebrate the people we love."

Ava looked at Shirley's face and then back at the others in the room.

"Does that mean they love me?" she whispered.

Shirley nodded. "Do you know what love feels like?"

Ava shook her head.

"It feels like the best, biggest hug ever. It feels safe and makes you happy, and you never want the feeling to go away."

Ava stilled, listening to the words coming out of her grammy's mouth, and in the midst of a story she was telling, there was a loud boom outside, like an explosion, and Ava jumped. Had it not been for Shirley, she would have fallen out of the chair.

The moment Wiley heard it, he turned, looking for Ava. She was already afraid of drive-by shootings, and then he saw his mother pulling Ava into her lap.

"It's just fireworks at the campground, honey. Silly people being noisy. Nothing to be afraid of."

"Fireworks?" Ava said.

"Yes, like on the Fourth of July," Shirley said. "You're safe."

Ava was quiet for a moment. "I'm safe and Bubba loves me because he chose me."

"Bubba chose you because you're his little sister. Because he wants to keep you safe. We all chose you, darlin'. You'll figure it out in the days to come. Now...I think I need to go wash up before I eat. Will you show me where the bathroom is?"

Ava was suddenly all business. She slid out of

Shirley's lap, then took her hand, and slowly walked her out of the room. When they came back, Ava was still holding her hand, but chattering away.

Wiley sighed. *There are angels on earth, and tonight, one's name is Shirley.*

We're ready to eat!" Wiley said. "We'll have yummy stuff to eat and then cake."

The kitchen island had become a buffet of little sandwiches and an assortment of mini-quiche, and chips and dips, and little wieners wrapped in warm, yeasty bread. There were two huge flat-pan pizzas cut in squares, and in Ava's honor, mac and cheese in the blue box, because it was familiar. But when it was time to make her plate, it was immediately obvious that she was too small to see over the counter, so Wiley sat her on a barstool.

"You point to what you want, I'll put it on your plate, then you can sit back in your spot at the table. How's that?" he said.

But her gaze was riveted on the cake, and Wiley paused, because there were tears rolling down her face. He put down her plate and picked her up. When he did, she tucked her face against his neck.

"Give us a moment," he said, then walked away from the island. "It's all a lot of fun at once, isn't it?"

She clung tighter.

"What are you afraid of, Ava…being happy?"

She nodded.

"Look, Sister, here's the deal. Corina is the reason

you're afraid to be happy. I'm not Corina. She tied you into tiny little knots, and my job is to untangle them. Now you sit in your spot, and I'll bring you a little bit of everything, okay?"

"Okay," she said. "I can walk, Bubba. I want everything and cake."

"I can do that," Wiley said, then set her back on her feet and watched her scramble back to the table.

B.J. stared at Wiley. "If you didn't still have that face, I wouldn't know you."

Wiley shrugged as he began making her plate. "It was a knee-jerk reaction that turned into a rescue, that's turned on every father instinct in me."

"All you need is a woman to go with it," Sean said.

"He has one, and he's opted out of pursuing her to take care of Ava," Aaron said.

"She's already met her," Wiley said. "It was a chance meeting, but there aren't any problems other than priority, because right now, I save the one who's drowning."

After that, food shifted the party into fun and laughter. Ava had opinions about square pizza, scarfed down her mac and cheese with delight, took one bite of a chicken salad sandwich and then set it aside, and went for the little wiener roll-ups.

"Remember to save room for cake," Wiley said.

"I'm saving room right here," she said, pointing to her stomach.

And when it was time to cut the cake, they cleared off their plates and carried the cake to the table.

This time Ava was beaming. "Aunt Annie made my name pink!"

"Can you read what it says?" Dani asked.

"Yes! The big word is *Ava.* That's me. And then the other words are *Welcome to the family.* That's my Bubba and all of you."

"Right you are," Dani said.

"I have plates and forks," Amalie said as she carried a stack to the table.

Wiley moved up behind where Ava was sitting and leaned over her, with the cake knife in his hand.

"Ava, this is your party, so you get the first piece. Where do you want me to cut?"

"My name! I want to eat my name!" she cried.

Wiley grinned. "That's my girl. Jumping right into the middle of things." He cut from the edge all the way to her name, removed the piece as neatly as a surgeon, and put it on her plate.

Amalie handed her a fork, and there they sat, holding their breath as they watched the tiny blond take a bite. There was a smear of icing on Ava's upper lip, but her expression was one of pure ecstasy.

"What's the verdict?" Wiley asked.

She looked up at him and smiled. "It's yummy, Bubba."

———————

Long after the food had been eaten, the puzzle played with a half-dozen times, the books read, the new

necklace replaced in her jewelry box, and she'd tried
every color of crayon in the box, Wiley had her tucked
in bed and she was sound asleep, with Pinky shoved
beneath her chin.

He stood in the doorway to her room, looking into
the shadows at the tiny child curled up in a ball beneath
the covers, and saw his future. It was about as perfect
as a man could want. The only thing missing was the
woman who would lie with him and grow old with him.
He sighed before turning around and retreating to his
bedroom. He was tired but restless, so he picked up his
phone and texted Linette.

> We had a welcome-to-the-family party for Ava
> tonight. It was a success. Please don't feel
> abandoned. I miss you. But this child was wrecked,
> and we're still pulling her out of the debris.

He hit Send, then put the phone on the charger and
went to bed.

———

Linette saw the text the next morning and sighed. All
was well with her and Wiley, and he had his priorities in
the right place. For now, it was enough.

> Don't forget I love kids, too. Next date we have, it
> will be me and you and little sister make three. We

don't leave her out of anything but our bed. She's
right where she belongs.

━━━━━━━━━

Wiley read the text at breakfast and nearly choked on
his coffee.

Ava looked up, frowning. "You okay, Bubba?"

"Yes, yes, I'm okay, sugar. My drink just went down
the wrong way."

"Miss Mattie always says, 'Slow down, girlie. You
ain't goin' nowhere.'"

Wiley laughed. "I'm sorry I never got to meet Miss
Mattie. She sounds like a smart lady."

Ava frowned. "Miss Mattie didn't like Corina, and
Corina got mad at Miss Mattie for droppin' dead."

"Why didn't Miss Mattie like Corina?" Wiley asked.

Ava thought about it, took another bite of toast, and
chewed. "Miss Mattie said Corina wasn't a nice woman.
Miss Mattie said Corina was a witch. After that, I was
afraid she would turn me into a toad."

Wiley sat there in shock again, listening to the
matter-of-fact rendition of a day in the life of Ava and
kept thinking, *I will never know all the shit she's seen and
heard, which means I will never be able to completely disin-
fect the poison that was Corina Dalton.*

"Being called a witch doesn't mean you are one.
Sometimes it means the same thing as being mean and
sneaky," he said.

Ava nodded. "Like Corina," she said, and licked jelly off her thumb. "What are we gonna do today, Bubba?"

He pushed his plate back and grinned. "Well, I have a friend in Bowling Green who sells playground equipment, and he's coming over here today to put up a swing set in our backyard for you to play on."

Ava gasped. "Do you think it might have a slide?"

"Oh, it not only has a swing and a slide, but it has a little playhouse on top of it, and stairs to climb to the playhouse."

Ava squealed!

Wiley flinched and then grinned. He'd just gotten his first real kid reaction, and at a pitch high enough to shatter crystal. Life was good.

———

The crew arrived with the playground setup just before 10:00 a.m., and after a few words with Wiley, they began carrying everything into the backyard to assemble.

Ava was beside herself to the point that there was nothing for them to do but go to the back porch, crawl up in the porch swing together, and watch the progress. Ava went from sitting beside him, to crawling in his lap, to abandoning him altogether and sitting on the back steps, just to be closer to the action.

"Ava, honey, you're gonna sunburn and I didn't put any sunblock on you. Let's go inside a minute and do that. And while we're there, we'll get a cold pop to bring back out with us."

"Okay," she said, and followed him inside. "The little house has a blue roof! Did you see that, Bubba?"

"I did," Wiley said as he got a bottle of sunblock from his medicine cabinet, stood her up on the lid of the commode, squirted some of the cream in his hands, and started with her face and neck. "Gotta put some here, right? We don't want that pretty little face to get burned."

Her chatter shifted back to a whisper. "Am I really pretty, Bubba?"

He paused, cupped her cheeks, and looked her straight in the eyes. "Yes, you are. And even better, I love that you're my sister." Then he squirted another dollop into his hands. "Now your arms and legs," he said, and rubbed the cream into the skin. "All done," he said, and turned to wash his hands as she climbed down.

"You didn't do you, Bubba," Ava said.

"I don't burn," Wiley said, then held his arm up against hers. "See the difference in the color of our skin?"

"Mine's white. Yours is tan, Bubba."

"That just means the sun can't hurt my skin as fast as it can hurt yours."

"Why is our skin different if we have the same daddy?"

"Because we have different mothers."

He watched the understanding dawn and realized Dani was right. This little girl was smart and, it appeared, had a really good memory, too.

"Your mother wasn't an ass."

He laughed. "No, she wasn't, but we're not gonna say that word to anyone else. That's just a secret between you and me."

She nodded. "I can keep secrets. I know Corina's secrets about Clyde."

Wiley froze. He didn't know whether he wanted to pursue this or not, and reached for her hand.

"Ready for that cold pop now?"

"Yes!"

"I like orange," she said.

"I know, Sister. And what kind do I like best?"

"Coca-Cola in a can."

"I'll race you to the kitchen," Wiley said, then watched the delight spreading across her face as she took off running. He made a lot of noise coming up behind her, but purposefully lagged.

"I win!" she shouted as she reached the refrigerator first.

"You sure did, and the winner gets a cookie. We can eat them outside."

She danced around him like a puppy and then settled in the swing beside him with the cold can of orange soda between her legs, periodically breaking off a piece of cookie and stuffing it into her mouth. It would take longer than a couple of days to get past having nothing, to having it all.

They sat for a few minutes enjoying the treats, but after she was through eating, he heard himself ask,

"What did you mean about knowing secrets about Corina and Clyde?"

"Corina made a mistake."

She made a whole fucking bunch of them, baby girl, Wiley thought, but he didn't say it. "What kind of mistake?"

"She gave Clyde bad pills. It made him do crazy things."

The skin suddenly crawled on the back of Wiley's neck. "How do you know this?"

"I heard Corina tell Janie when they were drinking too many beers. The pills made Corina see spiders in her hair, and Carl saw them, too, and cut it all off and ran away. She was bald for a long time until her hair grew back."

Wiley nodded, imagining the woman in a full-blown hallucination.

"And what did the pills do to Clyde?" Wiley asked.

"He tried to kill his old lady and made two people dead. They never got to go home again, and the police put him in prison forever."

The day was as still and hot as it could be, but in that moment, Wiley felt a cold wind blow through him. He set their drinks aside, pulled Ava into his arms, and held her, pulling her close. The words she knew. The life she'd witnessed, and now he was processing the answer to a question they'd had ever since Clyde Wallace nearly beat their mother to death, and why he shot two random people that day. They'd always known he was a mean drunk. And they'd always known he messed with drugs. But this put a whole new light on the why and how of it. Ava sat up, pointing. "Look! The man is hanging the swing, and the slide is there! Will I get to play on this today?"

"Yes, you will," Wiley said.

"Will you take a picture?

"I will take a picture and send it to all of your brothers and sisters, and to Grammy."

She shivered with excitement. She'd never been lauded before. Never posed for pictures for anyone. Never felt seen. Until Bubba.

She wrapped her arms around his neck and hugged him.

Wiley smiled as he returned the hug.

"Thank you for such a good hug," he said.

"Thank you for my swing."

Chapter 13

THE CREW WAS STILL WORKING WHEN LUNCHTIME arrived, so Wiley coaxed Ava inside long enough to feed her, and then miracle of miracles, there was a knock at the back door, and when Wiley answered, the crew boss was there.

"It's up and ready for testing," he said. "Got a spare kid around here who might be willing to do that?"

"Me!" Ava shrieked. "I would be willing!"

Wiley laughed. "Then wipe your hands and face and let's do this," he said.

An hour later, Wiley and the crew were all still out in the yard, watching Ava try out all of the attachments on the swing set to make sure they were safe and secure. Once they were good to go, Wiley paid them, but Ava was launched into perpetual motion, sitting in the swing, going back and forth, and higher and higher. She had a death grip on the ropes and a gaze fixed on the sky above, and in her mind, she was flying, and Bubba was the wizard who'd given her wings.

She played until Wiley went out to bring her inside.

"Ava, you need to come in, get a drink, and cool off," he said.

She didn't argue. She didn't beg. She just slid down the slide into his arms.

"It was fun, Bubba," she said.

"Good. It's not going anywhere. The swing is here now and so are you. It'll be ready to play on after you've rested."

She nodded and let him carry her into the house. He carried her to her bedroom, sat her on the bathroom counter and washed her face and hands with a cool, wet washcloth, gave her a big drink of water, then carried her to bed. Her head was drooping as he took off her shoes and tucked her and Pinky in beneath a blanket.

"Sleep good, Ava," he whispered.

"Bubba?"

"What, honey?"

"You'll still be here when I wake up?"

"Yes," he said.

She sighed, pulled Pinky beneath her chin, and closed her eyes.

Wiley went back to clean up the kitchen, but then his phone rang. When he saw caller ID, he quickly answered.

"Hello, darlin', and the answer is yes."

Linette laughed. "You don't even know why I'm calling."

"Doesn't matter. For you, the answer is always yes," he said.

She sighed. "Wiley Pope, you make me crazy."

"I'm not discussing what you do to me. What's up?"

"I'm getting off work in about an hour. I have a little gift for Ava. If you're going to be home, I'd like to drop it off."

"What are you doing this evening?" Wiley asked.

"Just going home."

"Stay and eat an early supper with us. I'm not cooking this evening. We're having pizza, but she doesn't know it."

"I would love to," she said. "But I think I'll go home and get out of the nurse duds and into comfortable clothes before I come over, okay?"

"Yes."

She laughed. "Is your answer always going to be yes?"

"Only for you," he said.

"How are things going with Ava?"

"Better than expected, and still sifting through the shock of what comes out of her mouth."

"What do you mean?" Linette asked.

"The revelations of her daily reality. She doesn't even know how horrifying some of them are, or how neglected she was. What she knew was all she knew. I'm working on fixing what I can. Today, we got a swing set put up in the backyard. She wore herself out playing on it. I just peeled her off the slide and put her to bed. You know what she asked me before she closed her eyes? Will I be here when she wakes up?"

"Oh lord, Wiley...bless her heart. Bless her heart. Are you sure I won't be an intrusion? I don't want to mess up what you have going."

"You can't be an intrusion, darlin'. And you can't mess up what's going on in my life, because part of it is you."

"You had me at *darlin'*," she said, and disconnected.

Wiley groaned. He wanted her in his arms—lying beneath him in a bed. But right now there was a little-bit-of-nothin' child who needed him more. And the upshot of that, which surprised him most, was how much he needed to be there for her.

———

Ava slept two hours, and the moment she woke up, she went to find Wiley. He was watching TV in the living room and smiled when he saw her. She crawled up in his lap and laid her head on his shoulder.

"Hey, sleepyhead. Did you and Pinky get a good rest?"

"Yes. Is it time for cartoons?"

"It's always time for cartoons somewhere," he said. "Let's see if we can find some."

She'd just settled in at the corner of the sofa when their doorbell rang.

"Do we have company?" she asked.

"Sounds like it," Wiley said, and went to the door, knowing it was likely Linette.

Ava's interest in cartoons suddenly shifted when the dark-haired lady walked in. It was the almost wife—the woman who'd helped her in the bathroom, and she was carrying a little gift bag with a bow on it. She watched Wiley kiss her on the cheek, but Ava's sudden silence reflected her concern as to whether the woman would like her, too.

Linette immediately caught on to Wiley's intention.

"Ava! Hi, sweetheart! It's so good to see you again. May I sit beside you?"

Ava nodded.

Linette sat and handed her the gift bag. "This is for you."

Wiley sat down in a chair to watch Ava's response to Linette entering their world.

Ava might not know what to think about an almost wife, but she knew what to do with presents. She pulled the tissue paper out of the top and then looked down into the bag and gasped.

"Bubba! It's hair stuff!"

Wiley was expecting maybe shampoo, but when she dumped the contents into her lap and began sorting through them, he realized it was stuff of a different kind. Colorful hair bows with little clips attached. Barrettes of different shapes and colors, and a pretty hairbrush.

Ava's baby blues were swimming in tears. "I never had hair stuff before."

"And now you do," Linette said. "I think you should pick one out now, and I'll put it in your hair for you."

"My hair is sleepy," Ava said.

"Then we'll fix that," Wiley said, picked up her new hairbrush and tamed the flyaway curls, while she and Linette went through the barrettes and bows.

"I choose this one!" Ava said.

Linette removed the bow from the packaging, got down on her knees in front of Ava, and after a few moments, clipped it just off-center at the top of her head, where it settled within the mop of blond curls.

"You look beautiful!" Wiley said.

"I need to see," Ava cried, and bailed off the sofa and ran.

Wiley reached down, pulled Linette up from the floor and into his arms, and kissed her hard and fast.

"Gotta take it when I can get it," he said, and grinned when that made her laugh. "You're the best, Linnie. Let's go admire the new bow with her."

Ava was staring at herself in the full-length mirror hanging on the door to the bathroom. But she wasn't smiling or twirling around, like a little girl might do. She was too still and too solemn.

"Uh-oh," Wiley muttered.

Linette didn't know what was happening, but obviously Wiley did.

"Ava?"

"Can you still see me?" Ava asked.

"Yes, I still see you. Why are you so quiet?"

"I'm looking for me," Ava said.

"That is you, little sister. This is how you look when

you don't have to be quiet anymore to disappear. This is the real Ava. Go say hi to her. Tell her she doesn't have to hide or disappear ever again, and then tell her she's gonna have pizza tonight with Bubba and Linette. And when you're through talking to her, we'll be in the kitchen ordering pizza, okay?"

"Yes! I like pizza."

"Just about everybody in the whole world likes pizza."

Ava patted her bow and gave Linette a shy glance. "I like my bow, too. Thank you for my present."

Linette was struggling not to cry. "Oh, honey, you're so welcome. Come on, Wiley. We need to get that order called in, so the wait time isn't too long. Ava looks like she's getting hungry."

"Right," Wiley said. They stepped out of the room and, as soon as they were out of sight, stopped to listen.

Ava was giving herself the lowdown on her new life, her new look, and that pizza was on the menu.

"She's okay now," Wiley said, and reached for Linette's hand as they walked back to the kitchen.

"I'm ordering pepperoni for Ava, but I plan to order another kind, too. What's your favorite, pretty lady?"

"As long as it doesn't have anchovies or pineapple on it, I'm good to go," she said.

He laughed. "I knew we were a good fit," he said, and called in an order for a pepperoni and a supreme pizza with extra cheese, then kissed Linette again. "Just making sure you still taste as good as you did while ago."

"Wiley Pope, you are outrageous," she said.

"So I've been told. We have sweet tea, Coca-Cola, and orange soda in a can. Name your poison."

"I'll have the tea, and don't float my ice," she said.

"Lots of ice. Got it!"

Moments later, they heard little footsteps in the hall, and then Ava appeared and crawled up into her seat at the table, eyed the two adults, and then glanced out the window. The sun was already on the other side of the mountain. Dusk was imminent.

"Bubba, can I show her my new swing?"

"Absolutely," Wiley said. "I'll turn on the porch light, and the streetlights will be coming on anytime now."

Linette was on her feet within seconds. This was an invitation she did not take lightly. They went out the door hand in hand, and Wiley could hear Ava talking all the way across the yard.

A few moments later, Ava was coming down the slide with a smile on her face, with Linette standing at the bottom to catch her. Ava giggled, then moved to the swing to show Linette how high she could go, and then how she climbed the little ladder to get to her playhouse. As soon as she was up, she leaned out the window and waved down at Linette, and to Wiley's delight, Linette waved back and blew her a kiss. The look on Ava's face was pure joy.

By the time they went back inside, Ava had decided Bubba's almost wife was nice. After the pizza arrived, they were all at the table, trading bites of the different kinds of pizza, and laughing at the stringy cheese that just kept stretching and stretching, when Ava suddenly announced, "Miss Mattie couldn't eat this."

"Who is Miss Mattie?" Linette asked.

"She was Ava's babysitter back in Conway," Wiley said.

Ava picked up a piece of cheese and slurped it into her mouth like a noodle, then added to Wiley's explanation.

"Miss Mattie dropped dead. That's why Corina was losin' her mind tryin' to figure out what to do with me."

Wiley needed to shift the conversation. "So, why couldn't Miss Mattie eat pizza?"

"No teeth," Ava said. She picked a piece of pepperoni off her slice and popped it in her mouth.

Wiley took a quick drink to keep from laughing, and Linette was suddenly wiping imaginary sauce from her chin. They couldn't look at each other for fear they'd lose it anyway, and didn't want to laugh about the only woman in Ava's life who'd been kind to her.

"Well, that explains a lot," Wiley said. "Mac and cheese in the blue box. Soup in a can, and burglar meat. Easy food to chew."

"And sometimes a pudding cup," Ava added.

Wiley smiled. "Right. Sometimes a pudding cup."

Linette was so taken with the way Wiley dealt with this child—his little sister. And the longer she watched them, the more she realized how alike they were. Neither one of them had a filter when it came to saying what they were thinking. They were both matter-of-fact.

Ava had learned how to deal with adversity all on her own, and Wiley was the dark horse of the Pope brothers. Quick to act and react, and both of them had saved their own lives, just in different ways. That's when she knew in her heart how much she needed them to love her, because they needed her to find the way to love themselves.

Ava was savvy about adult relationships in a way most children weren't. She'd seen Corina flirting, and men coming and going from their apartment her whole life. As far as she was concerned, that was how the world of adults worked, but this was Bubba, and his world was different, and she needed to know where her boundaries were now, so she asked.

"Bubba, is she staying over?"

Wiley blinked, then looked at Linette. She wasn't giving him any signs of helping, and that was the last thing he'd expected her to ask.

"Uh, well, we hadn't planned on it. Why?"

"Well, if she's your almost wife, I thought you would sleep together. Grown-ups do that," she said, and peeled a slice of pepperoni off her pizza and took a bite.

"Right. Well, sometimes she does," he said.

Ava nodded, and then looked straight at Linette. "I will be good when you come over. I don't bother anyone. You can ask Bubba. I know how to be quiet."

Linette was overwhelmed by Ava's constant need to please. "You'll never be a bother. I don't need you to be quiet, just happy."

Ava gave Wiley the side-eye. "If she was married to you, then would she be my sister, too, like Dani and Amalie?"

"Yes, she would," Wiley said. "Would that be okay with you?"

"Yes, but would I still go to Dani's house when you're at work?" Ava asked.

"Yes, because Linnie works, too. She's a nurse. And she goes to work every day like I do," Wiley said.

Ava thought about that a minute. "But then when you came to get me, Linnie would be home with us? And we would be a whole family, like a mommy and daddy, only not?"

"Yes, that's how it would work. Would you be okay with that?" Wiley asked.

"Yes. I would like that," Ava said. "Bubba, I'm full."

"Then hop down, go wash your face and hands. You can play until bedtime, okay?"

Ava gave the both of them a look. "Linnie could stay. Bubba has extra toothbrushes," she said, and then she slid out of her chair and left the room.

Linette was in tears. This child was breaking her heart. It was apparent how badly she wanted to belong to people, but she needed the reassurance that whatever changed in her life, she would still be loved.

"Oh, Wiley. She's discovered family, something she never had, and she is so afraid she'll lose it. I've purposefully not popped in and out like we've been doing, because I thought you two needed bonding time. But now it seems like knowing I exist in your life, she needs me to be in her space, too. You won't hurt my feelings, whatever you decide, but what do you want me to do?"

"You already know I want you here. All the time. But I don't want to force you into anything. It's totally your call."

Linette hugged him. "Your 'almost wife' misses being with you, too, and I think the sooner we provide a united front, the easier it will be for Ava to feel like every other little kid who has a home and two parents."

"She's never had either. You're giving up all of the honeymoon phase and jumping into the life of a parent without so much as a ring on your finger, let alone a wedding."

"All that will come in its own time," Linette said. "I think I can tough out the burden of having to come home to a sexy man and an adorable child every night. Do I still have a toothbrush and a change of clothes here?"

He grinned. "Yeah."

"May I share your bed tonight?" she asked.

He cupped her face, brushed a kiss across her lips, and then wrapped his arms around her and pulled her close.

"I don't know how I got this lucky, but you have no clue as to how much I love you. You were the entirety of my world, and then Ava showed up at the police station with that monster of a woman. Her eyes were wide with fright, and she was sitting so still I thought she was about to pass out. Instead, I find out that was Ava being quiet so we couldn't see her, and once again, another female had taken hold of my heart. Now I have the best of both worlds. A little sister and the woman who holds my heart in her hands. Thank you for not quitting on me."

Linette laid her head on his shoulder, feeling the power and strength within him as he held her close.

"Love you, too, Wiley Pope. Now, you clear off the table and I'll load the dishwasher. And if I'm moving in here, then I'll have to get out of my lease."

"I know the landlord," he said, thinking of PCG Inc., the company that owned Jubilee. "You'll be fine."

That night, they both put Ava to bed and kissed her good night, and the light in her eyes had gone all the way to the smile on her face.

And their journey began anew, becoming a family for Ava and making love in the dark.

———

Johnny Knight and Carey Eggers were happy to be back in their house in Bowling Green. When they didn't think about it too hard, it was almost like their life before. They ate together at their table, then watched TV in bed after it got dark.

They were holding hands and half-asleep with a show still playing, when a car roared past the house, then slammed on the brakes and skidded around a corner. The sound was startling enough that Carey jumped, thinking it was someone coming after her, when Johnny grabbed her arm.

"It's the Wilson kid, remember? You're okay, love. You're safe," Johnny said.

Carey's heart was still pounding. "Do you really believe that? That the man won't try to find me and finish the job?"

"I do believe it. Tom said Gardner crossed you off the case completely as far as being any help in solving it. There is no reason for anyone to care what you're doing now."

She sighed. "Yes, okay. You're right. It's just hard not to be afraid."

"I cannot imagine what you went through alone. And when I think about it, it makes me crazy, knowing how helpless I felt when we couldn't find you."

"But we're here now, and we're together again," Carey said. "I have a phone appointment with the lawyer tomorrow. Maybe we'll know more then."

"Right," Johnny said. "Now scoot back over here. I need to feel you beside me."

She eased back beside him, threaded her fingers through his, and fell asleep. It was almost like old times, except for the healing bullet hole in her back.

They didn't talk about their situation because until she spoke to Billy's lawyer, they didn't really know what their situation was. It would be another month before she'd heal enough to carry heavy trays of food to tables again, and Johnny had to be able to walk and drive before he could go back to work.

His disability payments had finally kicked in, back

pay included, so they weren't going to starve. All they knew was that whatever happened next, they would face it together.

———

Carey was in the shower when Tom called the next morning. Johnny muted the TV and reached for his phone.

"Hello."

"It's me," Tom said. "How are you two doing? Are you okay?"

"We're good. Thanks for the DoorDash supper you sent to us. It helped not having to cook. And Carey is calling the lawyers this morning."

"Okay. I'm on my way to work. It'll be a full day, but I'm good for any errands you need run after six."

"We should be fine, but thanks, buddy," Johnny said.

"Any time, and I mean it," Tom said, and disconnected.

Carey came out of the bathroom wearing sweatpants, and no bra under her T-shirt to accommodate the healing wound.

"Want some cereal?" she asked.

"Yes, please. I'll get myself in there in a bit. I want to shave first," he said.

Carey leaned over the bed and brushed a kiss across his lips, then ran the palm of her hand against the black stubble on his face.

"Love you," she said.

"Love you more," Johnny said, and watched the way

she was moving as she left the room. She was still favoring her sore ribs and the wounded shoulder, but the bruises on her face had nearly faded away, and the hair they'd shaved from her head was growing back. He was frustrated by his own inabilities right now, but after all they'd been through, he was grateful for small favors.

A couple of hours later, breakfast was over, and the dishes had been loaded into the dishwasher. They gathered themselves at the kitchen table. Johnny had pulled up the online site for the Williams and Williams law office on his laptop, and Carey's phone, which had been part of the contents from the wreck that Sheriff Woodley had given her, had been recharged. One small piece of her world had been returned, and she was grateful.

Johnny turned the laptop around so she could see the phone number to the law office and made the call. After a quick explanation to the receptionist, she was immediately put through to Billy's lawyer, Lee Williams, Sr.

"Miss Eggers. My condolences on the loss of your brother. We understand you've been in the hospital, and we're pleased to know you're on the road to recovery."

"Thank you," Carey said.

"I'm guessing you're calling about your brother's estate. He did leave a will, you know. Are you able to come to the office?" he asked.

"I am not allowed to drive at this time, but I could catch an Uber to get there and back."

"Can I be so forward as to assume time matters here?" he asked.

She sighed. "Yes, sir, it is. My fiancé was recovering from surgery when all this happened, so he's still unable to drive, and now I'm out of commission as well. He gets compensation because he was injured on the job. I found out this morning that I was fired weeks ago for not showing up at work."

"Then I will tell you now, you are the sole heir, and your brother has taken good care of you. Fret no longer. I wish we could just handle this through a Zoom call, but there are papers you need to sign, so we'll go over details in the office."

Carey started to cry. "I'm so grateful, but at the same time so sad he's gone."

"Yes, ma'am," Lee said. "I'm going to transfer you back to my secretary. You two can figure out a time that's convenient for you to come in, and we'll have the papers ready. We'll also need a copy of his death certificate to apply for his life insurance on your behalf, and a copy to go to his car insurance. We understand the insurance company declared the car totaled, so that payoff will go into his estate, which will go to you as well."

"He had life insurance?" Carey asked.

"Yes, a five-hundred-thousand-dollar policy."

Carey gasped. "Oh my God! I had no idea. I'll see to getting those certificates and bring them with me," she said.

"He also owned his home and forty surrounding acres. In the current market, being a seller is definitely on your side, unless you plan to live there, of course. But you can be deciding that on your own. He also has two healthy bank accounts. One personal. One business. You will inherit those as well. His earthly belongings will be yours. In the interim, take care, and I'll be seeing you soon. Now hang on while I transfer you back to Linda."

Carey gave Johnny a look, and then the secretary came online, and after some discussion, Carey settled on an afternoon appointment three days hence and disconnected.

"Billy had a five-hundred-thousand-dollar life insurance policy, and I'm the beneficiary. His house and forty acres are paid for. He has two healthy bank accounts. One personal. One business."

"Good lord," Johnny said. "I would never have imagined."

"Me neither," Carey said, and then leaned her head on Johnny's shoulder. "I have to go to the lawyer's office three days from now to sign papers, and I need to bring copies of Billy's death certificate." Her voice broke. "I can't believe those words just came out of my mouth."

"You don't have to go through this alone. I have a doctor's appointment tomorrow. It's more of a checkup. I'm hoping they'll finally put me in a walking cast so I can ditch these crutches. If they do, I'm going with you."

"Thank you, Johnny."

"No thanks needed, sweetheart. I will always have your back," he said.

———

Detective Gardner had the latest forensic reports on the Eggers murder back from the lab. Junior Henley's truck had been wiped clean. There wasn't a fingerprint on it anywhere. Not even Junior's. There was no DNA. No remnants of grass or dirt. No lingering scents of anything. As far as the police were concerned, that pointed to an attempt to hide a murder. But it did not point to a particular killer, and at this point, they had three possible suspects—Carl Henley, Junior Henley, and a thug for hire named Lonny Pryor.

They had Lonny Pryor's DNA under Eggers's fingernails. That was solid evidence. And Pryor's DNA was also found on the scene at the house where Eggers died, but as Eggers's cryptic phone call mentioned, in the grand scheme of things, it meant little. A good lawyer could easily explain that away, considering the fact that the men knew each other and Pryor was a periodic visitor to the property.

The police were looking at security footage all over the area where Pryor had lived to see if they could catch him driving the truck. They finally found footage at a car wash, dated just before Lonny Pryor went missing.

So, he had been in the truck at some point. And Pryor's DNA was under Eggers's fingernails. It might pin Pryor to the murder, but it still did not eliminate the Henleys from abetting, because the truck belonged to Junior and the murder weapon belonged to Carl. What they needed was to find Lonny Pryor and get him to implicate who hired him.

At that point, their entire focus shifted back to Pryor, and acting on the assumption that he'd left town, they began checking airport reservations and bus stations. They had security footage from the bus depot but no one matching Lonny's description was visible, until they applied facial recognition to the footage and he popped up with a bald head and a vandyke beard.

A couple of detectives paid a visit to the bus station and, after visiting with employees, discovered the man from their video had purchased a one-way ticket to Miami, Florida.

Finally, a trail to follow!

The next step was to check deeper into Lonny's background. Did he go there simply to disappear, or did he have connections there? It didn't take long for them to find a Roly Pryor listed as next of kin from one of Lonny's stints in prison, and his last known address was a rural route address in Miami, Florida. Now all they had to do was find the cousin. And to do that, they notified the Miami PD that there was an arrest warrant out for a man named Lonny Joe Pryor, whom they suspected might be hiding out with a relative in the Miami area named Roly Pryor, and asked if they would go to the residence, check out the premises, and interview the owner.

The order to search for Lonny at Roly Pryor's residence was given to Homicide Detective Wesley Davis. He took two units and four officers with him, and then drove out of Miami and into the rural area of the county to the address they'd been given, with an arrest warrant in hand.

═══════════

Lonny Pryor had been at Roly's for only a short time. Long enough to feel like he was settling, but not long enough to stop looking over his shoulder. He knew the Bowling Green PD would keep looking for him. There was that thing about his DNA being all over a dead man. After hearing nothing about the woman he'd killed on Pope Mountain, he had assumed they'd never connected the incidents. And whatever guilt he still harbored, he blamed it all on Eggers.

Looking back, he was firmly convinced that Eggers's overreaction to his presence had to do with the sister being in the house—something Lonny had no way of knowing about. Seeing the gun had made Eggers fear for his sister's life, and for that reason, Billy had jumped him. He sighed. If he'd only known she was there, none of this would have had happened. But he hadn't known, and it had happened, and here he was.

It was nearing noon, and Roly had been readying his airboat for an afternoon tour when he came in the house.

Lonny had potatoes frying on the stove and a plate of fried fish already done and sitting on the counter.

"Smells good," Roly said, and went to the kitchen sink to wash his hands.

SHARON SALA288

"Just fish and taters," Lonny said.

"That I didn't have to cook," Roly added, and they both grinned at the comment.

"I'll fix the glasses," Roly said, and headed for the cabinet.

Lonny heard cars driving up and turned away from the stove to look out the kitchen window. When he saw the Miami PD logos and the men climbing out of the vehicles, his heart sank.

"Better skip my glass," Lonny muttered.

Roly turned. "Why? What's wrong?"

Lonny sighed. "They found me."

Roly frowned. "Who found you?"

"The cops. Got myself in a bit of trouble. I'm sorry, cousin."

Roly's eyes widened. "Holy shit, Lonny."

Lonny turned the fire off from under the potatoes and wiped his hands.

"I'll get the door. Don't worry. I'll make sure they know I duped you," he said, and went to answer the knock.

Chapter 14

DETECTIVE WESLEY DAVIS FROM MIAMI PD WAS PREpared for an interrogation or a fight, whichever came first. What he did not expect was for their suspect to answer the door. Yet there he was, yellow shirt, blue jeans, and sneakers, head shaved bald, and sporting a vandyke beard.

"Officers. I'm Lonny Joe Pryor. I believe you've come for me?"

Davis was startled. "Mr. Pryor, step out of the house, hands up. Turn and face the wall."

Within moments, he had Lonny cuffed. Just as he was about to hand him off to other officers, Lonny spoke.

"I lied to my cousin, Roly. This is his place. He doesn't know anything about my life. We haven't seen each other in over twenty years. I was using him to hide. He did not know he was harboring a fugitive. He's innocent of any wrongdoing."

Davis pointed at the officers. "Take him to the station."

At that point, Roly appeared in the doorway, pale and shaken.

"He's my cousin. I thought he'd just come to visit. I didn't know y'all was looking for him," Roly sputtered.

"State your name, sir," Davis said.

"Roly Pryor. I've lived here all my life. I ain't never been in trouble. I take tourists out on my airboat. That's all I do."

"Do you live alone?" Davis asked.

"Yes, sir. Been divorced awhile," Roly said.

"If we have further questions, we'll be in touch," Davis said.

Roly stood in silent shock as they drove away, then went back into the house and shut the door. He stared at the fish and fried potatoes as the silence of the house settled back around him. His wife had cheated on him. His cousin had lied to him. He thought he didn't want to be alone, but now he wasn't so sure. At least he trusted himself. He glanced at the clock. He had a tour to take out in a couple of hours, and it would be late before he got home.

He didn't like cold fish. Might as well eat it while it was hot.

———

As soon as Detective Davis got back to Miami PD, he called Detective Gardner at the Bowling Green PD. While he was waiting for the call to be answered, he bent over to pick grass seed from the leg of his pants. He'd noticed the yard around the Pryor property was in dire need of mowing, and now he'd brought some of it back with him. He was still picking at the sticktights when his call was finally answered.

"Homicide. Detective Gardner speaking."

"Detective, this is Detective Davis, Miami PD. Wanted to let you know that we picked up Lonny Joe Pryor today. We have him in custody."

"That's the best news I've had in days," Gardner said. "Was he where we thought he might be?"

"Yes, sir, and it was the craziest thing. Pryor opened the door to greet us, identified himself, and said he supposed we'd come to pick him up. He cleared the relative he'd been staying with of any guilt, and I believe him. The cousin was stunned. They hadn't seen each other in twenty-some-odd years, and he thought Lonny had just come to visit. Lonny admitted he'd lied to him just to have a place to hide."

"Okay then," Gardner said. "We'll get the paperwork rolling to extradite. The U.S. Marshals Service will transport, so you can tell your people we're coming to get him. Thanks a lot."

Davis chuckled. "For once, I can truly say, it was not a problem. I wish all the perps we go to serve warrants on were as compliant."

"That bodes well for us. There's more involved here than what meets the eye, and we need him to talk."

As soon as they disconnected, Gardner called Sheriff Woodley to let him know they'd picked up their suspect. There wasn't anything Woodley could do toward aiding their case, but if Pryor copped to killing Eggers, then that would mean he'd also come after Carey Eggers, and that would clear Woodley's case as well.

But what Gardner did not do was spread the word about Pryor's arrest around the station. He'd long suspected that Carl Henley had someone on the inside there, and he didn't want Carl or Junior to know that Lonny Pryor was in custody. He needed to interrogate Pryor to get his story of the missing Beretta and Junior's truck.

———————

Woodley notified Chief Sonny Warren that they'd served an arrest warrant on Lonny Pryor, so the mystery of who shot Carey Eggers might soon be solved.

"That's good news," Sonny said. "I'll let my men know. At one time or another, a good number of them stood guard duty while she was in the hospital. They said she was a real sweet woman. Thanks for calling."

He walked down to the break room to get some snacks from one of the vending machines, and saw Lilah Perry pulling a cold can of soda from a machine.

"Afternoon, Lilah. Like minds, here. It's snack-thirty, isn't it?"

Lilah grinned. She admired the chief and appreciated that he was congenial to everyone, regardless of their rank.

"It was for me. I'd looked at dates and numbers and

logs all day until everything was running together. Thought I'd take a quick break and get a snack while I was at it."

"I'll likely add to your work in a day or so when I finalize an open report on that woman who was shot a few weeks back."

"Oh. The one from Pope Mountain, right?" Lilah said.

"Yes, it appears the person who shot her had killed her brother the same day. She was a witness he chased down. But the DNA they pulled off the brother's body matched to a man named Lonny Joe Pryor. When they went to arrest him, they found out he'd done a runner. They finally found him in Florida. We'll extradite him back and hope he coughs up a confession."

"Oh my God," Lilah mumbled as the room began spinning around her.

Sonny saw her eyes rolling back in her head and bolted. He caught her before her head hit the floor and was about to call for help when Bob Yancy walked in.

"Chief! What happened?" Yancy asked.

"I have no idea. We were just talking, and she fainted. Help me get her up on the sofa."

She was already regaining consciousness by the time they laid her on the sofa, but the moment she woke up, she began struggling to sit up, then grabbed Sonny's wrist.

"Chief! I know Lonny Pryor. We dated briefly when I still lived in Bowling Green. And the night of that rainstorm—the one when the girl was shot—Lonny called me out of the blue. He said he needed help. That he'd had a flat during the storm and hurt himself as he was changing it. Said his knee was bleeding. I told him to go to the ER. He said he didn't have the money, and I believed that. He just wanted help with some bandages and then he'd drive home and deal with it there."

"What did you do?" Sonny asked.

"What anybody would do in such a situation. He asked me if I lived in the same place. I said yes, and ten minutes later, he's at my door. Ten minutes. How far up was it from Jubilee where the girl was shot?"

The hair on the back of Sonny's neck crawled. "About fifteen minutes or so."

"That's about right," Lilah said. "I think he thought he'd drive home on his own, but he was in pretty bad shape when he got here, so I guess he changed his mind and that's why he called me."

"Was he shot?" Sonny asked.

"Oh no! Nothing like that or I would have suspected something. He just had a deep gash in his knee and some severe bruising. Like he'd fallen on something sharp."

Sonny nodded. "Chasing down a woman on the mountain in the dark, in a rainstorm, will do that to you."

Lilah moaned and covered her face with her hands.

"I didn't know. I had no idea. I would have said something sooner!" she said.

"Of course, you wouldn't know. All the details of that incident were going through the sheriff's department. But this is valuable information they'll need to know when they interrogate him, especially if he tries to deny being in the vicinity. I'll need to take your statement. Are you okay with this?"

She frowned. "Of course, I'm okay with it. I'm just thanking my lucky stars he didn't consider me a witness he needed to remove."

Sonny nodded. "Yancy, would you help Lilah up and walk her to an interview room so we can get that statement? And Lilah, don't open that pop you just bought. It'll spew all over. I'll bring you another one when I come, okay?"

Lilah nodded. "Yes, Chief, and thank you."

Sonny gave her arm a quick squeeze. "No, ma'am. Thank you."

Yancy helped Lilah up and walked her out of the break room, while Sonny hurried back to his office. He made a quick call to the sheriff's office, and as soon as Rance Woodley answered, he unloaded the latest news.

"I'll get a copy of her statement to you as soon as it's typed up and signed. You can let Bowling Green PD know. It might help with their interrogation."

"Will do," Woodley said. "I'll tell you one thing. This is the most convoluted case I've worked on in a while, and this just added another knot."

They disconnected, and while Sonny headed to the interview room with a fresh can of soda from the dispenser, Woodley made a quick call to Detective Gardner to fill him in.

Lonny Pryor was kicked back in the Miami jail cell, going over and over the story he intended to spin. He was confident to the point of cocky. And after a discussion with a jailhouse lawyer, he opted not to fight extradition. There was no purpose in it. His DNA had tied him to a murder.

Two days later, two U.S. Marshals arrived to transport him back to Bowling Green, Kentucky. They walked him out of the PD in leg irons and handcuffs, put him in the back of a government van, and handcuffed him to the inner wall.

"Make yourself comfortable, Mr. Pryor. This is a fifteen-hour drive," the marshal said, then climbed out of the back of the van and shut and locked the doors.

"Well, hell," Lonny said. The bench he was on was hard and narrow, and it was going to get a lot harder and narrower before this ride was over.

———

Detective Gardner walked into the Bowling Green PD the next morning, ready for Pryor's interrogation. He knew Pryor had been booked into their jail sometime after midnight, and a lawyer had been contacted. They were just waiting for word that the lawyer was on-site, and it came just before 11:00 a.m.

Gardner took his partner, Detective Rainey, to the interview room with him and entered to find Pryor handcuffed to the table, his lawyer sitting at his side, and a guard in the room with them. Both Pryor and his lawyer looked up as the detectives entered.

Gardner and Rainey sat. Gardner opened his file, sifted through a couple of papers, then nodded to his partner, who turned on the recorder.

"For the record, Detective Gardner, and Detective Rainey, in the interview room, beginning interview at 11:12 a.m. with Lonny Joe Pryor, and his lawyer, Ellis George. Mr. Pryor, for the record, please state your name, age, and occupation."

Lonny was ready. He wanted this over with, and hedging would only delay the inevitable.

"Lonny Joe Pryor. Fifty-seven years old. Self-employed."

"And what kind of work do you do in that capacity?" Gardner asked.

"I served in the military. I have worked as a bouncer, a security guard, and a bounty hunter. For the past four years, I've worked for Carl Henley."

Gardner's heart skipped. "Exactly what did you do for Mr. Henley?"

"Oh, delivered messages, ran errands...pretty much whatever he needed done that he didn't want to do for himself."

"Did you work for Junior Henley, too?"

Lonny snorted. "To a degree. Junior Henley is his daddy's mouthpiece. He delivers orders, but he does not give them."

"What was your relationship with Billy Dean Eggers?"

Lonny blinked. "Was that his middle name? I never knew. We knew each other. Sometimes we ran in the same circles. We often played poker at the same club. Sometimes at the same table."

"Would you consider yourself Eggers's friend?" Gardner asked.

Lonny shook his head, and then remembered the tape. "I don't have friends. I have acquaintances."

"Then, let me ask this another way. Did you and Billy Eggers have a fight on the day he died?"

"Yes. We'd been playing cards most of the night at my place. We had a row. He accused me of cheating. We roughed each other up a little. He left before daybreak."

"Were you cheating?" Gardner asked.

Lonny grinned. "Yeah. Billy was smart. He was on to me before I knew it, and I didn't have the balls to admit it. That's why we had the ruckus."

"When was the last time you were at Billy's place?"

"Maybe the week before. I don't remember exactly," Lonny said.

"You were seen driving Junior Henley's truck. We have video of you in it at a car wash."

"Yeah, Junior wanted it washed. I took it to the car wash and then drove it back to his place."

"Junior says you won it off him in a poker game."

"Well, I did, but he never gave up the title, and he's the boss's son, so I didn't challenge him on it. Anyways, I haven't owned a car in some years. I like to drink. So I take an Uber to get where I need to go, or someone picks me up."

Gardner was worried. This wasn't going the way he'd planned. It was time to quit pulling punches.

"Billy Eggers is dead. Your DNA was all over his body and beneath his fingernails. You were seen driving Junior Henley's truck prior to the murder. That truck was seen at Eggers's property the morning of his murder. You called in to the station hinting that Carl and Junior Henley were people to look at in the death. Would you like to explain that?"

Lonny's gut knotted. Who in hell had seen him at the house besides the girl? He glanced at his lawyer, then sighed.

"What I know is that somebody put a bug in Carl Henley's ear about a new crew trying to muscle in on Carl's territory. Carl thought Eggers might have heard something specific about it. I know he told Junior to deal with it. But Carl Henley did not, by God, tell me to do anything to Billy Eggers. He did not send me to his house. I had not even talked to Carl Henley in at least four days before Eggers was murdered."

"What do you call Carl Henley's business dealings?" Gardner asked.

Lonny shrugged. "He buys and sells stuff."

"What kind of stuff?" Gardner asked.

Lonny shrugged. "I don't know for sure."

"For someone who thinks he's in the know, you don't know a lot, do you, Lonny? Did you know someone else was in the house when Eggers was murdered?"

Lonny blinked. "I can't say as I did."

"Well, there was. She was Eggers's sister, and she got away. Or at least she tried. Someone trailed her all the way through two counties, then into the woods during a storm up on Pope Mountain, and shot her in the back."

"That's a terrible thing to hear...brother and sister dying like that on the same day."

"Oh, she didn't die," Gardner said. "She survived. Tough little thing. Oh...I see you are favoring your left knee. Did you hurt it?"

The skin was crawling on the back of Lonny's neck. *The girl was alive?* "Yeah, fell and cut it on a rock while I was changing a flat."

Gardner leaned forward. "Do you know a woman named Lilah Perry?"

Lonny had a good poker face, but his gut just tied itself into a knot.

"Yes, I know Lilah. What's she got to do with anything?"

"She can place you within ten minutes of Jubilee on the same night Carey Eggers was shot, that's what. You called her for help. Said you cut your knee and she felt sorry for you and helped you. But when she found out your DNA was all over a murdered man, she didn't feel sorry for you anymore."

Lonny hadn't prepared for these two revelations, and he was backpedaling, trying to come up with reasonable excuses for all of it.

"So, it's common knowledge that you issued an arrest warrant for me, and she read it in the papers or something. So maybe she just wants to get back at me for when we broke up."

"Nope. We did not publish your name. Her boss told her."

"Her boss? What are you playing at here?" Lonny asked.

"Oh, we're not playing. Lilah Perry is a records clerk for the Jubilee PD. Her boss is the police chief. He mentioned it in passing, and she put two and two together."

Lonny blinked. *The police? Lilah works for the police?*

"So, Mr. Pryor, do you have anything you want to add to your statement before I charge you with the murder of Billy Eggers and the attempted murder of his sister, Carey?"

Lonny froze. His eyes widened as he sat there, absorbing the reality that his witness was still alive and that Lilah worked for the enemy. Then he leaned over and whispered something into his lawyer's ear.

At that point, Ellis George spoke up. "Mr. Pryor might have more information to share, but it would involve charging him with lesser offenses."

"We can't ignore murder," Gardner said.

"Manslaughter on Billy Eggers," George said.

"And ignore the bullet in Carey Eggers's back? I think not." Gardner said.

Lonny whispered in his lawyer's ear again.

"That's the deal," Ellis George said.

"In return for what?" Gardner asked.

"Testifying against Carl and Junior Henley for running drugs in and out of the country," George said.

Gardner's eyes narrowed. "Mr. Pryor, would you care to revise the elaborate story you just gave us now?"

"Not until I have your word regarding the charges," Lonny said. "Otherwise, I'll take my chances in court. You can wave your security footage in front of the jury, and I'll repeat in court what I just said to you."

Gardner eyed his partner. "I can't make that call. I'm pausing this interrogation to consult with my superiors. The time is 12:02 p.m."

Then he and his partner got up and left the room.

Lonny glanced at his lawyer. "I'm just gonna rest my eyes a bit. I'm a little short on sleep." Then he scooted his chair back just enough to lay his head down on the table and wished himself to hell.

Gardner was in the conference room with his captain and the Bowling Green police chief, on a Zoom call with the district attorney. It didn't take long for them to come to a consensus. Taking Carl Henley down mattered. A lot. They knew the court would agree that both Eggers and Pryor had fought, because Eggers's knuckles had been bruised and bloody. With a good lawyer on Pryor's side and evidence of a fight between the two men, the court would have a difficult time proving premeditated murder. But Pryor wasn't getting off of the attempted murder charge. That bit about tracking prey through a storm and shooting her in the back was in cold blood.

Gardner had his orders. He and his partner went back into the interview room, resumed the recording, and began again.

"Your charges will be reduced to manslaughter for Eggers, but you do not get a free pass on hunting down an innocent woman and shooting her in the back. That's attempted murder any way you look at it. And you can't admit to one and deny the other, because the same gun was used in both crimes. Now start talking."

Lonny sighed. It was the best he could expect, and he wasn't going down alone. If Junior Eggers hadn't sent him there with a gun, none of this would have happened. But he was glad the woman was still alive. That shit had bothered him to no end.

"Junior Eggers called me to come to the house, so I did. Carl wanted Junior to pay Eggers a little visit, and Junior didn't want to go, so he sent me instead. All I was supposed to do was talk to him. Tell him what Carl had heard and ask him if he was involved."

"What had Carl heard, and involved in what?" Gardner asked.

"Drugs. Word on the street was some new crew was about to muscle in on Henley's territory, and he wanted to know if Eggers knew anything about it, or if he was involved. So, as I'm about to leave, Junior hands me this gun. I didn't know it was Carl's until later, and yes, I was driving Junior's truck. I drive up. The only car there is Billy's. I didn't know anyone else was there, and it wouldn't have mattered to me anyway. I was just asking questions and delivering a message.

"Eggers let me in. I asked him about what Carl wanted to know and warned him that if he was involved, Carl would not let it slide. Billy freaked out on me. Started shouting, telling me I was wrong and full of shit. He took a swing at me. Then we fought, and I panicked in the fight and pulled the gun, thinking he'd back off and that would be that. But he jumped me. The gun went off. And he was dead. None of that was supposed to happen."

"So how did you come to go after his sister?" Gardner asked.

Lonny shrugged. "I didn't know until later that it was his sister. But I think that's why he freaked out on me. When he saw the gun, I reckon he was thinking about protecting her. I saw her running to his car from the living room window. By the time I got outside, she was already out of the driveway and flying. I ran back inside in a panic, grabbed Billy's phone to see if he had a tracking app on the phone for his car, and he did. That's how I found her. I couldn't let her get away and give me up."

"She never saw your face. She never heard your name. She didn't hear anything that was said between either of you. She just heard the gunshot and ran, like her brother told her to do. She could never have fingered you. Not in a million years," Gardner said.

Lonny sighed. "I'll be damned. Well, it don't matter. I'm glad she lived. I'm sorry about Billy."

Gardner kept pushing. "We need the names of Carl's fences and everything that has to do with his involvement. How does he transport the drugs? Where does he get them? Who are his suppliers?"

"I can answer some of that, and I will testify against the both of them in court."

Gardner nodded.

Lonny added. "Just know that you're gonna have to keep me alive to make all that happen, which means you better get Carl and Junior off the street before he gets a chance to put a hit out on me, and the moment they go to jail, the people he does business with are going to go to ground or disappear."

"So, start talking, Lonny. We need names. We'll make a sweep and pick the whole lot of them up at once. They'll be so busy trying to make deals for themselves, they won't have time to worry about you."

"Carl will want revenge. He'll want me dead anyway. If you want to nail him to the wall, Junior is the one who will break. He's only along for the ride on Daddy's money anyway. Daddy is the one who lowers the hammer on what's happening, and who lives and who dies."

"Duly noted," Gardner said. "So, we're listening. Start talking."

"I only know what I saw when I was with Junior, or what I heard him talking about. There are food trucks and a pawnshop he drops drugs off in. Carl has a storage unit on the outskirts of the city. I went there with Junior once to drop off some boxes, but I don't know what was in them, or what's in the storage unit. I've seen a couple of invoices from trucking companies, and I think he has a shell company somewhere around the seaports in Houston bringing stuff in from overseas. One night I drove Junior home from a club because he was too drunk to drive, and he kept talking about wanting to go on the next run into Mexico to pick up a new shipment. I thought he meant drugs, but he was talking about girls for the sex trade. That's about all I know for sure," Lonny said.

Gardner nodded, and ended the interrogation.

"Lock him up," Gardner said. "No visitors but his lawyer."

The guard took Lonny out in shackles and cuffs as Gardner began stirring the pot. They had but a short time to find the leads and evidence needed to get search warrants and arrest warrants before Henley got wind of what was happening and destroyed the evidence.

Gardner went back to the office, gathered a half-dozen detectives around him, and began issuing orders about researching properties in Henley's name.

"I want around-the-clock surveillance on both Carl and Junior. Take note of everywhere they go and who they meet with. Now get cracking. We don't have much time."

Linette was, as of today, officially moved out of her apartment, her furniture was in storage, and she was at the elevator with a briefcase containing her personal papers, waiting for her ride down.

When the elevator car finally arrived and the doors opened, Cecily Michaels was standing against the wall, staring at her.

Linette stepped inside and then leaned against the opposite wall and stared her down.

"I haven't seen you around much," Cecily said.

Linette shrugged. "I moved out today. Now, you won't be seeing anything of me."

"Leaving town?" Cecily asked.

"No."

Cecily persisted. "See Wiley lately?"

"I live with him," Linette said.

Cecily rode that gut punch like a boss and never blinked. "Heard he has a kid. You can have him."

Linette laughed. "He was never yours to give away, and the child is his sister. Have a nice life, Cecily...and while you're at it, grow up."

The elevator stopped. The doors opened, and Linette walked away, leaving Cecily so speechless that she forgot to get off.

———

Ava had been in Wiley and Linette's life long enough that she had settled to his satisfaction. He would go back on duty now, and she would be at Dani's house during the day. He'd already pre-enrolled her at school, and she'd been taken with the building and all of the new playground equipment. The idea of making friends appealed to her, but she was so easily hurt, and he was dreading it.

His mom told him that's how all parents felt with a new baby—when they had to go back to work, and leave the child in someone else's care—and to be glad that it was his sister-in-law, and not some random day care. But his separation anxiety was real, and there were times when he couldn't remember a day without Ava and Linette in it.

Last night, Ava had forgotten to panic about closing blinds and curtains when it got dark, and she'd giggled hysterically as Linette was helping her bathe and get ready for bed. Wiley heard both of them chattering as if they'd known each other forever, and she wasn't afraid now to ask for food when she was hungry. The first time she rejected a suggestion and asked to play in her room instead, he felt justified. Ava Dalton was becoming the child she was meant to be.

But what they'd planned to do today was over the moment he woke up to a downpour. There would be no playing outside, or going to Reagan Bullard's campground and playing on the waterslide, or riding a pony. That would have to wait for another day. Linette was off, too, and they could have just spent the day together in the house, but he wanted to do things with her, for her, while he had the time, so they opted to go up the mountain to visit Shirley and Sean.

"Are we climbing the mountain today, Bubba?" Ava asked.

"Driving. We're driving there," he said. He put her little yellow poncho over her head and buckled her in the back seat, as Linette slipped into her raincoat and got into the front seat.

"Does Grammy know we're coming? Does Sean know we're coming?"

"Yes, ma'am. I already called them," Wiley said.

He jumped in the car and lowered the garage door as they were driving away. The rain was steady enough that he had the windshield wipers on high as he drove through town and took the road headed up the mountain. Everything was lush and green around them, and the rain was blurring the landscape just enough that it wasn't long before it began to feel as if the greenery had swallowed them whole.

Chapter 15

AVA WAS BIG-EYED AND QUIET IN THE BACK SEAT, with Phillip, her little brown squirrel, tucked under her arm. She'd left Pinky at home because she didn't want to get her wet, but was certain Phillip would enjoy the ride. Now she was afraid to turn loose of him, for fear he'd jump out and get lost in all the trees.

Linette was a little nervous. This was her first inclusion in a family gathering, although the whole family knew she and Wiley were living together. Wiley kept glancing from Linette to the rearview mirror to check on Ava, making sure she was okay. He could tell she was a little unnerved and wished she was sitting in his lap, instead of in the back seat all alone.

"You okay back there?" he asked.

"I'm okay. Is it far?" she asked.

"Not too much farther."

Ava frowned. "Are you sure you know the way?"

He laughed. "Yes, honey. I lived with Grammy and Sean until I went to work for the police. Then I moved to town so I would be closer to work.

"There aren't any houses here," she said.

"Oh, there are lots of houses, but the families live off the road. You'll see. Grammy's house is like that. Do you see that mailbox?"

She peered out the window, squinting through the rain. "Yes, I see it."

"The road leading up into the trees beside it is how you get to that person's house. So, everywhere you see a mailbox, there is a house at the other end of that road."

"Does Grammy have a mailbox?" she asked.

"Yes, she does, but it's too early for the mail carrier, so we can't get her mail and take it to her," he said.

Ava thought about that. She knew what mailboxes were, but they'd never had one. Linette and Bubba's mail went in the mailbox on their porch, and all of Corina's mail had gone to a little box in the lobby of their apartment building, but then the thought of Corina made her frown.

Wiley saw the frown, but opted not to comment. Sometimes a person just needed to have a moment on their own without everyone wanting to know what was going on. He felt Linette's anxiety and gave her hand a quick squeeze.

"Love you, baby. You're fine, too."

Linette rolled her eyes.

He winked.

A few minutes later, he began slowing down and then turned off the blacktop onto the gravel road that led to home.

Ava was all eyes now, a little cowed by the heavy

growth of trees on either side of the driveway, but as they came out into a clearing and she saw a house with a big front porch that was as long as the house, she felt better.

Linette was in awe. This was anything but a simple mountain home.

"Is this home?" Ava asked.

"This is your grammy's home," Wiley said, and pulled up as close to the porch as he could get. "Stay seated, sugar. I'll get you out and we'll make a run for it."

She grinned, entranced by the idea. "Make a run for it, Linnie," she echoed.

Linette laughed. "I will," she said, and pulled up the hood of her raincoat and made a run for the porch.

Wiley pulled the hood of his windbreaker up over his head and jumped out, circling the car to get Ava and Phillip. He pulled the hood of her poncho up over her head, tucked Phillip into her arms, and yanked her out.

They were immediately hammered by the falling rain, and Ava squealed.

"Run for it, Bubba!"

Wiley laughed and was up the steps and under the cover of the porch in seconds. They left their rain gear on a chair by the door and went inside.

"Mom! We're home!" he called.

"I'm in the kitchen," Shirley called.

"Something smells good," Wiley said.

Linette sighed. *Here we go.*

Ava shivered with expectation. This house felt happy. She tucked Phillip back under her arm as they went.

Shirley was drying her hands at the sink when they walked in. "I'm so glad you all came to see me! Welcome to our home, Linette. You and Ava turned on the light in my very dreary day. The weather is a scandal, isn't it?" Shirley said.

Wiley grinned. His mom had always referred to bad weather that way. "Don't I turn on any lights?" he asked.

She swatted at his backside. "You light fires, Wiley. That's why I love you."

He dodged the swat. "What smells so good?"

"Brownies. I made a double batch."

"My favorite," Wiley said, then wrapped his arms around her, swung her off her feet and danced her across the floor, delighting in the laughter in his mother's eyes.

"Put me down easy. I'm still wearing this cast for another week," she said when he finally stopped.

Linette was seeing yet another side of the man she loved, and completely smitten by his playfulness.

Shirley was still shaking her head as she gave Linette a welcome hug. "I'm so glad you were finally off work on the same day. Welcome to the family."

Ava was transfixed. She'd never seen grown-ups dancing like this. Then Shirley sat down at the kitchen table and opened her arms.

"Grammy needs a hug and an introduction. Who's your little furry friend?"

Ava crawled up in Shirley's lap. All the tension from the drive up disappeared when Shirley hugged her.

"This is Phillip. He's a squirrel. Squirrels live in trees. I brought him to see the trees."

Shirley brushed the curls away from Ava's forehead and hugged her again. "What a good idea!" she said. "Are you and Bubba and Linette going to stay and eat lunch with us?"

Ava's gaze shifted to Wiley. He nodded.

"Yes. We are staying," Ava said.

"Sean and Amalie are in his office. You need to let them know you're here," Shirley said.

Ava slid out of Shirley's lap, waiting for Wiley to lead the way.

"Amalie's home today?"

Shirley nodded. "Amalie got up and announced that the weather was horrible. Said she didn't have any appointments and wasn't going to the office just to sit there all day and watch it rain."

"My brother married a smart woman," Wiley said. "Come on, squirt. Let's all go say hello."

Linette walked beside Wiley as Ava skipped her way down the hall to Sean's office. Amalie was sitting on the couch with her laptop, and Sean was at his desk on the computer when they walked in.

Amalie saw them first and began smiling. "Sean, we have company!"

Sean turned around, saw the tiny blond with the fuzzy brown squirrel under her arm, and grinned. "Linnie! Ava! What a fun surprise on this yucky, rainy day!" he said. He gave Linette a quick hug, then swooped Ava into his arms and kissed her cheek, delighting in her giggle. "What are you guys doing today?"

"Having lunch with Grammy," she said.

Amalie reached for Linette's hands, felt an instant connection, and smiled.

"We're going to be such good friends," she said, then gave Ava a hug. "Who's this little fuzzy-tail tickling my arm?" she asked.

"My squirrel. Bubba bought him for me. His name is Phillip."

"I have a penguin sitting on a shelf in our bedroom. His name is Frank. Would you and Linnie like to meet Frank?" Amalie asked.

Ava glanced back at Wiley.

"Go on, honey. I'm going to talk to Sean a little bit and then go back to the kitchen with Grammy. This is your home, too."

Ava blinked. "I have three homes?"

"Yep. Can you believe how lucky you are?" Wiley said.

Amalie winked at Linette, took Ava by the hand, and the three of them left the room.

Sean gave Wiley a look. "Everything going okay?"

"Better every day," Wiley said. "I'm going back to work tomorrow and dreading it. Mom calls it separation anxiety. I guess I'll get used to it."

"Once you realize that she is fine with you coming and going, you'll settle. You're both trying to find your footing."

"I guess. I'll just be glad when all the final papers

have been signed and I have no need to even think about Corina Dalton again."

"What about Linette? How's all this business with her?"

"She loves me. She settled into this like we'd been together all our lives and Ava was the cherry on the cake. She's amazing."

"Don't forget Ava is my sister, too, and we're available for sleepovers," Sean said.

"Again, here's me, with this gut feeling of not wanting to let her out of my sight," Wiley said. "The things she reveals about her life without even realizing the horrors of it are the things of which nightmares are made."

Sean frowned. "That bad, is it? Does she cry for her mother?"

"Hell no. The only time that child cries is when she's afraid I'll give her back," Wiley said. "But I did learn one funny thing. You remember me telling you what her old babysitter fed her? The mac and cheese in a blue box. Soup in a can. Burglar meat? Well, guess why? Miss Mattie didn't have any teeth."

Sean chuckled. "That's awesome. So, the old lady's food choices were limited to begin with."

"Yes, but it appears she was generous to a fault with what she had. Ava's food at Corina's house was scraps from her mother's plate. The first time I took her out to eat, I asked her if she liked french fries. She said no. Come to find out, it's because Corina was giving her the cold ones she didn't eat."

Sean frowned. "I can't believe you knew about her and Clyde."

"I knew about all of them. Corina, Ruby, Justine, and Della. I saw him out and about with all of them at one time or another."

"Good lord! You never said a word," Sean said.

Wiley shrugged. "What good would it do? Hurt Mom more by telling her? Damn sure couldn't confront Clyde without taking a beating. He gave out enough of those to all of us for no reason. I wasn't going to give him an opening to kill me."

Sean sighed. "I'm sorry, little brother."

"It was never your fault, I'm not little anymore, and Mom's safe. And now we've rescued Ava from that same pit of despair, and I'm at peace in the world in a way I never was before."

Then they heard laughter coming from down the hall and Sean grinned.

"I told you Amalie was going to be smitten with Ava. She sees herself in her."

"Well, you and Amalie found each other again, and then her father found her, and we found Ava and saved her, too, so I get it. Look, I'm sorry to interrupt your day. I'll go bug Mom for a while."

"I'll come with you. I'm not working on anything urgent."

Shirley was sitting in her recliner in the living room with her feet up and her eyes closed, but she heard their footsteps.

"I'm not asleep. I'm just reveling in the sound of a child's voice in this house, and the laughter coming up the hall. I've been longing for grandbabies, but I never imagined Wiley would be the first one to bring one home."

Wiley leaned over and kissed her forehead. "Thank you for taking on the job."

She looked up. "Oh, honey, loving that child isn't a job. It's a blessing."

Then they heard the sound of running feet, and Ava ran into the living room and went straight to where Shirley was sitting and plopped down beside her.

"There's my darling!" Shirley said. "What have you girls been doing?"

"Amalie showed me her pick-one named Frank, and she is just like me."

Wiley caught her pronunciation of the word *penguin* and hid a smile.

"How is Amalie like you?" Wiley asked.

"We thought we were all alone, but we were only lost. Somebody always wanted us. They just didn't know where we were, and now they do!" Ava said.

Wiley gave Amalie a grateful glance.

"And Linnie and I are so happy we found you," he said.

A gust of wind suddenly rattled the windows beneath the porch. Ava's eyes widened nervously.

"Is it a tornado?" Ava asked.

Shirley pulled her close. "No, honey, it's just wind and rain. You're safe."

Ava pulled Phillip up beneath her chin. "I'm safe," she echoed.

But Wiley knew Ava didn't feel safe. She was just making sure all the people around her thought she was because she didn't want to cause trouble.

He leaned forward, resting his elbows on his knees. "Ava…"

Her gaze shifted to his face.

"Are you scared?"

She nodded.

"When you are, it's okay to say that."

Ava looked up at Shirley. "Grammy, I'm not all fine."

Shirley pulled her up in her lap and wrapped her arms around her. "Then we'll just cuddle up until you are. Okay?"

Ava nodded, slowly settling against the soft pillow of Shirley's breasts. Grammy smelled good, and her voice wasn't angry or loud. The grown-ups started talking, and she stilled, trying to find that quiet space where she always disappeared, but fell asleep instead.

"Bless her sweet heart," Shirley said when she noticed Ava had gone to sleep. "Wiley, that wind's really come up. You better rescue your rain gear from the porch before it blows away."

"Oh, good call," he said, and headed for the door to retrieve it. All the excess rain had already dripped onto the porch, so he left the raincoats on the floor, just inside the front door.

As it neared noontime, Shirley laid Ava down on the

sofa and covered her with an afghan, while they went to finish lunch.

Shirley had been stewing a chicken, so while Amalie deboned it, she mixed up some dumpling dough and began dropping it into the boiling chicken broth by the spoonful, then turned down the heat and covered the pot, while Linette was setting the table.

Wiley was standing at the back door, looking out across the rain-drenched land and thinking how peaceful it was here, when Ava came meandering into the kitchen.

Still waking up, she leaned against Wiley's leg.

"Hey, baby girl. You woke up just in time to eat. Are you hungry? Grammy made chicken and dumplings."

"Do I like them?" she asked.

He picked her up. "Well, you like biscuits and you like chicken and you like soup. Chicken and dumplings is all of that in one dish."

"Yum," she said.

He grinned. "Exactly, and brownies for dessert."

She turned and looked at the table and all the chairs.

"Where do I sit?" she asked.

"By me. And you're going to need a booster in your seat, aren't you?"

Shirley heard them and turned around. "Wiley, some of Mom's old phone books are in the bottom of the hall closet. Grab some of those and put a clean towel over them for her to sit on. They're probably dusty."

"Yes, ma'am," Wiley said, and put Ava down. "Come on, sugar. Let's go find you a booster seat."

A few minutes later, Ava was sitting up at the table, waiting and watching, and when everyone sat down with their bowl of chicken and dumplings, Ava watched them, then picked up her spoon and took a bite.

"I like this!" she said, and ate her way down to the bottom of the bowl. By the time they got down to eating gooey chocolate brownies, she'd forgotten about tornadoes.

━━━━━━━

The rain let up before dark, but Wiley and his girls were already home. Ava was playing in bubbles in her bathtub. Wiley was across the hall folding a load of towels, and Linette was in the shower. He was close enough he could still hear Ava's chatter. The curtains were drawn, and the shades pulled down. One more day together, and then they'd have a new routine. He hoped she was better prepared for it than he was.

Tomorrow was all about Wiley going back to work. He'd already called in to the precinct to make sure they had him on the roster, and Dani had checked in to remind Wiley to pack a little bag for Ava so she'd have a change of clothes and whatever else he thought she might want while she was at their house.

Ava was excited. She was talking about bird feeders and learning how to feed birds, and playing with Dani, so Wiley rode the wave of her excitement with her. He kept reminding himself that Ava was used to being moved from place to place. And she had come to trust him enough to know that if he said he would pick her up after work and they'd go home, she believed him.

Dani told him not to worry about feeding her breakfast before he brought her over. She could eat there. Dani was excited. Ava was excited. Wiley was resigned to their reality.

———

The next morning was a whirlwind of hustling, and the first thing was getting Ava awake and dressed. He woke her with a pat on the shoulder while Linette was in the kitchen making coffee.

"Wake up, baby girl. Today you go to Dani's house and I go back to work, remember?"

Ava unrolled herself from the covers like a hatchling coming out of an egg. First one leg and arm, then another arm, and then her other leg before sitting up on the side of the bed.

"I get to feed birds," she mumbled.

He tousled her curls. "Yes, you do."

"What do you do at work, Bubba?" Ava asked.

"Oh…all kinds of things, but mostly just making sure people follow rules, like don't drive too fast. And don't take things that don't belong to you, and helping people who get hurt. Now hustle. Brush your hair and teeth and get dressed. You're having breakfast with Dani."

"Yay!" Ava said, and headed for the bathroom.

Wiley laid out clothes for her to put on, and got a kiss in passing from Linette, who was on the way into the bedroom to get dressed.

"Dani's making Ava's breakfast, and I'll grab something at the precinct before briefing. Don't try to cook for either of us. It will make you late," he said.

Linette wrapped her arms around his neck. "Okay, but I will definitely need hugs before I leave."

He lowered his head and kissed her until she forgot to breathe, then cupped her backside and pulled her close enough to feel what she was doing to him.

"Thank you for the reminder, and hold that thought," Linette whispered, and went to make sure Ava was getting dressed.

The next time Wiley came out of his bedroom, he was wearing his uniform and his gun and carrying his hat, and Linette was across the hall, talking to Ava and helping her make her bed. He poured himself a coffee to go, then went to check on both of them.

"You're going to have such a good day," Linette said. "You'll have to tell me all about it this evening, okay?"

Ava eyed her closely. "I will save my memories for you."

Linette hugged her. "That might be the sweetest thing anyone has ever promised me. Thank you, baby. I need a goodbye hug now. I have to hurry so I won't be late."

Ava wrapped her arms around Linette's neck, giggled

when Linette kissed the side of her cheek, then patted the bow Linette had clipped in her hair today to make sure it was still in place as Linette left the house.

Ava was putting on her backpack and tucking Pinky under her arm when Wiley appeared in the doorway. Startled by his gun and uniform, she stopped, suddenly remembering this was how he looked when she first saw him.

"Are you ready to go?" he asked.

"You look like before."

"Before?" And then he got it. "Oh. You mean when we first saw each other? Well, I'm supposed to look like this when I go to work," Wiley said. "You know policemen wear uniforms, right? This is how people know who we are."

"Corina hides from the cops."

Wiley resisted the urge to roll his eyes. "The only people who hide from the police are people who did something wrong, so that's her problem. We don't have a problem."

Ava nodded. "We don't have a problem."

"Right, and you sure look pretty today. Now, let's hit the road, missy. Dani's waiting."

The drive from his house to Aaron and Dani's was less than five minutes, and when he pulled up in the driveway, Aaron's car was still in the drive.

"Looks like Aaron is waiting to see you," Wiley said as he pulled up behind his brother's car. He got out, helped Ava out of the car, and was heading up the steps with her when the front door opened and Aaron came out in a uniform just like Wiley's.

"Good morning, little sister," Aaron said. "You and Dani are going to have the best day."

"We're feeding birds!" Ava said.

"I need a hug," Wiley said, and dropped down on one knee as Ava threw her arms around him.

"Bye, Bubba."

"Goodbye, sugar. See you this evening, okay?"

Dani appeared in the doorway. "There's my girl. Are you ready for today?"

"Wait!" Aaron said. "I need a goodbye hug, too."

Ava was all giggles, and that was all Wiley needed to see as he watched Dani and Ava go inside.

Aaron saw the look on Wiley's face and clapped him on the shoulder.

"Let's go, Brother. We don't want to miss the morning briefing."

———

Carey and Johnny were in an Uber on their way to the lawyer's office.

"You look pretty enough to marry," Johnny said, and rubbed the little engagement ring on her finger that he'd given her four months earlier.

"I saw myself in the mirror. I still have a fading purple eye and two scars on my head."

"I would love you if you were bald, but the hair will

grow back, and you know it. I'm hoping my bones decide to grow back together, too."

"Doctor said you're doing great. The X-rays showed a lot of healing."

"I know, and I'm so grateful to still have a leg," he muttered.

She gave his hand a soft squeeze. "Are you sad you can't go back to being a lineman?"

He thought about it a minute. "Truth? No. That fall killed the thrill of bird poop on my shoulders."

She laughed.

He winked, then leaned over and kissed her square on the mouth. A couple of miles further, and their driver was pulling into the parking lot. He jumped out, then circled his car, opened the door for Carey, then helped Johnny out.

"Call if you guys need a ride home. I'll let the company know so they can page me if I'm in the area," he said.

Carey nodded, handed Johnny his cane, and waited while he steadied himself in his new walking cast before they headed indoors and were immediately taken into their lawyer's office.

Lee Williams stood up as they came in, helped Johnny into a chair, and seated Carey before taking his seat.

"First, I want to tell you that you were your brother's world, and it is good to put a face to a name," Lee said. "Every time he came in to add to the will or update it, he talked about you, so take heart from how dearly you were loved."

Carey's eyes welled, but she was smiling. "It was mutual. He was all I had when I was growing up, and he never failed at making sure I wasn't in need."

"Okay then," Lee said. "Down to business. Everything I told you over the phone is here in writing. We'll go over it together, and then you'll sign in the necessary places. I'll file the documents and get the property deeds registered in your name. Did you bring copies of the death certificate?"

She handed him a manila envelope. "I wasn't sure how many I would need so I ordered ten copies."

Lee removed the number he needed and handed the envelope back to her, then began to read the will aloud, stopping in necessary places to explain a detail. He kept going until they were through. Carey signed everything.

"The estate will now go into probate," Lee said. "It's a lengthy process. It could take up to six months. But Billy was prepared for that and had a separate bank account in your name only. The money in it is yours now. All you have to do is sign the authorization card at the bank. He wanted to do that in case you needed it to tide you over while the rest was being settled."

"I never knew he was so smart about stuff like this," Carey said.

"The name of the bank is in the file I just gave you. It's near your address, so it should be easily accessible for you. I'll stay in touch with you throughout the process and keep you updated on progress."

"How do I pay you for all this?" Carey asked.

"Oh, that's already been taken care of," Lee said. "What I'm doing now is finishing up the services Billy paid for on your behalf."

Carey reached for Johnny's hand, too moved to speak.

"What about inheritance taxes?" Johnny asked.

"Good news for you," Lee said. "The State of Kentucky does not have an inheritance tax. If you sell property later, you will of course pay tax on that, but everything Carey inherited is free and clear."

Carey was sobbing now and laid her head on Johnny's shoulder.

Lee picked up the phone and buzzed his secretary. "Linda, would you please bring a couple of bottles of water into my office?"

"Yes, sir. Right away," she said, and a few moments later came in with two cold bottles of water and put them on his desk.

"Please, help yourself," Lee said as he pushed a box of tissues toward Carey.

She grabbed a handful and began wiping her eyes and mumbling apologies.

"No need for that, Miss Eggers. You don't apologize for grief or love," Lee said.

Johnny opened a water bottle and handed it to Carey. Taking a few sips was enough to stop the tears and gave her time to regain her composure, while Johnny sent a quick text to Uber. They were about ready to go.

"Thank you," Carey whispered. "Is there anything else I need to do now?"

Lee shook his head. "We have the ball rolling. Now it's just a matter of getting it pushed through the courts. There aren't any issues. It just takes time. I'll walk you out," he said.

She gathered up the file with all of her copies, then tucked her hand under Johnny's elbow to steady him on the way out. They sat down in the outer lobby until they received a text that their driver was outside, then walked out into the sunshine.

———————

Gardner and his team had been scrambling for the past two days. He had the evidence he needed for the search warrants being served this morning, and he was pulling Junior Henley back in for questioning at the same time, purposefully leaving Carl hanging, hoping he'd panic and head for wherever he was storing records.

Carl Henley was as antsy as a virgin bride on her wedding night. After being taken in for questioning, only to be released after his statement, he'd heard nothing, and Junior seem oblivious to the implications. His son seemed to think that just because they'd been let go, they were in the clear.

Carl knew better. It felt more like a ticking time bomb, with no way of knowing when it would blow. He had no idea they had Pryor in custody, and his snitch on the inside wasn't communicating. This was not a good sign, either.

He and Junior were at breakfast when the doorbell rang, and before he knew it, the police were taking Junior back in for questioning.

"Daddy! Call the lawyer!" Junior kept shouting, as they walked him out the door, but Carl was already on the phone, doing just that.

No sooner had he disconnected, than his cell phone began to ring. His contacts were being hit with search warrants and being taken in for questioning, and they'd just hauled Junior off again. This didn't look good. For the first time in Carl Henley's life of crime, he panicked, and made a crucial mistake.

All he could think of was getting rid of evidence, and he headed for the old rent-controlled apartment that had been his childhood home—the one place he kept for himself after his parents died that not even Junior knew about.

At first, keeping it had been nothing but a sentimental gesture. Sometimes he'd go there just to disappear from the world he'd created, surrounded by his parents' old furniture and the simplicity of the tiny kitchen and old dining table and chairs. He even slept in his childhood room, rather than the master where his parents had been.

But after a while, he realized it was the perfect place to turn into a stronghold, and began the work to make it one in increments. He began by hanging a bulletproof door, then turning his parents' bedroom into his workplace, and having a steel door with combination locks installed. He soundproofed the room to make phone calls on burner phones, and considered himself unbreachable and untraceable.

But now that his world was crumbling, the cops would start digging through everything. They would eventually find out about the place, and it was that fear that sent him out the door. His phone kept ringing, but he didn't take the calls. He couldn't help them when he couldn't even help himself.

Only he was mistaken in believing his stronghold was still a secret. The cops *had* already discovered the property in his name. They also knew the apartment was vacant, but that he had been seen coming and going from there, and when nothing of consequence was found in the storage unit, this information prompted them to get a search warrant for that address.

The detective they'd had tailing the Henleys witnessed the police hauling Junior off the estate, and when he spotted Carl leaving the estate in haste and heading to the seedier part of the city, he called it in.

Police were already nearby, waiting for orders, and when they got them, they quickly moved into the building and took cover in an empty apartment across the hall from Carl's stronghold, waiting and watching through the peephole until Carl unlocked his door and was walking inside.

They came storming out with their guns drawn and followed him in, served the search warrant, and then handcuffed him to a table, put a guard on him, and began to search. At that point, Detective Gardner arrived.

Carl began cursing him, and shouting. "You have no right to do this!"

"That search warrant on the table in front of you says we do," Gardner said. "You have about two minutes to decide whether you're going to give us the combination to the locked room and open your safe, or we'll get a locksmith and a blowtorch and blow the hinges off this place and let ourselves in."

"Where's Junior? What have you done with my son?"

"He's being interrogated as we speak," Gardner said.

"You don't have anything on either of us!" Carl shouted.

"Well, yes, we do. After we picked up Lonny Pryor a few days ago, he decided it was in his best interests to cooperate fully with our investigation. And now we know that the fact you were worried about a new gang invading your territory is part of what got Billy Eggers murdered and connects you to the whole ugly mess of attempted murder on his sister as well. One thing led to another, and here we are."

Carl's expression froze, and then as Gardner watched it melt to one of dismay, he suspected Carl was sadly facing his future.

"So, which will it be? Blow the doors off the hinges, or the combination? And blowtorch the safe, or the combination?"

"I want my lawyer," Carl muttered.

"Well, he's at the PD with Junior, who's already peed his pants. They're making bets on how long it's going to take for him to break. It's in your best interests to cooperate now," Gardner said.

"I'm not helping you do anything," Carl muttered.

"No problem," Gardner said, and waved down a couple of officers. "You two, Mr. Henley is ready to transport to the PD. Book him in for abetting a murder and an attempted murder, and for buying and selling illegal drugs. We'll add other charges as the need arises."

Carl Henley already knew he was a dead man. His death would be in his contacts' best interests. Junior was probably going to wind up some goon's girlfriend in prison, and it would serve him right. All of this chaos was his son's fault. Every stinkin' bit of it. When they put Carl in the back seat of the police car and drove away, all he kept thinking was that he should have let Junior drown.

Chapter 16

JULY WAS ALMOST OVER, AND WITH AVA AND LINETTE settling into his space like they'd always been there, Wiley felt like the world was beginning to make sense again.

He was coming out of the morning briefing and waiting for his partner, who'd gone to pick up a warrant they needed to serve, when he saw Lilah Perry coming up the hall with an armful of files. Usually, she was all smiles, but this morning she appeared distracted.

Someone banged a door behind her, and when they did, she flinched, lost hold of the files, and then watched in dismay as they fell to her feet.

Wiley ran toward her, but when he knelt down to help, he saw that she was crying.

"Hey, hey, honey, no harm done here. Let me help," he said, and began gathering up files and handing them to her, then helped her to her feet. "See, all done and no harm, no foul."

"Thank you, Wiley. It's been a rough week," she muttered.

"Why? What happened?" he asked.

She rolled her eyes. "Everyone knows, and I feel like a fool."

"I don't know. I went away for a week dealing with family stuff and still playing catch-up. What's wrong?"

Lilah sighed. "Oh, I forgot. Anyway, you know about the girl who was shot up on Pope Mountain a few weeks back?"

"Yes. Carey Eggers. I was put on guard duty at the ICU when she came out of surgery."

"Long story short, they figured out who did it and arrested him, and I didn't know anything about it until weeks later, when the chief said something in passing. When I heard the name of the man they'd arrested, I fainted from the shock, and I am not a fainter. I not only knew the man from when I used to live in Bowling Green, but he called me the night the Eggers woman was shot, gave me some big story about hurting himself trying to change a flat in that rainstorm, and begged me to help him get bandaged up so he could drive home.

"I hadn't seen him in years, but relented. And when he showed up at my house about ten minutes later, I fixed him up and he went on his way. And then after hearing what the chief said, I was horrified that I had helped a murderer escape. I told the chief everything. My statement helped put Lonny Pryor at the location of the attempted murder and verified the timeline of when she'd been shot."

"But that's good, Lilah! Why would you be embarrassed?" Wiley asked.

"I'm embarrassed that I even knew someone who was capable of murder, let alone help him in any way."

"Try being related to a killer and living it down," Wiley muttered. "You just got played because you have a good heart. There's no shame in that."

Lilah didn't know what Wiley was talking about, but she guessed it was personal. "You're right. I was making a big deal out of nothing after all."

"No. It was a big deal to you, and how it made you feel matters. Now, I better hustle before Leedy drives off without me."

He took off at a lope, caught up with his partner outside, and jumped into the cruiser. "Sorry. Lilah dropped a bunch of files in the hall. I stopped to help her pick them up."

"No problem," Doug said. "We're just doing a welfare check on a man. His neighbors haven't seen him in days and he's not answering his phone."

Wiley groaned. "Please God we don't find a body in a state of putrefaction. I'll take a house full of cats and fleas before that."

Doug grimaced. "Damn, Wiley. Those are some god-awful choices."

"Yes, they are. My two worst fears for welfare checks, and so far, so good, but I don't want to encounter one today."

They left the precinct and headed east out of town

toward Reagan Bullard's campground, then turned south at the first section-line road and drove into a trailer park, and noticed the rows of mailboxes.

"What's the address?" Wiley asked.

"It's trailer number eleven," Doug said, and slowed down so they could read the numbers as they passed.

"That one!" Wiley said, pointing to a rusting white and turquoise single-wide with the front half of the skirting lying on the ground.

They pulled up in the drive behind a black Dodge truck. The hood was up, and the engine block was hanging on chains from a nearby tripod.

"If he's gone, he left afoot," Wiley muttered, carefully eyeing the concrete blocks stacked up for steps as he went up onto the stoop and knocked.

No one answered.

Wiley knocked again, and then called out, "Mr. Carlisle, it's the police. Are you able to come to the door?" He knocked again, but heard nothing.

"Try the knob," Doug said, and to their surprise, the door was unlocked.

"Here goes nothing," Wiley muttered, and stepped over the threshold.

The trailer was hot. Dirty dishes were in the sink and on a table, and flies were rampant all over the kitchen. But there was no one home. And after a quick check of the bedrooms, it was evident that Mr. Carlisle was no longer in the residence.

"No clothes and nothing in the bathroom," Doug

said. "Not even a toothbrush. We'll check the bus station when we get back into town to see if he took the bus, but it appears he left of his own accord. The only crime here is stinking garbage and dirty dishes, which is a reminder to me of why I do not ever want to be a landlord."

"Then we're done here, and I need some air," Wiley said.

After a quick trip by the bus station to check the records, they learned Sam Carlisle left Jubilee two weeks ago on a bus bound for Denver.

"Welfare check completed," Doug said as he got back into the car. You call and notify the chief ASAP so the family will at least know that much. I'll write up the report later."

"Will do," Wiley said, and made a quick call off radio to give Chief Warren the details.

───────────

Linette was on duty in a patient's room, administering a pain med via the shunt in the patient's IV.

The patient, a twelve-year-old boy who was two days out of surgery for the repair of a compound fracture to his leg from a rollover on his ATV, was miserable. His leg was in a cast from the ankle to just above his knee. He couldn't get comfortable, and when she'd entered the room with his meds, he was alone and in tears.

"I'm sorry you're having such a rough time, Davey, but these pain meds will kick in very soon."

He swiped at the tears on his face, embarrassed to be caught crying. "I know. Thank you, Miss Linnie."

"You're welcome, honey. Looks like someone moved your table too far away to reach the water. Are you thirsty?"

He nodded.

"We can fix that," she said, and poured some cold water into his cup, held the straw up to his lips, and watched as he drank.

As soon as he'd had his fill, he sank back into the pillow and glanced at the clock.

She saw the frown on his face. "Where is your mother this morning?"

"She got a phone call from Dad. Said she had to run home for a bit, but she'd be right back. That was three hours ago."

"Hmm, there are a dozen reasons why she might be delayed. I'll bet she shows up soon. In the meantime, why don't you just close your eyes and let those pain meds do their job?"

Davey was already getting sleepy and closed his eyes.

Linette straightened his covers, gently brushed her hand across his forehead, and then waited until she knew he was out. But as soon as she left the room, she went straight to the nurses' desk.

"Anyone here know why Davey Andrews's mother suddenly left this morning? He said she got a phone call. Said she'd be right back, but that was three hours ago. He's worried. I administered his pain meds, so he's asleep now, but this is unlike her. She has hardly left his side since they brought him in."

Then a nurse behind the desk looked up and pointed. "There she comes now, Linnie, but I think something's wrong."

Linette turned around, saw the panicked look on Shelly Andrews's face as she reached the station.

"I saw a man in the parking lot getting out of his truck with a gun in his hand. I don't know who he is, but I saw him entering the lobby just as the elevator doors closed on me."

Before any of the nurses could react, they began to hear gunshots, and then a lockdown alarm. Linette's first thought was Wiley, and then she thought of their patients. Who the hell was this man and who'd he come after?"

"I'm shoving the recliner against the door to my son's room," Shelly said, and ran.

The RN jumped into action. "We have twelve patients on this floor and six nurses. Get anyone who's mobile into a bathroom. Tell them to lock the door and stay in there. The rest of you, get in a room with a patient, bar the door as best you can, and wait for an all clear on the intercom."

The nurses turned and ran.

———————

The dispatch went out to every police car and to every handheld radio.

"Active shooter inside Jubilee Hospital. Proceed with caution. Hospital is on lockdown."

Wiley was in the passenger seat of the patrol car, and Doug Leedy was driving when they received the dispatch. Doug hit the lights and sirens and made a U-turn in the street before speeding off toward the hospital with more than a dozen other police cars doing the same thing, coming from all over town.

Wiley tried to call Linette, but when the call went to voicemail, his heart sank. He told himself it was because she was likely involved in securing her area and patients, but that didn't alleviate his fears.

They reached the hospital in less than two minutes and saw people pouring out of the front entrance on foot, trying to get to their vehicles. Wiley and Doug got out of the patrol car on the run.

A man came running toward Doug and Wiley, carrying a small child.

"How many shooters?" Wiley shouted.

"One man. Big, heavyset. Long gray hair in a ponytail. Black T-shirt and jeans. Black and white baseball cap," the man said, then kept going.

Wiley gave the description over a handheld radio. "People running out of the hospital. None appear to have been wounded. We're entering the front lobby now."

Aaron and Bob Yancy came in right behind them, as did a half-dozen other officers, while more were still en route, including Chief Warren and his driver.

Inside the lobby, a security guard was sitting against

a wall, bleeding from a bullet wound in his arm. Aaron stopped to apply a tourniquet. Calling for help was futile. Everyone on-site had taken cover.

"I'm going to move you behind the front desk," Aaron said, and helped the guard into a hiding spot. "Stay down. I'll radio your location to the EMTs."

"No! Don't!" the guard said. "He has a two-way. He can hear all of your traffic."

"Shit," Aaron muttered. "Do you know him?"

"Gene Terry, ex-EMT. Got fired and went to prison for stealing and selling drugs. I didn't know he was out," the guard said.

"Do you see where he went?" Yancy asked.

"Into the stairwell."

"How many security guards on duty?" Aaron asked.

"Three, so there's two more besides me. One might be in the ambulance area and one patrols the perimeter."

Wiley overheard the conversation and took off running while Aaron sent a cryptic message over their handhelds.

Go to emergency channel.

Then he issued a second warning there.

Shooter has ears. Took the stairwell. Maintain radio silence or use emergency channel.

Wiley paused in the stairwell to listen, trying to see if he could hear footsteps, and heard nothing. He sent Linette a brief text, knowing she'd pass the info along to the nurses.

One shooter in the building. Took the stairwell.
We're searching floors. He has a two-way. We're
maintaining radio silence to keep him from knowing
what we're doing. We'll find him. Stay safe.

━━━━━━━━

Linette read the text, then forwarded it to the hospital link
that would automatically send an alert to every employee's phone. It put all of them on the same page with what
was happening. But it didn't make her job easier.

She was holed up in a room with a ten-year-old
patient named Crystal, who was recovering from a
car wreck. She and her family had come to Jubilee on
vacation, then had a wreck outside of town before they
arrived. Her mother was in a room on a different floor,
recovering from hip surgery. Her dad had been flown to
Bowling Green for burn treatments.

Linette had been particularly empathetic toward
the little girl for having to be alone throughout her
ordeal and had headed straight for Crystal's room for
lockdown.

Crystal had heard the alarms, and people running
and shouting, and was already terrified and sobbing
when Linette came running into her room.

"What's happening?" she cried.

"We're going to hide from a bad man," Linette said.
"But don't worry. I'm going to be right here with you
the whole time. Okay?"

Crystal froze. "Is this like school lockdown? Does the man have a gun?"

Linette nodded. "Exactly like that. So, we know what to do, right?"

"I want Mama," Crystal sobbed.

"I know, but your mama is on a different floor, and she's in bed, too. Someone is taking care of her, just like I'm taking care of you, okay? Now you can watch me while I push this empty bed across our door."

Once she had blocked the door, Linette moved back to stand beside Crystal. She'd already come to terms again with the possibility of dying, and it made her sad. But she knew her role in this chaos, and if the shooter came into this room, he would have to go through her to get to the child.

She glanced down at the little girl again and could tell her pain meds were still making her sleepy. "Just relax, sweetheart. Close your eyes and rest. I'm here with you."

———

Wiley knew Linette worked on the third floor, but he had no idea which room she'd taken shelter in. It took everything in him not to storm up the stairs and go find her, but he couldn't. They had to clear floors in order, going one hospital room at a time before moving up to the next level.

They had officers on guard at every stairwell and at every elevator, on the off chance that the shooter slipped past the searchers and tried to escape the building. It was a tedious and tension-filled search. They'd heard no more gunshots. And there was no one talking anywhere. The officers were communicating with hand signs as they cleared the first floor, and then the second.

They were back in the stairwell on their way to the third floor when Doug Leedy caught a glimpse of movement above him and saw the backside of a man in a black T-shirt and cap dart into an exit door onto the third floor. But it was the long gray ponytail that solidified the ID.

"He's on the third floor!" Doug shouted, and immediately radioed the message on the emergency channel so the other searchers in the building could converge.

Wiley leaped past two other cops on the stairwell, hit the latch on the exit door, and flew into the hall. He caught a glimpse of the man running down the hall on the left, and took the right junction instead and started running parallel, while following the sound of the man's footsteps.

———

Gene Terry knew the cops were coming. He'd heard them in the stairwell. He'd already knew he would be going back to prison if they caught him, but he'd made his peace with dying. He just had payback on his mind. He'd already taken out the security guard and ambulance driver who'd ratted him out to the cops, and the only one left standing was an RN on the third floor. He'd put a bullet in her head, then one in his own, and be done with it.

The moment he exited onto the floor and heard nothing and saw no one, he headed for the nurses' station. He saw the corner of the desk from twenty yards away and increased his speed, but as he took the turn, he realized the desk was empty.

"Connie Parsons! Where the hell are you? Come out now or I'm gonna start shooting at everyone!" he roared, then aimed his gun at the first door in front of him and fired, and then kept firing at every door as he ran.

He turned the corner at the nurses' station on the run, still shooting at doors, and didn't know there was a cop coming down the hall behind him until he was tackled from behind. He went down hard, hitting his chin on the floor and biting his tongue in the process. His gun went flying, and he was struggling to breathe when someone grabbed his wrist, yanked his arm behind his back, and pushed it so far up he could feel his own hair.

The cold snap of steel around his wrists was shocking, and he began trying to resist with his free arm until the yank on his cuffed wrist was so sudden and hard it made him scream.

Then there was a voice in his ear, speaking with a calm that made him shudder.

"You move like that again, and I'll yank that arm off your shoulder."

The pain was still rolling up Gene's back and neck when the man twisted his other arm behind his back and cuffed it, too.

At that point, Gene began banging his head against the floor, screaming in frustration, and then began seeing the boots and legs of a dozen uniformed officers and realized he was surrounded. And again, he heard that voice, deep and sarcastic this time.

"Normally, boys, you'd pay money for the sideshow freak, but this one is giving you a performance for free. It's called, 'How long will it take for the asshole to knock himself out?'"

Three officers yanked Terry up from the floor. Blood was pouring from his forehead, his nose, and his chin. He spit blood on the floor and then looked up into the face of the cop who'd run him down, and thought, *No wonder I couldn't breathe. He's a fucking giant.* And then he blinked and saw another cop approaching and thought he was seeing double, until he realized there were two of them.

Unaware Aaron was coming up behind him, Wiley stared until Terry was the first to look away.

Aaron radioed an all clear, and moments later, the hospital relayed the all clear through their intercom.

But all clear meant nothing to Wiley until he heard Linette's voice. He was on the phone, listening to it ring, but it wasn't until he heard Linette's voice that he breathed easy again.

"Wiley?"

"It's over, honey. Shooter's down. What room are you in?"

"Three thirty-four."

He looked around and then shuddered. One door away from where he stopped the shooter. That door would have been next.

"I'm coming in," he said, and pushed past the crowd to get to her.

Linette was already dragging the bed away from the doorway when he came inside. He took one look at her face and wrapped his arms around her.

She was trembling but silent, and she was afraid to turn him loose for fear her legs would go out from under her.

And then Wiley saw the little girl asleep in the bed behind them and immediately thought of Ava.

"Who's your little friend?" he asked.

"Her name is Crystal. Oh my God, Wiley. Oh my God," she whispered, and hugged him again.

"I know. I've never been so scared," Wiley said. "Losing you wasn't an option. I'm sorry, baby, but I've got to go. We're still in cleanup mode."

Linette nodded. "Understood, and thank you for that text. It was a lifesaver for all of us. See you at home later."

"Absolutely," he said, and went to tend to business.

The relief of confirming that no one had been injured on the third floor from Terry's random shots was huge. The wounded security officer was in the operating room getting a bullet dug out of his arm. They found one deceased ambulance driver in the ambulance bay and two wounded visitors hiding in an elevator.

It was late in the day by the time everyone was accounted for and then, for the cops, the paperwork began.

Linette got off work before Wiley and went by to pick Ava up. Seeing that sweet little face as she picked her up was all the medicine Linette needed. She and Wiley had lived to fight another day, and then had the gift of coming home to her.

"Did you have the best day ever with Dani?" Linette asked.

"Oh, yes! We made cookies to take home and I read a new book. We played outside and we watered the flowers. I played in the sprinkler and my swimming pool."

Linette glanced at Dani and saw the level of fear she'd hidden from Ava while worrying about her own husband and family, in the midst of today's chaos.

"Go get your backpack and we'll head home," Linette said and put Ava down.

She took off running, and as she did, Dani reached for Linette and held her close.

"I was so scared for all of you," she whispered. "Was it bad?"

Linette nodded. "They caught him on our floor. He was shooting into the doors of patients' rooms as he ran down the hall."

"Aaron said that Wiley caught him."

Linette nodded. "In a flying tackle, stopping him

one door away from me and my ten-year-old patient. I'm still having nightmares about the bank robbery."

Dani saw tears in Linette's eyes and hugged her again.

"I said prayers. We love you. You are the best thing that could have ever happened to Wiley and Ava. I hope you know that," Dani said.

Linette sighed. "They're the best thing that's ever happened to me."

And then Ava came running back. "I'm ready!"

Dani handed Linette the sack of cookies on the hall table as she walked them to the door.

"Ava helped cut out the dough and decorated every one of these herself," Dani said.

Ava beamed. "All by myself. Dani did the oven. I'm not old enough for the oven."

"Amazing," Linette said. "How did Bubba and I get so lucky?"

Ava reached for Linette's hand. "'Cause Corina's an ass," she announced, and led the way out the door.

Linette could hear Dani laughing as she shut the door, and rolled her eyes. She could almost hear those words coming out of Wiley's mouth. This tiny blond and her black-haired wild man were two peas in a pod. She couldn't wait to get home. Love and sanctuary awaited.

That night, after their supper was over, Linette was in their bed in her pajamas watching TV, with Ava tucked up beside her. Wiley came out of the bathroom, fresh from his shower, and saw them sitting side by side, their gazes glued to the screen. After the drama of the day, and the fear he'd had that something would happen to Linette before he could find her, the sight of such a simple scene was a gut punch. Then she looked up.

"We're saving you a seat," she said.

Wiley took a deep breath and crawled into bed. Now Ava was sandwiched between them. He reached over Ava's head and put his hand on Linette's shoulder. *Love you,* he mouthed.

Love you more, she mouthed back.

"What are we watching?" Wiley asked.

"*A Bug's Life,*" Ava said.

"Is it good?" Wiley asked.

"Oh yes. So good, Bubba."

"And why is this movie so good?" he asked.

"Because they know how to be little and hide, so people can't see them—like me," Ava said.

"I don't want you to hide. I want everyone to see how pretty and how special you are," Wiley said. He scooped her up in his arms and hugged her until she giggled, then dropped her back down between them. "We need popcorn. Can't watch a movie without popcorn," he said. "Be right back."

Linette watched him lope out of the room with a longing to be lying in his arms.

"We're a-havin' popcorn, Linnie!" Ava cried.

Linette laughed. "We sure are. Bubba is the best."

Ava scooted herself beneath Linette's arms. "You're

my best, too," she said, and then giggled again at the scene on the screen.

Linette gently ruffled Ava's curls. "Thank you, sweetheart." The scent of popcorn wafted down the hall.

A few minutes later, Wiley was back with a big bowl of popped corn. He sat it in Ava's lap and then scooted in beside her.

Ava's eyes widened. "I get to hold the bowl?"

"Yep, and you get the first bite, and then we'll help you eat it," Wiley said. She picked up one kernel and put it in her mouth. "Yum, Bubba!"

Wiley winked. "Okay, Linnie, my love, Ava says, 'Yum.' I guess that means it's good enough to eat."

All of a sudden, a little Pixar movie had turned into an event, and by the time the movie was running credits, Ava was asleep with her hand still in the popcorn.

"Poor baby," Linette said. "I'll get the popcorn. You carry her to bed."

Wiley scooped her up into his arms and carried her across the hall. The bed was already turned down, and Pinky was on the pillow, waiting for her sleeping buddy. He tucked the doll in her arms, watched as Ava rolled over onto her side, and then covered her up.

He stood for a few moments, making sure she had settled, then leaned over and brushed a kiss across her forehead.

"Love you, baby," he whispered, and was starting to leave the room when he heard a sleepy little voice mumbling behind him.

"Love you, Bubba."

"Love you more," he whispered, and walked across the hall.

The lights were out. The covers were turned back on their bed, and Linette was stretched out beneath them, wearing nothing but a smile.

Wiley closed and locked the door behind him and stripped out of his gym shorts as Linette turned out the lamp, leaving the room lit by the bathroom night-light and the fire between them.

He slid into bed beside her and pulled her close.

"No talking," Linette said. "We've already said it all and it's over. We don't make love like it might be our last time together. We make love because we're here."

He said nothing as he slid over her. He was already hard, and she was so hot he could feel it, even before he slid inside her.

Chapter 17

Two days later, Corina Dalton received a notice from the Faulkner County Courthouse to appear before the judge to officially cede custody of her daughter. She read the letter and then threw up her hands in glee and began dancing around the apartment, shouting, "I'm free, I'm free. I'm free at last."

This cleared the way for her job on the cruise ship and cut the last link she'd had to Clyde. It would be like before she ever met him. No Clyde. No kid.

To celebrate, she made an appointment at a hair salon to get her hair and nails done, and maybe she needed a new outfit, too. She didn't want to look like white trash. It never occurred to her that every nuance of her existence was a symbol of that phrase.

The only downside would be having to face Wiley Pope. He had a hair-trigger temper and was as unpredictable as they come. She was a little bit afraid of him, but confident that nothing would happen in the judge's chambers, and when it was over, she'd never have to see him again.

Wiley received a notice to appear on the same day and immediately contacted Ray Greeley, his lawyer in Conway, and agreed to meet outside the judge's office before the hearing. In four days, he would officially become Ava's legal guardian. As soon as he got the notice, he chartered a chopper to fly him to Conway on that day, then went to talk to the chief.

Sonny Warren was at his desk, gathering up notes for the morning briefing when Wiley knocked.

Sonny waved him in. "Morning, Wiley. What's up?"

"I just received papers about the court hearing for my guardianship of Ava. I need next Monday off."

"Done, and none too soon," Sonny said. "I've held my breath, wondering what fresh hell that woman might come up with before this was made final."

"As have I," Wiley said. "I've chartered a helicopter. The hearing is at eleven a.m. I'll be there and back in time for supper and on the job bright and early Tuesday morning."

Sonny blinked. "Can you afford that?"

"I have friends," Wiley said.

Sonny laughed. "Let me guess. You have a cousin somewhere."

Keeping the family secret about being the owners of the entire town of Jubilee was nonnegotiable. Every business owner knew the land and buildings, along with a share of the profits, belonged to PCG Inc. But only family knew that PCG stood for *Pope, Cauley, and Glass*, and that every family member on the mountain received sizable quarterly dividends, which were banked in a different city and in a different bank.

"Something like that," Wiley said. "Besides, Ava is worth it."

"She's settling in then, I take it?"

Wiley nodded. "Linnie and me and Ava make three. They're my ride or dies. Thanks, Chief. See you in the briefing room."

Sonny smiled to himself as he watched Wiley walk out, remembering how pretty Shirley Pope was when they were in school together, and how crushed he'd been when she married and moved away. Whatever hell she'd gone through in life, the Pope gene held true. She had raised four of the finest men he'd ever met.

———————

Linette got off work before Wiley and picked Ava up and took her home.

After a short burst of chatter in which Ava told Linette everything she'd done in the day, she went outside to play on the swings.

Linette could see her through the windows as she worked, and marveled at Ava's continuing transformation. She was gaining weight, her skin and hair looked healthy now, and the most important change of all was Ava's manner. She didn't hide in the shadows. She wasn't afraid to speak up. She was learning to give hugs and kisses first, instead of tolerating the reception of them from other people. She was happy, and it showed. And for Linette, who dealt with sick and suffering children all day long, coming home to this child was like a breath of fresh air.

While she was peeling potatoes, her phone rang. She glanced down at caller ID and then quickly wiped her hands to answer.

"Mom! I'm so glad you called," she said.

Just hearing her daughter's voice always made Angela Elgin smile.

"Well, I'm calling to find out more about this Wiley Pope. Your texts are full of him and Ava."

"He's fabulous. She's adorable. I love them so much. How's Dad?"

Angela laughed. "Did you just change the subject?"

"Maybe," Linette said. "All I'm going to say about them is if you want to meet them before the wedding, then you'd best find time to pay a visit. We don't have a spare room, so book a room in one of the hotels, and let me know so I can take off a couple of days while you're here."

Angela gasped! "Wedding! I didn't know things had gone that far!"

Linette sighed. "I have loved him since the moment I saw him. We had one date that went haywire, and then no contact with each other, which was all my doing, until that attempted bank robbery."

"That was horrifying, but how was he connected to—"

"He's the one who stopped the robbers. He saved our lives and took a bullet in the chest for his troubles. I thought I was watching him die, and then I realized he was wearing body armor. Long story short, he proposed on our second date. I do not want to do life without him. Ava came later. We're already a family. He's in the process of becoming her legal guardian. Once all that's done, then we come next."

Angela was silent for a moment. "Understood, and I'm happy for you. Does he have family in the area?"

Linette laughed. "A whole mountain full, plus a bunch in the valley. He's one of four brothers. One's a policeman like him. One is the head pastry chef at the Serenity Inn, and the other one is an IT specialist. His mother was a Pope, as in Pope Mountain... Remember it from when we came here on vacation?"

"Oh, my goodness. Well, then I won't worry about you not having family close by anymore," her mother said.

"You and Dad are retired. I'm not. So, you two have to come see me." Then she glanced out the window and saw Ava limping toward the house. "Gotta go. Looks like Ava needs me. Love you."

She disconnected and hurried outside. "Honey, did you hurt yourself?

"Something's in my shoe," Ava said.

"We probably should have changed from sandals to sneakers," Linette said as she picked her up. "Let's get in out of the sun and see what's happened."

They were coming in the back door as Wiley was coming in the front.

"I'm home!" Wiley shouted.

"We're in the kitchen," Linette said as she sat Ava on the island and began taking off her shoe.

Wiley walked into the room just as Linette dropped the little sandal on the floor.

"What's going on?" he asked.

"Something hurts my foot," Ava said.

"It's a little pebble," Linette said as she brushed it off the bottom of Ava's foot. Then she took off the other sandal and brushed the bottom of that foot, too, making sure it was okay. "How about you play inside barefoot for a while?"

Ava nodded. "Miss Mattie took off her shoes so her feet could take a breath."

Wiley grinned. "Miss Mattie was a wonder. She took good care of you, didn't she, Sister?"

Ava nodded. "Sometimes I got the last bite."

"Thank God for Miss Mattie," Linette muttered, and brushed sweaty curls off Ava's forehead.

Wiley lifted Ava down from the counter. "Go tell Pinky about your day. I need to change out of my uniform."

"Okay, Bubba," Ava said, and ran out of the room.

Linette immediately turned and wrapped her arms around Wiley's neck. "Welcome home, my love," she said, then kissed him.

His hands slid around her waist, then down her hips,

pulling her closer. She was in his blood, and he had things to share.

"The guardianship thing is happening. I'm flying to Conway on Monday. I chartered a chopper. The hearing is at eleven a.m. One last face-to-face with Corina, and then she's out of our lives forever," he said.

Linette blinked. "You can afford to do that?"

"Yes, and darlin', once we say, 'I do,' I have a story to share."

"More secrets?" she said.

"Only one, but it's a good one. Let me get changed, and I'll help you with supper."

Linette cupped the side of his face. "Well, however you get to Conway, this is great news."

"The best," Wiley said, and then bolted out of the room just like Ava had, only with longer, louder steps.

Linette shook her head. "Two peas in a pod," she muttered, and went back to peeling potatoes, but as soon as he returned, the first thing she told him was about her mother's call.

"I told her if they wanted to meet you before the wedding, they had to come here. They're retired. We're busy. She laughed."

"Are they coming?" Wiley asked.

"I'm sure they will, but I also told them to book a room at one of the hotels because we don't have an extra bedroom, which is, for us, a blessing. Dad's a control freak, and Mom enables him. It works for them, but by the time I was fourteen, it was driving me crazy. I love them to death, but I could never be married to a man like my father."

Wiley rolled his eyes. "I get it. Most boys want to be just like their fathers. I wanted mine to disappear. Anyway, I can't wait to meet them. If they made you, then they're fine with me. Now, what are we doing with this hamburger meat?"

"The decision has yet to be made. But something that goes with potatoes, because Ava wanted potatoes like Bubba makes, which I take to mean fried potatoes."

Wiley smirked. "Yeah, fried potatoes are my thing. See, B.J. has nothing on me. Just because he can turn cake into art doesn't make him the only brother who can cook. How do you feel about plain hamburger steaks?"

"I have a deep fondness for beef in all incarnations. Do we have Worcestershire sauce?"

"Yes."

"Then do the patties. I'll douse mine with the sauce and pretend it's a rib eye."

"And I'll call mine a T-bone. For Ava, it's just burglar meat dipped in ketchup."

Linette laughed, and the sound carried through the house and down the hall into Ava's room, where Ava had Phillip the squirrel, Teddy the bear, and Pinky the doll lined up on her pillow and was sitting on the bed beside them, reading aloud when she heard Linette laugh.

She paused in the middle of a sentence, looked up at the open doorway, and listened.

That is a happy laugh. Not a mean one like when

Corina made fun of me. Bubba kept his promise not to yell. Linnie is his almost wife. Almost like a mommy. I have a family now. Corina is an ass.

Satisfied with the security she felt, Ava looked down at her book and picked up where she'd left off.

———

Wiley tucked Ava into bed Sunday night, then sat down beside her.

"I have to go to work really early tomorrow, so you'll still be asleep when I leave. Linnie will take you to Dani's house like always, and I'll be home in the evening like always, okay?"

"Why do you have to go early?" she asked.

"Oh, it's a very important meeting. I'll tell you all about it when I get home. Go to sleep, honey. Everything is fine and you're safe. I love you."

She blinked. "Because you wanted me, right?"

"Yes. Because I wanted you."

She snuggled a little deeper into the covers. "I wanted you, too," she whispered, and closed her eyes.

Wiley got up and turned out the lights, leaving her in shadows. But for the tip of her head, the covers had swallowed her. She was already disappearing before his eyes.

Linette was in the shower across the hall. Wiley went into the bedroom, locked the door behind him, and stripped as he headed for the bathroom.

The room was warm and steamy. The shower doors

were covered in condensation as he pushed them aside and walked in behind her.

Linette felt a waft of air and turned around. Her body was slick with soap as he took the cloth from her hands and stepped beneath the spray with her.

With the water pummeling them from head to toe, he took the cloth and slowly began to wipe the soap from her skin.

"Close your eyes," he whispered.

Linette grabbed hold of his shoulders and felt her world go dark. Her senses became focused on nothing but his touch and the swipe of the cloth, wiping off the soap on her face and her neck, moving down like an avalanche, from her breasts to her stomach, to the valley between her legs.

She shuddered and then moaned and held on tighter as her forehead dropped against his shoulder, then, *Oh God*, he slid his hands around her hips. Cupped his palms against her backside, then slid the washcloth through the downpour from the showerhead, all the way up the length of her back until every inch of her body was free of soap.

"Wiley," she moaned.

"I know, darlin'," he whispered.

He'd washed her clean and then set her on fire.

Water was dripping from their bodies when he carried her to the bed.

"Wet," she mumbled.

"Yes, you are," he whispered, and slid between her legs.

Wiley left them both sleeping and was out the door before daybreak. He headed for the heliport, stopping at Granny Annie's Bakery on the way for coffee and a sausage biscuit. It never paid to go to war on an empty stomach, and that's how it felt, knowing he was going to have to deal with Corina Dalton again.

He ate on the way to the helipad and finished his coffee in his SUV as he waited for the chopper to arrive, and when it did, it appeared with the sunrise, coming over the mountain and down into the valley like a dragonfly coming to land upon a pond.

As soon as it was down, he started toward it at a jog, jumped into the open bay, and slid the door shut behind him.

"Morning, Mr. Pope," the pilot said. "Conway, Arkansas, still the destination?"

"Yes, it is," Wiley said. He settled into a seat behind the pilot and buckled in.

The chopper rose, hovered for a second, then shot forward in an easterly direction, and they were gone. Wiley had a brief glimpse of the roof of their house before they flew out of sight.

It was hot and windy on the morning of the hearing, and the air conditioner in Corina Dalton's car wasn't working. By the time she pulled into the parking lot of the Faulkner County Courthouse and got inside, half her makeup had melted off her face and the hairdo she'd spent money on looked like it had been sucked backwards into a vacuum hose.

She had to pass through security in that condition before she could get to a bathroom to repair the damage, and it did nothing to ease the knot in her stomach. She had finally faced her truth. She was afraid of Wiley Pope. What he might say. What he might do.

The only hold she had over him was guessing how much he wanted what she'd given up. But she had no idea what Ava had been telling him, and she might be in deeper trouble than she knew.

It was a quarter to eleven when she reached the judge's quarters. Her lawyer, Frank Ashton, was waiting. He had a spot on his tie, and he'd combed his hair with his fingers. She knew, because his hair was oily enough that it had not fallen back into place, and she could see the grooves where his fingers had been. But she'd paid him with sex, her only commodity, and had no room to complain.

She sat down on the bench beside him. "Do they call us in or what?"

"No, we can go in. I was waiting for you," Ashton said.

"Is he already here?" she asked.

"If you are referring to a black-haired giant of a man in gray slacks and a white long-sleeved shirt, then maybe."

She grimaced, and when he opened the door for her,

she led with her chin and strode in like she owned the place. She caught a glimpse of Wiley from the corner of her eye, but refused to make eye contact as she sat down. Ashton informed the secretary they were present, and then joined her.

━━━━━━

Wiley looked up as the door opened, and within seconds, he felt her fear and knew it was still nothing to the extent of fear she'd put in her child. Moments later, the secretary buzzed the judge's office to let him know all parties had arrived, and they were escorted in.

There were four chairs, placed in groups of two, in front of the judge's desk. Corina and Ashton sat in one group, Wiley and Ray Greeley in the other.

Judge Beale had read all of the paperwork regarding both parties. On paper, the mother had offered no hardship reasons other than that she didn't want the child, and the half brother's immediate willingness to take her to raise was commendable.

He had Corina Dalton's rap sheet and Wiley Pope's résumé, his commendations, which were many, and a glowing letter of recommendation from his chief of police. He also knew that Wiley Pope and Ava Dalton were the children of one Clyde Wallace, a convicted murderer now residing in a state-run Arkansas prison.

Beale was a God-fearing man who kept his personal life within the teaching of the Holy Bible, but he was also a man who did not believe that the sins of a father should be carried upon the shoulders of his children and was reserving judgment until meeting them face-to-face.

And then they walked into his office.

The Dalton woman appeared nervous, but angry.

But he couldn't read Wiley Pope.

And so he began.

"I am Judge Beale. You have both come before me with a common interest. The well-being of a seven-year-old girl named Ava Joy Dalton." He turned his gaze to Corina. "Miss Dalton. It is 'Miss,' right?"

Corina's face flushed. "Yes, Your Honor."

"Will you please tell the court why you wish to give up all rights to your daughter, Ava?"

"Yes, Your Honor. Miss Mattie, her regular babysitter died. I didn't have anyone to watch her while I worked. Miss Mattie watched her for free. I can't afford to pay, and I'm leaving the first of September to go to work on a cruise line. I had to do something, so asking her half brothers to help was my solution. And I'll be honest, Judge. I never wanted kids."

Judge Beale turned to Wiley.

"Mr. Pope, what prompted you to make this offer?".

Every muscle in Corina's body went on alert, but she stayed silent. No matter what he said, she couldn't be forced to keep Ava if she wanted to give her up.

Wiley knew she was worried, but he wasn't about to sugarcoat anything.

"We didn't know we had a half sister until Corina

showed up at the police station where my brother Aaron and I are officers in the Jubilee PD. She came to file charges against Aaron for abandonment of her and her child. She told our police chief that Aaron was the father and had skipped town and changed his name to hide from her and pulled out a DNA report she'd had made on Ava when she was just a baby. Aaron didn't know who she was, but I did. I knew she was one of our father's side pieces.

"I told our chief right then that Ava was likely related, but she'd be our half sister, not Aaron's child. At first, all I felt was anger on my brother's behalf, and then I saw the child Corina had dragged into the station with her. She was bone-thin, pale, shaking and covered in bruises, and so quiet I hadn't even noticed she was there. Later, I found out that was one of Ava's behaviors when she wanted to disappear. When grown-ups yell and throw things, she told me, she just gets really quiet, and then they can't see her anymore."

The judge gave Corina a look, then refocused on Wiley. "Please continue, Mr. Pope."

Wiley nodded. "While everyone else was dealing with accusations and DNA reports and researching the parents' names on Ava's birth certificate, I took her to the break room to get something to eat. She inhaled a doughnut and a carton of milk so fast she didn't even chew. I took a picture of her then. I've taken several pictures since. They are in the file you were given. At first, she wouldn't talk, and she didn't want to be touched. It broke my heart. I asked her what she wanted most in the world. It was the first time she looked me square in the eyes. She said, 'A bed and a pillow,' and that she'd never had one. I told her we were brother and sister and asked her would she like to live with me."

Beale was stunned. He'd heard a lot of stories in his life, but this was a hard one.

"Why did you not bring her with you today?" he asked.

"Because the entire first week Ava was with me, her biggest fear was doing something wrong that would make me give her back to Corina, and those were her words, not mine. My concerns weren't just for her emotional well-being. I was concerned about what she'd gone through physically, too. I asked her if the random people Corina left her with had ever hurt her or touched her when they shouldn't. She assured me that they had not, and they mostly just ignored her. I asked her about the bruises, and if Corina hurt her. She said sometimes Corina threw stuff at her, and that it hurt, but it never bled. The fact that her point of reference for being abused had to do with how much you bleed nearly killed me. And bringing her back here today would have destroyed her faith in me. I promised to keep her safe. I promised to love her forever, and I do. We all do. My brothers. My mother, and me."

Beale jumped on the reference to Clyde Wallace's wife. "Your mother has no problem with the child belonging to another woman?"

Wiley looked back at the judge. "Why would she? We all belong to the man she married. She's the first one I called. She's the one who urged me to follow my heart and said she'd back me all the way. Ava calls her Grammy now."

Corina shifted nervously in her seat and stared at the floor.

"Does Ava ask about Corina?" Beale asked.

"No. She talks about Miss Mattie. She always refers to her old babysitter as 'Miss Mattie, who dropped dead.' But she does not inquire about Corina. She does ask from time to time if I'm still gonna keep her."

"Are you married, Mr. Pope?" Beale asked.

"I have a fiancée. Her name is Linette Elgin. She's a nurse on the children's ward at the hospital in Jubilee. She and Ava bonded instantly. She has fulfilled Ava's desire for the mommy she never had, and I have stepped in as the daddy figure. The first thing Ava asked me was could she call me Daddy? I would have given the world to say yes, but I explained how that wouldn't work because we are brother and sister. So, we are Linnie and Bubba to her, and I will die on that hill and dare anyone to knock me off it."

Wiley didn't know there were tears in his eyes until his lawyer handed him a handkerchief.

Judge Beale shifted focus back to Corina.

"Do you have anything you want to add?"

Her face was expressionless, her voice as cold as the heart within her. "No. I don't want the kid. I'm willing to give up custodial rights."

Beale said nothing more as the papers that took away Corina's rights to her child were signed and given back to her lawyer.

"Miss Dalton, the fact that no one has pressed charges against you does not make you innocent. If you ever show up in my courtroom again, I will remember you."

Then the papers giving Wiley Pope full custody and legal guardianship of Ava Dalton were signed and given back to his lawyer.

"Mr. Pope, I saw the pictures. I commend you on your desire to do the right thing for your sister and to want the best for her. I have every faith that will be so. I wish you and your family the best." He cleared his throat, then gave Wiley a long look. "If only every lost child had a bed and a pillow, and a brother like you. You are both dismissed."

Corina snatched the papers from Frank Ashton's hands and walked out without a word.

Wiley took the papers Ray Greeley gave him. "Thank you, Judge Beale. Thank you," he said, and then they left the courthouse.

Greeley went one way, and Wiley took an Uber another. He had something to pick up before he left.

———

They had a tailwind in the chopper flying back to Jubilee and arrived fifteen minutes faster than the trip out. He thanked the pilot, then walked back to his SUV. He got in and watched the chopper as it lifted off and disappeared. The silence wrapped around him like a hug as he reached for the phone and sent Linette a text.

I'm back. No challenges. She's ours. Corina didn't
even blink. I'll pick Ava up. I need to hug her...and
you...so tight. See you at the house. We're going
out to eat tonight. We have much to celebrate.
Love you.

Linette got the text, sent him back a big heart emoji,
and glanced at the clock. Her shift was almost over, and
it was a good day.

The monkey was off Wiley's back.

———

Wiley rang the doorbell at Dani's, and as he waited, he
heard little footsteps running toward the door. Then it
opened and Ava threw herself into Wiley's arms.

"Bubba! I didn't see you all day!"

He swung her up and hugged her, then kicked the
door shut behind him. "I know!" he said, then heard
music coming from the kitchen and danced her up the
hall toward the sound, with Ava giggling in his arms.

Dani heard all the merriment and turned toward the
doorway as Wiley two-stepped in with Ava stuck to him
like a little monkey, and thought, *The joy on their faces is
a beautiful thing.*

"So, little brother, you look happy today," she said.

"Best day ever," he said, and put Ava down. "Go get
your stuff, sugar. Linnie will be home soon, and we're
going out to eat tonight."

"Yay!" Ava said, and flew out of the room.

Dani arched an eyebrow. "So?"

"I just flew in from Conway. The guardianship hearing was today. Ava's mine. Signed, sealed, and delivered. Corina Dalton is now nothing but a bad memory."

Dani clapped her hands. "Oh my lord! This is wonderful news! Ava is such a precious little soul. Thank God she's safe. You are her hero. I'm so proud of you and so happy to be a part of her life."

"You've helped tremendously," Wiley said. "I couldn't have done my job as easily as I have been without knowing she was with someone I trusted."

"And I will continue to do so," Dani said. "It won't be long before school starts. You'll be dropping her off at school instead of at my house, but I'll be there for her every day and bring her home with me until you're both off work."

Ava came running back into the room with her backpack hanging off one shoulder and Pinky tucked under her arm.

"I'm ready, Bubba! Bye, Dani. See you tomorrow."

"Where's my goodbye hug?" Dani asked.

"I'm a-holdin' it," Ava said, and opened her arms as Dani leaned over for a quick hug and kiss.

"Thank you for being such a good helper today," Dani said.

Ava beamed, and then she went out the door talking, telling Wiley all about her day.

Chapter 18

As soon as they got home, Ava dropped her bag in her room and came running.

"Bubba, Linnie's not home. Can I go swing?"

"Yes, you can. Be careful, though. You're my best little sister, and I don't want you hurt."

"I'll be careful!" she said, and flew out the back door with her curls bouncing.

He watched from the doorway, thinking about how she'd changed, and did not have one regret about the decision he'd made to fight for her. He was still watching her play when he heard the front door open, and Linette called out, "I'm home!"

"In the kitchen," Wiley said, and then her footsteps were behind him, coming closer, and then her arms were around his waist, and her cheek against his back, hugging him.

"I'm glad you're back," she said.

He turned in her arms and pulled her closer. "And I'm glad to be here. No cooking tonight, love. We're going out. We have much to celebrate."

She slid her hands across the front of his chest and

looked up at him. Those black eyes. Hair always in need of a cut. Shoulders six ways wide to Sunday. And that stubborn jut of his jaw. Too good-looking for his own good, and he didn't care about any of it. All that mattered to Linette was that he loved her. "Ava's secure in this family now. That *is* something to celebrate."

"There's one more thing. I know you don't wear rings at work for obvious reasons, but I'm putting one on your finger now, because when you wear it, I want the world to know you're taken."

Linette gasped at the sight of the ring he pulled out of his pocket.

"Wiley! Oh my God! It's magnificent!"

"So are you," he said. "I proposed before you barely knew me. I have been calling you my fiancée ever since. You already know I cannot live life without you. This just makes it official," he said, and slid the ring on her finger.

"It fits! Oh, Wiley! I love you...so much," she cried, and threw her arms around his neck and kissed him.

At that moment, they heard the back door open. They turned. Ava was standing in the door, watching.

Linette immediately held out her hand. "Look Ava. Bubba and I are engaged!"

Ava was still staring. "Is that the same as 'almost a wife'?"

"Yes, it is," Linette said.

Her eyes welled. Her chin quivered. "Will I still be Bubba's girl, too?"

Wiley crossed the room in three long strides and swooped her up. "You're ours forever, and I have the papers to prove it. Today, a judge told me I am forever and ever your legal guardian. Linnie and I are always going to be your family. No more worries, okay?"

Ava's eyes widened. "What did those papers say about Corina?"

"Nothing," Wiley said. "Because she doesn't count. She can't bother you. She can't come get you. She can't ever, ever hurt you again."

"Not ever?" Ava whispered.

"Nope. Not ever," Wiley said.

Ava hid her face in the curve of Wiley's neck and started to cry. He panicked.

"Ava, honey, are you sad?"

She shook her head, but wouldn't look up.

Linette walked up beside them and wrapped her arms around both of them. "I think these are tears of relief."

"Will she still be in my dreams?" Ava whispered.

Wiley frowned. "I didn't know she was. Was she scary in the dreams?"

Ava nodded.

Wiley hugged her close. "Dreams aren't real, baby girl. They're just stories in your sleep. Like movies we watch. And when the movie is over, then so is the story. When you wake up, you always know the dream wasn't real, right?"

She didn't answer, but she was listening, and then Linette leaned over and whispered in her ear.

"Next time you have a scary dream that wakes you

up, you don't have to be scared alone. You come tell
Wiley and me, and we'll hug it away. Okay?"

"Absolutely," Wiley said. "Now, let's go wash your
face and pick out something to wear so we can go eat.
I'm starved. Are you starved?"

Ava nodded. "I'm starved."

"And I need to change out of my scrubs before we can
leave. I'll hurry," Linette said, gave Ava a quick kiss on the
cheek, and then one to Wiley. "I want to look pretty for my
two favorite people," she said, and hurried out of the room.

"I want to look pretty, too," Ava said.

Wiley nodded. "Then let's go pick out one of your
new dresses to wear."

"Yes! I want to wear the one with blue and yellow
flowers," she said.

"I knew you'd pick that one," Wiley said as they
headed up the hall and into her room.

"How did you know that?" she asked.

"Because your eyes are blue, and your hair is blond.
You'll look fabulous in that dress," he said as he took it
out of the closet.

"And can I wear my B.J. necklace?" she asked.

"Absolutely." Wiley said as he was pulling her T-shirt
over her head.

Ava wiggled out of her shorts, then held up her arms
as he slipped the little dress down over her head. "And
lipstick? Can I wear lipstick?"

He gave her a look. "We'll do lip gloss."

"Yes, that," Ava said.

Wiley sighed. *The girlie girl is strong within her. She is going to be a heartbreaker one day, but not today, Lord. Today, she's just my little sister.*

———————

Linette kept looking at her ring as she showered and dressed. She was officially Wiley Pope's almost wife, and that diamond he'd put on her finger proclaimed it. But she had questions, like how he had afforded chartering a helicopter for a one-day trip, and now the square-cut diamond on her ring. It was stunning. Something was going on with him, with all of them, but she wasn't sure what. What she did know was that she trusted him with her life, and the rest would be revealed.

She was checking her makeup in the mirror when Wiley walked in. She noticed he'd changed clothes, then he kissed the back of her neck, and she forgot what she was doing.

"You're gorgeous, darlin'."

The husky whisper in her ear made her shiver. "I don't know about all that, but you make me feel pretty, and that's all any girl needs. I'm ready. I just need to get my purse."

"Ava just told me the same thing. I am so outnumbered in this house," he said.

"You should never worry about that. Something tells me when we have babies, they're all going to be mini versions of you."

Wiley's eyes narrowed. The idea of making babies with her was an enticing vision of the years stretching out before them, but he was curious. "Why would you think that?"

She shrugged. "Just a hunch."

He rubbed his thumb across her ring finger, then kissed the back of her hand. "Love you, Linnie."

"Love you more," she said.

Then Ava bounced into the doorway. "I'm ready!"

Linette turned. "Oh, honey, how pretty you look, and I'm ready, too. I don't know where Bubba's taking us, but it sounds like a celebration."

"We're going fancy. Eating in the high-end restaurant at the Serenity Inn, where B.J. works. He knows we're coming, so let's get this show on the road," he said.

─────────────

As they were walking through the lobby of the Serenity Inn, Linette pointed to the rock wall and the fountain beneath.

"Wiley, let's get someone to take our picture in front of the fountain! I want to send it to Mom and Dad."

Ava's heart skipped. More people to let into her world? It was getting crowded. But she said nothing as Wiley turned to look for someone to take their picture, just when Ray Caldwell, the hotel owner, approached.

"Wiley…Linette…good to see you outside of work."

Then he looked down at the little blond between them. "This must be Ava. Brendan told me about her coming to live with you."

The moment Ava heard her name, she took a slight step closer to Bubba's leg.

"Welcome to the Serenity Inn!" Ray said. "Your brother Brendan told me you were coming. Is there anything I can do for you?"

"Would you mind taking a picture of us?" Wiley asked. "We're celebrating tonight, and we'd like to mark the occasion."

"I'd be honored," Ray said, and took Wiley's phone, then waited while they moved to the fountain. "Tell me when you're ready."

They stood Ava on the rock bench surrounding the fountain, and then moved into place beside her, holding hands behind Ava's back.

"Hold that pose!" Ray said, and took several shots before stopping. "Picture perfect," he said, as he handed back the phone.

"Thanks, Ray. Much appreciated," Wiley said.

"Always. Enjoy your evening," Ray said.

Wiley immediately pulled up the pictures and thought, *My first family photos.*

"Send those to me," Linette said. "I'm going to pick one and send it to Mom and Dad."

"Will do," Wiley said, and quickly sent the photos to her phone, then showed them to Ava. "See how pretty you look! Which one do you like best?" he asked.

She leaned her head against him. "I like all of them. We look like a family."

"Because we are a family," Wiley said. "Now let's go find that elevator. I don't want to walk up all those steps to get to the top floor."

"Miss Mattie's apartment had an elevator. Her knees didn't like steps," Ava said.

Linette nodded. "I'm not a huge fan of steps, either. I run up and down them all day at work, and I like to ride up once in a while. Come on. You can press the Up button for us."

Ava beamed. "I can do that."

A couple of minutes later, they exited the elevator onto the floor of the restaurant and headed toward the hostess desk.

"Wiley Pope. Reservation for three," he said.

"Yes, sir! Right this way," the hostess said, and picked up their menus before leading them into the dining area.

Heads turned at the elegance of the tall dark-haired man in black and white, the little blond walking beside him, and the beautiful dark-haired woman in blue on his arm.

Men noticed the ring on the woman's finger.

Women noticed the man.

But it was the tiny child with them that stole the show. Big-eyed and quiet, with a look of wonder on her face as she took in her surroundings.

The hostess paused at the wall of windows at a table

set for three, with a booster seat already in place. As soon as they were seated, she put the menus at their place, then paused.

"Mr. Pope. I was at the bank that day. Thank you for saving our lives, and Miss Elgin, thank you for everything you did for us afterward." Then she glanced down at Ava and winked, before walking away.

Wiley glanced at Ava, and then Linette. "We've come a long way in a short time since that day, haven't we, darlin'?"

"The hardest journeys are the ones most worth it," Linette said. "Thank you for bringing us here. The food is amazing, and just look at the view!"

"Spectacular," he said, but he was looking at his girls.

Then they began discussing food and giving Ava suggestions of choices they knew she might like, but Ava was overwhelmed by the decor and the chandeliers and shining lights and crystal. She leaned toward him, whispering, "Bubba, is this a palace?"

"No, just a really fancy restaurant, but if it was, you would be the perfect princess," he whispered back.

"And you would be the king and Linnie would be the queen and we'd live happy ever after, wouldn't we?" she asked.

Linette brushed a stray curl away from the corner of Ava's eyes. "We're already living 'happy ever after.' Oh look, I see someone we know coming to say hello!"

Ava turned to look, then started smiling. "It's B.J.!"

B.J. was already well-known as the head pastry chef,

and the rare times he emerged from the kitchens to come greet a guest were noted as special occasions. Wiley had called him about the reservation, but said nothing about what they were celebrating. B.J. was happy to get a chance to see Ava again, and when she smiled and waved, he waved back and hastened his step.

"Hi, little sister," he said, and gave her a quick kiss on the cheek.

"B.J., I'm wearing my necklace," she said.

"I see. I'm happy that you like it. You and Linette look beautiful. I don't know how Wiley got so lucky. So, Brother...what are we celebrating?"

"I have legal custody of Ava and an official fiancée."

Linette held up her hand and wiggled her fingers.

B.J. smiled and clapped Wiley on the back. "Congrats, Brother, and an official 'Welcome to the family,' Linnie."

Linette beamed. "Thank you, B.J."

"Have you ordered yet?" he asked.

"We're about to," Wiley said.

"Well, whatever you order, save room for dessert. I made something special for your table," B.J. said.

"What is it?" Ava cried.

B.J. winked. "It's a surprise. The waiter will tell me when you've finished your entrées. I'll come back with it then. Enjoy!" he said, and left the dining room.

The elegance of the place kept Ava subdued. Even her normal chatter had gone back to a whisper. She was awed by her surroundings and the notion of being a princess. But when food arrived at the table, she plowed through it like a starving pup, giving Wiley pause to caution her twice.

"Slow down a little, Ava. Chew before you swallow. You're gonna choke yourself," Wiley said.

"I'm a-hurryin' to get to the surprise!" she said.

Linette eyed Wiley and grinned. "Never tell a woman there's a surprise waiting, and then make her wait to get it."

He sighed. "Right. I know that now."

Then finally the moment arrived. A waiter emerged, pushing a cart with a small, but elegant two-tiered cake covered in an elaborate Swiss meringue, with tiny blue sugar flowers and a single little sparkler sticking up from the top tier. B.J. was walking behind him.

As soon as the cake was placed on the table, B.J. lit the sparkler. People at nearby tables began to applaud the cake and the display, but B.J.'s focus was all on his family, and Ava was beaming with delight.

Wiley looked up. "This is perfect, Brother. Thank you."

"Completely my pleasure," B.J. said, and personally served cake to each of them. "The waiter will box up what's left for you to take home. Love you guys." And then he was gone.

"My cake is good," Ava said. "It tastes like Miss Mattie's lemon drops."

"Thank God, for Miss Mattie," Wiley said, and took a bite.

Linette sighed. "It's delicious! I love anything citrus!"

"My Sunshine State girl! I thought you might," Wiley said.

They went home with their cake in a box and a night full of memories.

Linette sent her parents a picture of her, Wiley, and Ava taken at the fountain, then helped get Ava into bed. Once she was asleep, Wiley and Linette shut their door on the world and had a celebration of their own.

———

Angela Elgin was curled up on the sofa watching a movie. Her husband, Chuck, was snoring loudly in his recliner, with the remote held loosely in his hand, when her cell phone dinged a text.

She glanced down, saw it was from Linette, and quickly opened it, then gasped when she saw the photo.

"Oh my God!"

Chuck roused. "What's wrong?"

"Linnie just sent us a picture of her new family to be. They are officially engaged, but would you look at the size of that diamond in her ring?"

Chuck got out of the recliner and moved to the sofa beside her. "Show me," he said, and then peered closer as Angela enlarged the area on Linette's hand. "That guy is really tall. Do you reckon that gem is real?" Chuck asked.

"I'd say yes, and he's seriously good-looking," Angela added.

"Is that the little sister?" Chuck asked.

"Yes, and isn't she just the cutest thing? Linnie looks so happy," she added. "I can't wait to meet them."

Chuck sighed. "Well, she's obviously not coming back to Florida. I wonder where she'd be now if we hadn't taken her to Jubilee for her birthday."

Angela frowned. "Oh, for pity's sake, Chuck. Some things are just meant to be. I'm happy for her. Now get over yourself and go make reservations at one of the hotels. We need to go meet our future son-in-law."

———

Corina's job on the cruise ship was presenting problems she hadn't planned for. She was to board the cruise ship in New Orleans, which was a nearly eight-hour drive from Conway, Arkansas. But if she drove herself there, then she had no place to park her car for the six-month contract she'd signed. So, she either sold her car and then came back to no apartment and no means of transportation, or she stored it and paid a six-month storage bill in advance.

In a knee-jerk decision, she decided to sell the car after she got there and bank the money. So, she arrived a day early, spent half a day selling her car, then went to the hotel and waited for tomorrow to happen.

She'd been given instructions about minimal packing, the option to bring her own bed linens, rules about her work and her behavior, and the need for a passport, but she hadn't read the fine print. All she knew was she was escaping from her past. She was excited about the adventure and elated beyond words that her parental responsibilities had come to an end.

That night after she went to bed, it was hard to sleep. New Orleans was a city that came to life after the sun went down, and she wanted to party. But she didn't want to show up for her new job with a hangover, so she went to bed.

She was awake before daybreak the next morning, got dressed in a hurry, and grabbed a breakfast sandwich before checking out. Then she took an Uber down to the Julia Street Cruise terminal. The driver let her out, unloaded her luggage, and drove away. Now all Corina had to do was board, and according to her instructions, there would be people waiting at the top of the first deck, directing her as to where to go.

The sun was shining, and the wind off the gulf was brisk. She felt cute and carefree as she moved with a growing crowd of people, also in the act of boarding. But when she reached the top and presented her passport and the letter stating she was staff, she was cut out of the crowd like a steer headed for market and followed a different group being led into the bowels of the ship, out of the sunlight, and down long narrow hallways with artificial lighting and not a porthole to be seen.

It wasn't quite what she'd expected, but she was busy listening to the guide calling out names and cabin numbers as they moved down the hallways of the sleeping quarters, dropping workers off as they went. Then she called out another name.

"Corina Dalton."

"I'm here," Corina said.

"This will be your cabin. Take note of the number because everything looks alike. Your bunkmate has already checked in. Staff meeting in the staff mess hall after we sail. You have a map in your paperwork to direct you there. No wandering about the ship. You are not here to sightsee. You are here to work."

Corina's mouth opened, but no words came out. *Bunkmate? Belowdecks?*

She opened the door and walked into a small austere room with no portholes, a set of bunk beds, a sofa, a little desk, and an empty mini fridge, and the aforementioned bunkmate stretched out in the bottom bunk.

She was a thirtysomething redhead with a face full of freckles and shy on height, which explained why she'd chosen the bottom bunk. She rolled out to greet Corina.

"Hi, I'm Patsy. I snore. That's our closet. We share. The head is through that door. It's tiny, so it's a good thing you're not fat. What's your name?"

Corina blinked. "Corina Dalton. I didn't know we'd share a room."

Patsy laughed. "You didn't read the fine print. This is my fourth trip out. Unpack before the ship weighs anchor. The thrusters make a hell of a noise when we depart, but then they level off. You get used to the noise."

Corina was on the verge of pissed. "Noise? They didn't mention noise."

Patsy sighed. She had a feeling this was going to be a long six months, and she was right. By the end of the first day, although they were working side by side, they hadn't spoken six words to each other.

Corina was angry and sullen and slept with the pillow over her head, trying to drown out the sound of engines. They had fourteen-hour shifts, their own mess hall, and their own store to buy toiletries and cleaning products for their own cabins. By the end of the week, her hands were cracked and bleeding. A trip to the ship's doctor confirmed her allergy to the industrial-strength cleaning solutions, and she was sent to laundry instead.

After that, the only time she saw Patsy was in their cabin at night. Corina wasn't mad at Patsy. She was mad at herself, but everyone who came within range of her was sucked into her misery by her attitude alone. Finally, her boss called her into the office and read her the riot act about her behavior, what was acceptable and what was not.

Corina stood there, listening.

"Do we understand each other now?" her boss asked.

"I heard you. If we were anywhere but at sea, I would have already quit."

"You signed a contract!" he said.

"Yes, I did, to work on a ship. Not scrub shit off floors or try to sleep with that god-awful thumping noise! I wake up tired and mad because I can't get a decent night's sleep. So, what's next? Throw me overboard? Make me walk the plank?"

He stared her down. "What's next is you're fired. You can either continue to do your work until we dock again in New Orleans, at which time you will be escorted off the ship with your pay docked for reneging on the contract you signed, or you can quit now and you will be confined to your cabin."

Corina frowned. "Like jail?"

"Basically, it's you not getting to roam around while waiting for a free ride home," he said.

The stark reality of the choices was, once again, a reminder of her life. Every fucking choice she'd made had resulted in worsening her situation. She thought getting rid of Ava would end her troubles, but they'd just become worse, and so had her attitude. She leaned forward in the chair, staring at her boss with all the hate in her heart.

"Then laundry it is. Not too much starch in your shorts, right?" she said, and walked out.

———

Detective Gardner was smiling as he hung up the phone, then looked around the room at the collection of detectives who'd helped them solve this case.

"Heads up!" he said.

They all stopped what they were doing and looked up.

"Good news! Carl Henley and his son have both been indicted on multiple charges, and the evidence against them is insurmountable. Junior is testifying against his father for a lighter sentence. Lonny Pryor has agreed to plead out. Doesn't want a trial. And the associates we pulled in who were connected to Henley are facing charges ranging from the distribution of drugs, to fencing stolen property, to prostitution, and more."

The collective let out a whoop, then began to clap.

Gardner leaned back in his chair, smiling. They'd done it! They'd finally taken down a major player who'd blithely thumbed his nose in their faces for years. So much for being untouchable.

On the day that Johnny Knight ditched his last walking cast and cane, he and Carey went to the courthouse to get a marriage license. After all they'd endured, all they wanted was to belong to each other. They didn't belong to any church. They didn't have family left to invite. They chose to get married by a justice of the peace, with Tom Wheaton as their witness.

Probate was nearing closure.

Neither of them wanted to live in the house where Billy was murdered, so they'd decided to sell the property when Carey was able to claim full ownership and then buy their own house somewhere else in the city. Something small and cozy. Something they could call their own.

She still had nightmares of running through the woods in the rainstorm, and Johnny's dreams were all about falling, but they had each other to wake up to, and thanks to a brother who'd loved her to the end, they had enough.

———————

Linette's parents arrived at the end of the first week of August. Ava was already amped up about her new school, and now she was faced with meeting more new adults when she just wanted someone to play with.

But they had not come unannounced. Wiley and Linette knew they were coming and had them over to the house for supper on the evening of their arrival.

Ava was playing in her room when the doorbell rang, but she knew it meant company was here, and she left the room running. Bubba was her rock, and she was in uncertain waters again.

All of a sudden, Ava had wrapped herself around Wiley's leg, and Linette was looking nervous. He burst out laughing. "You two are something else. Linnie. It's your parents, for God's sake. Let them in."

Linette sighed and headed for the door, while Wiley peeled Ava off his leg and picked her up. "Is that better?" he whispered.

Ava nodded.

"Mom! Dad! Come in! Come in!" Linette said.

Chuck and Angela Elgin entered smiling, greeting their daughter with hugs and kisses, then eyed the big man and the tiny girl at the end of the hall. Before Linette could introduce them, Wiley approached.

"Welcome! I'm Wiley, and this is my little sister, Ava. It's great to finally put faces to the names. You raised a most exceptional woman, and she talks about you often."

Angela was smitten.

Chuck was overwhelmed by Wiley Pope's size. He wasn't just tall. He was built like a linebacker with a pretty face.

"We're happy to be here," Angela said, and immediately dug a small package from her purse. "Ava, I'm Linnie's mother, so when she and Wiley get married, that will make you my granddaughter. I've been waiting a long time for my first grandchild, and now here you are! I brought you a little gift."

Ava took the little package, then looked at Wiley. "I can have two grammies?"

"Yes, you can. Might want to call this one Grandma, or Nana, so we'll know which one you're talking about."

"Nana would be perfect!" Angela said. "And this is Linnie's daddy. You can call him Papa if you like."

Ava gasped. Her eyes welled. "Bubba...I will have a Papa, too?"

Wiley sighed. "Wanting to call me Daddy was her deepest wish, and we couldn't make that happen. But having a man in her life who she can call Papa is going to ice this cake. Welcome to the family, Chuck."

Chuck Elgin had been hesitant about the man, but Ava sealed the deal.

"I'd love to be called Papa," he said.

Linette sighed with relief. She'd known her dad was

going to pull the "Daddy's-girl routine, and Ava had just saved her from that.

"Ava, honey, let's go to the living room and sit down so you can open your gift, okay?"

Ava led the way, chattering, but the moment she sat down, she noticed the shades were up and the curtains still open.

"Bubba, the curtains," she whispered.

"Ah…right!" Wiley said, He began lowering shades and pulling curtains shut, then went through the house doing the same to all the windows, while Ava began tearing into her present.

"What's happening?" Angela whispered.

"It has to do with where Ava lived before. She doesn't feel safe until all the windows are covered. Drive-by shootings and gang-related neighborhood, I think."

Chuck frowned. "Bless her heart."

"And bless Wiley's, too," Linette said. "He's the one who rescued her from it."

And then Ava squealed just as Wiley came back into the room. "Bubba! Jewelry! Now I have two necklaces! Thank you, Nana. Thank you, Papa." She jumped up and ran to Linette. "Linnie, look! It has a pink jewel! Can I wear it for a while?"

"Absolutely," Linette said. She put it around Ava's neck and fastened the clasp.

The moment she did, Ava shot out of the room.

"Where's she going?" Angela asked.

"To look at herself in the mirror," Wiley said. "I keep

telling her she's pretty, but she has a hard time seeing that in herself."

"Why?" Angela asked.

"Because the woman who gave birth to her told her daily that she was a mistake. Because she was ignored and abused for the entirety of her seven years, and it breaks my heart. We didn't know she existed until just a couple of months ago," he said.

Linette walked up behind Wiley and put her hand on his shoulder. "I'm going to tell you now," she said to her parents. "Ava and Wiley may not look alike, and the age difference is obvious, but they are two peas in a pod when it comes to honesty. They didn't come with filters. We laugh daily at Ava's view of the world."

"And other times say to ourselves it's a damn good thing Corina Dalton lives a long way away," he muttered. "Oh. FYI…if she mentions Miss Mattie tonight, just know that's the old neighbor who used to look after her for days on end when Corina would disappear."

"My God," Chuck muttered. "Where's Miss Mattie now?"

"Ava just says, 'Miss Mattie dropped dead.' We don't really know what prompted it, but from Ava's standpoint, Miss Mattie was good. Corina was mean."

"Ava also says Corina was an ass, which I am certain came straight out of her brother's mouth first, but one cannot deny a truth," Linette said.

Chuck burst out laughing. His estimation of Wiley Pope was rising.

"Supper is ready. Wiley, will you please tell Ava it's time to eat?"

"Yes, ma'am," he said, and was out of the room in three long strides.

"Lord, but he's big," Chuck said.

"All the Popes are big, Daddy. He's one of four, and the youngest brother is taller than all of them. There is also a whole mountain of giants just like them. If they are related to the Popes, they grow tall. Come to the kitchen. I made your favorite entrée and Mom's favorite dessert."

"Meat loaf and mashed potatoes?" Chuck asked.

"Poppyseed cake with pineapple filling and cream cheese frosting?" Angela asked.

Linette smiled. "Yes, to both of you. Follow me."

Chapter 19

"Is Ava asleep?" Linette asked, as Wiley slipped back into their bedroom and closed the door.

He nodded. "Yes, curled up in her covers. All you can see of her is from the nose up. Do you think your parents liked us?"

Linette patted the empty side of the bed. "Lord yes. Mother is besotted with you. You have charmed her straight to hell and back. Daddy begrudgingly approves of you, but he'll die before he admits it, because he's jealous. But Mama will take the starch right out of him for his attitude tonight, and the next time you see him, he'll be your long-lost friend."

Wiley laughed as he crawled into bed beside her. "Well, that's quite a lot to live up to."

"You don't have to worry about them another second. I'm the woman you need to please, and it would please me greatly to die a little bit in your arms tonight."

He reached across her and turned out the lights. "I hear and obey," he whispered as he slipped his hand between her legs.

"They're happy," Angela said, as she pulled back the covers and crawled into bed.

Chuck Elgin sighed. "I saw that."

"He's different, Chuck. Different from any men I've seen in years. Like a throwback to a different time. He's not pretending to be something he's not, and he's a bona fide hero. Did you know about that hospital lockdown?"

Chuck shrugged. "She talked about it tonight after they put Ava to bed. It's the first I knew."

"He saved her life in that bank robbery, and he saved her life in that hospital. All you have to do is see the way he looks at her to know she is his heart. He is loyal to the core. I am never going to worry about our daughter again."

"I don't know about all that," Chuck muttered. "A father is always gonna worry about his daughter."

"Well, that's your prerogative, if you feel the need. But Linette is a grown woman, and the man who will look after her and love her now is Wiley Pope. I can't wait to meet the rest of the family."

"Is that tomorrow?" Chuck asked.

"Yes. Tomorrow is Saturday. We're having lunch— they call it dinner—at his mother's house. Apparently, his immediate family will be there," Angela said.

"Good. You can tell a lot about a man by the woman who raised him. I'll reserve judgment," he muttered.

Angela plopped down into bed beside him and turned off the light. There was a brief moment of silence before she fired her last shot in a voice devoid of emotion.

"Charles Elgin. You do not go up that mountain with judgment on your mind. You will pretend you are not an occasional bigot. If you see something that you disapprove of, you will keep it to yourself, or you will answer to me when we go home, and it is a long-ass drive from here to St. Petersburg. Do you get my drift?"

Chuck hadn't heard that tone in her voice in years, but he knew what it meant.

"Yes, honey. I didn't mean anything I said as an insult to the man. I'm just—"

"You're just jealous. So, grow up. We made her. We loved and raised her, and she'll always be our daughter. But she is his now. He cherishes the ground she walks on, which is more than I can say for how you treat me."

"But, honey—"

"You take me for granted and you know it," Angela said. "But I love you, so I put up with it. Now shut up and go to sleep. Tomorrow is an important day for Linnie, and we aren't going to embarrass her. Understand?"

"Yes, ma'am."

Angela snorted beneath her breath, then rolled over on her side and closed her eyes.

———

Shirley Pope knew Linette's family was coming to visit, and that they were coming to her house for dinner tomorrow. Even B.J. was taking off a day, leaving the assistant pastry chef in charge. Aaron and Dani were coming. Amalie was closing her office for the day.

Shirley had also invited Cameron and his family, Aunt Annie and Uncle John Cauley, Marcus Glass, and Ray and Betty Raines and their son, Charlie. It was the first get-together she'd hosted since Aunt Ella's passing, and her absence would be felt by the people who'd loved her.

Shirley had baked a ham yesterday and would make the beef roast and vegetables today, along with a half-dozen sides to go with it. Amalie and Sean had helped her last night and were at it again this morning, and Aunt Annie was bringing desserts from the bakery. It was also Shirley's first big meal to cook since she'd gotten rid of the walking cast, and it felt good to be whole again.

As always, family began arriving early, women bringing a side dish and an extra pair of hands, while the men were shooed out of the house onto the long front porch to swap stories to their hearts' content.

Sean had an ice chest full of cold pop and bottles of water, and the ceiling fans on the porch stirred the air enough to keep them cool, while the women had the air-conditioned house to cool their labors.

Aaron and Dani arrived, with B.J. right behind them, and then Cameron, Rusty, and Mikey came after, while the rest came stringing in. Finally, the only people left to arrive were the guests of honor.

"There they come!" Cameron said, pointing at the

appearance of Wiley's SUV, and right behind it was a car they didn't recognize. It had to be her parents.

Sean got up and opened the door. "Mom! They're here!" he shouted.

Shirley dropped what she was doing, wiped her hands, and went out to greet them.

―――――――

When the house came into full view, Linette gasped. "Who are all those people?"

"Kin," Wiley said. "You'll meet them all and love them. Anyone I love, they love."

"Will they love me, too?" Ava asked.

"Especially you," Linette said, as she unbuckled her seat belt.

"I'll get her," Wiley said. He jumped out, opened the door for Linette, then got Ava out of her car seat. "Two prettiest girls in the county, and they're mine," he said.

Chuck and Angela got out and hurried up to where Wiley and Linette were waiting.

"Jesus was a carpenter," Chuck muttered. "We just walked into the land of giants."

Angela sighed. "And aren't they something? Lord, but the blood runs true in all of them. I've never seen so many good-looking men, from the youngest to the oldest, with such strong family resemblances."

"Come on, Mom," Linette said, and they headed to the house together.

Shirley emerged from the house as they came up the steps. The strands of gray in her dark hair looked like silver, and her sons wore varying versions of her face. Because her sons were so tall, she never thought of herself that way, but found herself towering over both of Linette's parents.

Linette immediately began introductions. "Mom... Dad...these are Wiley's people, some of whom I have yet to meet. Everyone, this is my dad, Chuck Elgin, and my mother, Angela."

"And for those who have yet to meet them, these two beauties are my fiancée, Linette, and my little sister, Ava."

Cameron's son, Mikey, had been drawing pictures in the dirt when the strangers arrived and had gone back to the porch to stand beside his daddy. But then he saw the little girl with blond hair get out of his uncle Wiley's car, and he stared. And kept staring.

Even after everyone had gone inside and even more introductions were made, Mikey was still and quiet, something Rusty had never seen happen.

"Cameron, look at Mikey," she whispered.

Cameron quickly scanned the room, expecting to have to dig him out of a corner he wasn't supposed to be in, and then saw him sitting on a rock bench in front of the fireplace, staring. He followed his son's gaze, straight to the little blond sitting in Wiley's lap, and sighed.

"Well, damn," he said.

"I've seen that look before, but you were wearing it when we first met," Rusty said.

"He's barely seven," Cameron said.

Rusty shrugged. "So's she, but going into second grade, I hear."

"That doesn't happen this young," Cameron said.

Rusty shrugged. "I'm not advocating for anything. I'm just pointing out the obvious. Pope men love once. You've told me that a thousand times."

Cameron looked down at her, seeing the woman she was now, but remembering the wild, reckless woman who'd chosen undercover work for the FBI as her livelihood. And there was a part of her in their son, too.

"Well, we'll see what we will see," Cameron said, "and I think Shirley just rang the dinner bell. I'll gather up Sir Lancelot, while you go make him a plate."

———

Wiley heard the same dinner bell and scooted Ava off his lap. "Dinner's ready, sugar. Grammy has a whole bunch of good stuff cooked for us to eat. Would you like Linnie to make you a plate? She knows what you like."

"Where do I sit?" Ava whispered.

"I think there's a little table set up on the back porch for you and Mikey. And there are tables set up out in the yard beneath the shade trees, and chairs on the porch, too."

"We don't sit inside?" she asked.

"Not today. Too many people. We took all of the chairs outside to the big picnic tables and put all of the food on the kitchen table and the desserts on the kitchen island. We'll all be outside with you, okay? It will be just like eating lunch with a classmate at school. And Mikey will go to school where you go, too, so you're going to have a friend already on the first day of school."

Ava nodded. The idea of a friend was reassuring, even if it was a boy.

Cameron grabbed Mikey's drink and took it and him to the little table. Rusty was right behind them with his plate of food.

"Where's the girl gonna sit?" Mikey asked.

"Right here with you," Rusty said. "You be nice to her. She doesn't know all these people like you do, and she might be a little bit scared."

The little boy's eyes narrowed. "I know how to be good. I'll take care of her, Mama."

"Thank you," Rusty said. "Daddy and I are going back to get our plates, and then we'll be eating out here, too."

They went inside as Wiley was coming out with Ava and her drink, and Linette was behind them with Ava's plate. But before they could say a word, Mikey raised his hand.

"She's a'pposed to sit here, Uncle Wiley. I'll take care of her."

Wiley blinked. *What the hell?* "Well, that's really nice of you, Mikey."

Ava stared at the little boy with the black eyes and dark hair, and then slipped into the other little chair at the table without an argument.

Linette set the plate of food in front of her, handed her a fork, and then took Wiley's hand.

"Let's go get our food. We kind of need to sit by my folks. Can't abandon them in the middle of a houseful of strangers."

They looked back as they were going inside and saw Mikey eating and staring at Ava as if he'd just found the mother lode, while Ava was primly picking at the food on her plate and eating like a little princess.

"Where the hell did she learn to do that?" Wiley muttered.

"Do what?" Linette asked.

"Flirt. I swear to God, she knows he likes her."

Linette laughed. "We're born with it. Calm down. They're just kids meeting for the first time. I need to go rescue my parents before Dad makes an ass of himself."

Wiley laughed, and the moment passed.

By the time they got to dessert, Mikey was doing his dead-level best to make Ava laugh.

Linette watched Wiley among his family and saw him anew, and by the time they left, her parents were as sold on Wiley Pope and his people as Linette was. They left Jubilee the next morning accepting of the fact that their daughter was marrying into a clan.

———

Wiley went to work. Linette headed for the hospital, and Ava was at Dani's house, talking about a little boy named Mikey who could whistle between his teeth and make himself burp. The ultimate accomplishments for a seven-year-old boy.

Dani didn't know what to think. This was the most interest Ava had shown about anything since Wiley put up her swing set and Aaron bought her the little swimming pool for their backyard. Ava was finally blossoming as the normal little girl she should have been.

Corina ended her fourteen-hour shift and dragged herself back to the cabin. The ship was docking in New Orleans tomorrow morning, and she was getting the hell off of it. This was the most miserable seven days of her life. She hadn't been sober this long since she was fourteen. Between her dissatisfaction and the noise, she'd turned into a bitch, and she knew it.

She packed her stuff and then fell into bed without eating or showering. All she wanted was an escape, and that came with sleep. When she finally did sleep, she dreamed of before—of Clyde Wallace, and the times they got high together, and the times he used her for a punching bag. And sometimes, a little face would pop into the dream. Ava. Staring at her. Watching her. Eating the scraps from Corina's plate. Scurrying into the shadows like a little rat. And then Corina would wake up in a panic, thinking the kid was still there, haunting her. Then the dream morphed to Miss Mattie's doorstep. Corina was beating on the door, begging her to open it, when she woke up remembering Miss Mattie was dead. Ava was gone. And Corina was on a return trip from nowhere, coming back to nothing.

Maybe she'd just stay in New Orleans. It held possibilities that Conway, Arkansas, did not. She could start over. No one knew her or her story. She glanced at the time. It was almost 5:00 a.m. She groaned, threw back the covers, slipped down from the top bunk past Patsy's snores, and staggered to the bathroom, stripped, and finally showered off the smell of yesterday.

A short while later, she was dressed and digging in the mini fridge for something to eat. Her hair was still wet from her shampoo and shower when there was a sudden hammering on the door.

Patsy rolled over. "What's happening?"

"I don't know," Corina muttered, and opened the door. Two ship's officers were on the threshold.

"Corina Dalton?"

"Yes, that's me," she said.

"We are your escort off the ship. Get your things."

"Uh.. I'll need my passport and—"

"You will be given what is owed to you. Come with us."

Patsy stood up. "You're leaving?"

"As fast as my legs will carry me," Corina muttered. "I'm not the type to play Jonah in the belly of a whale. This is the worst damn job I ever had, and believe me, sister, I've had a few. I'd rather fuck a duck for free than do this again."

And then she was gone.

Within the hour she was on the streets of New Orleans with her passport in her purse and less than two hundred dollars for the ride she'd just taken. She had no place to live. Next to no clothes. No car, and four thousand dollars in the bank for having sold it. It was time to regroup.

Two hours later, she was in a motel with a newspaper, a breakfast sandwich, and a bottle of beer, going through the help wanted section before heading out into the city, making the rounds of jobs that needed no résumés.

By the time the sun went down, she was in a bar down in the French Quarter. The leather on the barstool was a little cracked on the edge. She could feel it rubbing against the leg of her pants, but her beer was cold and the place was lively. Right down her alley. She was looking forward to getting back to her room. Tonight, she would sleep in quiet, with the air-conditioning blasting cold air. No snoring roommate. No throbbing sounds of the powerful engines below. Just silence.

———

He'd been watching her all night. She'd had five beers and flashed cash when she paid. She was just shy of too drunk to know where she was going, and he needed a

fix, so when she left the bar alone, he followed, staying far enough back in the crowded streets not to be
spotted, and kept with her all the way to where she
was staying, then into the building and down the hall
behind her.

He watched her fumbling for her key card, and then
the moment she got the door open, he leaped, pushed
her inside so hard she hit the floor face-first.

———————

Corina never knew what happened. One moment she
was facedown and tasting blood, and then a man was
on her back. She tried to scream, but her front teeth had
been driven into her lower lip, and all she could muster
was a choking moan. The man grabbed her by the hair
and yanked her head backward so hard it broke her
neck. She was dead before the pain could fully register,
and he was already going through her purse.

Fifteen minutes later, he scored what he wanted and
headed for his flop. The woman was forgotten. She
didn't matter to him. She was just a means to an end,
and he was riding out his high.

———————

Housekeeping found her body the next morning.

Just another stranger who was now the responsibility of the New Orleans PD. It didn't take them long to

find out she had priors. They also found a bar tab in her purse. While they were waiting for the coroner, the team from the crime lab was gathering evidence in the room and found her paperwork from the cruise line.

"She was staff on a cruise ship."

A guy from the lab looked up. "One of the Carnival Cruises docked yesterday morning."

The detective in charge pointed at an officer. "Find the manager. I want the security footage from the time she entered the building to the moment she went into her room."

The police began working the case just like they did every random murder in their city, but the world was through with Corina. Her whole life had been about choices, and she'd rolled snake eyes every time.

———

A couple of days later, Wiley was on patrol. He'd dropped his partner, Doug Leedy, off at a dentist about an hour earlier and was on his own until he got the call to come pick Doug back up. So, when his phone rang, he thought it would be Doug. Instead, it was from the chief.

"Chief, what's up?" he said.

"Wiley, when you get a second, I need you to swing by my office," Sonny said.

"Yeah, sure. Be there in a few," Wiley said. He took the turn at the next corner and headed back to the station.

The door to the office was open, but he knocked anyway.

Sonny looked up. "Come in, Wiley, and close the door, will you?"

Wiley frowned. "What's wrong. What happened?"

"I just got a call from a detective in New Orleans. Corina Dalton was murdered there two days ago. Robbed in her hotel room. They picked up the guy who did it."

Wiley blinked, then took a deep breath, but said nothing.

Sonny didn't know how to read the man. The Pope brothers gave nothing away. He glanced down at the notes he'd made from the phone call and continued.

"They were looking for a next of kin and found the recent court records regarding the legal guardianship between you and her. This is a weird situation. Legally, they have to notify next of kin, but she's only seven. So, I'm telling you. And you can decide when, or if, you ever tell her. They want to know if anyone is claiming the body."

"Hell no, we're not claiming the body. And I know I'm not running home to tell Ava anything. If she ever asks...I might. But honest to God, Chief, she has nightmares about the woman. She got herself killed there. They can bury her there."

Sonny nodded. "They said she'd recently sold her car and banked the money in New Orleans. There's a little less than four thousand dollars in that account."

A muscle jerked at the side of Wiley's jaw. "Then they can bury her with it. Ava's never going to need that money. It's tainted, just like the woman it belonged to. Is that all, sir?"

Sonny sighed. "Yes, that will be all."

"Sir," Wiley said, and walked out, but the moment he got back in the car, he called Linette. She was off this afternoon and had gone to Bowling Green, so he knew he wasn't disturbing her at work. The call rang three times before she picked up.

"Hey, honey," she said.

"Are you where you can talk?" Wiley asked.

"Yes, I'm driving home. What happened?"

"Corina Dalton was murdered in New Orleans two days ago. They were trying to track down next of kin. They saw my name and Ava's connected to her most recent court case."

"Oh my God! So do we have to do anything?" she asked.

"Hell no."

"Are we going to tell Ava?" Linette asked.

"Hell no, again," Wiley said. "Not unless she ever asks about her, and then I'll take it into consideration. That woman gave away her child. That nullifies her existence. She chose the path she walked, and now it's finished."

"Okay, and I agree," Linette said.

"I just needed to tell you now. I don't want to talk about it at home and have her overhear any part of it. You and I are in this together. I'll always have your back."

"And I'll have yours," Linette said. "I'm just now coming over the mountain. It's so pretty up here. God, what a place to grow up. I love you. I'll see you soon."

"Love you, too. Drive safe, sweetheart."

He'd no sooner disconnected than he got a text from Doug to pick him up from the dentist, so he put the car in gear and drove away.

———————

Linette picked Ava up from Dani's house as soon as she got back to Jubilee, and then they spent the rest of the afternoon trying on school clothes Linette had purchased.

Ava was so excited she couldn't stop talking.

"I don't have to wear the same thing every day?"

"No, ma'am, you do not. We have a few dresses, and shorts and tops, and some jeans and sweatshirts, and a new jacket, and a new winter coat, and a sock cap and mittens, and another pair of sneakers. Bubba wanted to make sure you have everything you might need."

"And I can wear my hair stuff?"

Linette nodded. "A pretty bow or hair clip every day if you want it. Did you always eat in the school cafeteria before?"

Ava nodded. "Yes. Corina didn't make me lunch. I got a free lunch. I cost her plenty. She was broke because of me."

Linette was horrified by the wording. She knew

immediately that Ava had not made those determinations on her own. She was just repeating what she'd heard.

"That was then, and this is now," Linette said. "We aren't broke. And we'll make sure your meals are already paid for every month, okay?"

Ava nodded. She'd already learned that when Bubba and Linnie said something, they meant it. It was one of her biggest revelations. Grown-ups who kept their word.

"I'll hang up the rest of your things," Linette said. "Why don't you go outside and play in your playhouse for a while? Bubba will be home later, and we'll make supper."

"I'm going to take Pinky with me. She likes to slide," Ava said, and left the room with her rag doll tucked under her arm like she was carrying a pillow.

Linette watched her walking away and, in that moment, realized it was how Ava carried everything. She wondered again how Ava's prior environment had given her the idea that this was how to carry something, then decided she didn't want to know.

———

The board of directors of PCG Incorporated was having a meeting. Cameron Pope, the CEO of the corporation, had called it because they had business to discuss that had to do with Aunt Ella Pope's passing.

Rusty had taken Mikey and gone to visit Cameron's younger sister, Rachel. She knew what the meeting was about, but it was strictly board member business, and Mikey settled in to play with his cousin Lili, while she and Rachel visited.

Cameron was outside on the porch with Ghost at his side, waiting as the members began to arrive. One representative from each of the three families served on the board. John Cauley. Marcus Glass, and Cameron Pope. They knew why the meeting had been called, but there had to be a consensus among them before they could act. It was how peace was kept among so many people.

John Cauley was the first to arrive.

"Uncle John, thanks for coming," Cameron said, as John came up the porch steps.

"Sure thing, Son. We've let this go awhile. It's time to finish it," John said. He gave Ghost a pat on the head and got a head bump on his leg in appreciation.

"There comes Marcus," Cameron said, and waved as Marcus got out of his car.

"I got delayed by a phone call," Marcus said, scratched a spot behind Ghost's right ear. He got a tail wag for his troubles and then joined the others.

"No problem," Cameron said. "Let's go inside where it's cool. Rusty baked, and there's plenty of sweet tea."

They followed him in, laughing and talking as they moved to the kitchen, grabbed a couple of cookies, and each poured themselves a glass of tea before sitting down at the long kitchen table.

Ghost settled on the floor beside Cameron's chair, and then Cameron leaned forward.

"As you know, this isn't official PCG business. It has nothing to do with Jubilee. Aunt Ella left a will. You know the gist of it. She had no direct heirs. We're all, in some way or another, kin to her, but one no more than another. There is no direct heir to her property, but she stated in her will that she wanted the members of the board to decide the fate of her property. I don't think any of us want to see it sit empty. It will soon fall to ruin if that happens. Agreed?"

Both men nodded. "Agreed," they echoed.

"I asked you to bring names from each of the families who you think might want to take possession. And I understand the consensus is no one wants to live that far away from town, or they don't want to live where she died."

"That's true for the Cauley bunch," John said. "They're all already satisfied with where they are, and there aren't any young'uns in our bunch anywhere near needing their own place."

"All of the Glass families are settled. The young ones who have married either have put up houses on their parents' property or are afraid they'll be living with Ella's ghost. They choose to live in town to be near their jobs."

"The Pope family had dwindled to Rachel and me, then cousins from Mom and her sisters. But that was before Shirley came home and brought her sons with her. They've put new blood into the family, for which we are grateful. Aaron and Dani are committed to staying in Jubilee for the time being because of their jobs. Sean and Amalie are fully committed to staying with Shirley. None of the boys want her living alone. That leaves Wiley and B.J. B.J.'s work is at the hotel and often fourteen-hour days."

"What about Wiley?" John asked. "Annie says he's engaged to that pretty nurse from the hospital. And he's got his little sister to raise. Would they want to live up here and drive into town every day?"

"Have you talked to him?" Marcus asked.

"No. I chose not to mention anything to B.J. or Wiley until I talked to you two to see who else might suit. Ella loved all of you."

"But she was a Pope," Marcus said. "In my mind, by rights, it should go to a Pope. Shirley's daddy was a Pope. Her boys took her name, and well done for doing so. She inherited her homeplace when Helen died. That leaves Ella with no Pope to claim her land unless one of Shirley's boys wants it."

"Since Sean and Amalie are settled with Shirley, and Aaron and Dani don't want the long drive, I say you talk to Wiley and B.J. Feel them out about where they live, and if they'd even want to be that far away. And warn them that the house is in need of updates," John said. "It suited Ella, but it falls short of serving the needs of a family."

"Okay, if that's what you want, then I'll do that and let you know the end results," Cameron said. "Now help yourself to more cookies, because if they're still here when Rusty and Mikey come home, it's going to be a fight to keep him out of them."

"That one is you all over," John said.

Cameron grinned. "So says my wife."

"You need to give him a little brother or sister to play with," Marcus said.

"He is a solid handful right now. Besides, he has plenty of cousins," Cameron said, and thought of the current fascination his son had with Wiley's little sister.

A short while later, they left, and Cameron sent a text to Rusty to let her know the meeting had ended and that he was headed to Jubilee.

Chapter 20

As soon as Cameron started down the mountain, he called B.J. to see when, or if, he had time to talk.

B.J. answered on the second ring. "Hello."

"Hey, B.J., this is Cameron. I'm on my way into town and I need to run something by you. Do you have time to talk?"

"Yes, I'm at home. I'm off today."

"So, I can be there in about fifteen minutes. Is that okay?" Cameron asked.

"Sure thing. See you soon," he said.

Cameron disconnected and kept driving, wondering what he was going to do if both brothers said yes, or if both brothers said no. He needed one of them to be on board to settle the last of Ella's wishes.

B.J. was watching for him, and wondering what was going on, when Cameron pulled up into his driveway and got out. B.J. met him at the door.

"Good to see you. I don't have a lot of company," B.J. said. "Come sit. Would you like a cup of coffee?"

"I'm good," Cameron said as he sat down. "I'm

going to cut to the chase. We have a dilemma regarding Aunt Ella's property. She had no immediate heirs, but she wanted her place to go to someone in the Pope family, and you and Wiley are the only ones I haven't talked to yet. Aaron and Dani don't want the drive because of their jobs. Sean is already committed to staying with your mom. I inherited my family's home and don't want to move, and my sister, Rachel, loves the place she and Louis have on some of the Glass land. So, I need to know if you have any interest in living that far up the mountain in the old two-story house."

B.J. was shocked and, at the same time, honored. But he knew it wasn't meant for him.

"I'm single. I work fourteen, sometimes fifteen hours a day, and my days begin early. I would never be there. As it is, all I need now is a place to sleep. I pretty much live at the hotel. If this was ten years down the road and I had a wife and family, I might feel different, but I have to say, as much as I love this family and how much we loved Aunt Ella, the property isn't meant for me."

Cameron nodded. "I guessed you would feel that way, but I had to ask. What do you think Wiley is going to say?"

B.J. shrugged. "It's hard to say. He and Linette are getting married soon. He's raising our little sister. I don't know how they'd be about that drive into town every day. What I do know is that when the sun goes down in Jubilee, they have to pull all the curtains and shades for Ava because she's terrified of drive-by shootings. Wiley has reassured her many times those things don't happen here, but she's not convinced. Who knows? Maybe they'd move for her."

"Poor little girl. I didn't know that," Cameron said.

B.J. nodded. "The stories Wiley has shared with us would curl your hair. That child is lucky to be alive, and luckier still that Wiley got full custody of her. He is now her legal guardian."

"Thanks for the info," Cameron said. "Now I have to run Wiley down and see what he has to say."

"He won't make a decision like that without Linette present. I think this is her day off, and Wiley will clock out around five."

Cameron glanced at his watch. It was a quarter to four. "Thanks, B.J. I'll make some calls," he said and stood up. "Good to see you again. You're the only Pope on the mountain I can look up to."

They both grinned. B.J.'s height was a constant topic of conversation within the family.

"I wonder how big Brendan was," B.J. said.

"We'll never know for sure, but he had to be something big for that gene to stay so strong within us," Cameron said.

Watching Cameron walking away left B.J. with a pang of regret. But what he wanted and what he needed were two different things.

———

Wiley and Doug were headed to Trapper's Bar and Grill with their siren blasting and lights flashing. Another patrol car with two officers was right behind them. They came to a flying stop in the parking lot, entered the building on the run, and headed for the fight in progress.

Three men were trading punches, and Louis, the bartender, had a cut under his eye and a stream of blood running down his cheek. He was coming out from behind the bar with a baseball bat when they arrived. When Louis saw the officers, he breathed a quick sigh of relief and backed off.

Wiley grabbed the first one from behind and yanked him backward so hard he hit the floor on his butt, while Doug headed for the two rolling on the floor.

The other two officers were coming in the door on the run as Wiley rolled his drunk facedown on the floor and cuffed his hands behind him so fast he never knew it was happening, then leaped toward the third one, who was about to punch Doug in the back of the head.

"No sir!" Wiley said. "Facedown! Now!" When the man protested, Wiley just rolled him over and straddled him like a riding horse as Aaron and Yancy ran up. "Hey, Yancy! I need another pair of cuffs. This dude thinks he's Muhammed Ali."

Aaron had already seen the blood on Louis's face and radioed for an ambulance, before helping Doug cuff his perp.

Wiley stood up, then looked at Louis. "Are these the only three?"

Louis had a bar towel pressed against the cut on his face. "Yes. They came in drunk. I didn't let them get like this in here."

Wiley frowned. "You mean they were together?"

"They walked in together, sat down at the bar together, and began arguing about whose turn it was to buy a round. But they were obviously very drunk, and when I wouldn't serve them, one of them grabbed a beer mug from the hands of the customer beside him and threw it in my face," he said.

Wiley pivoted, then walked to where the three men were lying.

"Which one of you threw the mug at your bartender?"

They said nothing.

"Fine. Then all three of you will be charged with assault, drunk and disorderly, and liable for the damages you caused."

At that point, the skinny man with the bad comb-over hanging down the left side of his face started talking.

"Frank threw the mug. Ronnie punched Frank for doing it. I punched Ronnie for hitting Frank, because Frank's my brother-in-law, but I'm not taking the blame for his bad temper."

Aaron looked at Wiley and grinned. "Brotherly love."

Wiley rolled his eyes.

The ambulance arrived, and as soon as they began tending to Louis, the officers hauled the drunks out to their cruisers and took them to jail, while the employees started cleaning up the mess. It was just another day in paradise.

By the time they got the men booked and jailed, and then wrote up their reports, it was after five o'clock, and the next shift was already on duty.

Wiley had just left the precinct and was walking to his car when his cell phone rang. When he saw who it was, he stopped to answer.

"Hey, Cameron."

"Wiley, hope I'm not catching you at a bad time," Cameron said.

"Nope. I just clocked out and am about to head home. What's up?"

"Nothing's wrong. But we have an issue to settle among the Popes and you're one of them, so I need to get your feedback. Would it be okay if I came by your house to talk? And since you and Linette are getting married soon, I think her opinion should factor in."

"Yes, sure. No problem," Wiley said. "I'll let her know you're coming."

"Thanks. I'm already in town. I'll see you soon."

Wiley frowned as he was getting in the car, then called Linette as he was leaving the parking lot.

She answered on the second ring. "Hi, honey. Are you on the way home?" she asked.

"Yes, but Cameron just called. He's coming by the house in a few. Said he needed to ask us something, but I have no idea what's on his mind. Just wanted you to know."

She laughed. "You mean, this is a heads-up to make sure Ava hasn't dragged all the stuffies to the sofa to watch cartoons with her again?"

He chuckled. "Something like that."

"No problem. She's outside in her playhouse. We should be fine. See you soon."

Wiley pulled up in the driveway with Cameron right behind him.

"That's timing," Wiley said, and they walked into the house together. "Hey, Linnie! We're here." Then he gestured toward the living room. "Have a seat, Cameron. I'm going to lock up my weapon. Be right back."

"Take your time," Cameron said. "I'm fine."

Linette walked in, smiling. "Hi, Cameron, would you like something to drink? We have Coke, sweet tea, and orange soda."

"I'm fine, Linnie, but thanks. Where's the punkin?"

"Outside in her playhouse. I just checked on her," she said, and sat down. "School starts Monday. Is Mikey excited about going back?"

Cameron nodded. "Yes. He likes school. He's going into first grade. Ava's going to be in second grade, right?"

"Yes. She's a little anxious because she doesn't know anyone. However, getting to meet your boy at Shirley's was a plus. Now she at least knows one, even if they won't be in the same grade. And Dani has been her babysitter ever since she arrived, so having a sister on-site as one of the teachers is a big boost."

Wiley came back into the room and sat down on the

love seat beside Linette. "Okay, fire away, and know that at any moment Ava could appear."

"Then I won't mince words," Cameron said, and once again explained the situation to them, just as he had to all of the others.

Wiley was stunned, but Linette's eyes were glowing. It was all she could do to stay silent, because ultimately, it was Wiley's family and his choice to make.

"What did my brothers say?" he asked.

"Aaron and Dani felt like their jobs worked better by not having so far to drive. Sean and Amalie are committed to staying with your mom. B.J. said he doesn't do anything but sleep where he lives now, and a two-story house so far up the mountain, coupled with his working hours, was not feasible. I don't want you to feel like you have to accept, but the fact that I was possibly going to have to make a choice between the four of you has been whittled down to you and Linette. B.J. told me Ava is afraid of drive-by shootings here, but I don't know how she'd feel about being uprooted again so soon."

"She will adapt to wherever we are," Linette said.

Wiley looked at her then, remembering what she'd said about the mountain when she was coming home from Bowling Green.

"To inherit a piece of my family history is something I would never have imagined. But this isn't just about me anymore. What do you think, Linnie? It would add a good twenty minutes to our drive to work every morning, and we would need to do some remodeling first."

Her voice was trembling as she reached for his hand. "Oh, Wiley. I think this is the most wonderful wedding present we could ever receive. If you want this, then I'm with you. Wherever you go, we go," she said. "As for Ava, as long as she has her bed and pillow, and a pink room to put her things in, she'll be fine. But can we afford all that remodeling?"

Wiley glanced at Cameron and then looked away.

Cameron knew the predicament of keeping a secret from someone you loved. He'd faced it with Rusty. "Let's just say the Pope family has investments that we all benefit from. You'll be fine," he said.

Linette's eyes widened. The secret she had yet to be told.

"Okay then. I have absolutely no objections, but it's Wiley's decision."

"Then we accept, with undying gratitude," he said.

Cameron breathed a sigh of relief. "Thank God. You have just helped me fulfill Aunt Ella's last wish. I'll set the wheels in motion to transfer title and deed to you, and I'll let you know when it's officially yours. But in the meantime, I'm going to give you an extra key to the house. When you get a chance, you three take a drive up the mountain to see it, and just know that land was the first and oldest claim on Pope Mountain. Enjoy it for the treasure it is."

Wiley took the key Cameron offered, too emotional to speak, and then the back door slammed.

"Ava's in the house," Linette said.

"Bubba! Linnie!"

"We're in here!" Linette said.

Ava came running, holding Pinky by the arm, then slid to a halt when she saw the visitor and sidled up to where Wiley and Linette were sitting.

"Did Mikey come to play?" she asked.

Cameron grinned. "No, not this time, honey. Sorry."

Satisfied she hadn't missed something, she nodded and slipped out of the room.

"She's a little obsessed with her first friend," Linette said.

"And he's a little obsessed with her at the moment," Cameron said, and then stood. "Thank you, both, and I'll keep you abreast of the legal stuff. In the meantime, have a good evening. Don't get up. I'll let myself out."

As soon as the door shut behind him, Linette was in Wiley's arms.

"I can't believe this is happening," she said.

"Neither can I, but I feel like we've just won the lottery," Wiley said.

"That's how I felt the first time we made love," she whispered. "Like I'd just found my place in the world."

"Are you going to feel weird knowing Aunt Ella died there?" he asked.

She rolled her eyes. "Wiley. I'm a nurse. Every day I go to work where people die. It's the living who are scary."

Then they heard Ava coming back up the hall.

"Somebody's getting hungry," Linette said. "I think it's time to start supper."

Ava appeared in the doorway, saw that company was gone, and ran to where they were sitting. "Are we going to eat tonight?"

Wiley grinned at Linette. "You sure have her number, and by the way, what *is* for supper?"

Linette grinned. "S'gettie with meat sauce."

"Yum!" Ava said. "S'gettie is my favorite."

"It's my favorite, too!" Wiley said. "And you're my favorite little sister. I think we should help Linnie, don't you?" Then he swooped her up in his arms and began dancing her out of the room.

Linette sighed. *Just when I think I can't love him more, he does something like that,* she thought, and followed them to the kitchen.

———

It was two days later before Linette and Wiley had another day off together. They took Ava with them and headed up the mountain.

"Where are we going, Bubba? Are we going to Grammy's house?" Ava asked.

"No. We're going to a different house. You'll see when we get there."

"Will there be kids there?" she asked.

"You're a kid. You'll be there," Wiley said. "You and Pinky talk it over."

Ava leaned back and pulled Pinky up beneath her chin and closed her eyes. The next time Wiley glanced up in the rearview mirror to check on her, she was fast asleep.

"I'm timing the drive for future reference," Linette said, eyeing the scenery as they passed. "It's so beautiful up here. I can't imagine what it would have been like to grow up here."

"Me neither. When it comes to peace and quiet, the mountain is it. Usually, the loudest thing at night will be someone's hound baying on a trail in a far-off holler."

Linette frowned "Holler?"

"Mountain talk for a hollow. There are hollers all over the Cumberlands, places drastically smaller and more secluded than a valley. Jubilee used to be a valley before our ancestor, Brendan Pope, came here and started a trading post. The town grew out of that, and then turning it into a tourist attraction turned it into something else yet again."

"What's the cell service like?" she asked.

"The higher up you go, the better," Wiley said. "But Sean can fix us up. He runs his entire computer business from the house. Whatever we need to stay connected to our jobs, he can make happen." Then he pointed to a red mailbox on the road ahead. "See the red mailbox? That's where we turn."

She shivered. "I'm full of excitement and anticipation."

"Besides the house, the land around it is beautiful. A big open pasture at the back. Outbuildings, probably also in need of repair, but they're built of logs that were trees on this mountain and have been standing for well over a century."

"I can't wait," Linette said.

When Wiley began to slow down to take the turn, Ava stirred, opened her eyes, and then looked around.

"Is this where we're going?" she asked.

"Yes. To the house at the end of this gravel road," Wiley said.

"Who lives there?" Ava asked.

"Nobody now, but we're going to. We'll fix it up, then move your playhouse and swing set and all of our furniture to this house. You'll have a big fenced-in yard to play in, and lots of shade trees with birds everywhere. You and Linnie can feed birds here, and we'll get a cat who will live in the barn and catch mice, and you will have kitties to play with."

"And we can grow a garden," Linette said. "One for flowers, and one for vegetables, and when we go to bed at night, you can look out your window and see stars and moonlight. You will feel safe knowing there will never be cars driving by or people who would shoot into windows."

Ava's eyes filled with tears. "Never?"

"Never," Wiley said.

"I will like it," Ava whispered.

"And there it is," Wiley said, pointing to a white two-story house with a porch that ran the length of the house. Grass had grown up in the yard, and the house looked lonesome.

"Do I get to sleep upstairs?" Ava asked.

"All of the bedrooms are upstairs," Wiley said.

Ava heard, but said nothing, still absorbing this news, while Linette was already picturing their life there.

They walked up the rock path to the porch, then up the steps. Wiley unlocked the door and led the way, with Linette and Ava holding hands behind him.

He stopped to flip on the lights and, for a moment, felt as if he'd just been hugged.

"We're here, Aunt Ella. Thank you for the gift. We'll fill this house with so much love and laughter, and keep the home fires burning. I promise you."

———

School began before the remodeling, and it was just as well. Too many new things could have been a problem, but Ava soon found out that being Mrs. Pope's little sister was all the cachet she needed to fit in at her new school. And once Mikey informed all of the cousins at school that Ava was Uncle Wiley's little sister, she had her own built-in security squad without even knowing it, and she thrived.

Her giggle became commonplace. Her fears about everything began to recede. She hadn't known there was a world like this, with people like this. Bubba and Linnie were her touchstones to sanity, and school was her safe place to be, but she still feared night in the city and had worn out two questions. "When will we move to the mountain?" and "When are you getting married?"

And then finally the day arrived.

———

It was the first week of October, and Linette's parents arrived two days prior to the wedding. They had been taken aback by the news of the location of the venue, and then finding out Wiley and Linette were moving to the mountain.

And then they saw the locations.

They were in awe of the ancient Church in the Wildwood.

And even more so by the remodeled house Wiley had been bequeathed.

After that, they settled in at their hotel and, on the day of the wedding, drove up the mountain to the church, where the entire bridal party was getting dressed. The mountain was ablaze in color. The sun was bright, but this high up, the day was cold.

Wiley, who was usually wired and bordering on tense, was calm to the point of placid. It was the first time in his life that he knew this was exactly what he was supposed to do, and he wore what he'd been told to wear—a black suit, a white shirt, and a bolo tie with a large turquoise stone in the setting. His black boots had silver tips on the toes, and as always, his hair was brushing the edge of his collar.

His brothers were all getting ready to stand with him at the altar. Aaron as best man, and Sean and B.J. as his groomsmen. Cameron was in the room with them getting Mikey dressed, but this time his son was old enough to be trusted not to bolt down the aisle, and Ghost wasn't needed to keep him in line.

"Be still a minute, Son," Cameron said as he was fastening Mikey's tie.

Mikey stilled, but his gaze was focused on his daddy's face, and he was full of questions.

"Daddy?"

"Hmm?"

"How old do you have to be to get married?" he asked.

Cameron paused. "Old enough to have a job and money enough to take care of the woman you marry."

"How old is that?" Mikey asked.

"Older than twenty-one, for sure," Cameron glanced up. "Why?"

Mikey was counting on his fingers. "Then in fourteen more years, I can marry Ava."

Cameron stared, shocked that his son had that grasp of numbers, and that, at the age of seven, he'd already picked a girl.

"You can't just pick someone out and marry them. They have to agree to marry you. They have to love you and want to spend the rest of their life with you, too."

Mikey frowned. "Daddy. It will be fine."

Cameron frowned back. "And how do you know that?"

Mikey shrugged. "I just do. Sometimes you just know stuff, right?"

"Right," Cameron muttered, but he was bothered. Mikey was starting to sound like Aunt Ella.

"It's time. Is everyone ready?" Aaron asked, and when they nodded, he motioned to Wiley to get in line. The moment the pianist began playing music, they filed out in order and walked to the altar, then looked up the aisle.

Moments later, Dani, the maid of honor, came down the aisle, followed by Amalie and Amy, a nurse who was one of Linette's oldest friends from work. They took their places at the altar and then looked up the aisle.

Ava appeared in the doorway—a tiny blond in floor-length pink tulle, walking beside the little boy with black hair who was sedately carrying the ring fastened to a white satin pillow. He had one eye on the little blond scattering flowers beside him and the other on their progression.

But Ava wasn't ignoring anything. She was aware of herself in a way she'd never felt. She felt pretty, and important, and most of all, she felt loved, and her best friend, Mikey, was walking with her, whispering as they went, "You're doing good."

———

Wiley saw it all as if watching it all through a veil, because he was waiting for Linette, the woman who made his life matter.

And then the music changed, and when it did, everyone in the congregation stood and turned to look up the aisle.

The bride and her father appeared in the doorway.

Wiley took a deep breath and found himself blinking back tears. They were moving toward him, and it was all he could do to wait. The rest of the ceremony was a blur of words and rituals and flowers and a ring, and the vow of promising to love her forever and beyond.

And then it was over.

He heard Brother Farley pronouncing them husband and wife, and then he kissed her.

And in that brief moment of silence, as they were turning toward the congregation, Ava spoke her delight.

"You're married!" she cried. "No more almost wife."

The congregation erupted in laughter, and Linette and Wiley laughed along with them.

"I've got Ava," Aaron whispered. "You two head into the dining hall. You have a cake to cut and a first dance waiting to happen."

The cake and punch happened, and then the band began to play an old Willie Nelson song, "Always on My Mind," as Wiley led Linette out onto the floor. His arms went around her. Her hand was on his shoulder. Their eyes locked into each other's gaze. And as the music swelled around them, he swung her into a waltz and whispered in her ear.

"The family has a secret. Only spouses are allowed

to know, and it can never be told to outsiders. All of us on the mountain—the Pope, the Cauley, and the Glass families—own Jubilee, lock, stock, and barrel, and the mountain on which we're standing. PCG Incorporated, the company you pay rent to, the company that owns the hospital and every building in the valley, is all of us, and Cameron is the CEO. We make a buttload of money and get quarterly dividends that will keep us solvent for the rest of our lives. So, mum's the word, my love. Mum's the word."

Linette gasped. "Talk about classified material and a need to know! Holy crap, Batman!"

Wiley threw back his head and laughed, then kicked into high gear and spun her around the floor, dipping and swaying, until others joined in. He looked once to make sure Ava wasn't feeling left out and saw her sitting with Dani.

Then the brothers began cutting in, and he reluctantly gave Linette up and went to get Ava. He bowed at where she was sitting and then held out his hand.

"Miss Ava, would you like to dance?"

She giggled. It was all Wiley needed to hear. Moments later she was in his arms, and he was swirling her across the floor.

"We got married today, didn't we, Bubba?"

He grinned. "Yes, we did, honey. Yes, we did."

"Am I gonna sleep in my new room soon?"

"Yes, but not tonight. You're spending the night with Grammy and Sean and Amalie, remember? We move in two more days, and then we'll all be sleeping in our new house."

Her voice segued back to the whisper she'd come with as she tucked her head beneath his chin. "Corina can't find us there, right?"

He hugged her closer. "Honey, don't ever worry about her again. Corina is gone forever, understand?"

Ava blinked. "Did she drop dead like Miss Mattie?"

"What would you think if that happened?" he asked.

"I'd think I was safe."

"You're safe, Ava. Forever and ever."

Ava sighed and laid her head on Wiley's shoulder. "Nobody can hurt me now. Nobody can shoot at me through the windows. You and Linnie keep me safe."

"Yes, baby, Linnie and I keep you safe."

"Safe, just like at Grammy's house."

He grinned. "Yes, and I better dance you back to Grammy."

Watching her slide into his mother's lap was a blessing in itself. Shirley could have resented the child, and instead she'd welcomed her with open arms. Then he turned to look out across the dance floor, located his wife, and went to reclaim her.

———

They snuck out of the dancing, changed out of their wedding stuff, packed it up and dressed in street clothes, and left the church, only to drive down the mountain in a car with a *Just Married* banner across the trunk.

They arrived at the Serenity Inn, went straight up to the bridal suite, and hung a *Do Not Disturb* sign on the outside of the door.

Then they stood for a few moments, looking out at the valley and the town below and then turned and looked at each other.

"You really own that?"

"Me and every other Pope, Cauley, and Glass."

"What is my role in that world?"

"The same as mine—to stay silent."

"Do you think Ava is okay?" Linette asked.

He nodded. "She likes being at Mom's house." Then he took her by the hand and led her to the sofa. "Tonight she asked if when we moved, could Corina find her. I said no. That Corina was gone forever."

"Bless her heart. Even when we think she's forgetting, it's all still in her head. What did she say?" Linette asked.

"She gave me a look and then asked, 'Did she drop dead like Miss Mattie?' Then I asked her what she would think if that happened? And she said she'd feel safe. So, I told her she was safe forever."

"Oh, Wiley, was she sad?"

"Not even a little bit. All she said was when we move, no one can drive by our house and shoot in the windows."

Linette put her arms around Wiley's neck and tucked

SHARON SALA

her cheek against his shoulder. "You make Ava feel safe. You make me feel safe. Where does that come from? How did you get to be this knight in shining armor?"

"I'm no hero, sweetheart. I'm just a man who wants nothing more than to make love to his wife."

Then he got up and turned off the lights, but left the curtains open to the inky-black sky and the stars scattered across the heavens. When he turned around, she had pulled back the covers and was lying on the bed waiting for him, naked to the world.

He moved to the foot of the bed, watching her watching him, and slowly began taking off his clothes. Moments later, he slid into the bed beside her. Kissed the ring on her hand, and then her lips as he moved over her, then into her.

He was hard, and she was ready.

After that, it was nothing but fireworks.

The movers had packed up everything from the house Wiley and Linette had been renting and were on their way up the mountain with Sean leading the way for the van.

The rest of the family was already at their new house. It had been painted inside and out in a fresh coat of white, except for the pale-pink walls in Ava's room. They'd added a new bathroom attached to her room and remodeled the one in the master bedroom. Appliances in the kitchen had been replaced, the huge

propane tank outside refilled, the porch patched, and
the chimney cleaned. They'd kept all of Ella's antiques.
The sideboard and pie safe in the kitchen. The grand-
father clock in the hall. The old long-barrel rifle hanging over the fireplace. The handmade oak dining table
with twelve chairs. Family things. Irreplaceable things.
Things to cherish.

Ava had been up and down the stairs so many
times that she'd worn herself out and fallen asleep in
Shirley's lap.

Wiley was standing at the kitchen window, looking
out across the open pasture beyond the fencing, when
he noticed something along the hedgerow.

"Well, I'll be damned," he whispered.

Linette walked up behind him. "What?"

"Aunt Ella's old cat is back. They said she disappeared the day Ella died. Ray and Betty kept coming up
to look for her and left out food, but they never saw her.
I guess she was waiting for the new people to arrive."

"Ava will be so happy," Linette said. "She's talked
about the barn cat you promised for weeks."

Then they heard the screen door bang at the front
door. "The movers are here!" he said. "Cameron and
Marcus just drove up, and Ray and Betty are on the
porch. Let's do this!" Aaron said.

The shout woke Ava. "Is it happening, Grammy?"

Shirley laughed. "Honey, right now, everything's
happening at once, but you'll be sleeping in your own
bed again tonight. Are you excited?"

Ava nodded. "I won't be afraid anymore."

There was nothing to say that could follow the poignancy of that comment, so Shirley just hugged her.

The movers began unloading, and Linette and Wiley began indicating where to put the boxes they brought in, and then furniture came in, some downstairs, some up. Once they had the beds put back together and the mattresses in their places, the movers left.

And that's when the family got busy.

The women began putting up dishes where Linette wanted them to go, and unpacked pots and pans to add to Ella's cast-iron skillets and Dutch ovens that they'd kept, and slowly the house began to look like a home.

Sean hooked up all their tech equipment and put a booster on their Wi-Fi, then looked up as Wiley walked in.

"The signal is good up here," he said. "I've got your televisions hooked up to the satellite dish, so you'll have cartoons at the ready, and your Wi-Fi signal is good. Just plug in your laptops and sign on, and you should be good to go."

As soon as the kitchen was set up, the women moved to the bedrooms, made up the beds, hung towels in the bathrooms, and put the rest in the linen closet in the hall.

They moved food into Ella's freezer and filled up the new refrigerator, and when they were done, ate sandwiches at the big dining table and sat within the silence of the house, remembering Ella and giving thanks that

Linette and Wiley had accepted the task of keeping the old house alive.

Ava ate fast and bolted up the stairs. She needed to see her new space and make sure all her things were where they belonged. After a quick check, she was satisfied all was well and walked to the windows overlooking the back pasture. It was trees and pasture as far as the eye could see.

"I'm safe now," she whispered. "Forever and ever."

———————

That night, when Linette helped her with her bath and Bubba read her a story, then put her to bed, Ava didn't need any shades pulled down or curtains drawn across her windows.

She was high on the mountain and high up in the sky. And the last things she saw as she was closing her eyes were a patch of moonlight lying across the foot of her bed like a yellow blanket and about a bazillion stars up in the sky.

About the Author

New York Times and *USA Today* bestselling author Sharon Sala has over 135 books in print, published in six different genres—romance, young adult, western, general fiction, women's fiction and nonfiction. First published in 1991, her industry awards include the Janet Dailey Award, five-time Career Achievement winner, five-time winner of the National Readers' Choice Award, five-time winner of the Colorado Romance Writers' Award of Excellence, the Heart of Excellence award, the Booksellers Best Award, the Nora Roberts Lifetime Achievement Award, and the Centennial Award in recognition of her one hundredth published novel. She lives in Oklahoma, the state where she was born.

Website: sharonsalaauthor.com
Facebook: SharonSala_
Instagram: @sharonkaysala_